Pathway Home

OTHER BOOKS AND BOOKS ON CASSETTE
BY MICHELE ASHMAN BELL:

An Unexpected Love

An Enduring Love

A Forever Love

Yesterday's Love

Love After All

Love Lights the Way

Written in the Stars

Without a Flaw

Pathway Home

a novel

MICHELE ASHMAN BELL

Covenant Communications, Inc.

Cover Image ©2003 Comstock, Inc.

Cover design copyrighted 2003 by Covenant Communications, Inc.

Published by Covenant Communications, Inc.
American Fork, Utah

Printed in Canada
First Printing: March 2003

10 09 08 07 06 05 04 03   10 9 8 7 6 5 4 3 2 1

ISBN 1-59156-186-8

This one is for
Rachel.
Heavenly Father sent
one of His most special angels
when He sent you.

PROLOGUE

September 10, 1846

"There's a light up ahead!" Hawkins shouted when he saw the silhouette of the rocky outcropping lit up by the sudden flash from the lighthouse.

It was daybreak, but the thick, black covering of storm clouds made it seem as dark as the middle of the night. The torrential downpour and churning, white-capped sea made it difficult to row the small, wooden lifeboat toward the shore. With the hope of finding solid ground soon, the other two men struggled on with slackening strength.

"Come on!" Hawkins commanded them. "Row harder!"

He'd sailed long enough on the unforgiving sea to know that once she had you in her clutches, she wouldn't let go. If they were going to survive, they had to keep moving, had to get to shore.

He glanced back for one last look at the *Shark*, the three-hundred-ton U.S. Naval survey schooner, which had already been broken up and swallowed by the angry, dark water. She was gone, buried at sea, along with the captain and the crew.

As far as he knew, only he and the two men with him, Jonathan Reese and Sean McTavish, also passengers on the ship, were all that were left—along with the trunk of Spanish gold coins they'd been hired to deliver to the First Bank of San Francisco. Spanish doubloons made up almost half of the coins in the Oregon Territory, which was quickly becoming an area booming with growth and commerce. They would receive a tidy sum for the safe delivery of the gold, an amount Hawkins aimed to acquire no matter what the cost.

The light flashed again, giving him another chance to get his bearing. "Keep rowing, men!" he called over the roar of the waves and storm. "We're almost there!"

With all the strength they possessed, they dug their oars into the angry sea and pushed for shore. Thoughts of their shipmates going down to a watery grave propelled them forward. Some had tried to climb aboard their lifeboat, but had been snatched away by the hungry waves. Others had managed to climb aboard other lifeboats, but there was no sign of them anywhere. Hawkins shuddered to think what had happened to them.

"Straight ahead," he instructed, urging them toward the rugged coastline.

Minutes later the lifeboat ran aground, coming to an abrupt halt.

Even though the chest containing the gold was no bigger than a hatbox, the treasure it contained caused them to struggle with its weight.

"Over here," Hawkins called, guiding them to a rocky overhang, where they found momentary reprieve from the raging storm.

Once they found cover, Hawkins laid out his plan. "We'll hike up to the lighthouse. Maybe the keeper will give us lodging and a warm meal."

The lighthouse provided the only shelter within miles. "We can't make it much farther carrying this chest," he added, without voicing his concerns about the bands of wild Indians and petty thieves who roamed the territory. The gold made the men a prime target, and they knew they needed to find a safe place for that chest as soon as possible. Weak from their ordeal at sea, Reese and McTavish nodded, shivering from the icy wind and rain blowing in.

Although he had every intention of carrying out his orders and getting every solid gold coin to San Francisco, Hawkins knew there was great risk involved in transporting the gold. Reese and McTavish weren't the most trustworthy men he'd ever known. He wouldn't put it past them to want at least some of that gold, if not all of it, for themselves.

But Hawkins was a man of his word—a gentleman. His reputation preceded him and had garnered him the trust of the most wealthy settlers, bankers, and politicians. And he needed Reese's and McTavish's help. He also had to admit that without them, he wouldn't have escaped the sinking ship. He had to trust them for now, but he would still watch them closely, sleeping with one eye open and his revolver cocked and ready.

It was difficult and almost impossible to hike the steep trail leading to the lighthouse. But they managed to claw and scramble their way along the mud-slick, craggy, tree-lined cape until they finally reached the structure.

Bracing himself against the gale-force winds pounding the cape, Hawkins headed for the keeper's quarters and knocked loudly on the door.

There was no answer.

Hawkins tried again with no luck. Testing the locked door, he wondered where the old man was.

"Must be down at the lighthouse," Hawkins told his men. "Probably having a hard time keeping the light going."

Grumbling about the weight of the chest, the men followed Hawkins as they leaned into the wind and trudged their way back to the lighthouse.

Hawkins pounded on the door and waited. The keeper had to be inside.

But again, there was no answer.

He recalled that there wasn't a settlement even close by and wondered what they should do. They wouldn't make it far in the storm, which seemed to be getting worse by the minute.

Not one to let a situation get the better of him, Hawkins scanned the area quickly to find shelter from the storm. Next would be food. He didn't have high hopes for the latter, and he wasn't so sure about the former. Except for trees and rocks, there was nothing.

Then his gaze landed on a raised mound around the back side of the structure. Following the curve of the lighthouse, he inspected the mound and found a latched wooden door nearly flat on the ground. A storm cellar. Hawkins figured that the lighthouse keeper was down in there. In a storm like this, Hawkins wouldn't blame him.

"Reese!" Hawkins yelled. "McTavish!" He motioned for them to join him and then set to opening the door. The latch was padlocked shut, but he managed to kick the lock with his boot until the entire latch came loose, the lock still holding fast. No matter. He could offer to fix that later. Right now they needed to get inside. They could barely stand up against the fierce wind that drove the torrents of rain so hard it felt as though the drops sliced through their skin.

"Down here!" Hawkins yelled. He lifted the door, which the wind immediately ripped from his hands and tore from the hinges.

Reese descended first, then McTavish handed him the chest and followed him into the shelter. Then, just as Hawkins was about to step in, a sound as harrowing as the devil himself rose above the fury of the storm. A tree barely twenty feet in front of him was uprooted and crashed to the ground.

With a mighty leap, Hawkins dove into the shelter and landed in an exhausted heap at the bottom of the ladder.

"We could've died out there!" Reese yelled over the noise of the storm.

"We could die in here," McTavish answered.

"We'll be fine," Hawkins answered. "Have you found the keeper?"

"There's a door leading inside the lighthouse, but it's locked tight," Reese told him. "Maybe he's in there but can't hear us knocking over the noise from the storm."

It was a possibility Hawkins had considered. But no matter where the keeper was, they were finally out of harm's way.

"Is there a lantern or candles in here?" Hawkins asked, feeling around the dark interior of the cellar.

The other men helped search, and to their relief, McTavish found a lantern hanging near the door.

They managed to light the lantern, and the glow spread invitingly across the barren room.

"Any food?" Reese grumbled, shivering in his wet clothes.

There was nothing inside the cellar by way of food or dry clothing. Still, they were grateful to be out of the fury of the storm, even though rain poured through the open hole where the outside door had been stripped away.

"Maybe the keeper will join us soon and provide us with something to eat." Hawkins remained optimistic.

Reese went to the door and pounded on it to no avail. Collapsing back against its wooden planks, Reese slid to the floor, sitting on his haunches. "This is a fine mess you've gotten us into, Hawkins."

"'Tis a mite better than being at the bottom of the ocean, now, isn't it?" McTavish countered.

The men scouted around the room for other provisions.

"Here's another doorway," Reese exclaimed as he scooted a wooden shelf away from the wall. "It looks like some sort of tunnel. Take a look, McTavish."

"Aye, 'tis a tunnel. Where d'you suppose it leads?"

"Let's find out," Reese said, crouching down to look inside.

Just then, all three men stopped and looked upward as the sound of another tree being pulled by its roots resonated through the cellar.

"It's as if the fury of hell's been loosed," McTavish said, covering his ears. "I tell ye, we're goin' to die down here."

Hawkins didn't know how safe they were either, but he knew they still had a better chance of survival where they were than being outside.

"What was that?" McTavish bolted upright, straining to listen.

The howling wind had ceased for a moment.

"Maybe the worst is—"

Reese didn't get to finish. As if slammed by the greatest force of the universe, the ground shuddered, and a wall of water poured through the hole, filling the cellar.

But that wasn't the worst of it. An explosion as loud as a thousand sticks of dynamite filled the air. Then the walls, the stones, the very foundation of the lighthouse began to crumble, and within minutes the men were buried alive, their fate sealed in a grave of water and debris.

CHAPTER 1

Present Day

It had been the longest year of Cami's life. The longest, the hardest, and easily the worst year she'd ever lived through.

Living without her husband, Dallin, was like trying to learn to breathe without oxygen or to experience a sunset without having eyes.

They'd only had eighteen months together. Eighteen wonderful, blissful months. Cami had never known such happiness was possible. Dallin had been the love of her life. And then, one night, everything had changed . . .

* * *

"I don't understand why he's so late, Ashlyn." Panic filled Cami's heart as she spoke. The storm outside seemed to rage with heightened intensity. Icy drops of sleet pounded the windows. The wind howled through the trees. "I just talked to him a few minutes ago, and now he's not answering."

"Maybe he stopped for gas and can't hear the phone ring," Ashlyn offered. "Or he's on a call. I'm sure he's fine."

Cami wanted to believe her friend's words of comfort, but something inside of her wouldn't let her.

"Why was he in Portland anyway?" Ashlyn asked.

"You know how he's been looking for a new job and went to interview with an accounting firm."

"A job in Portland!" Ashlyn exclaimed.

"Don't worry," Cami said *with a laugh. "He'd be able to work in their branch here in Seamist."*

Ashlyn *expressed her relief, then she asked, "How did the interview go? Did he get the job?"*

"The interview went great, and they said they'd call in a few days. When I find out, I'll let you know." If he ever gets home, *she thought.*

"Well, call me as soon as he shows up so I'll know he made it okay."

"I will," Cami said. *"Thanks."*

"He's going to be fine," Ashlyn assured her. *"I bet you hear from him any minute."*

Cami *hung up the phone and went to the window. The storm had pounded the coastline the entire day, and the wet roads had turned into sheets of ice.*

Pacing *from the window to the front door, Cami wrung her hands with worry, hoping that any minute Dallin's car would pull into the driveway.*

Twenty *minutes passed. Thirty.*

A *constant prayer ran through her mind, but still, fear for the worst consumed her.*

Just *when she thought she'd lose her mind, the phone rang.*

A *chill tore up her spine. She stared at the phone.* Please, Father, *she prayed,* let it be Dallin. Let him be okay.

The *phone rang several more times before she answered it.*

"This is Sergeant Bridger. I'm trying to reach Mrs. Dallin Gardner," a voice said.

Tears *filled Cami's eyes, and her knees went weak. "This is Mrs. Gardner."*

"I'm sorry to have to tell you this, ma'am, but your husband was involved in a fatal car accident on Highway 26," he said. *"His body . . ."*

Cami *didn't hear the rest of his words. Her mind went blank, her body went numb, and bit by bit, her world crumbled around her.*

* * *

Tears filled Cami's eyes even now as she remembered the shocking news that had seemed unreal and impossible to accept. Today marked the anniversary of Dallin's death. She'd survived the first Christmas without him. She'd made it through his birthday, her birthday, and even their wedding anniversary. But today felt like she was reliving that awful day exactly one year ago last April.

Now, here she was, twenty-six years old and wondering what to do with the rest of her life. If one year had seemed like eternity, how was she supposed to live the rest of the years of her life?

Wiping at her eyes, Cami opened the front door of the Sea Rose Bed and Breakfast and stepped outside. The inn had started out as a bed-and-breakfast, but because of its exquisite location and accommodations, along with the delectable and unusual cuisine it served, it now offered full-service meals three times a day. Cami managed and lived in the inn with her grandfather.

She stepped over the morning paper onto the lovely, wraparound porch and pulled in a breath of fresh air . . . then froze. Turning back to the paper, she read the headline, "Heceta Head Lighthouse Murder Suspect Brought in for Questioning." A sense of relief washed over her. The news of the brutal murder several months ago had struck terror in the hearts of everyone living along the coastline. Every resident lived in a constant state of suspicion. Any stranger, any unusual activity, didn't go unnoticed.

"Thank goodness," Cami said as she set the paper back on the doorstep, knowing that her grandfather would be out shortly looking for it. She was grateful there had been a break in the case. The circumstances surrounding the murder had left authorities baffled. Many of the lighthouses along the coast were inactive, giving up their services to new, technologically sophisticated but decidedly less attractive structures. Some had become tourist destinations, complete with gift shops and tour guides giving the historical background of the lighthouses, just as the Misty Harbor Lighthouse had done. But the Heceta Head Lighthouse had become a bed-and-breakfast, along with being a favorite stop for tourists.

The murder of a local fisherman who was found at the bottom of the rocky point below the lighthouse had been front-page news in all the papers throughout the state. Along with being the scene of the murder, the lighthouse had also been broken into and vandalized. Strangely enough, nothing had been taken. But even more curious was all the digging along the coastline below and around the light-house.

Authorities didn't come out and say it, but people talked and speculated about what was going on. Many believed it was treasure hunters. It had happened before—money-hungry treasure seekers digging for buried gold after hearing various legends of sunken treasure ships and buried treasure boxes. But never before had someone been murdered in the process. Thankfully, the town of Seamist hadn't seen any suspicious activity since the incident. The police force, county sheriffs, and alert townspeople kept a constant, watchful eye over the town.

Cami was grateful for their safe little community. The close-knit, small town gave her a sense of support and security that had helped her get through the last difficult year.

She walked across the expansive lawn, which was already lush and green, and headed for the stairs leading to the beach. *The least it could do is rain,* she thought wryly, wanting the weather to match her mood. Instead, flower beds danced with beautiful white and yellow daffodils. Pink and red tulips nearly blinded her with their vivid colors, and birds chirped merrily in the blossoming apple trees as a warm breeze floated around, fragranced with the heavy combination of flowers and sea spray.

Descending the wooden steps that led to the rugged beach nestled at the base of the jutting precipice, Cami turned and looked back at the Sea Rose Bed and Breakfast towering stately above Douglas fir trees. She then drank in the beauty of the crashing surf and the long, sandy shore stretching north toward Misty Harbor and the town of Seamist.

It seemed like yesterday that she and her best friend, Ashlyn, had come to Seamist after Cami's graduation from college. She'd returned to her hometown, a place she'd missed dearly, and her beloved grand-father, and she was happy to be back with loved ones once again.

That summer had been magical. Not only had she and Ashlyn helped restore the crumbling Davenport Mansion to the beautiful inn it now was, but Ashlyn had met Mitch Bradford, the man of her dreams, a man who was now her husband, and Cami and Dallin had been given a second chance at love.

They'd dated before she went away to college. She knew she loved him then, but the timing just hadn't been right. He'd gone his way, and she'd gone hers. But the heavens had smiled down upon them and had helped their paths cross again, and this time they'd found true love. The day they got married in the Portland Oregon Temple had been the happiest day of her life. It had been a fairy-tale day, a perfect day.

Their first and only year and a half of marriage had been the most joyful and wonderful time of her life. She hadn't known such bliss was possible. It was as if they couldn't get enough of each other. Indeed, she hadn't gotten enough of him, at least not enough to last her the rest of her life, not enough to make up for the fact that he was gone.

She was so empty inside she ached.

The wind kicked up and whipped Cami's shoulder-length blonde hair into her face and tugged at her windbreaker. She tilted her face toward the sky and shut her eyes.

Please help me, Heavenly Father. How do I go on?

Her prayer echoed in her thoughts. It was the same prayer she offered morning, noon, and night. She pleaded constantly for God to help her.

"Cami!"

The voice startled her. She'd heard it as plain as the biting wind on her face. Someone had called her name. Had the heavens finally answered her?

She forced herself to turn slowly toward the sound of the voice.

"Hey there," Ashlyn called, and waved as she scurried down the steps to the beach. "I've been looking all over for you."

Cami returned the wave to her friend, decidedly disappointed that her prayer hadn't summoned a heavenly being to answer all her questions.

"What are you doing?" Ashlyn asked. Her long, curly hair was pulled back into a ponytail that was tucked underneath a baseball hat, probably one of Mitch's hats. The man was obsessed with baseball, but he wore many hats for all the things he was involved with in Seamist—everything from high school coach and schoolteacher to volunteer firefighter and occasional clerk at his family's hardware store.

"Just going for a walk," Cami answered with a shrug.

Ashlyn studied her friend's face for a moment, then said, "I've been thinking about you. How are you doing?"

"Oh," Cami pulled in a long breath then released it, "I guess I'm okay. Heck, I don't know. I mean, am I supposed to be over him after a year?" she asked Ashlyn pointedly, not necessarily expecting an answer. "Am I supposed to just tuck his memory in the back of my mind and forget about him?" Her voice continued to rise as she spoke, growing in a crescendo of emotion. "Because I can't, Ashlyn. I don't know if something's wrong with me or what the deal is," her voice broke, and she began to cry, "but I just can't stop thinking about him."

Ashlyn took her friend in her arms and hugged her. Cami released her tears and fought for control. Not a day had gone by in the last year—not one—that she hadn't shed a tear for Dallin.

Ashlyn stroked Cami's hair and spoke soothingly. "I'm sorry. I am so sorry. This must be so hard for you."

Without the strength, help, and support of friends and family, Cami knew she would never have survived this long. Their compassion and love had rescued her from despair many times. She didn't know about angels in heaven, but she did know there certainly were angels on earth.

Ashlyn gave her an encouraging smile. "You know what I think?"

Cami gave her a questioning look.

"I think we need to do something to get your mind off things. Go out to lunch, go shopping, anything to give you a break from all of this," Ashlyn said enthusiastically.

"I don't know." Cami shook her head. "I won't be much fun."

"That's okay, I'll be fun enough for both of us. Besides, Mitch is going to be gone until late this evening, and I'll be all alone. You'd be helping me out too. Please?"

Cami stared at her friend's insistent expression and realized she wasn't going to win this argument. Ashlyn wouldn't give in. Maybe Ashlyn was right—perhaps getting out would do her some good. It certainly couldn't hurt.

* * *

Over shrimp salads and bowls of clam chowder, Ashlyn and Cami enjoyed the view of the Misty Harbor Bay from a picturesque window at the Bayside Diner. They were ahead of the lunch crowd and had the place to themselves except for a rough-looking biker couple wearing black leather pants and vests, the woman wearing heavy makeup and studded with jewelry, and the man sporting a collage of tattoos on his forearms.

"Hey, did you read the paper this morning?" Ashlyn asked Cami as Ashlyn crumbled a cracker into her chowder.

"I just glanced at the headlines. They've finally found a suspect in that murder. I sure hope it's the guy who did it," Cami said. "I'll sleep much better knowing he's behind bars."

"Me too!" Ashlyn exclaimed. "I'm so tired of worrying about it. I mean," she nodded toward the couple in the corner and said, "We used to be so tourist friendly, but now I'm suspicious of every stranger I see. Heck," she lowered her voice, "for all we know, it could be that guy over there."

Cami chuckled. "They've already got a suspect, remember?"

"Yeah, but until they can pin it on him or he confesses, anyone could be a suspect."

"I guess. All I know is that I wish things could get back to the way they were." Cami meant before the murder, but her thoughts extended beyond that to another death—Dallin's.

Ashlyn obviously sensed her thoughts. "I know. Me too."

"We were going to have babies together," Cami reminded Ashlyn. "Build houses next to each other. Go on vacations together." Then she spoke softer, slower. "The four of us were going to grow old together."

Ashlyn looked at Cami with sadness in her eyes. They'd had fun planning their futures together. "I'm sorry," Cami said. "I don't know why you even hang out with me anymore. I'm such a downer to be around. I feel like part of me died with Dallin, like there's no life left inside of me."

Ashlyn reached across the table and took ahold of her friend's hand. "I know. I want so much to help you. I just don't know how."

"I don't either," Cami told her friend tearfully. "I've had heartache before, but this time my heart is broken. And I don't think it's possible to fix it."

"But Dallin wouldn't want you to just sit here and be miserable, would he?"

Cami shrugged and shook her head with despair.

"Well, I know he wouldn't. He would want you to find happiness, joy, and fulfillment in life. I'm sure of it."

Cami gave her a weak but appreciative smile. "Thanks."

Ashlyn didn't hear her. Her gaze was fixed on something behind Cami.

"Ash?" Cami said.

Ashlyn blinked. "What? Did you say something?"

"What are you looking at?" Cami twisted in her seat to see what was behind her.

"No!" Ashlyn exclaimed, grabbing Cami's arm. "Don't look."

Cami turned back around. "Why? What is it?" She was curious to know what Ashlyn was looking at.

"Those two bikers," Ashlyn whispered, trying to look interested in her chowder. "In the corner."

"What about them?"

"I don't know. There's something about them that doesn't seem right, like they could jump up any minute and hold up the place or something."

Cami chuckled. "Ashlyn, that's silly. Just because they're dressed like that doesn't mean they're criminals. I've heard that bikers are some of the nicest people around. They're the first ones to help someone else in need, especially on the road."

Ashlyn shook her head. "I don't know . . ." She suddenly grabbed a packet of saltines and ripped open the cellophane wrapper. She motioned with her eyes and a slight tilt of her head for Cami to look over.

Cami turned and watched as the tall man stood, adjusted his sunglasses, and strode toward the rest rooms.

"I wonder what they're doing here," Ashlyn said.

"Probably just driving their Harleys along the coast. A lot of bikers do that. A lot of normal tourists do that."

Ashlyn's shoulders slumped. "You're right. They were looking at a map, probably figuring out their route."

Cami agreed, but took one last look toward the corner just as the man returned from the rest room several minutes later. She glanced away, but not before her eyes met the shaded glare of the stringy-haired man. A chill went through her, and she quickly turned to face Ashlyn.

"Okay, you're right. The guy is creepy. Let's get out of here," Cami said.

Ashlyn was more than happy to oblige. "Hey!" she exclaimed. "I have a great idea! Let's go to Portland."

"Portland!" Cami couldn't remember the last time she'd been to the city. "Why Portland?"

"I don't know. I just think it sounds fun."

Cami reviewed her day in her mind, realizing that she had no pressing obligations. After a moment's hesitation, she said, "Okay, why not?" Doing something was better than sitting around feeling sorry for herself. "I'm game."

Leaving a tip for the waitress, they left their table, but Cami remembered that she had left her purse under her seat and turned back to get it. She reached down for her bag, and when she stood up, the leather-clad man was staring straight at her, causing the hair on her neck to stand up.

She couldn't get out of there fast enough.

CHAPTER 2

Cami couldn't remember the last time she'd enjoyed herself more or laughed so hard. The trip to Portland had been just what she'd needed. A change of scenery, crowds of strangers, the hustle and bustle of a fast-paced city—it was perfect.

For the first time in months, Cami actually bought herself some new clothes. All the spring fashions were out, and the bright, fresh colors lifted her spirits and lightened her mood. She bought a new pair of jeans, a new skirt, two sweaters, a shirt, and three pairs of shoes.

It was almost eight o'clock when they returned home and pulled up to the Sea Rose mansion. An unfamiliar car was in the driveway— a handsome, misty gray Volvo S80. Ashlyn and Cami looked at each other when they saw the car, then burst out laughing for no reason.

"I'll come in with you," Ashlyn told Cami as they climbed out of her car. "I want to say hi to Pearl and your grandpa."

"Good, I need you to help me carry in all my packages anyway," Cami told her, amazed that she didn't feel guilty for all the things she bought. She knew that buying something new only gave momentary pleasure, but for right now, she was grateful to get pleasure in any way and for as long as she could.

They both clamored up the stairs with their arms full and practically stumbled into the entryway.

A man jumped to his feet when they came inside, startling Cami for a moment.

"Hello," he said quickly. "Can I help you with that?" He reached for the stack of shoe boxes she balanced with one arm and caught them just as they tipped over.

"Thanks," Cami exclaimed, grateful the man had been there to catch them.

He placed the boxes on the registration desk, making sure they were stacked securely.

Cami looked at the man suspiciously. She'd expected a guest to check in that evening, a history professor from back east, but she'd anticipated an older, bearded man with wire-framed glasses and a pinched expression. This man was young, in his midthirties, wearing a chocolate-brown leather jacket, a light blue, button-down oxford shirt, jeans, and cordovan-colored loafers. He was boyishly handsome, with dark, curly hair, startling blue eyes, and a warm, friendly smile. She liked how his cheeks had a rosy tint to them, as though he'd just come in from the cold.

"You don't happen to know if the owner is around, do you?" he asked politely.

"Actually yes." Cami smiled, shifting her packages into her left hand so she could extend her right one to him. "I'm the owner, Cami Gardner." She extended her hand and they shook. "Sorry to keep you waiting. Usually my grandfather is somewhere close," she commented, glancing around for any sign of him.

"I saw an elderly man outside in the trees with something that looked like a BB gun. Could that have been him?" the man asked.

A smile broke onto Cami's and Ashlyn's faces. "That's him," they said, giggling.

"We've had a bit of a squirrel problem," Cami explained, piling her packages into Ashlyn's arms.

With her vision blocked by boxes and bags, Ashlyn mumbled, "I'll just take these to the other room," as she attempted to go to the dining room without bumping into anything. Cami stepped around the desk and took out the registration book. "Welcome to the Sea Rose Bed and Breakfast," she told him. "I hope you didn't have any trouble finding us."

"No," he said. "I just followed the map in the brochure. This is a beautiful place you have here. It's much bigger than I expected. The view must be magnificent from the upstairs rooms."

"It is," she assured him. "This home has been in our family now for over a hundred years."

"Well, it's very impressive."

Cami smiled her thanks. "Let's see." She looked down at the book. "May I have your name please?"

"It's Josh. Josh Drake," he told her, fishing his wallet out of his back pocket.

She found his name and remembered that he'd booked the room for an entire week with an option to stay longer if desired. She took his identification and entered the necessary information into their computer, then handed him back his credit card and driver's license, noticing how handsome his picture was. Hers looked like she'd just stepped out of a spook alley.

"We've put you in the Nautical Room," she told him. "It has a beautiful view of the north shore and the Misty Harbor Lighthouse." She came around the desk and paused. "Do you need help with your bags?"

"No." He lifted a suitcase and a briefcase off the ground. "This is all I have."

She led the way up the stairs and down the hallway. They stopped several times as interesting art pieces and collectibles caught his eye. She told him about Pearl, who was the cook and gardener at the inn. When Pearl was younger, she'd worked as a freelance photographer, having many of her pictures in *National Geographic, Time,* and *Life* magazines. Cami listed some of Pearl's world travels and how she'd donated most of the items to the inn for display.

"Does Pearl live here?" he asked with interest.

"No, she has a little cottage just east of the mansion," she answered.

"Does her family also work for you?" he questioned further.

"She doesn't really have any family. She was never married," Cami told him, wondering why he was so interested.

She was afraid he was going to ask more personal questions about Pearl when, to her relief, he stopped and admired a vase along with other knickknacks on a shelf in the corner of the hallway.

"That is a very lovely vase," he commented.

"Thank you," Cami said, admiring his taste. From what Pearl had told her, the piece was from seventeenth-century Austria and quite valuable. "It's one of Pearl's favorites."

"May I?" he asked.

She nodded, and he carefully picked up the delicate piece and turned it over to see the bottom. "Just as I thought," he said. "A Dzierzon original. This is priceless."

"It is?" Cami replied, shocked at Mr. Drake's announcement. She knew many of Pearl's pieces were valuable, but she'd never thought any of them were priceless. "Are you an art dealer?"

"Not really, although I've studied art quite extensively. I'm a history professor at Bucknell University, but my mother was from Italy. She was an artist."

In Cami's opinion, Mr. Drake didn't look Italian. His skin was fair, and if it weren't for his dark hair, she would have thought him more Nordic, or perhaps even Irish, than Italian.

"We lived in Europe when I was young and traveled all over to museums and universities to see famous artwork," he continued.

"That must have been fascinating," Cami said, trying to imagine such an unusual childhood. "Is that why you studied history?"

"Walking through ancient Roman ruins, seeing sculptures and artwork created before the time of Christ, makes history come alive. As a child, these things became real to me. They weren't ancient, forgotten pieces of rock, but carvings and structures crafted by men thousands of years ago. I have an appreciation and a love for history that I owe to my mother."

"She must be so proud of you," Cami commented.

"She died when I was ten," Mr. Drake said, his voice edged with pain.

"I'm sorry."

He drew in a quick breath and released it. "Anyway," he placed the vase down gently on the shelf, "if you don't mind me saying it, this vase should be locked up somewhere or even put in a museum."

"Really?" It had never occurred to Cami that one of their guests might be tempted to take the vase or any of the other valuable pieces in Pearl's collection.

"Absolutely. It's very rare, and it would be a shame to see it stolen or accidentally knocked off the shelf and broken."

"You're right," Cami said, picking up the vase and protecting it carefully in her arms. "I've got a locked curio cabinet downstairs in the front parlor. I can put it there for now. But let me first show you to your room."

She led the way to the Nautical Room. Mr. Drake was thrilled with the decor, but even more so with the view from his window. The last few rays of the setting sun glowed on the horizon. The outline of the coast and the lighthouse were still visible.

"This is perfect," he said. "Thank you."

"We're happy to have you with us, Mr. Drake. And if you'd like something to eat before bed, just come down to the dining room when you get settled. Pearl keeps the pantry stocked full of all kinds of goodies."

Mr. Drake smiled gratefully. Cami returned the smile and, looking at his face, noticed a hint of emptiness in his eyes. Or was it loneliness?

"I'd like that," he said.

* * *

Cami found Ashlyn, Grandpa Willy, and Pearl in the kitchen enjoying some of Pearl's thickly iced cinnamon rolls along with cold glasses of milk. Putting one of the jumbo-sized confections on a plate, she joined them.

"So, did Mr. Drake get settled?" Grandpa Willy asked.

Cami nodded as she chewed and swallowed a bite of the roll. "He really liked the room. In fact, he likes the whole place. He knows a lot about art and history and identified many of Pearl's collectibles as priceless pieces of art. I put the vase from the shelf in the hallway into the locked curio after he told me how valuable it is."

"How valuable is it?" Pearl asked.

"He says its priceless," Cami told her. "Maybe you should get some of your things appraised. You could put them in museums or display the most valuable items of your collection at the art center in Portland."

"Priceless!" Pearl exclaimed. "I had no idea some of this junk was worth so much!"

"Mr. Drake seems to think so," Cami said.

"Wouldn't mind a ride in that car of his," Grandpa Willy said. "It's a beauty."

Just then the phone rang. Pearl answered and handed it to Ashlyn. It was her husband, Mitch. Cami noticed by Ashlyn's replies that Mitch was telling her about something exciting that had happened. With his work as a volunteer fireman and member of the town council, he was aware of all the activities in the community.

"Guess I better get home," Ashlyn said after she hung up the phone.

"Is something going on?" Cami asked.

"Mitch just got back from spending the afternoon with Fred Granger—you remember his friend who's a county sheriff?"

Cami nodded.

Ashlyn looked at them, hesitating a moment before saying, "Someone tried to break into the Misty Harbor Lighthouse last night."

"What?" Cami didn't want to hear that.

"Some kids in a Jeep were near the lighthouse spotlighting deer and saw someone running from the lighthouse. They tried to chase the guy in the Jeep, but he took off down the trail to the beach and they couldn't follow. They think he got away in a boat."

"What happened to the lighthouse?"

"The lock on the door was pried open with a crowbar and the place was trashed, like the person was looking for something. Nothing was taken."

Cami remembered the break-in at the Heceta Head Lighthouse. Nothing had been taken there either. The thought of a connection between the two incidents spooked her, and suddenly Seamist didn't seem as safe anymore.

"Maybe it was treasure hunters," Pearl announced, speaking what was likely on everyone else's mind.

Grandpa Willy accidentally knocked over his glass of milk. "Dad blast it!" he exclaimed, jumping to his feet and grabbing a handful of paper towels.

"Here, William," Pearl assisted with a hand towel. "Let me do that. Go on, Ashlyn. Tell us more."

"Enough about all this treasure business," Grandpa Willy objected. "There's not a word of truth to any of it. They're all just a bunch of folktales."

"Apparently someone doesn't think they're just folktales," Ashlyn said.

"Some people are willing to do anything for money," Pearl said. "I hate to think of what a person who's obsessed with trying to find a buried treasure would be willing to do."

"Did you say you needed to be getting home?" Grandpa Willy asked Ashlyn. "I'll walk you partway, just to make sure you get there safely."

"That would be nice," Ashlyn replied, glancing out the window.

Before Ashlyn left, she gave Cami a giant hug. "Are you going to be okay?"

Cami nodded. "I think so." She flashed a brave smile. "Today really helped. Thanks." This time Cami hugged Ashlyn.

"I'll call you tomorrow," Ashlyn said in parting, and left with Grandpa Willy.

Cami told Pearl she'd straighten up the kitchen, and Pearl bid her good night. In no time at all, Cami had the plates and glasses washed and the table wiped off.

The grandfather clock in the hallway chimed the hour, and her mind drifted back to the same time last year. It was right about now that Dallin had been driving home in that terrible storm. Her heart ached as she thought about how quickly everything had changed, how delicate life's balance really was.

She wiped off the chrome faucet so it would shine the way Pearl liked it.

Pearl. Cami didn't know what she would have done without Pearl this last year.

Pearl herself had suffered a great loss as a young woman. Frederick, the love of her life, had been killed before they'd been able to get married. Pearl had never loved again.

Tears stung Cami's eyes as she thought about how much she missed having Dallin's arms around her. How she missed his kisses, his voice, his laughter.

Her heart ached, and the tears came faster, cascading down her cheeks. She swallowed a sob that threatened to spill out and clutched her fist to her aching heart.

A noise startled Cami, and she turned suddenly at the sound of footsteps behind her.

Mr. Drake had just stepped into the room, but his cheerful expression quickly faded as he saw her tearstained face.

CHAPTER 3

"I'm sorry," he said, taking a step back toward the door. "I didn't mean to bother you."

Cami wiped her eyes and cheeks with the dish towel. "No, it's fine. Really." She tried to be cheerful but knew she was failing miserably. "Here." She motioned toward the table. "Please, sit down."

"It's okay," he said. "I'll be fine until morning." He moved closer toward the door.

It was obvious he didn't want to bother her, which she appreciated, but she also welcomed a distraction from her thoughts.

"I insist, really," she said with more determination. "Pearl made these cinnamon rolls just for you."

"Homemade cinnamon rolls?" he asked.

She nodded, practically seeing his mouth start to water.

"Alright then, if you're sure it's no trouble." He looked at her, and in his eyes she saw understanding and kindness.

She smiled at him and motioned for him to sit while she got a plate and a roll for him.

"I've got milk, juice, tea, coffee, or Pearl's special-blend herb tea to drink. What would you like?" she asked.

"Herb tea sounds wonderful, but I don't want you to—"

"It's no trouble," she cut him off. "In fact, I think I'll join you. Pearl's herb tea is very relaxing. She gathers the herbs herself from the fields behind us."

They didn't speak while she put the water on to boil, but a moment later Mr. Drake exclaimed, "These rolls are incredible!"

Cami turned and smiled at the look of pure heaven on his face.

"They're my favorite," she told him. "They're worth every calorie as far as I'm concerned."

"I agree." He licked his fingers, then took another bite, rolling his eyes with delight. "Mmm," he said as he chewed.

The pot whistled, and Cami dunked a cheesecloth bag of herbs into the boiling water. Soon the fragrance of comfrey, chamomile, and peppermint drifted through the room.

"Would you like another roll?" she asked, noticing that he had polished the first one off rather quickly.

"No," he said, shaking his head. "Not tonight. But maybe for breakfast?" he asked hopefully.

"I'll put one aside for you," she told him. She poured the cups of tea and handed one to him. "If you'd like, we can move into the parlor and sit by the fire. It's much more comfortable in there."

He readily accepted, and she led him into the back parlor, happy to have some company since she knew the minute she was alone again she would be consumed with her former thoughts.

They settled into two wing-back chairs facing the fireplace. An oval table stood between the chairs, just the right size for their cups and saucers.

"So," Cami said, after taking a sip of her tea, "what brings you clear to the West Coast?"

Mr. Drake sighed, his shoulders slumping wearily. He looked as though he were completely worn out. Cami guessed he probably was if he'd driven across the country, which she assumed he had since there were Pennsylvania plates on his car.

He didn't answer right away, which made Cami wonder if her question had been too personal.

"I'm sorry," she said. "It's really none of my business."

"No," he said quickly. "It's okay. I . . . well . . . I just needed to get away for a while." He sipped his tea, then placed it on the saucer on the table. "My father passed away a few months ago."

"I'm so sorry." Her words were heartfelt and sincere.

"Thank you." He smiled gently. "I appreciate that. It's been very difficult. I've had a hard time focusing on my teaching, so I decided to get away and get my thoughts together."

He leaned forward in his seat, resting his elbows on his knees, watching the flames dance in the fireplace. "I arranged for time off work, loaded up my car, and began driving."

"How did you end up here?" she asked.

"I found out about your place on the Internet, so I decided if I got this far west, I'd check it out," he said. "And here I am."

Cami nodded, continuing to listen.

"Funny thing about death," he said, his voice distant. "It forces you to really evaluate your life and your existence. Do a bit of 'soul searching.'" He shifted his gaze to the fire and said, "Some things suddenly seem so meaningless and a waste of time, while other things suddenly become vitally important."

She knew exactly what he meant. His words described her own feelings.

"My job, my interests, the day-to-day grind, just seemed to go out of focus for me. I decided that I needed to figure out what I wanted out of life and what I wanted to spend my time on. I couldn't go on like I was, so I took off. I'm sure my colleagues and friends think I'm nuts, but this is something I have to do for myself. My father's death has raised many questions for me. I'm looking for answers, but I'm not exactly sure where to find them."

Cami's expression grew solemn. How well she knew his feelings. For the last year she'd been doing her own share of soul searching and trying to find answers to her questions.

"I know what you're saying," she said softly, staring at the mesmerizing movement of the flames.

"How so?" Mr. Drake asked, glancing over at her, then back to the fire. He took a sip of his tea and waited for her answer.

Cami didn't know why she felt like answering his question. Maybe it was simply because they shared one thing in common—a grieving heart. Or maybe because he seemed so kind and understanding.

"Today marks the first-year anniversary of my husband's death," she said evenly, amazed that her voice hadn't crumbled or that she hadn't dissolved into tears.

"How difficult for you," Mr. Drake said. "I am very sorry."

"Thank you," Cami answered, pursing her lips together as she drew in a long breath to help keep her emotions in check.

"It will be good to get this day behind you, won't it?" he remarked.

She nodded.

"I already dread that day," he said. "And so many others." He placed his cup and saucer on the table. "Like holidays, or weekends in the fall when we'd go to football games together. But most of all I dread our birthdays. They're only three days apart," he explained, "and to celebrate we've gone to Alaska to fish every June. It was something we looked forward to every year."

"It sounds like you two were very close," she said, finding herself drawn into his story.

"We were. He was my best friend."

Cami didn't know what prompted him, but Mr. Drake got to his feet and walked over to the wall where a watercolor painting of the Misty Harbor Lighthouse hung.

He admired the painting for a minute before he said, "This is very beautiful. Is it an original?"

"Yes, a local artist painted it. The moment I saw the painting, I had to have it," she told him. "The artist based the scene on a verse from the Bible."

Mr. Drake lifted one eyebrow with interest.

"It's from the 107th Psalm, the 29th verse. It says, 'He maketh the storm a calm.'"

He looked back at the picture and nodded his head. "It's very powerful."

Just then there was a clamoring at the back door, and Cami heard her grandfather come inside the house.

"Cami?" he hollered. "Can you help me just a minute?"

Cami jumped to her feet. "That's my grandfather," she told Mr. Drake.

Rushing to the kitchen, she found her grandfather with a large, butcher paper–wrapped package in his arms. The package was over two feet long.

"What in the world? . . ."

"It's salmon," he told her. "Mitch asked if we could put it in our freezer. There's no place to store the blasted thing over at his place."

"Just a minute." Cami rushed to the utility room off the kitchen, where the deep freeze stood in the corner. Opening the lid, she adjusted the contents to make room for the large package.

"Here, sir," Mr. Drake said. "Let me help you with that."

"You the fellow who just checked in?" Grandpa Willy asked Mr. Drake.

"That's me," Mr. Drake said. "The name's Josh. Josh Drake."

The two men lugged the package over to the freezer and dumped it in. Cami closed the lid for them.

"Thank you, Mr. Drake," Grandpa Willy said, extending his hand in welcome to their guest.

"Please," Mr. Drake said, "call me Josh." He looked at Grandpa and at Cami.

"Alright, Josh," Grandpa Willy said. "You can call me Willy. Is there anything we can get you? Are you making yourself at home?"

Josh nodded his head. "Yes, sir, I mean, Willy. Thank you. I'm very comfortable. Your granddaughter has taken good care of me."

"That's my girl," Grandpa said proudly with a nod toward Cami. "Can we get you something to eat before bed?"

"Already done," Josh replied. "I had one of those delicious cinnamon rolls."

"That ought to keep you full through the night," Grandpa said. "I guess I'll bid you good night then. It's late, and I've got an early day tomorrow."

"Nice meeting you, Willy," Josh said.

Grandpa nodded, then gave Cami a quick peck on the cheek. "Don't stay up too late," he said. "Holler if you need me."

"I will, Grandpa," she told him, knowing that was his way of checking on her to make sure she was doing okay.

After Grandpa Willy left, Cami walked with Josh to the stair landing.

"Guess I'll also turn in," Josh said. "Is there a specific time I should be down for breakfast?" he asked.

"Nope, the kitchen's open any time. Just come down whenever you're ready," she told him. "You'll get a chance to meet Pearl in the morning. You're going to love her," Cami said.

"I have a feeling you're right," he said with a nod of his head. "I'm looking forward to hearing about some of her adventures."

"She'll be thrilled to have someone to share them with, and believe me, she's got plenty," Cami assured him with a smile.

He smiled in return, and for a moment Cami lost her train of thought. Then, blinking several times, she realized she'd been staring at him. "Well," she stammered, "good night."

"Good night."

She turned to leave.

"And thank you, Mrs. Gardner. I have a feeling that perhaps I just might be able to do some 'soul searching' while I'm here. Maybe even figure out some of the answers to those questions I have."

Cami gave him a warm smile. "I hope you do. And by the way, you can call me Cami."

* * *

Early the next morning, Cami ran to the print shop in town to make changes on the new brochure they were getting ready to send out to advertise the Sea Rose Bed and Breakfast. She also stopped at the grocery store to pick up some things Pearl needed for dinner and to say hi to her father-in-law.

Dallin's parents were the original owners of Gardner's Groceries, and the store had been an anchor in the downtown area for nearly thirty-five years. Wayne Gardner was a wonderful man and treated Cami more like a daughter than a daughter-in-law. And to her, he seemed more like the father she'd never really had.

When she returned to the inn, she entered through the back door that led into the kitchen. She heard voices in the dining room. Pearl's contagious laughter filled the air, making Cami smile. Pearl had obviously met their houseguest.

Depositing her packages onto the kitchen counter, Cami stepped through to the dining room to see what was going on. There, sitting at the table, were Pearl and Josh, just as she had expected. Pearl rarely ever sat down with the guests when they ate, but obviously she felt as comfortable with Josh as Cami had.

"Good morning." Cami smiled at both of them. "I trust you got your cinnamon roll for breakfast." An empty dessert plate sat next to Josh's plate of bacon and scrambled eggs.

"Yes." He smiled. "Thank you. I woke up with quite a craving. I'm going to have to be careful while I'm here, or I'm likely to end up going home with more than a few seashells for souvenirs."

Pearl and Cami laughed.

"You look like you could use some good, home-cooked meals. A bachelor like yourself probably doesn't spend a lot of time in the kitchen," Pearl commented.

"You're right about that. Except for heating up a can of soup or grabbing a bowl of cereal for breakfast, I don't do any cooking. I eat most of my meals at the cafeteria on campus or at a restaurant near my apartment," he told them.

"Well, we'll just have to do something about that," Pearl said. She had a way of mothering anyone who stepped through the front door, and a lone man like Josh Drake was a prime candidate for some of her special attention. "If you have any favorites, I would love to fix something extra special for you while you're here," she offered.

Josh held up his hand to decline her offer. "I don't want to be any bother," he said.

"You might as well just tell her," Cami instructed. "If I know Pearl, she won't give up until she's tracked down your nearest relative and found out what she wants to know."

"Alright," he said with a chuckle. "How can I turn down an offer like that?" He thought for a moment. "I guess if I had to pick a favorite meal, it would be roast beef with mashed potatoes and gravy."

"Roast beef!" Pearl exclaimed. "You're sure you don't want pheasant under glass or stuffed quail? They're my specialties."

"Even though my mother was Italian, she made roast beef for our family every Sunday when I was a little boy," Josh explained. "It was my father's favorite meal too."

"Well, if it's roast beef you want, then it's roast beef you'll get. I've got a beautiful roast in the freezer. You just wait until dinner tonight," Pearl told him. "You're going to think you've died and gone to heaven."

"I think I already have," he said. "I had no idea I would get such royal treatment at your inn. I feel like the Queen of England," he told them.

"Well, even she couldn't turn up her nose at my roast beef dinner. In fact, when I dined with the Queen, we had a steak-and-kidney pie that tasted like something they'd saved from the reign of King Henry. It was awful." Pearl pulled a face, which brought a laugh from Cami and Josh. "I'd much rather cook for someone young and handsome like yourself," she told their guest.

Cami noticed a flush of red color Josh's cheeks. He was probably used to lecturing in front of hundreds of students, but judging by the way he got embarrassed at Pearl's compliment, it was obvious the man was also shy.

"So," Pearl asked him, "have you got any special plans for today?"

"I thought I'd take a walk along the coastline toward the harbor and see what's downtown. Is there anything I should see while I'm there?" he asked both of them.

Cami suggested a nice gallery that displayed a lot of local artwork, and she and Pearl both recommended he have a bowl of clam chowder at the Bayside Diner, and maybe even take a trip to the Misty Harbor Lighthouse.

Hoping that the weather cooperated, Josh set off for his outing and left the two women to take care of business at the inn.

"That's one fine hunk of a man," Pearl exclaimed after he left.

"Pearl!"

The woman shrugged. "I call 'em like I see 'em. I may be getting old, but I'm not blind!" She pulled the roast from the freezer and put it in the microwave to thaw for dinner. "He seems lonely though. I could see it in his eyes."

Cami told her about Josh's father dying and how hard it had been on him.

"That explains it," Pearl said, her forehead creasing with concern. "I want his stay here to be extra special. He's driven clear across the country looking for something, and he's run out of road. That man needs some time and a place to heal. I think the Sea Rose is exactly what he needs."

Cami didn't comment. She wondered why Pearl thought Josh would be able to heal his broken heart here when she hadn't been able to heal her own.

But for Josh's sake, she hoped somehow he did find the peace he sought.

CHAPTER 4

Cami cocooned herself inside the office and tackled several stacks of mail and paperwork that had piled up over the last few weeks.

While opening one of the envelopes, she managed to give herself a nice, painful paper cut and went to the bathroom for a bandage. Going back to her desk, she stopped momentarily to look out the window. She searched the long stretch of beach for a sign of Josh Drake, but the beach was deserted. And for good reason. A stiff wind blew a wall of low-hanging, gray clouds toward the coastline.

Wondering if Josh was going to get caught in the storm, she glanced at the clock on the wall and noted that it was one o' clock in the afternoon. Surely he had reached downtown Seamist by now and was safely inside the gallery or at the diner having some lunch.

Forcing herself back to her paperwork, Cami found her attention wandering and jumped when a crack of thunder split the air. Within seconds, rain pelted the glass and soon turned into a torrential down-pour.

The door to the office opened, and Pearl peeked inside. "Sorry to bother you, Cami," she said, "but do you think we ought to drive to town and give Mr. Drake a lift home? It's awfully soggy out there."

Cami smiled at Pearl, not surprised by the woman's concern and nurturing instincts. "I'll make a few calls and see if I can track him down," she offered.

Her friends at the diner hadn't seen him, and he hadn't been to the gallery either. Cami called several other places, still without luck. *He is a grown man,* she told herself. *There is no reason to worry.* But still she fretted.

"Any luck?" Pearl checked back several minutes later. There was a dusting of flour on her apron and a smudge on her cheek.

"No, but I'm sure he's fine," Cami said, trying to be convincing.

"The storm doesn't show any sign of letting up." Pearl gazed outside at the drizzles of rain running down the window.

"I should have told him to call if he wanted a ride back to the inn." Cami pushed herself away from the desk, walked to the window, and looked out, but there was nothing to see. The bank of gray clouds had swallowed up the beach and blanketed the entire coastline, giving it a good drenching.

Just then the back door opened and a clatter of footsteps caught their attention. Grandpa Willy was busily explaining to someone about one of his frightening experiences at sea during the storm of '67 that sank dozens of boats and took the lives of many men.

To their relief, a cold and dripping wet Josh Drake stepped inside the kitchen behind Grandpa Willy.

"There you are!" Pearl exclaimed. "We were getting worried about you."

"I was getting worried about myself," Josh said with a laugh. "I walked to the lighthouse, then thought I'd work my way back through town, but the rain came on so suddenly I didn't have a chance to find cover."

"How did you two meet up?" Cami asked, grabbing a fresh dish towel and handing it to him to dry his face and hair.

"I saw him on my way home from the marina," Grandpa Willy explained. "He was walking down the side of the road toward town. I didn't know it was Josh until I stopped to pick him up."

"I'm certainly glad you found him," Pearl fussed. "Now," she told Josh, "you go get out of those wet clothes, and I'll warm you up some soup. I'd hate to see you catch a cold being out in weather like this."

Josh didn't put up a fight, but removed his shoes so he didn't track water through the house.

"Just set your wet things by the door out in the hallway," Pearl called after him. "We'll put them in the laundry for you."

With their houseguest safely inside, Cami went back to her work. But try as she might, she was in no mood to sort through bills and answer inquiries about the inn. Part of her distraction was the mixture of voices and laughter coming from the kitchen. Pearl, Grandpa Willy, and Josh were at the table, eating soup and enjoying each other's company. Cami pushed the door shut but still heard the muffled sound of their lively conversation.

"Forget it." She dropped the handful of papers onto the desk and shoved back her chair. She'd try again later. She hadn't had any lunch, and a bowl of Pearl's minestrone soup sounded perfect on a cold, dreary day like today.

The threesome stopped talking when Cami stepped into the room.

"What?" Cami said, wondering why they'd gotten quiet so abruptly.

Pearl and Grandpa looked guiltily at each other, then back at her.

"Nothing," Pearl said. "I thought you were working in the office."

"I got hungry," Cami said, eyeing each of them. Something told her they had been talking about her before she came into the room. "Did I interrupt anything?" she asked.

"No," Grandpa Willy answered, wiping the inside of his soup bowl with a chunk of bread. "Josh here's been telling us about his fascination for travel and historical artifacts."

"I got my doctorate in history," Josh explained. "But as much as I enjoy teaching, I would rather be out exploring the world, discovering ancient cities and lost treasures."

Cami nodded and took a seat at the table as Pearl jumped up and filled a bowl of soup for her. Mumbling her thanks, Cami took several crackers and crumbled them into the soup. *Lost treasure?* Cami found his choice of words interesting, especially since there was a suspected treasure hunter out there who was also likely a murderer. Then she reminded herself the police had their suspect.

"So you want to be a modern-day Indiana Jones, is that it?" Pearl asked.

Josh chuckled but answered affirmatively. "Actually, yes. To find a thousand-year-old relic or discover an ancient buried city would be a thrill."

"Let's see." Cami licked a cracker crumb off her bottom lip. "We could call you Pennsylvania Drake. Hmm, doesn't quite have the same ring to it."

Josh laughed. "I'd have to move to another state that sounds a bit more rugged, I guess. Like Nevada or Texas. Texas Drake," he said. "Any better?"

"How about Dakota Drake?" Pearl suggested. "The Dakotas are rugged states."

"Dakota Drake doesn't sound too bad." Josh nodded thoughtfully. "I've got a friend who's a paleontologist. Maybe he'd let me tag along next time he gets involved in a project. By the way, how did you get started in all of this, Pearl? Did you take classes?"

"Heavens no," Pearl said. "I worked at the local newspaper office as a secretary for several years and helped out a few times reporting on small community gatherings like bake-offs and social functions. When I was twenty-three, I moved to Portland to work at the paper there and got bigger assignments. That's where I began my training as a photographer. I was quiet enamored with the photography side of reporting and went on assignment with as many photographers as I could. By the time I was twenty-five, I was covering some of the bigger stories in the Portland area and traveling around the state."

"That sounds pretty young," Josh said, apparently impressed by her accomplishments.

"For a woman it was," Pearl admitted. "I was in the right place at the right time when I was introduced to a representative for *National Geographic*. He was the one who offered me the opportunity to go to Egypt the first time as an assistant photographer."

"I'll bet that was a fascinating trip," Cami said.

"I never went with him," Pearl said.

"Why not?" Cami was shocked.

"We weren't leaving for a month, so in the meantime I handled an assignment in San Francisco, and . . . ," she paused, "that was where I met Frederick. He was in the import-export business. We fell in love the first time we laid eyes on each other."

Cami had never heard the full story of how Pearl and Frederick met, and she listened with fascination.

"He traveled a great deal, and I was on the road a lot too, so we only saw each other occasionally, going months at a time without being together. But we had something very special." Pearl's wistful tone struck a chord in Cami's heart. "We talked about getting married," Pearl said.

"But my work kept me on the road so often, we didn't really know when we could. I didn't see my family much, and I was rarely in the same city two weeks in a row, so I also had a hard time staying in the habit of going to church. Eventually I quit going altogether."

Cami sensed the regret in Pearl's voice.

"Anyway, by the time I was twenty-seven, I was ready to get married, settle down in Seamist, and start a family. But things didn't quite work out the way I had planned."

Josh looked at her with questioning eyes, apparently wanting to know the rest of the story.

"After Frederick passed away, I went through some difficult personal challenges. I wasn't sure how I was going to manage, but one day out of the blue the man from *National Geographic* called to see what I was doing. He was heading out on a tour of eastern Europe and northern Africa and needed an assistant. It was the lifeline I needed, and I grabbed onto it with both hands. That decision changed my whole life."

Josh stared at Pearl with the same amazement Cami felt.

Grandpa Willy broke the silence by scooting back his chair and clearing away his dishes. "Back then we learned things through the school of hard knocks," he said. "Not like you young ones now, going to college and learning in a classroom."

"That's true," Pearl agreed. "I earned every one of these wrinkles."

Grandpa chuckled. "Not to mention the gray hair."

"That's for sure." Pearl laughed and cleared her own dishes, then appeared to have remembered something. "I've invited Ashlyn and Mitch over for dinner tonight. I hope you don't mind, Cami. I thought Josh might enjoy meeting Mitch."

"Of course not," Cami replied, wishing Pearl would have kept talking. She loved to hear stories from Pearl's life. "I was thinking the same thing."

"You'll like them," Pearl told Josh. "They're a lovely couple."

"I'm looking forward to meeting them," he answered. "But don't forget, you promised to show me some of your scrapbooks. I'd love to see your pictures."

"Let me get the kitchen straightened up, and I'll dig them out for you," Pearl told him.

"Thank you for telling us your story, Pearl," Josh said. "You're quite a fascinating lady."

Pearl's cheeks flushed. "I was able to do and see some fascinating things," she said, "but my life hasn't been without its challenges and heartbreaks. It's been quite a bumpy ride. I guess that's why I enjoy what I'm doing now so much. Life is much smoother now, thank goodness."

* * *

After lunch, Cami noticed that Grandpa Willy took a nap in front of the television as he was prone to do. Josh and Pearl went into the back parlor to look at photo albums of Pearl's many adventures.

Cami found herself once again in her office, but instead of paying bills, she stared out the window at the storm breaking up outside. Streaks of sunshine peeked through cracks in the clouds, sparking the water's surface with golden glitters of light.

The last thing Cami felt like doing was the tedious task of book work. Dallin had always done the books for the inn while she took care of correspondence and advertising. She'd never been a real whiz at accounting, nor did she particularly enjoy working with numbers. But with Dallin gone, someone had to do it. Grandpa wasn't about to tackle a computer at his age, and Pearl already did the gardening, cooking, and light cleaning around the inn.

Glaring at the pile of work on the desk, she decided to put it off one more day and walk next door to see if Ashlyn was home. Ashlyn taught AP English at the high school every weekday morning, but she was usually home by noon, sometimes later if she stayed and had lunch with Mitch, who taught health, aside from coaching baseball and football.

Cami grabbed a jacket out of the coat closet and went to tell Pearl where she was going. Walking softly through the front parlor toward the back parlor, she listened as Pearl told Josh about one of her escapades and brushes with dangers during the exciting years she worked as a photojournalist. Cami had seen Pearl's collection of photographs, which numbered in the thousands, and had been amazed over and over again at the daring feats the woman had survived. She'd been nearly to the top of Mount Everest, she'd dived in the deepest caverns of the sea, and she'd traveled to the farthest reaches of the Arctic by dogsled. There was nothing the woman hadn't done, and Cami was amazed she'd survived all her adventures.

Pearl and Josh were so engrossed in their conversation that they didn't notice Cami for a full five minutes as she stood in the same room listening to them talk. And even then she had to clear her throat three times before they looked up.

"Cami!" Pearl exclaimed. "I didn't see you there. Did you need me?"

"No, no," Cami assured her. "I just wanted to tell you I was heading next door to see if Ashlyn was home."

Pearl nodded. "Tell her dinner will be around six-thirty."

"I will," Cami replied. Josh looked up from the pictures and gave her a smile, then returned quickly to Pearl's life in pictures. "See you later," she said as she left the room.

* * *

The breeze was fresh and cool as she walked through the thicket of trees to the house Ashlyn and Mitch rented from Grandpa Willy. Cami had lived most of her life in that house, and even with Mitch and Ashlyn living there, it still seemed like home. Sometimes she wished she could go up to her room, turn back the clock a few years, and find a way to alter the course of her and Dallin's life. If only he hadn't gone to Portland that day. If only she'd gone with him. Maybe they would've spent the night in Portland, or come home at a different time. Or maybe she would've died with him.

As morbid as the thought was, she wasn't so sure it was such a bad alternative to life without him. Certainly their loved ones would have struggled with the tragedy of both Dallin and Cami dying in the car accident, but Cami knew there would have been reason for comfort knowing that she and Dallin were together in heaven forever. Certainly that was much more desirable than the hell she tried to bear each day being alone on earth.

Knocking at Ashlyn's door, she noticed the pots of geraniums Ashlyn had planted and the cute welcome mat on the porch.

Sometimes it was difficult for her to be around Mitch and Ashlyn. Not that she didn't love them as much as if they were family, but seeing them so happy, so in love, brought an ache to her heart that took days to go away.

"Hey there," Ashlyn said when she opened the door.

"Mmm, smells good in here. Are you baking?"

"Are you kidding? It's a sugar cookie–scented candle." Ashlyn stepped aside so Cami could enter. "I was just going to call you and see if you wanted to run to town with me."

"Sure, why not? I'm not doing anything else. As usual," Cami said with a sigh.

"You know what? You need a hobby. Maybe you could take some correspondence courses. You need to work toward something, see some change and progress in your life," she suggested.

"A hobby?" Cami asked. "You mean like crocheting or scrap-booking?"

"Yes." Ashlyn nodded. "Hey, maybe we could take a cooking class together. Heaven knows I could use it."

"Cooking?" Cami shook her head. "Too boring."

"Okay, then how about painting? Or flower arranging?"

Cami got to her feet and walked across the room. "I don't know," she told Ashlyn. "Let me think about it. Right now, nothing sounds interesting to me."

"You need to do something besides your work at the inn," Ashlyn said. "Hey, maybe you could do something at the high school, like teach an interior design class or something. The kids would love you, and you would be so good. Mitch could pull some strings and get you on there."

The suggestion actually made Cami stop and think. Teaching. The thought had never occurred to her before. She mulled the idea over in her head a few times, then shrugged and said, "That does sound kind of fun. But let me think about it before you talk to Mitch, okay?"

"Okay," Ashlyn said with a smile. "Now, let's go run that errand."

"What do you need in town?"

"I need to go to the bakery," Ashlyn said with a sly grin. "I'm craving sugar cookies."

* * *

On their way back from the bakery, the girls rolled down the windows and let the fresh spring breeze fill the car. They had purchased extra sugar cookies to take home for dinner that night, even though Pearl would probably take offense that they'd actually bought something from the bakery when she could very well make it better at home.

"You know," Cami said, licking frosting from her fingers, "you shouldn't hang around with me anymore."

"Why's that?" Ashlyn asked, popping the last bite of cookie into her mouth.

"Because you might die," Cami said matter-of-factly.

Ashlyn choked on the cookie and began coughing. Luckily she was near a stop sign and could stop the car while she cleared her airway.

"See!" Cami said. "I'm bad luck. You're lucky you didn't croak just then."

Ashlyn gasped for air until she finally breathed without coughing. "What are you talking about?" she demanded.

"I'm talking about the fact that everyone around me seems to end up dying," Cami stated.

"My father, my mother, my grandma . . . Dallin. I just wonder who's going to be next?"

Ashlyn rolled her eyes with annoyance. "Cami, will you stop it? You are not bad luck, and I'm not worried that I'm going to die if I hang out with you. But I'd like to change the subject if we could please. All this talk about dying is freaking me out!"

"I'm sorry, but I just thought I'd warn you," Cami said.

"Okay, consider me sufficiently warned," Ashlyn told her. "Now, let's talk about something else." She pulled onto the interstate. "I know, let's talk about Mr. Drake," she said. "I mean, how cute can a man be? And nice. I thought Mitch had the market cornered on cute and nice, but Josh Drake is definitely a close second. Don't you think?"

Cami didn't know how to answer. Talking about another man made her feel uncomfortable and disloyal to Dallin. But she couldn't deny she'd had the same thoughts. He was nice and cute. But he was also someone the people of Seamist had reason to be wary of—a self-admitted treasure hunter.

CHAPTER 5

"That was about the best meal I've eaten in my entire life," Josh said, scooting his chair back from the table. "Honestly Pearl, that roast was so tender it melted in my mouth."

"He's right," Mitch said. "You managed to outdo yourself tonight, Pearl. And I ate way too much."

"I'm the one who had three helpings of potatoes," Josh confessed.

"You're welcome to come running with us in the morning to burn off some of those calories," Mitch offered. "Ashlyn and I hit the beach at 6:00 A.M."

Josh nodded. "Sounds like a good idea. I'd better do something or I'm not going to fit inside my car to drive back home."

Pearl assured him he could use some homegrown meat on his bones, then suggested they move to the parlor for dessert. Everyone complained that they were too full, but no one turned down her offer of fresh fruit and cookies.

"Now, mind you, I didn't actually make these cookies," she told everyone. "My cookies are softer and lighter, but these will do for now."

"So, Josh, how do you like the Oregon coast?" Mitch asked, taking a cookie off the tray.

"It's very beautiful," he answered. "I wanted to see more of it today, but I got caught in that storm. I got a pretty good drenching."

Ashlyn giggled at his comment, and Josh's expression grew confused. She quickly explained herself. "I'm not laughing at you," she told him. "It just reminded me of when I got caught in a storm when I first came to Seamist. I nearly drowned in the ocean."

"Really?" Josh asked with alarm. "How?"

She told him the story of how she'd gone for a walk around the cape, but a storm had hit the coast before she'd gotten back around. A sneaker wave caught her off guard and had pulled her into the churning sea. The memory of trying to fight her way above the surface but not being strong enough still made Ashlyn tentative about going into the water.

Cami remembered how terrified she'd been that day. Mitch had gone out to look for Ashlyn and found her unconscious on the beach. Although Ashlyn had recovered fully, Cami had never forgotten the fear she'd had for her friend, and as much as she loved the ocean, she knew of its power and unpredictability and had a sober respect for it.

Josh made the mistake of asking Mitch about the high school baseball team. Since baseball was Mitch's passion, the answer was long and lengthy, and finally Ashlyn broke in and said, "Honey, I don't think Josh needs to know the batting averages of each player on the team."

"Oh." Mitch smiled sheepishly and turned to Josh. "I guess not. We do have a preseason game this weekend if you want to come and watch."

Cami remembered that Josh had only reserved his room for five days, which meant he was planning on checking out Saturday morning.

"I'll have to see," he replied. "I was thinking of driving down the coast to San Francisco, but I might stay on through the weekend. If that's okay," he directed his comment to Cami.

"Your room is still available," she told him. They had several elderly couples coming for the weekend, so the inn would be much busier in a few days. But so far, his room hadn't been booked.

"Good," he said. "I'm not quite ready to take off yet. I never did get a chance to have clam chowder at the Bayside Diner or visit the galleries downtown."

"And we still have to grill Mitch's salmon," Pearl told him. "You can't miss that."

"Well," Josh said with a nod, "I guess it's decided then. I don't want to wear out my welcome, though."

"No chance of that," Grandpa Willy assured him. "Besides, I promised to take you out whale watching," he said. "If the weather's good tomorrow, we could go out then."

"Thanks, Willy," Josh replied. "I'm looking forward to that."

Ashlyn took Mitch's hand in hers and announced that they needed to be getting home. "I'll help you clean up the dishes, Pearl," she offered.

Pearl waved her offer away. "No problem. I washed pots and pans as I went along. I just have to throw the dishes in the dishwasher."

"Are you sure?" Ashlyn asked. "I feel guilty making you do all the work."

"Don't feel too guilty," Grandpa Willy said gruffly. "She had me working as a scullery maid all afternoon. I'm the one with dishpan hands." He held his hands up for all to see.

"Now, William," Pearl said, "I don't recall having to twist your arm too much to get you to help."

"She's got me working for my supper," he said. "I'm telling you, I'm outnumbered in this house. These women have me two to one."

"Most men would count themselves lucky," Mitch said, giving Pearl a peck on the cheek and thanking her for the wonderful meal. He and Ashlyn bid everyone good night and reminded Josh about their 6:00 A.M. run the next day.

Pearl also turned down Cami's offer to help in the kitchen, and Grandpa went to check the weather report for the next day's outing while grumbling something about if he didn't have bad luck, he wouldn't have any luck at all.

"You have wonderful friends and family," Josh told Cami. "And such a lovely place here."

"Thank you," Cami said, glad he liked it. "How did you enjoy your visit to the Misty Harbor Lighthouse?"

"It's an enchanting place. I enjoyed the tour, and Mr. McDougall told me the history behind the lighthouse."

"Fascinating, isn't it?" Cami said.

"The men who worked as lighthouse keepers back then had to be among some of the bravest in the world," Josh observed.

Cami agreed. "Did Mr. McDougall tell you all about the first lighthouse that existed and how it was destroyed?"

"He did. The storm of 1846 is still considered the worst in Seamist history," he remarked. "Imagine what a sight that must have been—to have a wave that large wash over the cape and literally destroy the light-house!" He shook his head at the thought. "That poor lighthouse keeper who died during the storm. Like I said, some of the bravest men."

He shook his head as if he still couldn't believe it, then he continued. "They never did find his body or clear away all the debris.

He told me that in 1882, when the city of Seamist was established, a new lighthouse was built in the same place as the old one. He showed me some pictures of the original structure. They duplicated the old lighthouse almost exactly. I think I wore out Mr. McDougall with all my questions."

"Doubtful," Cami told him. "The man loves to talk about the history of the lighthouse. One of his ancestors was the first lighthouse keeper when the new lighthouse was finished. He's very proud of his ancestry and eagerly talks about it."

"He took me downstairs where some of the original structure remains. Most people don't know this, but there's a hidden door leading to a storm cellar as well as a tunnel connecting the lighthouse and the caretaker's house. It was also used originally for a safe place to hide from Indian attacks."

"I didn't know that," Cami said, fascinated by the new piece of information.

"I've always had a fascination with lighthouses, but for some reason, they seem to have more significance than they used to."

Cami wondered if it was because they sometimes were connected with buried treasure.

He gazed at the fireplace, then said with quiet introspection, "My father's death has changed the way I look at things."

The pain in his heart was reflected in his voice, and Cami felt bad for her accusatory thought. "I know what you mean," she said.

He looked at her and gave her an understanding smile. "I imagine you do."

"So," Cami tried to lighten the conversation before the topic of Dallin or his untimely death came up, "how did you enjoy Pearl's photo albums this afternoon?"

"The woman's amazing. Jacques Cousteau had nothing on her," he said.

Cami laughed.

"I am amazed at the things she's seen and the places she's been. I may be an Indiana Jones wanna-be, but she's the real thing. She's lived more in one life than any ten people I know."

"She really is something," Cami told him. "I don't know what we'd do without her."

"I don't know how Pearl would feel about this," Josh weighed his words carefully, "but I have a good friend in New York who works for one of the big publishing houses back there. I'd like to talk to him about the possibility of doing a book with all her pictures and stories. How do you think she'd react?"

"A book? Pearl?" Cami exclaimed.

"Yes. Those pictures of wild animals in Africa, penguins in Antarctica, the top of the world from Mount Everest base camp . . . It would make a fascinating account of many of history's greatest moments and greatest places. And to think she experienced all of it!"

"It's a great idea." Cami was breathless at the thought of something so wonderful coming out of Pearl's hard work. "Do you really think your friend would be interested?"

"There's only one way to find out," Josh said. "I'll call him first thing in the morning and talk to him about it. There's no sense approaching Pearl with the idea until I know someone is interested."

Before she could respond, the clock on the mantle chimed the lateness of the hour. "Are you going running in the morning also?" he asked, changing the subject.

"Uh," she fumbled for an answer. How did she tell him that she'd rather have a root canal than go running? "I don't run," she said. "I love to go for walks on the beach, but I'm not much of a runner."

"You know what?" he confessed. "Neither am I. I guess it's a guy thing, but I didn't want Mitch to think I was wimpy when he invited me to go along."

Cami burst out laughing. She supposed it probably was a "guy thing," but it was refreshing to have a man actually admit it.

"You don't have to go if you don't want," she told him.

"I wouldn't mind getting up and going for an early morning walk, though," he replied with a look of invitation in his eyes.

She was shocked by her own reply. For once she didn't overanalyze her feelings or rethink them. She simply said, "Would you like some company?"

His blue eyes sparkled when he smiled. "I was hoping you'd say that."

Cami grinned, telling herself that there was nothing wrong with going on a simple, harmless walk with Josh. She found his company easy and his conversations interesting. She couldn't think of one reason not to go on a walk with him.

* * *

Cami couldn't sleep that night. Thoughts of Dallin filled her mind, and guilt filled her heart. She knew a walk with Josh was innocent and harmless, yet she couldn't help feeling as though she were doing something wrong.

Finally she went to the kitchen for a drink. Sitting at the table, she rested her head in her hands and tried to make sense of her feelings—those that were loyal to Dallin, and those that were attracted to Josh.

A squeak in the floorboards brought Cami's head up with a snap. Her grandfather walked into the kitchen, rubbing his eyes. "What's going on?" he asked, his voice thick and sleepy. "Is something wrong? Are you sick?"

"No, Grandpa," Cami answered. "I just couldn't sleep."

He patted her on the head as he walked by, then took a seat at the table. He'd patted her on the head like that for as long as she could remember. It always made her feel like a little girl—something, in a way, she wished she still was. Life had been so much simpler then. Feelings weren't so complicated.

"You got something on your mind?" he asked, but it sounded more like a statement than a question.

She shrugged and ran her finger around the rim of her glass. "Kind of."

"What is it, my dear?" he asked. "You can tell me what's botherin' you."

She smiled, knowing that it was true. She'd always been able to talk to him. Her grandfather was a good listener and always gave sound advice. She trusted his opinions and knew that they came from a great deal of wisdom, but they also came from his heart, and that made all the difference.

She wanted to be strong, to handle it on her own, but for some reason, as her grandfather looked at her with such love, concern, and true willingness to do anything in the world to help her, she found her resolve melt, and the words began to pour from her mouth as fast as tears fell from her eyes.

"I feel like Dallin is the only man for me, Grandpa. I love him with all my heart and look forward to when we can be together again. But sometimes I feel so lonely. I can't imagine how I'm going to go through the rest of my life alone." Then she grew alarmed and added, "Not that you aren't always there for me, Grandpa," she said. "And Pearl and Ashlyn and Mitch. You guys are the only way I've been able to make it this far."

"Does this have anything to do with Mr. Drake?"

She opened her mouth to say "no," but she knew it was a lie. "Kind of," she said, looking down at her glass. "Yes," she corrected. "And the guilt is eating me alive. I feel like I'm being untrue to Dallin."

Grandpa took a deep breath and let it out slowly. "My little Cami-girl," he said, calling her by her childhood nickname, "life shouldn't be so hard on such a young one." He patted her hand. "It breaks my heart to see you so worried. It's been such a long time since I've seen you smile, heard you laugh. Since you've been truly happy. That is, until . . ." He stopped.

Cami looked at him with anticipation, waiting for him to continue. "Until what, Grandpa?"

"Until Mr. Drake came," he told her matter-of-factly.

"Mr. Drake! What do you mean?"

"I mean it's been good to see you enjoy the company of someone else, someone your own age. Especially with a person who has a good heart like Mr. Drake," Grandpa Willy said.

"I've only visited with him a few times," she said in her defense. "It's not like we've spent that much time together, and it's not like I've been flirting with him or anything."

Grandpa Willy held up one hand. "Now, now, don't get yourself all worked up. I didn't mean anything by it. I'm just saying that it's nice to see you acting a little more like your old self."

"So what do you think I should do? He asked me to go walking with him in the morning."

Grandpa Willy thought a moment before he answered. "Let me put it this way. All the possessions I own, all the places I've seen, and all the money I have still don't fill up the empty space I have inside of me left by your grandmother. The only thing that's going to fill it is the love and companionship of another person. Same with Pearl. She has so much, so many material possessions, but I bet she'd give up all of them to have someone to share her life with."

"What are you saying, Grandpa?"

"I'm saying, what if the situation were turned around and you were the one in heaven and Dallin were the one on earth? Are you telling me that you wouldn't want him to find someone else? Maybe even get married again? Would you want him to spend the rest of his life, which could be fifty years or more, alone?"

She thought she had a ready answer for him, but his words sank deep. How would she feel if Dallin were the one down here, struggling and alone? Would she want him to prove his undying love and loyalty to her by staying single the rest of his life? Was that the price she would expect him to pay? Did she truly think that was what Dallin expected of her?

New tears sprang to her eyes. She blinked, and they overflowed onto her cheeks.

"Well?" Grandpa asked.

"As hard as it would be for me to see him meet and maybe marry someone else, I think it would be harder for me to see him sad and lonely, never letting himself love again. That's too much to ask—for someone to sacrifice their personal happiness for the rest of their life."

Grandpa Willy nodded. "That's why God's plan is called 'the plan of happiness.' That's what He wants for His children. He wants them to be happy. And that means you. I think Dallin probably understands that plan even better now than we do. I'm sure he wants you to be happy, Cami. Who knows—maybe Josh is all a part of Heavenly Father's great plan for you."

"Oh, Grandpa!" she exclaimed.

"Well, you never know. But going for a harmless walk with Josh is nothing to be ashamed of or worried about. You are young and beautiful, and I hate to see you spend the rest of your life alone. I, for one, wouldn't want that for you. I know Pearl would completely agree with me—for once in her life," he added, and they both chuckled. Then, on a more serious note, he added, "And I believe that Dallin wouldn't want you to be alone either. He loved you much, much more than that."

Cami's tears dried. Her heart grew calm and warm. "You always know just what to say to help me," she told him. "Thank you, Grandpa."

"Anytime, Cami-girl," he said, pushing himself up from his chair. He walked over to her and gave her a kiss on the forehead. "Now, you better skedaddle and get to bed. It's going to be morning before you know it."

Kneeling beside her bed that night, Cami approached her prayers with a different mind-set and goal. Instead of pleading for help to figure out what to do with her life now that Dallin was gone, she asked the Lord to help her have the strength and courage she needed to start moving on with her life. And she asked for the Lord to help her feel right in her heart about her decision to move on.

She also asked for one more thing. She asked the Lord to let Dallin know she still loved him with all her heart, and that while she might spend time with Josh, no one could ever take Dallin's place.

CHAPTER 6

Josh came down the stairs just as Cami stepped through her bedroom door. They looked at each other in the soft morning light and smiled.

"Are we out of our minds to get up this time of day?" Josh asked quietly.

Cami nodded and giggled softly. "You don't know how hard it was to get out of bed," she told him. "When my alarm went off, I thought it was the oven timer, and I couldn't figure out what Pearl was doing up baking so early in the morning."

Josh chuckled.

"Let's go out through the kitchen," Cami suggested.

Outside there wasn't even a breath of wind in the air, which was fresh and crisp. Cami pulled in several long breaths and felt the fog in her head clear away.

They emerged from the thicket of pines surrounding the inn, and the view of the coast northward appeared before them. "Look at that!" he exclaimed.

A gauzy mist cloaked the headlands and blanketed the sea. The beach was clear, but the fog hung low. It was mystical and magical and breathtaking. The sound of surf pounding the shore was the only evidence of the ocean beneath the blanket of gray.

Cami looked at the boyish excitement in his expression. His eyes were wide with wonder, his cheeks rosy from the morning chill. His wavy, unruly hair added to his charm, and she had to wonder why the man wasn't married. Of course, maybe he had a girlfriend. For all she knew he could even be engaged.

"Do you see any sign of Mitch or Ashlyn?" Cami asked as they descended the wooden stairs to the beach, where jagged rocks and driftwood collected in the half-moon-shaped bay below the jutting precipice.

"Nope," he said. He checked his watch. "Wonder if they slept in?"

"They better not have!" Cami exclaimed. "It's their fault we're here in the first place. I say we go bang on their door and wake them up."

Josh looked at her with amusement. "Or we could just enjoy this beautiful morning without having to jog."

"You're right!" she cried. "If they come, we might have to run."

"But still, we should wait a little longer since they were the ones who invited us," he said.

"Yeah, you're right," Cami agreed. She sighed and looked around the beach, tapped her toe on the hard sand, then said, "Okay, that's long enough." She grabbed his arm and pulled him down the beach. "Let's get going before they show up." He laughed as she dragged him along until they finally broke into a well-matched, briskly paced walk along the shoreline.

At his request, Cami told Josh some of the history of Seamist and answered questions about the school system, the close-knit towns-people, and about some of the celebrations the city had that had been traditions from the time she was a young girl.

"I haven't seen any churches around," he remarked. "What religion are the people around here?"

"There are a lot of Mormons in our town. Brigham Young sent pioneers to help settle Oregon in 1849. But it was the next President of the Church, John Taylor, who later sent Mormons here to Seamist. My great-great-grandparents were some of the first settlers in the area. The Sea Rose Bed and Breakfast was their home."

"I've studied the Mormons," he said. "They had quite a history of persecution in their early years."

"It wasn't until they finally moved to the Salt Lake Valley that they were able to live in peace," she told him.

"I actually stopped in Carthage, Illinois, on my way west and went through the jail where Joseph Smith and his brother were killed."

Cami's face registered surprise. "I've always wanted to go there."

"You have?" he said. Then he asked, "Are you—"

"A member of The Church of Jesus Christ of Latter-day Saints? Yes," she said.

"Wow, I didn't know that," he told her. "I had a lot of questions after the tour, but the visitors' center was closing, so I couldn't ask anyone. Maybe sometime we can have a talk. I'm curious about some things."

"Sure," Cami said. "I can't guarantee I'll have all the answers you need, but I'm sure Grandpa or one of the others can help."

"Are Pearl and Mitch and Ashlyn all members of the Church?"

"Yes," she answered. "You're surrounded," she said in a menacing tone. Then he said something that made her stop in her tracks.

"I was baptized into your church when I was eight."

"You're a member?" she asked, and started walking again.

"I guess, in a way, I am." He fell in step beside her. "But my mom died when I was ten, and my dad remarried a woman who was not a member. He lost interest in the Church after that, and we never went back," he said.

"Do you go to any other church now?"

"No," he replied. "But ever since my father passed away, I find I have all kinds of questions about the whole purpose of life. You know, why we're even here." He looked at her with a lost expression in his eyes. "I guess that's why I stopped at Carthage and then went on to Nauvoo," he told her. "I'm curious to know about the church I was baptized into. I mean, obviously it meant a lot to my parents when I was younger, or they wouldn't have had me baptized, right?"

Cami nodded.

"I can't really remember much about what I learned when I was younger. Bits and pieces mostly. I just want to find out what Latter-day Saints believe and find out if maybe your church has some of the answers I'm looking for."

"Church is at eleven o'clock Sunday morning. You're welcome to join us if you'd like," she invited.

He pondered her invitation for a moment, then nodded his head. "Maybe I will," he said. Then he smiled broadly. "I think I'd like that."

A sudden, warm feeling washed over Cami. The thought that he had been guided to the Sea Rose for a reason surfaced in her mind. She felt guilty even thinking he had any other reason for being there. The man admitted that he was searching for answers to his father's death, to his own questions about life. She knew those answers would come as he learned about the Church and the teachings of the gospel.

"Cami?" he said louder for a second time.

"Oh." Her attention snapped back. "I'm sorry, I was thinking about something."

"Is everything okay?" he asked.

"Everything's great," she answered with a warm, sincere smile.

* * *

They never did find Mitch and Ashlyn, and it was just as well because Cami truly enjoyed their walk together. Josh was easy to talk to. She had imagined a history professor to be a bit stuffy and narrow-minded, but Cami found Josh to be fascinating and affable. Even though he hadn't seen all the things in the world he wanted to see, he'd still traveled a great deal and had interesting stories to tell. She found herself captivated by his quest to learn from the past, from the people and experiences that had gone before. He felt much could be learned from ancestors, but was afraid that the way the world was, people wouldn't listen and would still follow destructive paths, paths already trodden by the people in the past, paths that didn't need to be trodden again.

Pearl pulled apple-cinnamon streusel muffins out of the oven just as they walked through the back door. The fragrance seemed like a warm welcome home.

She greeted them with a cheerful hello. "You're just in time," she announced. "How about a muffin and something warm to drink?"

Josh shook his head. "Pearl, you're spoiling me."

"I'm sure trying," she replied with a smile. "Now, both of you go wash up, and I'll serve you out on the porch."

Cami almost declined her offer since she wasn't a guest and had her own work to do, but she knew it was Pearl's nature to always be doing things for others. Pampering their guest obviously brought her a great deal of joy.

Minutes later, Cami found herself seated in a wicker chair next to Josh, a plate of muffins and steaming cups of herb tea on a table before them.

As they ate, they watched the morning unfold. The bank of clouds broke up, letting veils of golden sunlight shine through, burning off the misty fog hugging the coastline. A soft breeze, fresh and fragrant, tickled the blossoms on the trees. The morning was perfect, heavenly.

"So, tell me about Pennsylvania," she asked, turning to Josh.

He told her about the university where he taught, and confessed that he spent most of his time preparing for classes or grading papers.

"I'm sure it's not as boring as you make it sound," she countered. "I'll bet you do a lot of socializing."

"Not really. Jane and I go out occasionally to a movie or to dinner, but that's about all."

"Jane?" she asked, quickly scanning her mind for any previous reference to a person named Jane.

"Jane Covington," he told her. "My girlfriend."

Cami didn't anticipate the reaction she felt when he said he had a girlfriend. Certainly she didn't care if he had a girlfriend, a fiancée, or a wife for that matter. He was a guest at their inn. Period. Sure, they'd developed a mild friendship, but he had also done so with Pearl, Grandpa Willy, Ashlyn, and Mitch. Still, niggling at the corner of her brain was the tiniest feeling of . . . *Of what?* she asked herself. What did she feel?

She wasn't sure, but one thing she knew—she needed to distance herself from him.

"Well," she said, pushing herself to her feet, "I've got a lot of work, so I'd better go get showered."

Josh stood and thanked her for spending time with him. He said something about enjoying their walk and learning some of the history behind Seamist, but Cami wasn't really listening. Mr. Drake had a girlfriend. Named Jane.

* * *

Holing up in her office, Cami actually managed to get lost in some paperwork and was surprised to learn that several hours had passed. It was the first time in a long time that she'd kept her attention focused on a project for that length of time.

The mansion was quiet when she left her office. She wandered into the kitchen and grabbed an apple to eat. Pearl was nowhere to be found and neither was Grandpa Willy.

Stepping onto the porch, she cautiously looked around for their houseguest and was relieved when she found no sign of him outside. She did, however, find Pearl wearing a stylish denim skirt and bright yellow shirt, kneeling in the shade and digging at the base of a rosebush. She looked up when Cami approached.

"Taking a break from all that thinking?" Pearl asked her, well aware of Cami's loathing for bookkeeping and finances.

"I got a brain cramp," Cami joked. She sank to her knees and sat next to Pearl. The day had grown warm and sunny, but not too hot to work outside. "Where is everybody?"

"Your grandfather and Josh went sailing," Pearl told her.

"Sailing!" Cami exclaimed.

Pearl nodded. "They said they wouldn't be back until later this afternoon. I hope they're not late, because I'm grilling some of that salmon on the barbecue for dinner. Josh is anxious to try some."

"You seem to think a lot of our 'Mr. Drake,'" Cami teased.

"How could anyone not like him? He's warm, witty, and intelligent. Not to mention very handsome." Her tone hinted at something Cami chose not to pursue.

"Did you know he's LDS?" Cami said, giving the conversation a jump start in a completely different direction.

"He is?" Pearl exclaimed. "I had no idea."

"He told me he was baptized when he was eight, but when he was ten his mother died. After his dad remarried, they never went back to church," she explained.

"For heaven's sake, why not?" Pearl asked, appalled at the news.

"His dad remarried a nonmember and lost interest in the Church. They just quit going." Cami watched an earthworm wiggle its way through freshly dug soil. "He has a lot of questions. His father's death has gotten him thinking about the purpose of life and what the Church believes. He's trying to find answers," Cami said.

Pearl looked at her, wide-eyed. "That poor, sweet boy," she said. "He must feel so lost with his mother and father both gone now. We should invite him to church on Sunday," she said. "After one of Mitch's Sunday School lessons, he's bound to get even more interested in learning about the Church."

"Actually, I already mentioned it to him, but I don't know if his 'girlfriend' will appreciate it. I doubt she'd be excited to have him come home all religious and active in the Church."

"Are you sure she's not LDS?" Pearl questioned.

"No, but I think he would have said something if she were." Cami pushed herself to her feet and dusted off her knees. "Has he said any more about how long he's going to be here?" she asked Pearl. Josh may have been led to the Sea Rose Bed and Breakfast for a reason, but as far as Cami was concerned, the sooner he got his answers and left, the better.

"He said something about staying until next Wednesday. But we can find out when they get home," Pearl said. She packed the dirt around the rosebush and gave it a final pat. "I better get washed up and started on dinner." She pulled off her gloves, then stopped and looked at Cami. "Mr. Drake is a curious man. I can't seem to put my finger on it, but I get the feeling there's more to him than meets the eye."

"What do you mean?"

"Something mysterious. You've heard the saying 'still waters run deep.' I think that's our Mr. Drake."

Pearl left for the house, leaving Cami behind to digest her words. The image of an iceberg formed in her mind—a small piece of ice floating above the surface of the water, but below the surface an enormous, undetected, jagged chunk of ice. She knew what had happened to the *Titanic* and what kind of damage an innocent-looking iceberg could do. Was that what Mr. Drake was?

Cami decided she'd stay busy until Mr. Drake left the following Wednesday. She'd been meaning to do some cleaning in the attic and sort through some of the storage in the garage, and this would give her a reason to stay out of Mr. Drake's way.

Which, in her opinion, was the safest place to be.

CHAPTER 7

Cami worked in the attic until the sunlight coming through the window of the gabled roof became bronzed and dim by the setting sun. She'd gotten a lot done and had created several piles—things to keep, things for the dump, and things for Goodwill. There were still many boxes she hadn't had a chance to go through, but she resolved to work on those later.

Originally, the boxes had been stored in the basement, but after the renovation of the mansion, they'd been moved to the attic, which was roomy and big. Since there was no other need for all the space, they'd used it for storage. Still, Cami didn't like storing junk and decided to come up again the next morning and finish the project.

Dusting her hands on her denim-covered thighs, Cami came down the ladder and caught her reflection in the mirror. Streaks of dirt and black smudges decorated her face and arms. Her shirt wasn't even close to being the white color it was when she'd started. She looked as though she'd rolled down a mountain, especially with her hair falling out of her ponytail in complete disarray.

Before she hit the shower, she decided to check on Pearl and see how dinner was coming. She hated leaving the woman with so much work to do, but Pearl insisted that it wasn't work when she enjoyed cooking a nice meal for people she loved and the friendly visitors who stayed at the inn.

But Pearl was nowhere to be found. Pots boiled on the stove, and a tray of rolls had just come out of the oven while another tray baked, filling the whole house with its delicious aroma.

Cami's stomach growled, and without another thought, she quickly washed her hands and took one of the freshly baked rolls off the tray, knowing Pearl wouldn't mind.

She heard the side door open and, figuring it was Pearl, she called out, "Don't get mad! I snitched a roll." She took a big bite and reached in the fridge for a bottle of water.

With cheeks bulging, she turned to greet Pearl and nearly choked on the wad of food in her mouth.

Josh had just come inside.

She tried to swallow, but had taken such a big bite she felt like she was trying to swallow a golf ball. Straining to clear her mouth, she felt her eyes bulge as she swallowed several more times, finally succeeding in downing the mass of bread.

"Hungry?" Josh asked, his expression full of amusement.

She took a drink from her water bottle, feeling stupid because he'd caught her snarfing down food like a starving bulldog and looking as though she'd just bounced off the back of a cattle truck.

"A little," she replied. "Help yourself." Feeling color flame on her cheeks, she quickly excused herself to get cleaned up.

* * *

Over dinner that night, Josh gave a vivid account of his afternoon with Grandpa Willy.

"So here we are, floating a mile offshore," Josh said excitedly, "and out of nowhere this whale surfaces right next to us! He blows a fountain of water probably ten feet or more into the air. I mean," he used his hands expressively as he spoke, "I could feel the spray inside the boat. I watched as the whale's head and dorsal fin arched out of the water, then the ridges in his back, and then his tail broke the surface." He collapsed back into his chair. "It was the most incredible thing I've seen in a long time. And there were probably half a dozen more whales swimming with him. I couldn't believe I left my camera at the marina."

As many times as Cami had been whale watching, she'd never seen a whale up close like Josh had.

"It's true," Grandpa Willy echoed Josh's account. "Thought one of those fellers was going to jump right into the boat with us."

"I haven't been whale watching for years," Pearl said. "I'd like to go out with you sometime."

"Me too, Grandpa," Cami added. "Maybe we could go again before Josh leaves so he can take his camera and get pictures," she said, earning an affirmative nod from Josh.

"That would be great!" he exclaimed.

Ashlyn and Mitch also wanted to go out on one of the sight-seeing boats with the others.

As they finished dinner, a day was chosen for the outing, working around Mitch's and Ashlyn's teaching schedules.

"Well." Josh leaned back in his chair and gave a contented sigh. "That was another incredible meal, Pearl." Everyone around the dinner table agreed. The grilled salmon was mouthwateringly moist and delicious with the hickory-smoked flavor of the barbecue.

"I'm so full I may never eat again." Mitch rubbed his hand over his stomach.

"At least until you have your nightly mixing-size bowl of *Frosted Mini Wheats,*" Ashlyn said teasingly.

Cami insisted on cleaning up the dishes while everyone went out on the back porch and relaxed. To her surprise, Josh was just as insistent on helping.

As he swept the kitchen floor, she wiped off the counters and polished the chrome faucet until it sparkled.

Josh brought up the subject of his sailing again, his enthusiasm about the whole experience remaining strong.

Cami had to laugh at his boyish excitement as he recounted, once again, his amazement at spotting the whales. Maybe there was a mysterious side to him, but she couldn't deny there was also an incredibly charming side.

Josh went outside and emptied the dustpan just as the telephone rang. Cami answered it.

"Good evening, Sea Rose Bed and Breakfast. May I help you?"

A woman's voice came on the line. "Yes, hello, I'm trying to reach someone by the name of Josh Drake. I understand he's staying there."

The woman's voice sounded young. Cami knew a voice couldn't give a hint as to the person's physical appearance, but to her, the woman also sounded pretty. And classy. She had an East Coast accent—not exactly snobby, but very intellectual.

"Just a moment," Cami answered. "I'll check and see if he's available. May I tell him who's calling, please?"

"This is Jane Covington," the woman replied with a hint of annoyance to her words.

Wondering why Ms. Covington would get so uppity at having to give her name, Cami went to find Josh.

He was still outside with the dustpan, but he was leaning against the porch rail, gazing up at the sky. He looked over when she opened the screen door.

She hated interrupting him. He had a faraway, withdrawn look on his face. Was he thinking of his father?

"Sorry to bother you," she spoke softly. "You're wanted on the phone."

His brows knit together. "I am?" he said, as if he hadn't been expecting any phone calls.

Cami nodded.

"Do you know who it is?" he asked.

"Jane Covington," she answered.

His expression immediately changed to one of pure annoyance. She wondered if he was displeased that the woman would call him there. Perhaps some of his need for space was to put some distance between him and his girlfriend. Was Jane one of the questions he needed to find an answer to?

"I'll take it up in my room," he told her.

They walked back inside together until they got to the entry. He started up the stairs, and Cami blurted out, "Josh, thanks for helping out with the dishes tonight."

He stopped in midstep and said, "It was my pleasure." He smiled with genuine warmth in his eyes, then he was gone.

Cami joined the others in the parlor, but she couldn't help wondering about Josh and Jane. What kind of woman was this Jane Covington anyway? And what was Josh up to?

* * *

Friday morning, Pearl and Cami rushed to get ready for their coming guests. They had two couples booked for the weekend, and they wanted everything to be just right.

When the rooms were ready and food was prepared, Pearl spent some time outdoors pruning rosebushes and picking a bouquet of flowers for the entry. Cami decided to continue her work on the attic in hopes that she could finish the project that afternoon.

Wearing an apron this time to keep the dust off her clothes, Cami climbed the ladder to the attic and began sorting and organizing boxes of books, clothes, and small knickknacks. She found several pieces to add to the curio downstairs, including a lovely porcelain desk clock with a brightly colored mermaid curled around the face and a pair of brass bookends shaped like mallard duck heads, which was perfect for the bookshelf in the back parlor.

One small box tucked away in the slanted corner of the attic caught her eye, and though it was difficult to reach, she managed to slide it closer with her foot.

The sound of a car pulling into the driveway carried up through the attic vent.

"Oh great!" she complained. She'd hoped she would be able to finish her task before their first guests arrived. Knowing she had to leave the rest for later, she stacked the clock and bookends on top of the small box and carried them down the ladder with her. She could look through the box later in her office.

Removing her apron, she washed her hands in the bathroom, quickly fixed her hair, and rushed downstairs in time to greet their guests.

"Welcome to the Sea Rose Bed and Breakfast," she announced as they came through the door. Greeting them with a smile, she shook hands with Mr. and Mrs. Norman, an elderly couple from eastern Oregon coming to the coast for a weekend vacation.

Cami showed them their room, the Rose Room, which fit Mrs. Norman's taste to perfection. They loved the ocean view and the decor of their surroundings. Cami offered them a bite to eat, but since it was midmorning they declined, claiming that they'd grab something in town if they got hungry. Their first order of business was to take advantage of the clear, sunny day and visit the lighthouse.

Having skipped breakfast herself, Cami wandered into the kitchen to grab something she could take to the office to eat. She grabbed an applesauce bran muffin and a bottle of water, then wandered into her office and deposited her findings from the attic onto her desk to look at later.

She went through the mail and paid several bills that were due, then stopped to gaze out the window as she finished her muffin.

The day was indeed beautiful and sunny, and she felt the yearning to go outside for a breath of fresh air. Then she stopped. Outside, relaxing in a chair under the shade of a tree, was Josh.

She hadn't spoken to him after his phone call the night before, nor had she seen him yet that day. Stepping back into the shadows, she watched him for a moment. She could have sworn he was asleep, except that his eyes were wide open. Still, he stared off into space as if in a trance.

There definitely was something else going on. He seemed to have so much on his mind. The death of his father, yes, but there seemed to be even more.

Afraid of disturbing him if she went to the beach by way of the backyard, Cami decided to go out the front and cut through the woods between the mansion and Mitch and Ashlyn's place and access the beach from their backyard.

Pulling a baseball cap and sunglasses on, she stepped through the front door into the beautiful spring day.

"Hey there, sport," a voice from above called to her.

Cami looked up and saw her grandfather perched high on the rung of a ladder. He was pounding a nail into some trim that had blown loose in the last storm.

"Grandpa!" she exclaimed. "You shouldn't be up there! Mitch can do that when he gets home tonight," she scolded protectively.

"Criminy, Cami, I'm perfectly able to climb a ladder and take care of a little carpentry around this place," he countered. "But you did come outside at the perfect time. I need a few more nails out of that bag." He pointed to a container on the porch.

She got the nails for him and stretched up on tiptoes to hand them to him. Although he reached for them, he still came up a few inches short. Taking one step down on the ladder, Grandpa Willy reached for the nails again, but somehow the shift in weight caused the ladder to tip onto one leg, which startled him, making him jerk quickly the other direction to counterbalance the ladder. The abrupt movement sent the ladder teetering onto the other leg, causing Grandpa Willy to lose his grip. Right before Cami's eyes, she watched in horror as he plummeted to the ground.

CHAPTER 8

"Grandpa!" she shrieked as she rushed to his side.

A gash on his forehead bled freely, and the position of his left arm looked awkward and unnatural.

She panicked. "Grandpa! Are you okay?"

"I'm fine, I'm fine," he assured her, his face scrunching up with pain. "Just give me a second to get my bearings."

Just then, rounding the corner like a runaway train, came Josh. "What happened?" he cried. Seeing Grandpa Willy sprawled on the ground, he skidded to a stop. "Willy, are you okay?"

Grandpa Willy nodded, but Cami quickly told him what happened.

"Don't move," Josh instructed. "You might make it worse if your arm's broken. Do you hurt anywhere else? Your neck, your back, your hip?"

"Just my pride," Grandpa Willy said with a forced chuckle.

"Keep him calm and still," Josh told Cami. "I'll go call 911."

Grandpa opened his mouth to protest, but Josh quickly said, "It's just a precaution. I'll be right back."

Cami was grateful to have Josh by her side as they waited for the paramedics to arrive. He managed to keep Grandpa Willy's mind off the pain as he spoke calmly and soothingly to the older man still lying in the spot where he'd landed.

To their surprise, Mitch, who was a volunteer at the fire department, was on the truck when the emergency vehicle arrived. He was at the station when the call came and jumped on when he learned it was Grandpa Willy who'd fallen.

The emergency team did a quick check before they moved an argumentative and unhappy Willy Davenport to the hospital for further evaluation and a possible cast for his injured arm.

After they left a note for Pearl, Josh offered to drive Cami to the hospital. She accepted gratefully, knowing that she was too upset and worried to drive safely. A constant prayer ran through her mind as they traveled the twenty-minute drive to the hospital.

Grandpa was already in a room when they arrived and was complaining to the nurse that he was fine and she didn't need to bother taking his temperature. "I'm not sick, for crying out loud!" he growled. Luckily the doctor arrived shortly thereafter, and x-rays were promptly ordered. The scrape on Grandpa's head was not deep enough to require stitches and was easily mended with a butterfly bandage.

Cami paced the floor as they waited for Grandpa to return. Josh assured her that everything was going to be fine and she didn't need to worry. A panicked Pearl called from the inn to find out what was going on. Cami explained the situation and promised to call as soon as they found out about Grandpa Willy's arm.

To their relief, his arm wasn't broken, but he'd sustained a buckle fracture from the impact. Although it would heal, it would also be painful, and the doctor told Grandpa he would have to give it a two-week rest, or recovery would take even longer.

"I'm amazed you didn't break your arm or a hip in that fall, Willy," Dr. Campbell told him.

"I got good bones, and I'm tough as an old boiled owl," Willy replied. "Takes more than a tumble off a ladder to do any damage."

"Well, just the same, no more ladders," the doctor instructed. "You gave your granddaughter here the fright of her life, and next time, you might not be so lucky."

Grandpa did more grumbling as the nurse wrapped his arm and secured it in a serious-looking sling, which he hated immediately. With a large pack of ice on his arm, Grandpa was released from the emergency room. He complained grumpily all the way home.

"What a stupid stunt to pull right now," he scolded himself. "I've got that leak in the main bathroom to repair, those fence posts need fixin', and I was going to work on that flagstone walk out in the garden so it could be finished before Memorial Day weekend. I don't have a day, let alone two weeks to lose!"

"I'm pretty handy around the house and yard," Josh offered. "I can do some of that work for you, Willy."

"I can't have you working around the place, Josh. You're a guest," Grandpa Willy retorted. "It wouldn't be right."

"You guys have treated me like one of the family," Josh replied. "I would like a chance to repay you for all your kindness. Besides," he added, "it will give me a reason to stay on a little longer." He looked at Cami when he spoke, but didn't say more. Still, Cami felt her cheeks flush, and she quickly looked away.

Pearl was in a complete dither when they arrived. She gasped when she saw Grandpa Willy and wrung her hands with worry. By the way she acted, one would have thought Grandpa Willy had lost his arm in a shark attack.

"I'm fine, Pearl!" Grandpa barked. "Quit your fussin'."

"I just can't believe you fell!" she cried. "Just think how much worse it could have been!"

"Yes, but it wasn't worse. In fact, it feels fine now. I can barely breathe with this blasted harness strapped around my chest. I feel like an old cart horse rigged up like this."

"Grandpa, you heard the doctor," Cami reminded him. "You have to keep that on for two weeks."

"Two weeks!" Pearl exclaimed, slapping her hands onto her cheeks with dismay. Then her demeanor changed. "Alright, Mr. Davenport," she said with the tone of a drill sergeant, "off to bed with you. You need to rest and take care of yourself, and—"

"Good grief, woman," Grandpa interrupted.

"Don't 'good grief, woman' me," she said louder. "If you don't have enough sense to take care of yourself, then I'll do it for you."

Cami pursed her lips together to keep from smiling. She liked seeing Pearl get so protective of Grandpa. He needed someone to pamper and fuss over him, and Pearl was quite suited to the job.

"I'd do what she says, Grandpa," Cami said.

Grandpa Willy gave her a stern look and said, "I don't like this. I don't like this one bit!"

"Quit your bellyaching, William. You need to rest for a while. I'll get you some lunch shortly." Pearl issued her command with a firm but gentle voice.

"Oh, alright. But don't expect me to like this," he warned them all. "I'm not one for having someone wait on me, and I'll be danged if I'm going to sit up there on my bed like a corpse. I've got work to do and tours lined up."

"We wouldn't even dream of expecting you to like this, William," Pearl said patronizingly. She continued to sympathize with him as she guided him toward his room at the back of the house, promising him that she would make sure he got well quickly so he could get back to all his work. Cami was amazed at how well the woman handled Grandpa Willy. With skills like that, Pearl could tame wild beasts for a living. Josh shook his head, also obviously impressed with Pearl's handling of the situation.

"Now that was amazing," Josh said.

"I never thought I'd live to see the day that Grandpa let someone else tell him what to do. He's a sweetheart, but he's also very stubborn."

Josh smiled and said, "I'll change my clothes, then go outside and finish nailing up that trim."

"You don't have to," Cami said. "Really, Mitch can do it some other time. Besides it's almost two o'clock. We didn't even have lunch."

"I'm not hungry," he said. Then he looked her straight in the eye. "Cami, I'd like to do this. Besides, I'm doing this as much for me as I am for you," he said. "I find physical labor to be very therapeutic, and right now, I could really use a project or two."

Cami debated a moment longer, then said, "Okay. But please don't feel like you have to do all those things Grandpa was talking about. There are plenty of people we can hire if we need to. And between Pearl and myself, we can fix a fence and lay flagstone."

"That's good to hear," he said. "I'm sure I'll need the help, and," he said with a sparkle in his eyes, "I'd appreciate the company."

Cami felt her heartbeat quicken again—briefly, almost unnoticeably, but nevertheless, it had happened. Quickly she said, "I'll let you get to work then. I'll call you when lunch is ready."

Since the Normans were gone on their outing to the lighthouse and Pearl was still fussing over Grandpa, Cami made some hoagie sandwiches for everyone. But as she worked, she thought about the emotions percolating inside of her.

She'd thought her heart was sealed. Locked tight. And she thought only Dallin had the key. But somehow Josh had gotten through the hardened exterior. He'd gotten through the wall she'd layered with emotions and pain and loneliness. And without her permission, her heart had let him in.

She filled glasses with pink lemonade and pondered her feelings. She wasn't up to starting a new relationship, giving all of herself to someone else. It was too much work, and it was too risky. She never, ever wanted to get hurt again.

You're being ridiculous, she told herself. Josh wasn't even trying to get a relationship going with her. He had issues of his own to figure out, and he had a girlfriend who was apparently complicating his life. Plus, there was something else going on with him. Cami could tell. She just didn't know what.

For now, he was a guest at their inn who had become a friend. And they both were dealing with the loss of a loved one, which gave them something in common. It was that simple.

Yes, she thought again, it was simple. They were just friends.

Everything was fine.

Her nerves calmed. Her stomach calmed.

Taking a cleansing breath, she felt like she was back in charge of her life and her emotions. She picked up the tray of food and drinks to take to Pearl and Grandpa Willy and then to Josh, who was still outside working on the trim.

Everything was fine, she told herself one last time.

* * *

Later than afternoon, Cami was working at the front desk in the entry when a couple walked through the door.

"Good afternoon," the gentleman said. He spoke with an English accent, proper yet charming. "We're the Rothchilds. You have a reservation for us?"

The man and his wife bespoke aristocracy. The man, tall with broad shoulders, wore a tweed jacket with a silk ascot. He carried himself regally, with an intense gaze. He had a thick head of salt-and-pepper-colored hair that was parted on the side and styled perfectly. Too perfectly. Cami decided it was definitely a toupee.

Mrs. Rothchild looked every bit as royal as her husband in a light wool navy blue pantsuit with a paisley scarf fastened around her neck with a glittering diamond pin. Her honey-colored hair was cut in a stylish bob worn sleek and smooth, tucked behind her ears. She looked easily fifteen years younger than her husband, yet they seemed a perfect fit.

"What a lovely place you have here," Mrs. Rothchild complimented. "Is it original?"

As Cami filled out the necessary paperwork, she explained to them that the home had been in the family over a hundred years and was newly renovated but retained much of its original architecture.

Once the registration process was complete, Cami gave the couple a quick tour of the downstairs, including the kitchen, the dining room, and the front and back parlor. The couple admired the artwork, the collection of antique furniture, and the abundant decorations in the home.

The mansion had four rooms to rent: the Nautical Room, which was occupied by Josh; the Rose Room, where the Normans were staying; the Asian Room, which was vacant; and the Victorian Room, which the Rothchilds had requested.

She led them to their room, and much to Cami's relief, the Rothchilds seemed genuinely pleased with their accommodations. Cami was thrilled at their reaction, especially since their taste appeared to be expensive and refined. She imagined it took quite a bit to impress this couple, and she was glad the mansion did so. But then, she knew the inn was a magnificent establishment. The Oregon Historical Society had done a write-up in their monthly newsletter about the bed-and-breakfast, which brought an increased number of patrons to stay at the inn. Some people even came just to see the place and admire what the newsletter had called the "outstanding and unusual" art collection. Others came for the "exquisite and delicious" food served at the Sea Rose Bed and Breakfast.

Cami told them that dinner was served at seven o'clock in the dining room and invited them to make themselves at home.

With the Rothchilds settled and Pearl overseeing dinner, Cami found herself with time on her hands. Outside she heard the hammering and clanking as Josh worked in the yard. Knowing that she'd been a bit abrupt with him, she decided to go out and see what he was doing, maybe even take him a glass of ice water.

He was making so much racket when she approached he didn't hear her come up behind him. For a moment she watched him work. He knocked off edges of the flagstones to fit them into place to create a stone pathway around the side of the house through the vine-covered archway to the gazebo. Cami and Grandpa Willy had painstakingly staked out the path, and she wanted to make sure Josh was following it. It turned and curved in such a way that on nights when the moon was full, the pathway was completely illuminated by the silvery light.

Josh had taken off his light blue polo shirt and was wearing only a white T-shirt that was sweat and dirt stained. He wasn't a large man—just a little over six feet—but he was lean and trim. Cami noticed that he had a strong, broad back and fairly developed shoulders and biceps. He'd told Cami that he did a lot of rowing back home, and she could see the evidence of it.

He turned to grab the hammer and caught her looking at him.

"Oh, um, hi Josh," she stumbled over her words, feeling stupid. She hadn't meant to stare, and she certainly hadn't meant to have him catch her staring! "I thought you might be thirsty." She thrust the glass of water toward him, spilling some on the ground.

"Just what I needed," he said gratefully. He wiped at his sweat-stained brow with the back of his hand before he took a long, drawn-out drink of water. "Ahh, that hit the spot." Handing her back the glass, he picked up the hammer. "So, what do you think?"

She eyed his work, surprised at how much he'd already gotten done. She also noticed how beautifully the stone pieces fit together and how level they were. Either he'd laid flagstone before or he was a gifted craftsman. She guessed it was maybe a little of both.

"You're doing a wonderful job," she told him. "It looks great. Have you done this before?"

He explained that he'd worked a summer for a landscaping company while he was putting himself through school. Since now he didn't have a home or a yard of his own, he was glad to have a chance to get outside again. He hadn't done yard work for years, and it was something he missed dearly.

"I think if I spend the next two days on it, I just might get it finished," he said.

Cami pulled a face.

"What?" Josh asked with alarm. "Is something wrong?"

"No," Cami said quickly. "Nothing's wrong. It's just that I hate to see you working so hard. You're here on vacation, remember?"

Josh smiled, his wide, white grin contrasting against the golden tan of his face. Since he'd arrived he'd spent enough time in the sun to get a healthy glow to his skin, something he hadn't had when he first arrived.

"My vacation is taking a break from teaching and stress and relationships back home," he confessed, "not from hard work. Being outside in all this beautiful fresh air and around all these flowers breathes energy into my soul," he said, puffing out his chest and taking a deep breath.

With raised eyebrows, Cami looked at him, surprised at his declaration.

He burst out laughing. "That sounded pretty corny, didn't it?"

She laughed along with him. "Actually no. But it sounds like I need to get outdoors more, if that's what it would do for me."

"I could use an assistant," he invited.

Knowing she had nothing pressing inside at the moment, she realized that working outside on that beautiful spring day did sound appealing; plus working together would make the task go much faster.

"Sure," she said. "What do you want me to do?"

He handed her a pair of leather gloves and showed her how to shape and fit the rocks to each spot in the ground to form a smooth, solid pathway.

As they worked, Josh was full of questions, and Cami found herself telling him about her parents, who had passed away when she was young. She explained that her mother had fallen from the balcony of a second-story window, but didn't add that there was evidence of prescription drug use in her mother's autopsy. Her grand-parents had believed it was suicide, which was something Cami never wanted to believe.

Then there was her father, who had died at the hands of drug dealers within a year after he left their family. She told Josh what it had been like growing up with her grandmother and grandfather, and he, in turn, told Cami about his life in Pennsylvania.

She found out that, for him, teaching had been a secure profession to go into, but he'd always seen it as a temporary occupation because his first love was traveling and exploring. His plans for adventure, however, had never seemed to work out. Cami assumed that was why he had such an interest in Pearl and her world travels.

He stopped digging and leaned against his shovel to take a break. "I doubt this makes any sense to you," he said, "but right now I feel kind of like I did when I graduated from high school. Everyone asked me, 'So what are your plans? What are you going to do now? What are you going to study in college?' And the problem back then was I didn't know. I hadn't figured out yet what I wanted to do with my life." He shifted his weight onto his other foot. "That's how I feel now, except the difference is that I'm the one asking those questions of myself. I'm not content with my life, yet I don't know what I want." He looked at her with sad, confused eyes. "I need to find out what's missing."

CHAPTER 9

Sunday morning Pearl opted to stay home and take care of Grandpa Willy instead of going to church. She was supposed to teach in Relief Society, but she was able to get someone to substitute for her at the last minute. As much as Grandpa Willy had insisted that his fall was nothing to be concerned about, he finally confessed that his arm was causing him a lot of pain. Sitting through three hours of meetings was simply out of the question.

Cami put on a long rayon skirt made out of a soft lavender floral print, along with a matching lavender sweater. Her eyes were blue, but against all the light purple they took on a shade of periwinkle. She hadn't cut her hair since Dallin had died, and it had grown from the short, cropped cut she used to wear to a shoulder-length pageboy. She knew she needed to have it trimmed and styled. Up until now she hadn't been too concerned about her appearance, but she felt different having Josh around. She resolved to call and make an appointment with the stylist tomorrow.

When she emerged from her bedroom, she found the Normans and the Rothchilds seated at the dining room table with Pearl serving them a beautiful breakfast of mushroom-and-Swiss omelettes and fresh fruit. Both couples greeted Cami warmly, and she made sure they were enjoying their stay and that their rooms were comfortable. The Normans said they were planning to travel down the coast south-ward to seek out even more lighthouses. They were having the time of their lives and wished they didn't have to return home that evening. The Rothchilds were booked until Monday and were planning an outing to Cannon Beach and inland to Tillamook.

Cami wondered why Josh wasn't down for breakfast, but didn't have to wonder long. Just as she walked through the entry to go out the front door to her car, he bounded down the stairs, dressed in his Sunday best. He wore a pair of camel-tan pants, a navy blue blazer, and a pale blue pinpoint oxford shirt. He dazzled her with a smile, and again, Cami's heart skipped a beat. Her breath caught for a moment in her throat so she couldn't speak. But Pearl took care of that for her.

"Goodness gracious!" the woman exclaimed. "If you don't look handsome this morning, Josh."

"Thank you, Pearl. You look beautiful yourself," he complimented, joining Cami in the entryway.

Pearl blushed, touching her hand to her short, cropped curls. She'd battled her natural curl all her life and had recently gone to a shorter style that accentuated her lively, hazel-green eyes. The hairstyle was also stunning on her because Pearl loved chunky earrings and necklaces. She had beautiful smooth skin, tanned by working outdoors and hiking the many nature trails in the mountains to the west. "Well, thank you," she answered. "Can I get you some breakfast?"

"Actually, I was hoping I could catch a ride to church. It is at eleven, isn't it?" he questioned both of them.

"Yes," Cami answered. "I was just leaving." She hadn't thought to remind him about going, yet he'd remembered on his own. Keeping her reaction and emotions steady, Cami smiled and accepted his offer to drive.

As they drove to the church, Cami recalled the distinct feeling she'd had on the beach when she knew without a doubt that there was a reason Josh had come to the Sea Rose Bed and Breakfast. Now she just wondered exactly what that was.

* * *

Cami marveled at the messages given over the pulpit and in Sunday School. They all seemed designed specifically for the one guest in their audience who was looking for answers, who wanted to know what the purpose of life was. Josh sat spellbound through sacrament meeting as the speakers addressed the topic of prophets. The first speaker related the story of Joseph Smith and the First Vision. The man had served a mission in upstate New York and shared a strong testimony of his experiences at places such as the grove where Joseph had knelt to pray for answers to his own questions, and the Hill Cumorah, where the golden plates had been hidden until it was time to bring them forth.

A musical number, "Joseph Smith's First Prayer," was presented by the ward choir and, with embarrassment, Cami found herself wiping constantly at her eyes as a stream of tears filled them. The Spirit during the song was so strong Cami was certain Josh felt it, if not inside his own chest, then from her as he sat next to her in the congregation.

The second speaker bore testimony of modern-day prophets and the Twelve Apostles. The man had had the distinct privilege of working with the prophet while living in Salt Lake City. He shared many personal experiences and a powerful testimony of the prophet's divine calling, as well as a sure knowledge that the prophet did indeed receive constant direction from the Lord to lead and guide the Church.

Cami hated for the meeting to end but looked forward to Mitch's Gospel Doctrine lesson with anticipation. Mitch was a gifted teacher. Not only did he present an enjoyable and interesting lesson, but he brought the scriptures to life through gospel study and research. Even more powerful was his testimony, which brought a strong spirit into the room.

Several members, including the bishop, came up after sacrament meeting to greet Josh. He was warm and cordial toward them, but Cami could tell there was something on his mind. He seemed subdued and thoughtful, and she hoped he was thinking about the messages shared in the meeting.

Full of anticipation, Cami led the way to the Gospel Doctrine class. She looked forward to the spiritual feast she knew they were about to experience, and right now, more than anything, both she and Josh needed the Spirit to feed their souls.

Mitch introduced the topic of the day's discussion, which was a detailed account of Lehi's dream. Sketching each verse and symbol,

Mitch portrayed the account visually and with such clear and distinct explanations that Cami herself, after hearing and studying Lehi's dream all her life, still felt like she'd gained even greater insight and understanding into its meaning and purpose.

Sharing her scriptures with Josh, they followed along together as Mitch touched, point by point, each symbol and its meaning in the dream.

"You sure have underlined a lot of scriptures," Josh whispered.

"I underline the ones that have a special meaning to me, or that stand out to me when I'm reading them," she explained.

"May I look?"

She watched out of the corner of her eye as he thumbed through the pages, stopping to read some of the scriptures she had underlined. Then he turned from the Book of Mormon and found the section that contained the Old Testament. Wondering what he was looking for, she watched as he turned to Psalm 107. There she had the three scriptures highlighted that went along with the lighthouse painting at the mansion—verses 28, 29, and 30.

Along with Josh, she read:

Then they cry unto the Lord in their trouble, and he bringeth them out of their distresses.

He maketh the storm a calm, so that the waves thereof are still.

Then are they glad because they be quiet; so he bringeth them unto their desired haven.

Cami thought about the words. *How many times in the scriptures does the Lord offer to help those who come to Him with their troubles? Hundreds of times? Thousands?* The verses in Psalms said that the Lord would calm the storms and that He would bring them unto their desired haven. Her desired haven was to have peace in her life, and she imagined it was the same for Josh. He sought peace concerning his father's death. Josh also wanted answers. Receiving answers to his questions would certainly bring him peace.

She was lost in thought, not really listening to Mitch, when Josh nudged her with his elbow and asked, "So Mitch is saying you guys not only believe in a pre-earth existence, but a life after death?"

She looked at him blankly for a moment until his question sunk in. Then she nodded, realizing that he was asking a very important question. A fleeting prayer crossed her mind. She needed heavenly help if she were to answer his question properly.

"We lived in heaven with our Heavenly Father before we came here to earth. After we die, we will return to heaven and be with our family and loved ones," she told him in whispered tones.

His brows knitted together, and his expression grew serious. "Do you mean not only will I see my father again, but we will be able to live together?"

"Yes," she said with great sincerity. "For eternity. With your father and mother and all your loved ones."

He stared into her eyes for several moments. She felt as if he were searching her mind for more information, reading all her thoughts and feelings. A collective "Amen" startled her. They hadn't even noticed that the lesson had ended and the closing prayer had been offered.

"Cami," Josh said, an urgent tone to his voice, "how do you know these things? Do you really believe they are true?" His words caught her off guard, and she wanted to say that of course she believed they were true. "Because if they are," he continued, "you have just validated something I've felt deep inside for many, many years. And you have given me more comfort than I dreamed possible," he told her.

Before she could answer, Mitch approached Josh about going to priesthood with him. She wished she had a chance to pull Mitch aside and tell him what was going on, but the best she could do was pray that Mitch would be inspired to help Josh and that he would say the right things. If anyone could answer Josh's questions, Mitch could.

"Could we talk later?" Josh asked.

"Of course," Cami said.

She watched him walk away and realized how grateful she was for the gospel, for the sense it made out of life, for the hope and peace it offered. The Lord was willing to bear her burden, and He wanted to take it from her. He loved her. He was her big brother, someone she could count on and lean on. Someone who knew every feeling and emotion inside of her.

She didn't know where her path would take her, but with faith in the Lord she knew He would guide her and help her along the way.

* * *

Josh and Cami were both quiet at dinner. Grandpa Willy actually felt well enough to join them for the evening meal along with their guests, the Rothchilds.

Mr. Rothchild was fascinated with the coast, the history of Seamist, and the surrounding area. He asked dozens of questions about the first settlers and about the mansion, and Grandpa Willy was more than happy to answer all of his questions—at least he was until Mr. Rothchild asked him about the Heceta Head Lighthouse murder.

"I read in the newspaper about a fellow getting murdered south of here."

"What about it?" Grandpa Willy said curtly.

"I got the impression he was seeking some sort of treasure. I find it fascinating that there are still people looking for buried treasure."

"No one knows that for sure," Grandpa Willy answered.

Mr. Rothchild persisted. "I understand that a schooner actually went down somewhere along the coast around here over 150 years ago. Is that true?"

Everyone looked at Grandpa Willy to hear his answer.

He looked thoughtful for a minute, then said, "There are a dozen tales about all sorts of ships filled with all sorts of treasures going down in these waters." He adjusted the strap on his sling and shifted in his seat.

"Hmm," Mr. Rothchild answered. "I've heard of a legend about a sailing vessel with a chest of Spanish gold headed for San Francisco that sunk a few miles offshore."

"It's possible," Grandpa Willy answered.

"According to the story, most of the men abandoned ship and tried to swim ashore, but most of them died in the effort. But," he looked around the table at his captive audience, "some of the men hired as couriers to deliver the chest of gold managed to load the treasure into one of the dinghies and found their way ashore."

"I've lived here my entire life and nothing of the sort has ever been proven," Grandpa Willy told him. "There may have been some talk at one time, but nothing's ever come of it. And it's best left alone. Old ghosts, especially those who drowned at sea, don't want to be disturbed. Nothing good can come of it, I tell you."

Mr. Rothchild looked at Grandpa Willy with one eyebrow raised in interest. And to Cami's surprise, he didn't let the topic drop. "According to the source I heard it from, the treasure is buried somewhere along the coastline. Somewhere . . . ," he paused again, "near this mansion."

With an aggravated huff, Grandpa pushed himself away from the table with his good arm and got to his feet. "I'll believe it when I see it. But I wouldn't go wasting my time looking for a buried treasure that doesn't exist."

With that he left the room.

Pearl, in a flurry of concern that the meal had been ruined, apologized for Grandpa Willy's behavior, blaming it on his pain medication. Cami was puzzled by her grandfather's behavior. He was testy about all that had happened with the murder, but why would the topic of the buried gold upset him so much?

Gratefully, the topic changed as the group sat down in the parlor and had dessert. The telephone rang, and Cami stepped into the kitchen to answer it.

"Josh Drake, please," a man's voice asked.

Cami found Josh finishing the last bite of his blackberry pie à la mode and let him know the call was for him.

Josh took the call in his room while Cami helped Pearl clean the dishes and tidy up the kitchen. The Rothchilds decided to go on a nature walk, and to Cami's relief, seemed completely unruffled by her grandfather's outburst.

With the kitchen clean, Pearl went to check on Grandpa Willy. "Tell him if he weren't already confined to his room, I'd ground him to his bedroom for his behavior tonight," Cami said with a tone of authority.

Pearl laughed and said, "I've never seen his claws come out so quickly before. Why would he get so angry about a buried treasure? Especially if it doesn't even exist?"

"I don't know, Pearl," Cami said with exasperation. "If you find out, let me know."

Cami went upstairs to make sure there were plenty of fresh towels for their guests. She gazed out the window for a moment, enjoying the tranquility of the quiet evening and lovely sunset.

She turned to go back downstairs and nearly collided with Mr. Rothchild.

"Oh! Excuse me!" Cami exclaimed.

Mr. Rothchild seemed as surprised as she was.

"Pardon me, my dear," he said quickly.

"I thought you'd gone for a walk. Can I help you?" she offered, confused as to why he was coming from a different direction than his room.

"No. I was just . . . ah . . . looking around a bit," he finally said.

Cami smiled. "Let me know if you need anything. I'll be downstairs."

He dipped his chin and thanked her. "I'll do that," he said.

The man disappeared down the hallway toward his room, and Cami watched with interest, wondering why they hadn't gone on a walk like they'd planned. Then she shrugged and wandered down the stairs to the entry and looked at the guest register.

Cami checked phone messages and e-mail and straightened a stack of pamphlets and flyers. Then she looked in the kitchen and both parlors and couldn't find a soul.

She was bored. Not only that, she had a dozen thoughts swirling and colliding in her brain, thoughts of Grandpa and the treasure, but also thoughts of Josh and his questions.

Just when she thought she was going to start climbing the wood-paneled walls, she heard footsteps.

She turned to see a grinning Josh coming down the stairs.

"Are you busy?" he asked.

She chuckled at his timing. "Actually no, I'm not."

"Good," he replied. He grabbed her hand and pulled her to the front door. "I have to talk to you outside." He kept ahold of her until they got outdoors.

"Josh!" she cried, shaking her arm loose from his grasp. "What is all this about?"

"Let's go out to the gazebo, away from the house."

Cami shrugged and followed him to the white, lattice-trimmed gazebo crowning Pearl's flower garden.

They sat side by side on one of the benches bordering six of the eight sides of the structure.

"Now, are you going to tell me what's going on?" she stated directly.

"Max is interested in the book!" he exclaimed excitedly.

"What book?" Cami asked. "And who's Max?"

"Max Simons, my editor friend in New York. He said Pearl's book is just the type of book Lexington Press is looking for!"

"Pearl's book!" she cried. "You mean the pictures and the history and—"

Josh laughed and exclaimed, "Yes! All of it. He's completely thrilled with the idea."

"Pearl isn't going to believe this," Cami said, shaking her head and still not quite believing it herself. A book. All of Pearl's hard work and life-risking adventures would finally be captured in a historical picture book. "Josh," she turned, suddenly feeling his contagious excitement, "this is so awesome!"

"I know!" he agreed. He grabbed Cami in his arms and hugged her tightly. "I nearly dropped the phone when he said yes." He released his hug and smiled at her.

She sat there, looking at him, waiting for the tingling to go away. His hug, his touch, had stirred her for just the slightest moment—there was no denying it.

"So," she swallowed hard and attempted to change the subject to clear her mind from the memory of his touch, "what's the plan now? When does he want it? How is Pearl going to figure out how to write a book?"

Josh chuckled at her stream of voiced concerns. "She's got all the time she needs. Of course, he's hoping to get a first draft in six months, but he understands she's never done this before. That's why he asked me to assist her and help her any way I can."

Cami looked at him with surprise. "How will you be able to do that? Especially from Pennsylvania?"

He looked away at the wispy white clouds and deep blue sky.

"Josh?" she asked. "How long are you planning on staying, anyway?" She knew deep down part of her wanted him to stay longer, but the practical side of her brain reasoned that there was no way he could leave his job and life in Pennsylvania much longer.

When his gaze finally met her, there was a sadness about him, the same sadness he'd had when she first met him. "What is it?" she asked. "What's wrong?"

"I just can't leave right now. I'm finally beginning to understand some things that are very important. I may be risking my position at the college, but I feel strongly that I need to stay here. I hope I'm not wearing out my welcome," he said. "I wouldn't—"

"Of course you're not wearing out your welcome!" she interrupted. "You can stay as long as you'd like." Still, she knew at the rate he was paying every night, his bill would be outrageous. Cami decided she'd have a talk with Grandpa about approving a weekly rate that would help Josh out with his room charges. Plus, she figured, they could apply all the work he'd been doing around the place toward his bill. "I didn't mean to give you that impression," she clarified.

"Am I tying up a room that you need to rent out?" he asked with concern.

"No, no, that's not a problem," she assured him. "Really. I was just wondering about your plans. Pearl will love having your help with the book, and you've already been so much help around the mansion, especially with Grandpa's arm being injured."

He nodded his thanks. "Then I guess the next question is, when do we tell Pearl?"

"Why not right now? All our guests are taken care of, and she was just taking Grandpa some dessert. Let's go join them."

Cami led the way back to the house. She was so excited to see the look on Pearl's face.

CHAPTER 10

Pearl collapsed onto the foot of Grandpa Willy's bed like someone had just knocked her legs out from under her. "A book? Me?" she exclaimed. "Are you sure?" she asked Josh, who nodded happily.

"With my pictures and my personal accounts of world events and places?" She restated everything Josh had told her. "But he's never seen my pictures or met me! Why would he do this?"

"Because he trusts my opinion," Josh explained. "You've preserved history in-depth and in a very personal way. Your accounts, your stories, will make those places and events seem real and alive. You have so much to offer. This is your chance to offer it."

Pearl's eyes filled with tears. She shook her head as if she still didn't quite believe all that had happened. "I don't even know where to begin or what to do."

"Since I've worked with Max on a textbook I've written, he seems to think I could help you," Josh assured her. "So, I'm going to stay awhile longer to help you get started. And I think Willy can also be a great deal of help to us."

"Me?" Grandpa Willy exclaimed with surprise. "How did I get roped into this?"

"You've traveled as much as Pearl and been to many of the places she's been. I'm sure you'll be able to help her out with details and specifics regarding a lot of her experiences," Josh told the older man.

"It's true," Pearl concurred completely with Josh. "William, you have such a wonderful memory for detail. I know your help would be invaluable. You will help me, won't you?"

"Guess I don't have anything better to do," he answered gruffly, lifting his injured arm in explanation.

"This is so exciting." Pearl got to her feet. "I don't know how to thank you, Josh."

"I can think of one way," he said, reaching his arms out toward her.

Pearl joined him in a hug, and they both patted each other's backs with congratulations.

Cami tingled with excitement. Pearl had lived such a full, exciting life, but she'd also had her fair share of trials and challenges. Something so wonderful couldn't have happened to a nicer person.

Just then they heard the jingle of the front door opening. Cami expected one of their guests to be coming or going and stepped from her grandfather's room to see if they needed any help. To her surprise, Ashlyn and Mitch came inside.

"Hey, guys!" Cami enthused. "You're just in time."

She pulled them into Grandpa's room and let Pearl share with them her exciting news.

By way of celebration, Pearl offered to make peach smoothies for everyone. The crowd moved into the parlor to be more comfortable, and soon they were sipping fresh peach drinks and nibbling on Pearl's pecan sandie cookies that were melt-in-your-mouth delicious.

"Mitch," Josh said as he drained the last drop of smoothie from his glass and placed it on a tray, "I have a question about your Sunday School lesson this morning."

"Sure, Josh." Mitch straightened in his chair and focused his attention on Josh.

"It's about the plan of salvation you mentioned today. You touched on it briefly in your lesson and Cami told me a little about it before the meeting ended. But I wondered if you'd mind explaining it to me in more detail." Josh leaned forward, ready to listen to Mitch's explanation.

"I think I can explain it better with an illustration," Mitch replied.

Using paper and pencil, Mitch proceeded to map out the plan of salvation for Josh. He began with the premortal life, telling him of the fact that everyone lived in heaven before coming to earth. He also explained the reason they were on the earth and the purpose of trials. He assured Josh with words of power and conviction that the Lord was very aware of Josh, and all of them for that matter, and that He loved each of them very much. He also told Josh that even though trials were sometimes more difficult than one thought they could bear, the Lord was with them and wanted to help them have the strength to face those trials. All they had to do was ask for His help.

Mitch talked about earth life and having a mortal body—of being tested and tried, then of what happened after a person died. He drew lines and wrote words to help diagram the body being separated from the spirit and told about the spirit world, where people were taught the gospel and learned about the Savior. And when Josh asked about his father, Mitch assured him again that his father and mother were together again, and that they were extremely happy.

Cami watched as the etched lines around Josh's eyes and on his forehead visibly softened. His expression changed from one of strain and confusion to a peaceful understanding.

As Mitch explained the final judgement and the three degrees of glory, where all inhabitants of the earth would be placed after they were judged by the Lord, Josh relaxed against the back of his chair, his expression thoughtful.

"So," Mitch said, setting the pen down, "God's love is extended to everyone upon the earth. He wants all of His children to come home again, to live with Him forever. He's given us so many wonderful things to help us along the way. Like prayer."

Josh nodded.

"We've also got the scriptures," Mitch told him. "I've received so many answers to my prayers by reading the Book of Mormon."

"The Book of Mormon?" Josh asked, his gaze wandering off as if checking his memory bank. Then he looked at Mitch. "I haven't thought about the Book of Mormon in years. I remember the pictures. Pictures of men, strong and powerful. And an army of young soldiers," Josh said quickly, as if the memories were coming faster than he could process them.

Cami jumped up and walked to the bookshelf. They kept several copies of the Book of Mormon to give out to any guests who might be interested in learning more about the Church. Grabbing a copy, she quickly gave it to him.

He looked at it for a long minute, then opened the cover, leafed through several pages, and found the first picture. It was of young Nephi subduing his elder brothers. "I remember this!" Josh said, his face lighting up with the memory. He turned the page and looked at the next one. "And this!" They watched as he searched through the book for all the Friberg paintings depicting key moments in the Book of Mormon. "This is amazing," Josh said without looking up. "I remember all of these. And these things you've told me," he swallowed hard, "I've heard all of it before."

No one in the room said a word, but watched as Josh slowly digested all the information he'd just been given. Cami herself pondered and thought about Mitch's explanation over and over. She'd always thought she believed in the Atonement and the great plan of salvation. But it seemed as though it took an actual event, a trial or some sort of tribulation, to actually make those teachings come alive and seem real to her, for them to have significance in her life.

And now they did.

* * *

With Mitch and Ashlyn's departure, the evening came to an end, and before she knew it, Cami found herself alone with Josh.

They sat for a moment in silence, Cami trying to think of something to say or a gracious way to excuse herself, but her mind kept coming up blank. She was grateful when Josh finally spoke.

"This is really amazing," he said, picking up the sheet of paper Mitch had drawn on.

"What is?" Cami asked, stretching her neck to see what he was referring to.

"This whole concept changes everything for me."

"What do you mean?" she asked.

"At my father's funeral, when I took that one last look at him, it was as if my mind went numb. I couldn't believe that he was gone, that his life was over," he snapped his fingers, "just like that. I couldn't believe it was the end and that I would never see him again.

Yet, I couldn't imagine anything else. I thought of heaven, and I wondered about God and angels with halos and wings, but the image just wasn't clear. I couldn't seem to bring the picture into focus. But this," he held up the paper, "this makes so much sense. It seems right in here," he tapped on his forehead, "and it feels right in here," he placed his hand over his heart. "It's as if something inside of me is recalling something I've already known."

"You did know it," she told him. "You knew it all. Just like Mitch said, you were there in the Council in Heaven. You voted for the Savior's plan."

A smile grew on his face. "I guess I did, didn't I?" he said.

She nodded, recognizing the sincere joy in his eyes.

"I will see my mother and father again." His voice held hope and happiness. "Do you understand how much that means to me? Especially when I thought they were gone forever?" He looked at her with pleading eyes, eyes that begged for understanding.

Her heart filled with empathy.

"Of course you do," he said quickly. "You above anyone can understand how I feel. To know that you will see your husband again must bring you a lot of peace and joy."

Her lip trembled. Yes. This knowledge of the plan of salvation gave her peace and joy. She still missed Dallin, but she felt herself growing stronger, just a little bit, each day.

* * *

"Morning, Grandpa," Cami said early the next day. Pearl was nowhere to be found, but something wonderful was baking in the oven, and most likely their guests would be down momentarily for breakfast. The Rothchilds were checking out that morning, and then three women from Sacramento were coming to stay from Tuesday until Sunday. Two were sisters and one was a friend. They wanted to stay in the same room, so once the Rothchilds checked out, Cami and her grandfather planned to make up a rollaway bed in the Victorian Room for the extra guest.

When they had the room ready, they went back downstairs to the kitchen just as Pearl served up breakfast. Cami and her grandfather sat down at the table, where Josh and the Rothchilds already sat, enjoying a pleasant conversation about some of the antique pieces in the mansion.

"Tell me about the grandfather clock in the entryway," Mr. Rothchild requested. "Is it German?"

Cami waited for her grandfather to answer, but he remained tight-lipped for some reason. Cami couldn't figure out his odd behavior toward this couple.

"Yes," she answered their guests. "From the Black Forest. It was an anniversary present for my great-great-grandmother from my great-great-grandfather, just after they moved in. We actually didn't know it was still in here until we began remodeling. Then we found it tucked away in a corner of the parlor, covered by a sheet of muslin. It was quite a surprise when we uncovered it."

"It's such a treasure to have a family heirloom like that," Mrs. Rothchild exclaimed.

The Rothchilds, Cami decided, were an interesting couple. Even though Mr. Rothchild was a bit nosy and had startled Cami several times as she'd run into him snooping around the house, they were still warm and friendly. Why her grandfather didn't care for them was beyond her.

"Tell me," Mr. Rothchild directed his question toward Cami, "does this charming old mansion have secret passageways like so many of the old homes?"

Cami opened her mouth to answer, but Grandpa Willy cut her off.

"They've all been sealed shut," he said quickly.

Cami looked at him with surprise and confusion. None of the passageways had been sealed off.

"Well, actually, the few that we have are going to get sealed off as soon as my arm gets healed," he corrected himself, glancing over at his granddaughter with his brows narrowed and the expression in his eyes telling her to let him handle the question.

Mr. Rothchild's forehead wrinkled at Grandpa Willy's excuse. Cami could tell he wasn't sure he believed the explanation.

Gratefully, the conversation shifted as Josh told the Rothchilds his account of whale watching. On their way out of town, they said, they were going to the marina to take a tour of the harbor and hopefully spot some migrating whales.

After the meal, Pearl and Cami cleaned up the kitchen while Josh and Grandpa Willy went outside to discuss work on the flagstone pathway and the Rothchilds packed their bags for their departure.

"I have no idea what's gotten into Grandpa," Cami complained to the older woman. "I've never seen him act this way around anyone. Why do you think he was so rude to the Rothchilds?"

Pearl shrugged. "Hard to say. They are a lovely couple. But still," Pearl paused at the kitchen sink, "there's something. . ." She drifted off with her thoughts for a moment.

"What?" Cami asked.

"I don't know for sure." Pearl looked at her with a blank expression. "I can't really put my finger on it. Something about them just doesn't seem straightforward."

Cami didn't know what to make of that. "Well, I guess it doesn't matter now anyway. They'll be gone soon," Cami told her.

Pearl nodded. "You're right. No reason to stew about it."

They heard voices in the entryway and hurried out to find the Rothchilds carrying their suitcases out to their rental car.

"Here," Cami piped up immediately, "let me take those out to the car for you."

"Thank you, my dear," Mrs. Rothchild replied with appreciation.

"We certainly hope you've enjoyed your stay with us," Pearl said to the couple. "And we hope you'll come back to visit us soon."

Cami noticed Mr. and Mrs. Rothchild glance quickly at each other, and then Mr. Rothchild said in a pleasant tone, "We're already looking forward to it. Especially for more of your exquisite cooking, dear lady."

Mr. Rothchild took one of Pearl's hands in his and kissed her knuckles. Pearl turned a vivid shade of crimson and giggled.

Mrs. Rothchild smiled warmly and echoed her husband's compliment.

"Well, dear," Mr. Rothchild addressed his wife, "we'd better get going. Our plane leaves for Chicago at four."

Pearl wished them a pleasant trip home, and Cami helped them carry their luggage out to their car. The day was overcast, and a cool breeze blew.

With their luggage stowed away in the trunk, Cami watched as the older couple climbed inside the Buick. After a wave and a smile, they were gone.

"So, they're gone," a voice behind her said.

Cami turned. "Grandpa! Yes, they are gone. And why in heaven's name were you so rude to them? They are exactly the kind of people we want to attract to the inn."

"I know, I know," he said defensively. "I just didn't like all those questions and that shifty-eyed expression of his."

Cami shook her head hopelessly.

"I caught the old man sneaking around the mansion a few times," Grandpa Willy continued his defense.

"I'm sure it was nothing," she assured him, not telling him that she'd also caught the man exploring freely.

"Well, with all that's been going on lately, no one's above suspicion," Grandpa Willy said.

Cami chuckled. "And you really think Mr. Rothchild could be the murderer? I'm sorry, but I don't think he would muddy his expensive Italian leather shoes even for a buried treasure. He's much too proper."

"The man's a fake, I'm sure of it. And his wife too."

A commotion from the side of the house caught their attention, cutting off their conversation. Wearing rubber hip waders and carrying several buckets, Pearl waddled around the corner. Grandpa Willy and Cami looked at Pearl, then at each other, and started laughing.

"What in tarnation, woman?" Grandpa Willy exclaimed.

Pearl's gaze narrowed with an unappreciative scowl. "Now just what are you two laughing at?"

Grandpa Willy's eyebrows rose with amusement. "Isn't it obvious? We're laughing at you. You look like you're fixin' to bail out a sinking boat."

"For Pete's sake, William," Pearl fumed, "I'm going clam digging."

"Dressed like that?" he said with a chuckle.

"What's wrong with the way I'm dressed?"

"Nothing." He tried to suppress his laughter. "Not a thing. Just how deep are these clams buried anyway?"

Just then, Josh came around the corner wearing an identical pair of waders and carrying a shovel. "I'm ready, Pearl," he announced.

That was all Grandpa Willy and Cami needed. They burst out laughing and could hardly remain standing.

"What?" Josh asked with surprise, looking from Cami to Grandpa Willy, then to Pearl for an explanation.

"Just ignore them, Josh," Pearl told him. "You'd think these two had never been clam digging before."

"We've been before," Cami said, taking several gasps for air. "We've just never gotten quite so dressed up for the occasion."

"Well, where I'm going, you have to dress like this. That is, if you want the best butter clams on the West Coast," Pearl explained indignantly.

Cami loved butter clams. The clam shells were small—no bigger than a golf ball—but they were loaded with flavor and very tender. Her mouth watered just thinking about it.

"Don't you two want to come with us?" Josh asked, his gaze on Cami.

She hadn't been clamming for a long time. It did sound kind of fun to get outside in the fresh air and go dig in the mud.

"You know who loves clams?" Cami replied. "Ashlyn. Could we invite her and Mitch to join us?"

Josh looked at Pearl, who said with exasperation, "Of course you can invite them, but let's hurry it up. These waders are making my legs sweat."

"Grandpa, you're going to come, aren't you?" Cami asked before running into the house to call Ashlyn.

"Don't know what I can do with this blasted thing on my arm," he complained.

"You can hold a bucket or something, William," Pearl told him. "Now, go get your hip boots on and let's get this show on the road!"

Cami streaked into the house and grabbed the phone. It took three rings before Ashlyn answered the phone.

"Hello?" Ashlyn's voice sounded sluggish and strained.

"Ash? Are you okay?" Cami asked, suddenly filled with concern.

"Uh, yeah," Ashlyn replied unconvincingly.

"You don't sound okay," Cami told her.

"I've just got a touch of something," Ashlyn answered.

"I'm sorry to hear that. Do you need anything?" Cami offered.

"No, Mitch is home today. If I need anything, he can get it for me."

"I'll call you a little later then," Cami said. "Take care of yourself."

"I will," Ashlyn said raggedly.

Cami hung up the phone. *She probably picked up a bug at school.*

A honk from Pearl's old Subaru station wagon sent Cami scurrying to grab her own pair of waders and a pitchfork, the perfect tool for digging clams.

CHAPTER 11

With the tide out, the small harbor was a swampy sea of mud and puddles of seawater. Already there were dozens of people dressed in similar attire, digging and sifting through the mud for clams.

Pearl led the way through the mucky water and thick mud with Josh and Cami right behind. Grandpa Willy followed behind, grumbling to himself. Cami knew his sour disposition was due mostly to the fact that with his arm in a sling, his freedom and activities were limited. He had zero tolerance for inconveniences like a broken arm.

"Here we are!" Pearl announced as she dropped her buckets in the mud next to her.

Josh dug right in, using the long-handled shovel. He turned over shovelfuls of mud as smooth as melted chocolate and picked through it for any of the hard-shelled delicacies. Each time he found a clam, he cried out excitedly. His enthusiasm was contagious, and soon Pearl and Cami were knee-deep in mud, flinging handfuls of the stuff everywhere as they searched for clams. Even Grandpa Willy seemed to enjoy the process and helped with the sifting process using his one good arm. It didn't take long to fill the bottom of both buckets with the small, round clams.

Throwing muddy gear and equipment into the back of the car, Pearl drove them home as the coast displayed some of its finest scenery against a backdrop of solid blue sky for their guest.

"It would be a perfect day to go to the galleries in town, Josh," Pearl suggested.

"It would," he replied, "but I was thinking I should probably finish laying that flagstone."

"That flagstone can wait," Grandpa Willy told him. "You don't get beautiful days like this too often, son. Go and enjoy yourself. In fact," Grandpa went on to suggest, "why don't you take him around to some of the sights, Cami? I'm sure he'd enjoy some company, now, wouldn't you, Josh?"

Josh looked at Cami, who sat in the seat next to him. His brows lifted with anticipation. "I'd love some company," he said. "That is, if you're not too busy."

Cami wasn't sure she appreciated her grandfather arranging her day for her or volunteering her to be Josh's personal tour guide, but the truth was, she really didn't have much to do that day. "I guess I could show you around a bit," she said with slight hesitation. She didn't want him to think her anxious at the prospect of spending the afternoon together. She wasn't really sure how she felt about it.

A smile broke onto his face. "That's great!" he exclaimed. "To show you my appreciation, I'll buy you lunch at the Bayside Diner. I never did get there on my last outing."

* * *

After a light lunch of crab cakes and clam chowder at the diner, Cami and Josh wandered around some of the art galleries in downtown Seamist. The galleries displayed various forms of artwork from local artists. There were exquisite paintings of ocean scenes and mountain landscapes, sculptures of seagulls and other wildlife, and beautiful pieces of hand-painted Indian pottery. Josh was completely enthralled and impressed with the displays of local talent.

Cami had to admit that she enjoyed Josh's company. He had a way of putting her at ease and making her feel as though everything she said was important. Sometimes in the middle of the sentence, she'd stop and look at him, amazed at how intently he listened to her.

After stopping for an ice cream cone at the local sweet shop, they strolled down to the beach, enjoying the beauty of the day. A gentle breeze blew across the shimmering waves lapping at the shoreline.

"Thanks for coming with me," Josh said as he caught a drip of ice cream with his tongue. "I'm sure I wouldn't have had as much fun by myself."

"I'm glad it worked out. It's been awhile since I've visited the galleries myself. I haven't been out much since . . ." She didn't finish.

Josh nodded knowingly.

"Anyway," Cami tried to brighten her voice with some enthusiasm, "what do you think of our little town?"

"I think it's great," he replied. He finished his cone and wiped at the corners of his mouth with a napkin. "It's very peaceful," he said. "I find it easier to think here than back home."

Cami smiled at him, hoping that meant he was finding the answers to the questions that brought him here.

"Right after my father died, I was filled with such a sense of sadness. I was filled with grief too," he said. "I couldn't seem to get past the grief and sadness. That is, until Sunday night after we had that talk about life after death and the fact that I would see my father again. And I finally figured it out. I realized why I couldn't move on."

They stopped walking and faced each other as they talked. "What was it?" she asked anxiously.

"I didn't get to tell him good-bye," he said. "I didn't get a chance to tell him how much I loved him and what a wonderful father he'd been to me. I wanted so badly to have one last chance to tell him how I felt." He looked into her eyes, his gaze imploring, as if hoping she would understand his feelings.

"I think he knows, Josh," she told him. "He knows everything in your heart."

Josh's expression softened. "You think so?"

"I know so," she said.

Josh took in a deep breath and let it out slowly, looking out at the ocean. "I'd like to believe that."

Cami stood next to him, her shoulder brushing against his arm.

He turned to her again. "Thank you," he said.

"For what?" she answered softly.

"For listening. For understanding," he explained. "You're the only one I've been able to talk to. It's felt so good to have someone know how I'm feeling."

Cami swallowed. The appreciation in his eyes was so sincere, the longing in his voice so moving, she couldn't speak.

"I've been doing a lot of thinking," he said. "A lot." He reached out and took both of her hands in his. "I know now without a doubt that I was led here to Seamist to your inn."

Cami bit her lip, not knowing how to answer. She didn't have trouble believing that the Lord guided people's paths and that He put people in one another's lives to help each other. But her? How could she help Josh when she couldn't even help herself?

"I'm glad," she finally said. "I mean, that I can help," she added.

His smile was as bright as the afternoon sun. The loneliness that had filled his eyes when she'd first met him had vanished, and she could tell he was finding the answers he needed, and in turn, those answers were bringing peace to his life. She was indeed happy for him, but wondered if she herself would ever find the same peace.

* * *

"What's all of this?" Cami exclaimed when they walked into the office back at the mansion and saw Grandpa Willy and Pearl sitting at a card table in the corner up to their eyeballs in scrapbooks and boxes of pictures.

"We're starting on the book!" Pearl exclaimed happily. "William's helping me sort through pictures so we can categorize and put them in chronological order."

"Helping, my foot," Grandpa Willy grumbled. "Didn't know I had a choice."

"Now William," Pearl said, "you know I need you to help me remember and identify all these pictures. You've been to most of these places yourself. I can't do this without you."

"Alright, alright," he growled. "I'll sure be glad when I get this contraption off my arm so I can get back to work," he mumbled under his breath.

Josh and Cami smiled at Grandpa Willy and immediately launched into the stacks of pictures. Realizing that the project required more space than the card table allowed, Cami cleared off part of her own desk to make room for the piles of sorted pictures.

Throwing bills into a tray and gathering letters of requests for information about the inn, Cami gave up most of her desk space for

Pearl's project. On the corner of her desk she found the heavy shoe box she'd uncovered upstairs, and placed it on the bookshelf, making a mental note to go through it later.

"These really are incredible," Josh said as he studied a photograph of Pearl poised at the edge of a smoking volcano. "I've never known anyone who had the courage to stare danger in the face as often as you did."

"Well, what you're calling courage was really stupidity," she clarified for him. "I'd probably have been shaking in my boots if I'd known how much danger I'd really been in half the time." She looked at the picture, as if seeing it took her away from the present into another time and place. "When I see these pictures, I still remember how I felt at the time I took them."

"That's it!" Josh exclaimed.

Pearl looked at him with confusion.

"That's exactly what I want in this book—those feelings you had, those strong emotions behind each picture." He looked at Pearl with deepened respect. "I don't think you understand how powerful this book is going to be."

Pearl's eyes watered, and she nodded knowingly. Her understanding and Josh's expectation were apparently on the exact same level.

Between stories of Pearl's countless escapades and Grandpa Willy's tales of adventure, the four spent the next few hours digging through boxes of pictures and making notes of facts and memories to go with many of the photographs.

It was well past dinnertime when Pearl realized how late it was. "Oh my goodness! It's nearly eight o'clock. I fed our guests hours ago, but you all must be starving."

"Stay put," Cami told her as she got up from her chair. "I'll go in and make something for us."

"Are you sure?" Pearl asked.

"Sure—this way you can keep working. I don't want you to stop while you're on a roll."

"Thanks, Cami," Pearl replied as she opened yet another box of pictures.

Over grilled cheese sandwiches and tomato soup, Cami, Josh, Pearl, and Grandpa Willy continued working until after ten o'clock.

Finally, Grandpa Willy yawned so much Cami was afraid he'd fall asleep in his chair.

"This has been a lot of fun," he finally said. "But I'm so tired I can't see straight. I think I'm going to turn in. Cami, you'll make sure all the windows are closed? I think we're in for a storm tonight."

There was no rain yet, but the wind had blown mercilessly all evening long.

Pearl dropped a handful of pictures onto the table. "I'm bushed too. I'm starting to get the outback in Australia mixed up with Africa. We'd better stop for now."

Josh and Cami also agreed they could continue the project tomorrow.

Grandpa Willy kissed his granddaughter on the forehead and bid everyone good night. Pearl thanked them all for their help and went home to her cottage next door.

"Well," Josh said, looking around at the stacks and piles of pictures, "she had more pictures than I imagined."

"She said there's even more at home," Cami told him.

He looked at her with wonder, apparently having a hard time imagining more pictures. They already had thousands still to look through.

They organized the mess as best they could before turning in. Josh stacked cardboard boxes containing Pearl's pictures and travel papers against the wall. Cami placed the piles of photographs that had already been sorted by event into large manila folders.

Attempting to create just a little more room for the boxes, Josh tried to shoulder a file cabinet over to make space, but it was heavier than he'd expected.

"Here," Cami dropped the envelope, "let me help you."

Josh pushed from the bottom, and Cami from the top, and together they slid the cabinet. The movement caused a heavy, brass-plated clock sitting on top of the cabinet to inch its way to the back of the cabinet. Without warning, it crashed into the wall and landed on the floor with a loud thump.

Cami scrunched her eyes closed, not wanting to assess the damage. That was one of her grandfather's favorite clocks.

Josh retrieved the timepiece and looked it over.

"Hey," he pressed his ear to the face of the clock, "it still works."

Opening her eyes with a sigh of relief, Cami took the clock from him and looked at it closely, amazed that it hadn't missed a second. "I bet it left a huge dent in the floor, though."

Josh peered behind the cabinet. "Yeah, there's a gouge where it landed."

"I'm glad it's behind the cabinet," Cami commented.

"Hey, wait!" Josh exclaimed. "It looks like the wall—" He bent down farther to get a closer look at something behind the cabinet.

"What?" Cami asked, wondering what he'd found. "Did it dent the wall too?"

"No, it looks like—" He banged on the wood-paneled wall a few times. "It is! There's a passageway back here."

"What?" Cami rushed over to take a closer look. "I didn't know there was a passageway back here."

Sure enough, when she looked behind the cabinet, the seam in the paneling concealed by wood molding had given way several inches.

"Wow!" she exclaimed. "I thought we'd checked out all the secret passages. Somehow we missed this one. Let's move the cabinet and see where it leads."

Josh's eyes lit up with excitement. "This is so cool!" he said, sounding like one of his college students. "What if we find a skeleton or some priceless painting?"

Cami shook her head and laughed. "Don't get your hopes up too high. The only thing we'll find in here is dust and cobwebs. I'm sure this doorway's connected to the rest of the passageways, and I've wandered through all of them."

"You never know," he replied optimistically.

It took a minute to get the heavy cabinet out of the way, but finally they had enough space to access the secret panel. It was barely two feet wide and five feet tall, but it swung open easily into the eerie darkness of the passageway.

"There's a flashlight in that top drawer," Cami told Josh, who reached behind him and retrieved the light from the desk.

Testing the flashlight several times first, they paused at the edge of the doorway.

"Should I go first?" Josh asked, shining the light inside and illuminating drapes of gauzy cobwebs and the interior framework of the house.

"If you don't mind," she answered. "You know, just in case we do meet up with any skeletons or anything creepy."

Giving her one last backward glance and an excited smile, Josh stepped through the opening, then turned once he got on the other side and extended his hand to help her through.

"See anything creepy yet?" she asked as she climbed through the wall.

"Just me," he said, holding the flashlight under his chin as he pulled a scary face.

"Very funny," Cami told him. "On second thought, maybe I better lead."

"No, no." Josh turned the light into the open passageway. "I've got it." Then he asked, "Are you ready?"

Cami could tell this was just the kind of thing he loved doing. "As ready as I'll ever be," she answered.

Together they made their way into the darkness.

CHAPTER 12

The interior passageways were narrow, and the floorboards squeaked with each step. Cami sneezed several times and got chills as cobwebs stuck in her hair and brushed across her face.

"Watch your step—" Josh tried to warn her.

"Ow!" Cami's shin rammed into something low on the ground. She lifted her leg and rubbed her throbbing shin. "What was that?"

"Probably ductwork or a box for the electrical wiring," he offered.

"Couldn't they have found a better place to put it?"

"Are you okay?" He stepped toward her and shined the light onto her leg so she could get a look at her injury.

Pulling up her pant leg, she exposed the wounded area to find a large, purplish bump forming on her shin bone.

"We should get some ice on that," Josh said.

"It's okay," Cami replied, putting her pant leg down. "Let's keep going."

Even though there were several octagonal-shaped windows in the passageway, there was no light coming in from the already-darkened sky. Creeping through the main floor of the house, they came to a spiral stairway leading to the upper chambers. The stairs groaned under their weight.

At the top of the stairs they stopped.

"Which way?" he asked.

They stood close together in the shadows, talking in soft tones.

She pointed to her left. "I think that way leads to the Victorian Room and the Rose Room. And that way," she pointed the other direction, "goes to your room and the Asian Room."

"Let's go that way." He pointed in the direction of his room.

They walked along the passageway, stepping carefully, holding their breath as the floorboards complained against their weight.

"Here's another doorway," Josh pointed out. "Which room is this?" he asked.

"I think it's your room, but I'm not sure."

Josh easily unlocked the small latch holding the panel in place, and the door creaked open. But to their dismay, the six-drawer dresser and large dresser mirror were in the way. There was only a crack of space to see into the dark interior of the room.

"I'm pretty sure that's my room," Josh said as he shined the light into the room. "Yes, there's the bed and nightstand."

They closed the door, and the latch snapped into place, holding the panel firmly in position.

"So," Josh said, shining the light both directions. On one side was a dead end. On the other was the passage from where they came. "Looks like we've run out of road," he said.

"Guess so." Cami peered into the corners where the gabled roof angled down sharply. "It's getting late. We should probably head back down," she said.

They retraced their steps back to the stairway as the flashlight began to flicker and dim.

"Oh great," Cami exclaimed. "The light's not going out, is it?"

"I hope not. We've got a ways to go yet," Josh said.

"Here." She took the flashlight from him and banged it against her hand a couple of times. The light beamed stronger. "There," she said with satisfaction. "That's better."

Josh looked impressed, but that was the last of his expression Cami saw. The light suddenly disappeared.

"Josh!" Cami whispered.

"I'm here," he answered.

"Guess I hit the light a little too hard," she said, feeling foolish.

"It probably would've gone out on its own anyway," he answered.

"So, now what do we do?" she asked.

"We'll have to feel our way back until we can see the light from the office," he suggested. "Here," he said, "give me your hand."

She reached out and clasped his outstretched hand. He gave hers a reassuring squeeze, and they started down the stairs.

Moving slowly and carefully, they inched their way down the passageway, tripping on floor joists and abrupt corners.

"We should be seeing the light from my office by now. Where is it?" she asked.

"I was just beginning to wonder the same thing," he replied.

But there was nothing.

They continued a little farther until Josh bumped into a wall. Cami ran right into him.

"Sorry," she said.

"We've hit a dead end."

Cami thought for a moment. "We're just going to have to holler and wake up Grandpa."

"You think we can? Pearl said his pain medication made him sleep so soundly he wouldn't know if the roof caved in unless it fell on top of him," Josh reminded her.

"All we can do is try," she replied.

They counted to three, then yelled. Waiting thirty seconds for a reply, they tried again, but it was no use. Grandpa Willy was out for the night.

They made another attempt to find the opening in the wall, but in the absolute darkness, Cami had lost her sense of direction.

"What do we do now?" she asked him.

"Guess we make ourselves comfortable. We're going to be here awhile."

"Who do you think turned out the light?" Cami wondered out loud.

"Maybe your grandfather got up and saw it was on, so he turned it out," Josh guessed.

They took a seat on the floor next to each other and tried to get comfortable.

Outside, the wind beat against the house, and the branches from the trees scraped the siding.

"I hope there aren't any bugs crawling around," Cami said, shuddering at the thought of something long legged and hairy creeping up her backside.

"We might get a few visitors," Josh said, which did little to comfort her.

"It's a good thing it's dark then, because I do *not* like spiders." She leaned away from the wall and wrapped her arms around her legs.

"Sorry I got us into this. We should've waited until daylight to come in here," Josh said

"It's not your fault," she declared. "I wanted to see inside too."

Josh chuckled. "Your grandfather's going to have something to say about this, isn't he?"

Cami groaned. "He'll probably ground me." Grandpa Willy had never been one for spankings, but as a teenager she'd spent her fair share of time alone in her room, being grounded for dozens of things she'd done that she was glad she couldn't remember anymore.

"Think he'll ground me too?" Josh asked.

"Probably. But I'll make sure you're not charged for your room those days," she answered with a laugh.

Josh laughed along with her. Then, several seconds later, they laughed again, this time harder.

Cami didn't know what it was—the ridiculousness of the situation, the lateness of the hour, or the fact that they were both tired—but for some reason, the thought of Grandpa Willy grounding them to their rooms seemed extremely funny.

Wiping at her eyes, Cami couldn't stop giggling. She leaned against Josh weakly, still shaking with laughter.

But their laughter soon died down, and once again, silence surrounded them.

"You know what?" Josh said.

"What?" Cami answered, not liking how dusty and stifling the air was.

"You're the first person I've really laughed with like that since my father died."

Cami's heart grew warm, yet she didn't know what to say.

"Thank you," Josh said softly.

"For what?" she answered in the same tone.

"For your friendship. It's just what I need right now."

She wondered about Jane. Didn't he have that kind of relationship with her? And if not, why? Shouldn't a girlfriend be a best friend too?

"You know what?" Cami said.

"What?" Josh answered.

"It's just what I needed too." The words came from her heart. She truly meant them. She had friends and loved ones, but for some reason she didn't feel as close to them or as able to share her feelings with them. She knew that Josh understood the pain in her heart, the emptiness and the aching that accompanied her every day.

"Can I be really honest with you?" she asked him.

"Sure," Josh replied.

"I never thought I'd be able to have a friendship with another man," she confessed. "I never, ever thought I'd be comfortable with another man. But with you, I am. I don't really understand it, but I'm grateful to have you as a friend." She shifted positions, her back beginning to ache, her rear end going numb from the hard floor. "I know I'm not anywhere near ready to have a relationship with someone. I don't know if I'll ever be ready for a relationship," she told him, "but I'm grateful to know I can be comfortable having a man as a friend. Does that make sense?"

Josh didn't answer for several seconds, then he cleared his throat. "Um, yeah," he said, with an audible reticence in his voice. "It makes sense."

"Are you just saying that? Or do you really mean it?" she pressed him.

"No," he paused, "I mean it. I don't think I ever expected to become such good friends with a woman, either."

"But you're friends with Jane, aren't you?" she verbalized her earlier thoughts.

"Of course I am."

Cami sensed an abruptness in his voice. Did he feel defensive? Had he felt he needed to be protective of Jane?

"I'm sorry," she said, not sure what she was apologizing for. "I didn't mean to upset you."

"It's not that," he answered. "You didn't." Then in a quiet tone he added, "I'm just tired."

They sat in silence for a moment.

"I have something else to tell you," Cami said. She pulled in a deep breath, trying to relax. "I'm claustrophobic."

Josh chuckled. "Is there any reason why you're telling me this now?"

"Actually, yes." She sat upright. "The air is really heavy in here. I'm trying hard not to think about how close the walls are and how narrow this space is, but it's not working." Her words were edged with tension. Inside, her heartbeat quickened and her palms began to sweat.

"Cami." Josh's tone was calm and even. "Everything's okay. Don't get yourself worked up."

Cami grabbed the flashlight next to her foot and clicked it on, giving it a good shaking. Nothing. She clenched it in her hands, taking deep, even breaths.

"Maybe we should try and find our way out again," Josh said, getting to his feet. "Reach out your hand and I'll help you up."

Cami grappled for his hand in the darkness. Josh accidentally conked her upside the head with his hand. "Sorry, did I hurt you?"

"I'm fine," she replied. As she reached up and smoothed her hair, she heard a soft clink on the ground.

"What was that?" she asked. She felt her ear, and just as she suspected, one of her diamond earrings was gone. Dallin had given her those earrings when they got married. "My earring! Josh, my diamond earring fell out."

"Cami, I'm so sorry," he said. "Maybe if we feel around we can find it."

Together they ran their hands along the floor, finding dust, bits of wood, and nails, but no earring.

"It's no use," Cami fretted. "We'll never find it in the dark."

She pushed herself to her feet, and the flashlight dropped onto the floor. The minute it struck the ground with a resounding thump, the light beamed on, filling the passageway with light. And there, not five feet away from them, was the door leading to the library.

"There's the opening!" Josh exclaimed. "Now let's look for your earring."

Relief filled Cami. Now they'd be able to find the earring.

But try as they might, after scouring every possible inch of the floor, they couldn't find it.

Finally, when there wasn't another spot left that they hadn't searched, Cami gave up. "It's no use," she said. "It's gone."

"We can look again tomorrow when it's light," he suggested.

But Cami knew that in spite of their searching every obvious place—and every impossible place—they would still come up empty.

"Okay," she said, feeling defeated, having lost faith that they'd ever find it.

"I'm really sorry," Josh apologized again. "It must have come loose when I bumped you."

"It was an accident," she said. "You barely touched my ear. It probably would have fallen out anyway."

Somberly, they crawled through the doorway, leaving the passageway and her diamond earring behind.

* * *

Cami's eyes fluttered open for a moment as a dull clang outside pulled her from a deep sleep. She rolled to one side and snuggled deep into her down comforter. It was much too early to get up.

In her relaxed state, her body easily cooperated with going back to sleep, but her mind wasn't as accommodating. What was the noise she'd heard?

Probably nothing, she argued with herself.

She tried to go back to sleep, but curiosity got the best of her.

"Fine!" she announced as she threw back the covers, irritated at herself for not being able to ignore the noise. Yet she knew she couldn't sleep until she looked outside her window.

The sky was just showing the blush of a new day and was free of clouds. There was no sign of the previous night's storm. Everything was quiet—not a whisper of wind or hint of life. The earth still slumbered.

Satisfied, she was about to crawl back to the warmth of her bed when she caught a movement out of the corner of her eye. Emerging from the trees she saw Josh, with a shovel in his hand, walking toward the shed.

What in the world was he doing, digging so early in the morning? Her breath caught in her throat.

That's ridiculous. She chided herself for even permitting the thought to go through her mind. Still, Josh did know about the treasure, and he had admitted that he was fascinated with old relics and playing "Indiana Jones" or "Dakota Drake," or whatever he'd come up with. But surely he wasn't after any buried treasure around there, was he?

She forced herself to believe it was a coincidence. Just because it was barely six o'clock in the morning and he was carrying a shovel and coming from the direction of the beach didn't mean anything . . . did it?

* * *

Cami hadn't been able to go back to sleep, so she showered and went into her office to do some work. While she addressed brochures, she tried to make sense out of Josh's early morning outing, but there didn't seem to be any explanation.

About seven-thirty Cami heard Pearl come through the kitchen door.

Racing to the kitchen, she startled Pearl as she rushed into the room.

"You scared the starch right out of me, girl," Pearl scolded.

"Sorry, I've just been waiting for you or Grandpa to get up. I need to talk to you."

"Is something wrong? You look like you've seen a ghost." Pearl tied an apron around her trim waist.

Cami checked the doorways first.

"Who are you looking for?"

"I just wanted to make sure Josh wasn't around."

"Oh, didn't you know? He and William left this morning to go out whale watching. He wanted to try and get some pictures this time."

"When did they decide this?" Cami asked, feeling uneasy about Josh and her grandfather alone on the ocean.

"While you were making dinner last night. I guess we forgot to mention it to you."

"But Grandpa shouldn't be doing something like that with his arm."

"They're going on a motorboat, and Josh said he's done a lot of boating. Besides, you know how stubborn your grandfather is once he makes up his mind."

Cami nodded, knowing that there was no changing her grandfather's mind once it was made up.

"They said they wouldn't be back until late," Pearl said. "Now, what did you have to tell me?"

Cami decided to wait until her grandfather got home before she made any accusations. If anyone was a good judge of character, it was her grandfather. He seemed to see right through people. If Josh were up to something, Grandpa Willy would sense it.

* * *

Josh and Grandpa Willy still weren't home by dark, and Cami had paced every possible spot in the house waiting for them. Pearl saved some dinner for them and had retreated to the parlor to read a magazine on French cuisine.

Cami finally couldn't stand it any longer and decided to walk over and see Ashlyn. If she didn't talk to someone soon, she was going to explode. She hoped Ashlyn could help shed some light on the situation.

It was a dark and moonless night. Cami knew the path to Ashlyn's house like the back of her hand, but in the pitch dark of the night, she felt unsure of her steps. Still, she continued on, using Ashlyn's front porch light to guide her.

The wind picked up again and whistled through the pine trees, the eerie sound making Cami walk faster along the path. Her foot caught on a tree root, and she stumbled a little but managed to stay on her feet. The thought occurred to her to turn around and go home, but she pressed forward.

Whipping her hair into her eyes, the cold wind gusted around her and sliced through her lightweight windbreaker. She pulled the coat closer and wished she'd worn something heavier. A crackle of twigs caught her attention, and she turned to look behind her but saw nothing in the inky blackness.

Probably just the wind, she told herself as she picked up her pace.

Breathless, she finally broke through the trees at the edge of Ashlyn's property and sprinted towards the house.

Tromping up the front steps, she banged on the door and rang the doorbell, waiting anxiously for Ashlyn to answer.

No answer came, so she rang and knocked again and checked the driveway. Ashlyn's car was there.

"Why isn't she answering?" Cami asked out loud.

Ringing and knocking one last time, Cami peeked through the side window and saw a light on in the kitchen but no lights anywhere else in the house.

Where could she be?

Disappointed that Ashlyn wasn't there, she turned to head back to her house, then stopped. She was tempted to go the long way—which was near the street—but that was at least four times as far. She could be home in five minutes if she went back the way she came.

Taking a deep breath, she looked at the pathway through the trees and told herself, *Go for it.*

With a few tentative steps, she began the walk home. She balled her fists, steeled herself, and walked faster, telling herself there wasn't anything to be frightened about.

Pine needles and gravel crunched beneath her feet as she scurried along the trail. Lights from the mansion appeared in the distance. She was almost home.

Next time bring a flashlight, she told herself. Forging ahead, she walked faster, breathing easier when she saw the outline of the mansion ahead. It was just a few more feet until she reached the edge of the yard.

Suddenly, the hair stood up on the back of her neck. Footsteps? She swore she'd heard the footsteps behind her.

Deciding she wasn't about to wait around and find out if something was back there, she took off in a sudden burst of speed, charging through the trees until she broke out into the open expanse of the backyard. She took the porch steps two at a time and burst into the mansion.

Pearl shrieked and threw an armload of folded towels in the air. Grandpa Willy tipped a chair over as he raced from the kitchen to see what had happened. Holding her chest and heaving great breaths, Cami pointed behind her and gasped for air.

"What happened?" Grandpa Willy exclaimed, charging to the door and looking outside.

Just then, the front door opened and in walked Josh, startled by the scene before him. "Cami," he said, rushing inside. "Is something wrong?"

"No," she said, calming herself. "I was outside and something spooked me, that's all."

"Probably the wind," he said. "I just went out to make sure the windows in my car were up. I think we're in for another storm."

"Yeah," Cami said, "probably just the wind."

* * *

That night Cami slept fitfully. Dreams and images played in her mind, keeping her in a constant state of turmoil.

Over and over, her dreams became flights for her life—running and screaming, filled with panic and fear. They were nightmares that ran in a continuous loop. Each time, a man chased her through the forest as the limbs of the trees rose up to trip her or vines reached out to hold her.

Deeper and deeper into the dark, menacing forest she ran, with the branches getting closer and denser until she couldn't move forward, until she felt vines wrap themselves around her arms and legs, her stomach, and finally, her neck. With all her might, she grabbed at the vines and thick branches, trying to pull them away, but they held strong.

Cami woke up with a start, drenched in sweat.

Her room was empty and she was alone, yet she couldn't shake the feeling that someone had been in there with her.

What was even more strange was that her bedroom door was open. She always kept her door shut and locked when she went to bed at night. Always.

She shivered beneath her covers and prayed for morning to come quickly.

* * *

"I went into the office this morning," Pearl said over breakfast. Their guests had already eaten and were gone until lunch. "I noticed something interesting . . ."

Cami and Josh exchanged glances, and Grandpa Willy lifted one bushy eyebrow with interest.

Josh had greeted Cami that morning with the same friendliness and warmth he had since he'd arrived, and she almost forgot about her suspicions because a bigger part of her believed there was a reasonable explanation for any of his actions she questioned. With all the strange occurrences going on, she didn't want to jump to conclusions.

"William, did you know there's a hidden door in the office leading into the passageway? And I think someone's been inside."

Grandpa Willy looked at Cami with displeasure. "I know about the door, but I didn't think anyone else did. Cami?" he questioned. "Did you know about it?"

"Well, no," she stalled. "That is, not until two nights ago."

"Two nights ago?" Grandpa Willy questioned.

Cami and Josh confessed about their late-night escapade inside the house and the loss of her diamond earring.

"I knew we needed to seal off those doors." Grandpa Willy thumped his fist on the table. "As soon as I get this thing off," he lifted his elbow in the sling, "I'm going to take care of it."

"Willy," Josh was quick to offer, "I would be happy to take care of that for you. I'll do it right after I get the flagstone laid."

Grandpa Willy grumbled about the "blasted sling" and the "durned passageways" and his "dadblamed medication" while Pearl offered Josh more pancakes.

"Weren't those the earrings Dallin gave you?" Pearl asked.

Cami nodded, catching Josh's surprised expression out of the corner of her eye.

"You didn't say they were from Dallin," he said, sitting up in his chair. "I'll go look for that earring right now."

"Josh." She stopped him. "We can look later. It's okay. Really."

"You're just like your mother. You know that, don't you?" Grandpa Willy scolded his granddaughter. "She was always sneakin' up here to the mansion with her friends, exploring these passageways and getting into all sorts of mischief. It's a wonder she didn't get herself hurt playing around in this old place."

"Did she really, Grandpa?" Cami asked, always enjoying it when her grandfather shared memories of her mother.

"Good grief, yes! That girl had an overactive imagination. She spent most of her time daydreaming and exploring. She dragged more junk off the beach than the sanitation department. She called all that garbage her 'treasures' and hid the stuff everywhere."

Cami listened to her grandfather go on and on about all the seashells and strange things her mother used to hide under her bed when she was little.

Grandpa Willy shook his head as a gentle smile played on his lips. "Yep, your mother was quite a pack rat. Used to drive your grandma crazy too."

"Did you keep any of Mom's stuff, Grandpa? Is any of it in storage?" Cami asked, hoping he'd say yes.

"Not to my knowledge, Cami-girl," he answered. "Though we looked for some of her things after she passed away. Your grandma gave your mom some things from your great-great-grandmother, Olivia Easton Davenport. I'm not sure what they were, but probably things we would like to keep in the family. We just haven't found where they are yet."

Cami's shoulders dropped with disappointment. What she would give to have something that belonged to her great-great-grandmother.

"Maybe she hid it in the passageway somewhere," Cami offered. "We can search around for it when we look for my earring," she said as a tickle of excitement filled her. Maybe they would find her earring after all, and in the process they'd find items from her grandmother. Both would be priceless possessions.

"I don't want you going back in there," Grandpa Willy warned. "I don't think it's safe."

Cami knew the discussion was over for now. But she also knew she couldn't stay away. She wouldn't rest until she'd searched every inch of the passageway for anything belonging to her mother or her great-great-grandmother, even if it meant being sneaky so her grandfather wouldn't find out about it.

CHAPTER 13

"Cami, this is Mitch," the voice on the other end of the phone said.

Cami dried her hands on a dish towel and took a seat at the kitchen table.

"How serious are you about doing some part-time teaching at the high school?" he said, coming right to the point.

"I . . . ah . . . um," she stammered as his question sunk in. "I don't know. I mean, Ash and I talked about it briefly, but that's about it."

"Our interior design teacher broke her leg last night and had to have emergency surgery and have pins put in. She's going to be out the rest of the school year," Mitch explained. "School's out the end of May, so it's just for a little over three more weeks."

Cami couldn't think of one earthly reason why she couldn't help out, but she wasn't sure she was ready for something like this. She'd been secluded for so long that the thought of being out in public, up in front of a group of high school kids, terrified her.

"It's only three mornings a week," he explained. "I know the kids would love you."

Cami wasn't sure how he could "know" something like that, but she appreciated him saying so.

"We could really use you," Mitch said. "You're the only one we know even qualified to teach the subject."

"But I've never taught before," she said.

"Doesn't matter," Mitch answered. "You've got great people skills. You'll do really well."

"You must be pretty desperate," Cami said, letting down her guard a little.

"Cami, we've got plenty of substitute teachers to draw from. We just think you'd do the best job."

Cami had been intrigued with the idea when Ashlyn presented it to her originally. "Can I think about it and call you tonight?" she asked.

"Sure—but not too late. There's a nine o'clock class in the morning we need covered," he told her.

Cami thanked him for the offer and hung up the phone.

They wanted her to teach. She tried to picture herself in front of a class of students and felt her stomach muscles tighten. She couldn't do it. She wasn't ready for something like this. But part of her was still drawn to the challenge. She had a degree in interior design, so it wasn't like she didn't know the subject. Still, it was a lot to ask, and she didn't want to commit unless she was really ready.

* * *

Lost in thought, Cami sat in a wicker chair on the wraparound porch overlooking the garden.

"Cami?"

The voice startled her. It was Josh, his shirt sleeves rolled up and a baseball cap pulled low over his eyes.

"Hi," she said, giving him half a smile. "What are you doing?"

"Do you have a minute? I need a hand with some of these stones." He'd been working most of the morning to finish laying the flagstone.

"Sure." She pushed herself to her feet and followed him around the side of the house. Grandpa Willy had been pleased with the job Josh was doing, and Cami agreed that the pathway looked wonderful. The stones were smooth and even, and fit together perfectly, like a jigsaw puzzle.

Her thoughts of teaching school continued to crowd her mind as she and Josh worked side by side.

"Hey," Josh finally said, "are you okay? Did you have something else you needed to do?"

"Something to do?" she answered absentmindedly. "What do you mean?"

"I mean your body's here, but your mind is somewhere else. I just thought you might have something else you needed to be doing instead."

Leaning against the shovel while Josh brushed dirt off a flat stone, Cami sighed. She'd always considered herself strong and independent. She was the type who knew what she wanted and didn't let anything stand in her way of getting it. At least she used to be that way. Dallin's death had altered her personality, emotionally and spiritually.

"So, what's up?" Josh asked, brushing dust off the knees of his jeans. The question was casual but sincere. His gaze focused on her face, and she saw concern in his eyes.

"Mitch offered me a job teaching interior design classes at the high school, but I've never taught before. I'm not sure I can do it."

"Why not?" he asked.

"I'm afraid I'm going to get up in front of those kids and make a fool out of myself. I don't feel strong enough to handle humiliation right now."

"What if I told you that wouldn't happen? What if I promised that you would find teaching one of the most fulfilling opportunities you could have?" He spoke with conviction.

"How could you promise me that?" she asked.

"First of all, the kids will love you the minute you walk into that room. You probably know most of them anyway, so you'll be among friends. Second, you know what you're talking about. The subject matter isn't going to be a challenge for you. And last of all," he dipped his chin and stared into her eyes, "you only fail if you don't try."

Cami held his gaze for a moment and thought about his words, then looked away.

"You think I should do it, then?"

Josh spoke in a voice that was soft and gentle but full of encouragement. "I think you should do what you want to do, but I know," he reached forward and lifted her chin so she was looking right at him, "I know you would do a great job."

He spoke with such power he almost convinced her she could do it.

"Those kids would be lucky to have you for a teacher," he added. Then he took the shovel from her and began leveling off dirt for the last rock.

Cami sat on a wooden bench and watched Josh work. Beads of sweat collected on his forehead, and his face became flushed from the heat of the day. She wasn't sure what to think about him. He claimed to be searching for the meaning of life, but she wondered . . . was he really searching for a buried treasure? Her common sense leaned toward the treasure, but her heart disagreed. She'd seen pain in his eyes, pain that came from great loss.

"How about something cold to drink?" Cami offered him. "I think Pearl has some juice in the fridge."

"Sure," he said, not looking up. "If you don't mind." He chipped at the corners of the rock, trying to create a perfect fit.

Cami noticed that Josh was not only a hard worker but a conscientious one too. He took pride in his work. He cleaned up when he was done. And he consulted Grandpa Willy often, just to make sure the project met Grandpa's expectation.

A moment later, Cami brought Josh a tall glass of pineapple-orange juice on ice. He took several long draws from the straw with a final, "Ahh, that hits the spot."

Cami smiled at him, then took a thorough look at the rock path leading from the side of the house, through the grape arbor, across the backyard, and ending at the gazebo. It was lovely and beautifully crafted.

"You've done an outstanding job, Josh."

"You like it?" he asked, turning his head from one side to the other as he looked at his work.

She nodded. "It's perfect. Just what the house needed." She turned and looked at him, noticing the crinkles around his eyes and the angle of his strong jaw. He seemed like such a gentle man, but also very rugged. A nice combination. A rare combination. How she wished she knew who he was beneath the surface, deep down inside. Her mother had fallen in love with her father and then learned what type of man he was. Cami didn't want to take chances with any man—not after the heartache she'd already been through.

"How would you like to be the first to walk the completed pathway?" he asked.

She placed her hand on her chest in a gesture of surprise and delight. "Me? I would love to."

He stood and offered her his arm.

She looped hers through his, and together they strolled slowly up the rock path that curved and wound its way to the gazebo, where they found reprieve from the afternoon sun. They watched several birds dancing and twittering playfully on the grass until Pearl called out the back door that Josh was wanted on the phone.

While he took his call, Cami checked the reservation book to see what time their guests were scheduled to arrive that night. For the most part, the inn attracted couples, both older and newly married, but occasionally families stayed at the inn and groups of women came to shop, relax, and have a weekend getaway from the daily pressures of family and career.

Going through some of the papers that needed to be filed, Cami found copies of Josh's credit card information and identification that hadn't been put in his file. They liked to keep a personal file on everyone who stayed at the inn in an effort to increase returning guests.

Glancing down at Josh's date of birth, she noticed that his birthday was only three days away. The idea to throw him a birthday party dawned on her immediately. Pearl would love baking a special cake for him, and they could invite Mitch and Ashlyn and make it a real celebration.

Rushing in to the kitchen, Cami found Pearl polishing silver trays and humming to herself. She told Pearl about Josh's birthday on Friday, and just as she'd expected, Pearl immediately set in motion plans for a birthday barbecue and party for him.

* * *

That night Pearl, Grandpa Willy, Josh, and Cami gathered around the table in the office and continued their task of sorting through Pearl's pictures.

"I've been thinking of a title for your book," Josh said as he dragged another box off the stack and opened the lid.

"A title?" Pearl said. "For my book?" Her face beamed with an exuberant smile. "I still can't get used to saying that. My book. My book. Don't you just love the sound of that?"

"What have you come up with?" Cami asked, anxious to hear his idea.

"How do you like *Worth a Thousand Words—A Photojournalist's Journey Around the World*," he said.

"*Worth a Thousand Words!*" Grandpa said with a cough and a laugh.

"I love it," Cami said. "I think it's perfect. Have you suggested it to the publisher yet?"

"Not yet. I need to call him in a day or two, though. I'll tell him then."

"I thought maybe that was who you talked to earlier today," she said, slipping a pile of pictures into an envelope.

Josh rolled his eyes. "I wish I'd been talking to Max. No," he shook his head slowly, "it was Mr. Hawthorne from the university. He was wondering when I'm returning."

His words got Cami's full attention. "What did you tell him?"

"I told him I don't know yet. I said I needed more time, and since the quarter ends in two weeks, it doesn't make much sense for me to rush back now," Josh explained. "Of course he didn't agree, and I understand his concern, but the substitute is very capable of filling in for me and . . ." he paused and looked at the three faces staring at him, "I'm not quite ready to leave. That is, if it's okay with you that I stay."

Cami wasn't sure how to respond, but she was grateful that Pearl and Grandpa Willy spoke up and assured him he was welcome as long as he wanted to stay. Only after they'd spoken did she add her vote that he could stay as long as he needed.

But her reaction to his comment caught her off guard. She enjoyed having Josh around, but she still had doubts and misgivings about him. She was a small-town girl, but that didn't make her so naive that she didn't know appearances could be deceiving. Was Josh sincerely the person he appeared to be, or, like Pearl said, did still waters run deep? Was there a dark side to him that they hadn't seen before? Or was she just uncomfortable with her own feelings toward him?

Cami felt a sudden need to get out of that room, to get away from Josh. She felt as though she'd slipped into a grayish fog, where her vision and her feelings were unclear.

"I need to make a phone call." She bolted to her feet. "I'll be right back."

Dialing Mitch and Ashlyn's number, she waited for the phone to ring, then quickly hung up, deciding instead to go to their home and talk to Mitch in person.

"I'll be back in a little while," she called as she headed out the door. It was still light out, and the path to Ashlyn's house wasn't nearly so frightening in daylight.

"Please be home," she muttered as she skittered down the trail as quickly as she could without tripping over overgrown tree roots and shrubbery.

The lights were on, for which Cami was grateful. She needed to touch base with reality and was grateful to have a place to come and do so. Mitch and Ashlyn would take her mind off things. They would help her clear her head. Besides, she needed to give Mitch her decision about teaching the interior design class for the rest of the term.

She knocked quickly, then Mitch swung the door open wide.

"Hey, there," he said. "What brings you by?"

Cami noticed he didn't invite her inside.

"Are you busy?" Cami asked, looking behind him for any sign of Ashlyn.

"Uh, yeah, kind of," he answered. "I can give you a call later when I'm free if you want."

"Where's Ash?" Cami asked.

"She's busy too. She's in the tub. Long day," he explained, his words coming in choppy, quick sentences.

"Oh, okay," Cami said sadly. She'd been looking forward to talking to Ashlyn.

"Is there a problem?" Mitch asked, voicing what sounded like sincere concern.

"No, no problem. I just wanted to talk to her, and I wanted to tell you that I've decided to substitute that class for you—if you still need me to."

"Do we ever!" he exclaimed with excitement. "Are you okay to come in the morning?"

Cami felt her confidence slip a notch, but she remained solid in her decision. "I'll be there."

"I'll meet you in the front office at eight-thirty, then we can get all the paperwork taken care of and give you your class list and lesson plan." He gave her a grateful smile. "This is great of you to do this, Cami. And I have a feeling you're going to be glad you did."

"I hope so," she replied. "Tell Ashlyn I'll see her at school tomorrow."

Mitch promised to pass the message along and thanked her again. And that was it. She was a schoolteacher, starting tomorrow.

CHAPTER 14

"Okay, class," Cami said, her voice shaking as badly as her knees. "Some of you may know me. My name is Cami Gardner. I grew up here in Seamist." She gave them a little background on herself and her college degree.

A few warm smiles from some of the girls in the class helped calm her fears.

She remembered Josh's final words that morning before she left for school. *"Just remember, it wasn't that long ago you were their age. Relax and be yourself and everything will be fine,"* he'd said. Cami took a slow breath and gave them a tremulous smile.

"I thought we'd take some time today just getting to know each other and having you tell me what you've learned in class this year."

As each of the nineteen girls in the class took turns giving their names and involvement in school, Cami found herself relaxing bit by bit. By the time the bell rang, she felt she was among friends and had been accepted by the girls.

The girls hurried to their next class, and Cami breathed a sigh of relief. Of course, she hadn't taught the girls a blasted thing about interior design, but they'd had a fun time, and Cami actually found herself looking forward to her class on Friday.

"Hey there," a voice from the doorway said.

Cami looked up to see Ashlyn leaning against the door frame.

"Hey," Cami exclaimed, happy to see her friend after so many days. Dark circles under Ashlyn's eyes coupled with her pale complexion caused Cami to ask, "Are you sick?"

"I'm not quite myself," Ashlyn answered. "But I'll be fine." Then she asked, "So how did your first day go?"

Cami held her head triumphantly and raised the chalkboard eraser into the air. "It went great. The girls didn't walk out on me."

"I bet the class loved you," Ashlyn said, taking a seat at one of the desks as Cami erased her name and Friday's assignment from the board. "This is going to be so much fun having you at school," Ashlyn continued. "Mitch is excited too."

"He'd better be. It took everything I had to do this," Cami confessed.

"I know it must have been a hard decision, but you won't regret it."

Ashlyn couldn't stay long since she had a class in less than five minutes, but she promised to find Cami later.

Cami noticed when Ashlyn walked away she seemed thinner. *She must be sicker than I realized,* Cami thought.

* * *

Cami arrived home full of excitement. She knew it wasn't much, but the fact that she'd survived her first class and even enjoyed it was no less than a miracle, in her opinion.

Josh and Grandpa Willy were out in front of the house when she pulled into the driveway. Right off she noticed that Grandpa's sling was missing.

"Grandpa!" she called when she got out of the car. "Where's your sling? It hasn't been two weeks yet!"

Grandpa Willy looked at her with surprise and amusement.

"Well?" She stomped her foot and planted her fists firmly on her hips, not surprised that he'd finally gotten sick enough of the thing to take it off for good.

"We just got back from his doctor's appointment," Josh told her. "The doctor said he doesn't have to wear it anymore."

"Oh," Cami said, her hands sliding down to her sides. "I forgot you had an appointment today. Sorry."

"That's okay," Grandpa Willy replied. "The doctor was surprised at how well my arm healed," he told her. "I just have to keep it wrapped for another week."

"I'm glad to hear that." She gave her grandfather an affectionate peck on the cheek. "That just shows how healthy you are."

"So?" Josh changed the subject. "How did it go?"

"Well . . ." Cami paused for a moment, then she exclaimed, "It went great! I can't wait until my next class."

"That's my Cami-girl," Grandpa Willy said proudly.

Josh smiled broadly. "That's wonderful, Cami."

"Thanks," she said, feeling excitement bubble inside of her. "Where's Pearl? She wanted to hear all about my day."

"Inside somewhere," Grandpa Willy answered.

Cami rushed into the house to find her, calling Pearl's name as she burst into the kitchen.

"In here," Pearl answered.

Cami found her in the office, looking through pictures. The somber expression on Pearl's face told her something was wrong.

"Are you okay?" Cami asked, dropping her purse onto the desk.

Pearl drew in a long breath and nodded as she exhaled slowly.

"What is it?" Cami pulled up a chair next to her and tried to look at the pictures in Pearl's hand. "What's the matter?"

"Frederick," Pearl said. "I found some pictures of Frederick."

Cami's heart dropped. No wonder Pearl was upset. Frederick had been the love of Pearl's life, the person who had meant so much to her that she'd chosen to spend the remainder of her life alone. Frederick was the man she'd been engaged to, but he had been killed before they were married.

Pearl handed the pictures to Cami, who looked at them closely. She caught glimpses of Frederick in each picture, but in each one he was partially blocked by the billowing sail of a sailboat, turned just enough so his facial features were hard to distinguish, or standing behind a young, vibrant Pearl whose full, naturally curly hairdo hid part of his face.

Still, she saw enough of him to conclude that he was quite handsome, with wavy dark hair, chiseled jawbone, and deep-set eyes. He was tall, trim, and dressed in elegant attire. Very classy, Cami decided right off.

"There are some other pictures of him in here somewhere," Pearl said, resting her head on the back of the chair and looking dazedly out the window.

"He's a handsome man, from what I can tell," Cami said. "You two made quite a stunning couple."

Pearl smiled for a brief moment. "I wasn't the only girl who thought he was handsome. Every girl for miles had their eyes on my Frederick, but he always said he only had eyes for me."

"I can see why." Cami glanced at the pictures again. "You were very pretty," she said. "You still are."

Pearl gave her a level look and raised a skeptical eyebrow.

"Well, you are."

Pearl's gaze traveled back to the window.

"Is something wrong?" Cami asked, her heart full of sympathy. She knew how difficult seeing the pictures must have been for Pearl.

"It's interesting how a picture can bring back a thousand memories. I remember even the tiniest details of those moments—where we were, what we were doing, things we said . . . how it felt to be with him." Pearl closed her eyes, as if the memories were just too painful. "I think I'm just having one of those moments when your past suddenly floods in and things you've forgotten or tried to forget float to the surface."

Cami knew that Pearl had a lifetime of painful memories to deal with. Two of the most difficult were Frederick's death and the birth of their child whom she'd chosen to give up for adoption.

"What can I do?" Cami asked.

Pearl turned her head slowly and looked at Cami. Then she reached out and patted Cami's hand. "I'll be fine. I appreciate you listening."

Cami wished there was more she could do to ease Pearl's pain, to lighten her heart and mind.

"What time is it?" Pearl exclaimed as the grandfather clock began to chime. "I better get lunch started. We have guests."

Pearl hurried to the kitchen, and Cami took another look at the pictures and wondered why things turned out the way they did. Life seemed so unfair at times. It didn't seem to make sense, no sense at all.

Rifling through another stack of pictures, Cami looked for more photographs of Frederick and Pearl. She was interrupted when the phone rang. A couple in Seattle related that they were coming to Portland on business and wanted to spend a weekend on the coast. They had some questions about the inn.

Giving her best sales pitch, Cami told the husband about the history of the inn and described its location and the accommodations. While she talked, she went through a pile of mail and organized her desk. On the back corner she found the box she'd retrieved from the attic. She worked on the twine that had been tied around it to keep the lid on, but she couldn't undo the knot. She knew that somewhere in one of her drawers she had a pair of scissors, but she couldn't find them.

Telling the man on the other end that she would send him a brochure in the mail, she thanked him for calling and hung up the phone. She went into the kitchen in search of another pair of scissors, but Pearl needed help slicing fruit for lunch, and the scissors were forgotten.

* * *

Friday morning Pearl and Cami reviewed plans for Josh's birthday party. He wasn't expecting a party. In fact, as far as he knew, no one at the inn was even aware that it was his birthday. The element of surprise made it even more exciting.

At breakfast that morning, it was hard not to blurt out, "Happy Birthday!" to him, but everyone managed to remain aloof and not give away their plans. Grandpa Willy came up with half a dozen projects outdoors to keep Josh busy so that after Cami returned from teaching that morning, she and Pearl could decorate the house and prepare food for the barbecue. They planned on a huge feast that included Pearl's mouthwatering, marinated London broil and shrimp kabobs grilled on the barbecue, as well as a variety of salads, fresh vegetables, fruit, and an elaborate birthday cake.

Cami peeled and sliced cucumbers for the relish tray. "Have you heard from Ashlyn and Mitch yet? Are they coming?" she asked Pearl, realizing that neither of them had returned her call or mentioned anything earlier that day at school.

"No," Pearl answered. "I thought you'd already talked to them."

"I better give Ash a call." Cami finished her task and dried her hands on a dishcloth. Dialing Ashlyn's number, she waited for her friend to pick up the phone. Just as the answering machine clicked on, Mitch answered.

"Hey, Mitch," Cami said, happy to reach them. "Did you get my message about Josh's birthday party tonight?"

"Uh, yeah," he said with a slight pause. "Sorry I haven't called you back."

"We're eating around seven," she told him.

"I'm not sure . . ." He stopped. "I mean, we have a little conflict," he said, "but we'll try and stop in for a little while."

"A conflict?" Cami said with more volume than she meant to. "What kind of conflict?"

"A . . . um . . . just some family stuff," he told her.

Cami was confused. She and Ashlyn used to talk every day. They knew each other's schedules and daily comings and goings. But lately Ashlyn had been evasive and distant.

Feeling as though something was wrong, that maybe Ashlyn was upset at her or something, Cami tried not to take it personally. She forced her voice to remain cheerful, even though inside she felt her heart constrict in her chest. She told Mitch good-bye and hung up the phone.

Her expression must have reflected her confused emotions because Pearl looked at her in alarm when she saw her. "Cami, what's wrong?" she exclaimed. "They're coming, aren't they?"

"Yes, for a little while," Cami answered.

"What do you mean, 'for a little while'? Why can't they stay the whole time?" Pearl wasn't any happier about the news than Cami was.

"I don't know. Some kind of 'family stuff,'" Cami said, using Mitch's own words.

"'Family stuff'! What kind of 'family stuff'?"

Cami shrugged. "I wish I knew." Then she looked at Pearl and said, "I keep getting the feeling that I've offended Ashlyn in some way. She seems to be avoiding me."

Pearl's eyebrows narrowed. "Avoiding you! She wouldn't do that. You and Ashlyn are like sisters. If there was a problem, she'd talk to you about it."

"That's what I thought. I've gone over it in my head a dozen times and tried to think of anything I might have said or done that would offend either one of them, but I can't come up with anything."

"Maybe you should go over and talk to her," Pearl suggested.

Cami thought about Pearl's suggestion for a moment, then decided against it. "I think I'll see how she acts tonight before I say anything."

* * *

Grandpa Willy took Josh down to the dock with him for a while so the women could put the finishing touches on the party. They'd planned a small, intimate gathering, and the evening held the promise of an enjoyable time. Even Cami's concerns about Ashlyn faded slightly in hopes that a fun evening together with friends and family would repair any problems in their friendship.

Cami finished fastening balloons around the yard and took one last look before heading inside for a shower. With streamers and colorful tablecloths, tiki lamps and balloons, the yard looked bright and festive.

Josh was going to be so surprised!

Pushing her hair out of her eyes, Cami hurried inside just as the front door of the inn opened. She happened to glance outside and notice a red Buick Le Sabre in the driveway.

A woman close to Cami's age stepped inside. She wore slim-fitting beige pants, a crisp white cotton shirt, and a long, navy blue silk scarf that trailed around her neck and down one shoulder. She wore her auburn hair short and simple, which accentuated her fine features, especially her deep green eyes.

"Hello," the woman greeted Cami with an air of aristocratic refinement. "I'm looking for Josh Drake. I believe he's a guest at your inn."

It was Jane. Cami knew it before the woman even introduced herself.

CHAPTER 15

Wishing she didn't look like hired help, Cami became all too aware of her dirt-smudged capris and sweat-stained T-shirt, not to mention her lack of makeup and her disheveled ponytail.

Forcing a pleasant smile, Cami replied, "Actually, Mr. Drake isn't here at the moment. He's gone down to the dock."

"The dock," Jane said. "Oh, I see. Well," she said with a quick glance at her surroundings, "is there someplace I could wait for him?"

Cami opened her mouth to reply, but Jane added, "And I guess I should inquire if you have a room available?"

Even though it was a question, Jane's direct manner made it sound as if she expected Cami to boot out any guests that might prevent her from being able to stay at the inn.

"I'll have to check," Cami said, wanting to give her the impression that there was a chance that staying there *wasn't* an option.

Cami didn't know why having Jane there was rankling her so, but it was. It wasn't that having Josh's girlfriend there made any difference to her. It wasn't like she herself had any romantic interest in him. Because she didn't. They were just friends. She was just a little surprised by the woman. That was all.

With more force than necessary, Cami punched some information into the computer. She wasn't upset at Jane for showing up—she was upset with herself for caring. It didn't make sense. Being a widow was a full-time job in the emotional department. She had no room in her life for this sort of stuff.

Just as Cami expected, the Asian Room was available. They didn't have anyone booked in that room until Wednesday of the next week.

"You're in luck," Cami said without much enthusiasm. "We do have a room available. How many nights will you be staying?"

"That's a good question," Jane said. "Just a moment." She fished in her bag for something and pulled out a small, black, rectangular-shaped object. She flipped open the lid and tapped on a small screen with a stylus. "I've cleared my schedule until next Friday. But my plans won't be definite until I talk to Josh."

Cami booked the room and hoped Jane didn't end up staying the entire week. The woman reminded Cami of a high-class rich girl who'd grown up in the lap of luxury, going to preppy girls' schools and living off Daddy's income. Her flawless skin, perfect makeup, and slim and trim shape didn't make it any easier to like her. Of course, who else would Josh be interested in? An intelligent, attractive, classy woman like Jane seemed to be exactly his type.

As Cami showed Jane to her room, the woman's cell phone rang. She answered it by saying, "This is Jane," then launched into a conversation which sounded like university business. "Yes, yes," she said, and her abrupt tone made Cami step out of her way. In fact, Jane just nodded when Cami opened the door to her room and showed her inside, then ignored her while she finished her conversation. She didn't even notice when Cami slipped from the room and headed to her own room to shower and change for the party.

While she blew her hair dry, Cami thought about Jane. Even though Jane seemed a bit stuffy and formal, Cami reasoned that the woman obviously cared a great deal about Josh to come all this way for his birthday.

Cami groaned inwardly as she thought about seeing them holding hands, sitting on the sofa together, snuggling next to each other, or worse, kissing. She didn't think she could stomach that.

She pulled on a clean pair of white walking shorts and a coral-pink sweater. Clipping back some of her hair, she left the rest to hang softly around her shoulders. With just a touch of mascara and lipstick, she was ready to go.

Spritzing on her best perfume, she nearly dropped the bottle when she heard a loud *clank* echo through the vents. She listened, trying to detect what it was. Sometimes when Grandpa Willy worked outside, the banging of his hammer or whir from his table saw carried through the ductwork.

Hearing no further noise, she left her room to find Pearl, who was in the kitchen working silently at the counter. Cami paused in the doorway for a moment and watched Pearl slicing chunks of fresh pineapple onto a tray. Pearl's expression seemed less than festive. In fact, by the way she sniffed and wiped at her cheeks with the back of her hand, Cami would've thought she was chopping onions, not pineapple.

Pearl finished with the fruit and rinsed her hands in the sink. With the dish towel, she wiped her hands and cheeks, then held the cloth to her chest as she gazed out the window a moment. Cami tried to step back out of the room to let Pearl have her privacy, but the floor squeaked, announcing her presence.

With a quick turn, Pearl saw Cami and gave her a quick smile. "Hi!" she said with forced brightness. "You look nice."

"So do you," Cami answered. "Can I give you a hand?"

"If you want to mix the fruit dip for me, that would be nice." Pearl set out the ingredients for the dip and Cami went to work.

"Is everything okay?" Cami asked Pearl without glancing up from the mixing bowl.

"Everything's fine," Pearl answered. "Why?"

Cami didn't want to tell her she'd seen her crying, but she did wish that if Pearl had a problem, she would talk to her about it.

"You've just been working so hard getting things ready for the party, you seem a little tired," Cami answered.

"No, I'm fine," Pearl told her.

They continued working on their tasks.

"Oh." Cami suddenly remembered why she'd come to the kitchen in the first place. She spoke quietly so only Pearl could hear. "Did you meet our new guest?"

Pearl looked at her with surprise. "Did someone else check in?" She filled bowls with chips and salsa. "I thought we had a cancellation."

"We did. This is a walk-in guest. Her name is Jane Covington," Cami told her, watching for a reaction. But Pearl continued getting things ready, so Cami told her a little more about Ms. Covington. "Jane is Josh's girlfriend from back east. She came to surprise him for his birthday."

Pearl stopped dumping olives onto a sterling silver tray. "Oh," she said, finally understanding. "That Jane."

Cami nodded.

"Well," Pearl said thoughtfully, "we have a room available, and there's plenty of food. And," she added, "she *is* his girlfriend."

"Right," Cami agreed.

Pearl handed Cami a jar of pickles to open.

"So tell me," Pearl lowered her voice, "what does she look like?"

Cami glanced at the kitchen doorway to make sure they were alone, but she still spoke in a whispered tone. "She's beautiful, intelligent, and businesslike. She's dressed in very classy, expensive clothes and nice jewelry." Cami shrugged. "The exact kind of person you'd expect Josh to have for a girlfriend."

Pearl pulled a face. "Looks can be deceiving."

"I don't think so. She seems a little snooty maybe, but not snobby."

They heard footsteps in the entryway going toward the parlor. Looking at each other, they both knew it was Jane.

"I guess we should tell her about the party," Cami whispered. "I don't know what she has planned for Josh while she's here, but we've worked too hard for this party to not have it now."

"I'll go with you," Pearl replied in a hushed voice. "I want to meet this girl."

They walked to the parlor together. Jane stood when they entered.

"Hello," Pearl said stiffly. "Cami said we had another guest."

Jane extended her hand. "I'm Jane Covington. I'm Josh's, I mean, Mr. Drake's girlfriend."

"Nice to meet you, Jane. Is there anything we can get you?" Pearl offered in a tone that was less than inviting. Cami gathered that Pearl also felt uncomfortable having the woman there.

"Thank you," Jane answered. "I'm fine. When do you expect Josh?"

Pearl glanced at the clock. There was half an hour until the party started.

"Soon," Pearl answered. "We thought we should tell you that, since today is Josh's birthday, we've planned a little surprise party for him."

"You have?" Jane seemed genuinely surprised.

"We just thought that since he was—"

"That was very thoughtful of you," Jane interrupted. "I'm sure he'll appreciate it."

Pearl just smiled, apparently not sure what to think of Josh's girl-friend.

"I guess I'll go back up to my room and make some phone calls while I'm waiting." Jane stood.

"We'll call you as soon as he gets here," Pearl assured her.

No sooner had Jane left the room than Mitch and Ashlyn stepped through the front door.

"Is he here yet?" Mitch asked.

Cami gave them a welcoming smile, then greeted them each with a hug. "Not yet," she told them. "I'm so glad you could make it. We're having the party outside in the garden."

They walked through the kitchen to the side door, then followed the newly laid stone path around the side of the house to the back-yard. Ashlyn and Mitch both commented on Josh's fine workman-ship, then Mitch told Cami that he'd received a lot of positive comments from the girls in her interior design class at school.

"They like the fact that you're young and 'cool,'" he said with a smile.

"They think I'm cool?" Cami asked with surprise.

"I've been there a year, and I've never been called 'cool,'" Ashlyn said with a frown. "What's your secret?"

"My secret?" Cami laughed. "I wish I knew."

Pearl was delighted to see the guests had arrived. "William just called!" she said excitedly. "They're on their way."

"I better go tell *Jane*," Cami said as if she were getting sentenced to the electric chair.

"Who's Jane?" Ashlyn asked, taking a cracker off a tray and biting the corner.

"Oh, I didn't tell you," Cami answered. "Josh's girlfriend from back east showed up to surprise him for his birthday."

"She did!" Ashlyn exclaimed. "What's she like? Is she pretty?"

"I'll go get her and you can see for yourself," Cami told her, and dashed into the house. She was almost there when the door to Jane's room opened and the woman stepped out.

She wore a red linen sheath dress, sleeveless and slim fitting, with a pair of gold-strapped sandals. The outfit was very classy and tailored, yet casual and comfortable. Her perfume was delicate and fresh smelling.

"I was just coming to see if Josh had gotten back yet," she said.

"He should be here any minute," Cami told her, amazed at how smooth and creamy Jane's complexion was. It seemed as though the more Cami saw her, the prettier Jane got.

Jane followed her downstairs and asked about some of the interesting collectibles in the house. Cami noticed that Jane pointed out some of the same items Josh had when he first arrived.

When they walked into the backyard, Jane exclaimed how wonderful everything looked. "You've really gone to a lot of work," she observed. "And look at all that food!"

Cami couldn't tell if Jane was pleased or curious. Was she wondering about her boyfriend getting so chummy with the owners and operators of the Sea Rose Bed and Breakfast?

A horn honked as Grandpa Willy's white Toyota truck pulled into the driveway.

"They're here," Pearl said, glancing around quickly one last time.

Cami saw Jane's cheeks flush with excitement. For a moment, the muscles around Cami's heart constricted tightly. She remembered how excited she used to get when Dallin came home, especially when she had a special dinner or a romantic evening planned. She couldn't help the jealousy that crowded into her chest, making her breath shallow and tight. How she missed having butterflies in her stomach and the flutters in her heart that were such a wonderful part of being in love.

"Get ready," Pearl told them.

Grandpa and Josh walked around the corner and everyone yelled, "SURPRISE!"

Josh stopped dead in his tracks, his mouth hanging open in complete shock.

"I don't believe this!" he exclaimed as he looked at all the decorations. "How did you know? Why did you—Jane?!" He rushed over to his girlfriend and engulfed her in an enormous hug. Jane threw her arms around his neck and hugged him tightly.

Josh lifted her off the ground and swung her around. "What are you doing here?" he asked. He set her gently back down on the ground.

"You didn't think I'd miss your birthday, did you?" Her arms lingered around his neck a moment longer. Cami couldn't watch their display of affection. She spied the punch bowl and began filling glasses for the guests.

Josh laughed as he realized Grandpa Willy had played a huge role in the party preparations by keeping him away at the dock most of the afternoon. Josh gave him a hug with a hearty pat on the back. He then shook hands with Mitch and Ashlyn and thanked them for coming. He approached Pearl and gave her an affectionate hug and a kiss on the cheek. "I bet this was all your idea," he said.

Pearl denied the accusation, giving credit to Cami for most of the work involved.

Turning to Cami, Josh gave her a knockout smile, and before she knew it, he was lifting her off the ground in an enormous hug.

"Josh!" she cried. "It wasn't *that* much work."

Over her shoulder, she noticed Pearl wipe at her eyes with the corner of her apron.

"You guys are great," he said enthusiastically. "This is *really* a surprise. Thank you."

Jane stepped up next to him and he slid his arm comfortably around her waist.

Cami grabbed the lighter and started lighting the tiki lamps, somehow annoyed that Jane seemed to look even prettier standing next to Josh.

Since the food was laid out buffet style, Pearl instructed them on which end of the table to grab their plates. The London broil sizzled on the barbecue along with delectable shrimp kabobs.

Cami offered to tend the meat while everyone filled their plates and found seats at the table. Calypso music from Pearl's international library of tapes and CDs played in the background, lending a festive feel to the atmosphere.

Every once in a while, Cami glanced over at the table where everyone talked and laughed as they enjoyed the sumptuous meal. Most of the conversation seemed to be directed toward Jane, finding out about her and how she and Josh met. Cami caught enough of the conversation to learn that she was a professor at Bucknell University, teaching French, German, and Italian. Her father was an international businessman, and their family had lived abroad most of her childhood. In each of the countries they'd lived, she'd managed to pick up the language easily, and once her family settled back in New York City, she went to college, where she continued her studies of foreign languages.

She told how she had met Josh in the Metropolitan Museum of Art. They'd both been admiring *Hand of God,* a famous sculpture by Rodin on display.

Aside from both of them liking similar pieces of artwork, they both loved Broadway musicals, Italian opera, and Volvos. Jane drove the same make and model as Josh did, only hers was pearl white.

Cami couldn't help listening as Jane went on about their first meeting.

"We were both on vacation in New York," Jane told her audience, "and it seemed as if fate brought us together. I was just finishing my master's degree, and Josh was in Manhattan visiting some friends. But after that afternoon at the museum, we ended up spending the rest of his time in New York together. We went sightseeing and shopping during the day and saw a different Broadway play every night. It was . . ." she searched for the right word, ". . . magical." Jane reached over and placed her hand on top of Josh's.

Cami looked away in time to see that it was time to turn the kabobs over. It was then that Pearl called her to come and join them at the table.

Cami lifted the tongs in her hand and said, "As soon as the shrimp is done."

For a moment her gaze connected with Josh's, and she felt a jolt of electricity zip through her. It all happened so quickly she almost wouldn't have noticed except that it left her heart beating faster.

Taking a deep, cleansing breath, Cami checked the skewered shrimp and vegetables one last time and removed them from the heat. Carrying the steaming plate of kabobs to the table, she was greeted with oohs and ahhs.

"Cami, these are unbelievable," Jane complimented. "This whole meal is delicious."

Cami noticed that for a person as rail thin as Jane was, the woman certainly had a hearty appetite. Cami wanted to dislike Jane. But the more she was around her, the more she was beginning to like her. The woman was accomplished, intelligent, beautiful, and successful. Cami knew that if she was truly Josh's friend, she would have been glad to see him have such a lovely girlfriend. He deserved someone like Jane.

But Cami's feelings weren't that simple. She felt turbulence and conflict inside her, and she didn't like it.

"Cami?" Pearl said a little louder. "Would you mind helping me with the ice cream and cake?"

Cami snapped out of her thoughts and focused on the faces looking at her. "Ice cream?" she repeated.

"For the birthday cake," Pearl said again.

"Oh, sure." Cami pushed her chair back. "I'll go get it."

While Pearl sliced pieces of her moist carrot cake with cream cheese frosting—which she'd learned was Josh's favorite—Cami ran to the house to get the ice cream. Scouring the utensil drawer, Cami searched for the ice cream scooper, but couldn't find it. As she dug through all the different kitchen utensils cluttering the drawer, she felt a streak of anger grow inside of her. She pushed and shoved at the items in the drawer until she slammed it shut with a frustrated bang. She didn't have time to sort through her emotions, but she knew something serious was going on inside of her.

"Can I help you find something?" a voice from the doorway asked.

Cami's head snapped up so fast she was surprised she didn't break her own neck.

Josh took several steps into the room. "What are you looking for?" he asked.

A lump remained in Cami's throat. She swallowed quickly to clear it away. "Ice cream scooper," she managed to say.

"Here." He opened the drawer she'd been looking in. "Let me see if I can—" He reached into the drawer. "Is this it?" He held up the scooper.

Cami shut her eyes for a moment, feeling foolish, then answered, "That's it."

Josh handed the utensil to her and said, "You carry this. I'll carry the ice cream."

He picked up a half gallon of French vanilla ice cream in each hand and turned to her. "Is everything okay?" he asked.

Cami gave him as much of a smile as she could muster. "Everything's fine."

"I just wanted to thank you for going to all this trouble for my birthday. No one's ever done anything like this for me before." His eyes were sincere, his gaze holding steady on her face.

"Hey, we do this for all our guests' birthdays," she told him.

"Oh," he said, his expression fading. "Well, it's really nice of you."

She shrugged off his compliment. "Glad to do it. We better get out there before the ice cream melts."

Walking off without him, she hurried out the side door and down the walk. Her eyes misted over, and her heart ached inside her chest. Even though her vision was blurred, she could clearly see the reason for her emotions, a reason she didn't want to admit to anyone else, especially to herself. But she knew there was no denying it.

She cared for Josh Drake. She cared for him more than she wanted to, and certainly more than she'd ever admit.

CHAPTER 16

Cami kept her distance from Josh for the rest of the evening. Ashlyn and Mitch had left right after dinner. Ashlyn claimed she had a headache and needed to go home.

Josh opened the gifts they'd gotten him, which were mostly items from the area: a carved wooden seagull, a lovely, hand-tooled wallet, and a small but beautiful framed watercolor of the coast with the Misty Harbor Lighthouse in the distance.

"If I didn't know better, I'd think these wonderful people had adopted you, Josh," Jane joked.

"As much work as he's done around this place, he's earned a spot in the family," Grandpa Willy said.

Josh smiled at his new friends. "You've all made me feel so welcome and at home here. It's going to be hard to leave."

Cami sat up with a start. Was he telling them good-bye?

"You aren't taking off yet, are you, Josh?" Pearl asked. "I still need your help on the book."

"I'm not sure when I'm leaving," he said, "but it's probably time to start thinking about it. I've escaped from the 'real world' about as long as I can."

"I was beginning to think you weren't ever coming home," Jane said. She leaned toward him and snuggled into his shoulder. "It's lonely back there without you." She rested her hand on his cheek for a moment.

Josh glanced up and caught Cami's gaze, but she looked away and busied herself gathering up the dessert plates.

Pearl and Cami did dishes and put away food while Josh and Jane volunteered to put away the tables and folding chairs. Cami heard their voices and laughter float on the night air. She tried to ignore them, but the evening breeze seemed to magnify the sound.

Wiping at her forehead with the back of her hand, Pearl took a weary breath and flung the dish towel over her shoulder. "Well, I don't know about you, but I'm ready for bed."

"You look exhausted," Cami said. "You've had a long day." She noticed the weary lines around Pearl's eyes.

Pearl nodded. "Guess I'll head home. Thanks for all your help, deary." Pearl gave Cami a tender hug. She stepped back and looked Cami in the eye. "Is everything okay with you?"

Cami smiled. "I'm fine. I was about to ask you the same thing."

Pearl chuckled. "I'm just tuckered out is all. You seemed a bit distracted tonight. Are you sure you're alright?"

"Yes, I'm sure," Cami answered.

"She's a nice girl, isn't she?" Pearl said.

"Who, Jane?" Cami asked, knowing exactly who Pearl was referring to.

Pearl nodded. "Didn't think I'd like her at first, but she's as friendly as she is pretty. Seems genuine too."

Cami had to agree. "It's not hard to see why Josh cares so much about her."

Pearl bid Cami good night and left through the side door for her own little cottage just fifty yards from the main house. The cottage had been built by the original owners as servants' quarters for a couple they employed; the husband did yard work and maintenance around the mansion while the wife did the cooking and housecleaning. Cami's grandparents had sold the cottage to Pearl almost twenty years ago, and she'd lived in it ever since, but it was only in the last few years that Pearl had become like a member of the family. Cami treasured Pearl's friendship. She was easy to talk to and as supportive and loving as Cami's own grandmother had been. After Dallin's death, it was Pearl's shoulder Cami cried on. They'd shed many tears together.

* * *

Having Jane around made Cami uneasy. Not that Jane wasn't the perfect houseguest. However, Cami's first impression of Jane was that the woman was a snooty debutant who was born with a silver spoon in her mouth. But after spending more time with her, Cami realized Jane was down-to-earth and had a warmth and charm about her that made her enjoyable to be around. She brightened every room she entered like a breath of fresh air.

Cami couldn't help comparing herself to Jane. All of Jane's wonderful qualities, plus the fact that she was naturally stunning, intimidated Cami. Where Cami's hair blew in the wind, Jane's stayed smooth and unmussed. Jane had long, tan, shapely legs. Cami's were short, athletic, and muscular. Jane's laugh was musical and feminine, and Cami felt loud and unrefined around her.

After Jane's arrival, she and Josh spent most of their time away from the mansion, sightseeing and shopping. At least, Cami thought gratefully, she didn't have to watch them together, holding hands, gazing into each other's eyes.

Cami wondered if Josh might try to come to church while Jane was visiting, but he made no mention of it, and when Sunday morning arrived, Cami discovered that Jane and Josh were already gone for the day.

It took some effort, but Cami forced thoughts of Josh from her mind every time he managed to sneak into them. She'd grown used to his friendly conversation, his caring manner, and his contagious laughter. But apparently to him, Jane proved too great of a distraction, and she in turn kept Josh all to herself.

Even Pearl noticed it.

"Josh and Jane certainly are packing a lot into their time together while she's here, aren't they?" Pearl remarked to Cami as they worked together in the garden, thinning vegetables and pulling weeds.

"Have they?" Cami said, trying to appear uninterested. "I haven't really noticed."

Pearl looked at her out of the corner of her eye, but Cami quickly busied herself with a row of beets.

"I hate to admit it, but I've grown quite used to having him around. I'm going to have a hard time when he leaves," Pearl admitted.

Cami felt Pearl's gaze on her, but wasn't about to let on that she cared whether Josh stayed or left. At least with him gone, there wouldn't be any reason to believe he was involved with any of the mystery surrounding the lighthouse murder and buried treasure. She couldn't help but like him, yet if he was a self-proclaimed treasure hunter, how could she not suspect him?

"I'm thirsty," Cami said, sitting back on her heels. "Would you like something to drink?"

Pearl cast her a knowing look, but was kind enough not to press Cami with questions.

"Some lemonade would be nice," Pearl replied, adjusting the wide brim of her straw hat.

"I'll be right back." Cami pushed herself to her feet and hurried around the side of the house to the kitchen, but stopped when she heard Josh's and Jane's voices off in the distance.

"But Josh," Jane complained, "you've been here so long already. Don't you think it's time to come home? I miss you."

"I'm sorry," Josh replied. "I didn't intend to stay so long. You know how hard it's been for me since my father died."

"I know," Jane replied with a tone of softness and understanding. "But can't I be the one to help you through this? You know I'd do anything for you, Josh."

"That means a lot to me, Jane. Just be patient a little longer. I've still got some unfinished business here, okay?"

"Okay," Jane answered.

Cami stepped back from the house and hurried around the corner before they saw her. Unfinished business? What did he mean by that? But she didn't wonder long. She knew what he was after and why he was there.

She couldn't go into the house by way of the kitchen, so she headed for the back door leading to the garden. Out of habit, she glanced through the trees and caught sight of Ashlyn and Mitch's place. Ashlyn was on the back deck, shaking a rug over the banister.

Changing her plans, Cami hurried along the beaten path to Ashlyn's house. She'd missed the closeness she and Ashlyn shared, and right now she needed a friend.

It took a few minutes before Ashlyn answered the door. And when she did, Cami thought she looked like she was about to collapse.

"Cami!" Ashlyn exclaimed. "What are you doing here?"

"I saw you on the deck and thought I'd come say hi," Cami answered. She waited for Ashlyn to say something or invite her in, but Ashlyn did neither. "Um, hi," Cami said.

"Hi." Ashlyn leaned against the door as though it was the only thing holding her upright.

"Ash, you look like you're about to—"

Ashlyn didn't hear the rest of Cami's sentence. She ran from the room with her hand over her mouth.

Knowing now, without a doubt, that something was definitely wrong, Cami waited in the living room for her to return.

Looking pale and weak, Ashlyn came back, but stood silently in the room, looking down at her hands.

Cami confronted her. "Are you going to tell me what's going on?"

Ashlyn rolled her thumbs and licked her lips, then swallowed hard.

Cami stood up and approached her friend. "Ash?"

With her bottom lip trembling and her eyes filling with tears, Ashlyn looked up and met Cami's gaze.

"Oh, Cami," Ashlyn said, then broke down and sobbed.

Cami pulled Ashlyn close and hugged her. Her mind whirled with possibilities, and while she hoped for the best, she feared the worst.

"Ashlyn." Cami forced her friend away and held her at arm's length, looking her square in the eye. "You have to tell me what's going on. I'm so worried about you."

"Okay," Ashlyn sniffed, wiping at her cheeks and eyes. "I know." She nodded. "You're right—it is time."

They sat side by side on the couch, holding each other's hands.

"This is so hard," Ashlyn started. "I feel so bad."

"Bad about what?" Cami insisted.

"About being . . . " She paused, as if the words just wouldn't come out. "Oh, Cami . . . I'm pregnant." Ashlyn turned her face, unable to look Cami in the eye.

"Ashlyn!" Cami exclaimed. "That's wonderful." She hugged her friend, then said as an unexpected sob caught in her throat, "Congratulations." Cami fought back tears, but lost. "I'm so happy for . . . you," she tried to say.

Equally emotional, Ashlyn replied, "Thank . . . you."

A floodgate of tears released, and the two friends held each other and cried.

When their tears began to dry, Ashlyn finally spoke.

"I didn't want to tell you. I didn't want to hurt you," she confessed. "I mean, when we first got married, all we talked about was having our first babies together, you know?"

Cami nodded, remembering the many conversations they'd had about starting their families at the same time, hoping that they'd both have daughters who would be best friends like they were.

"I felt so happy when I learned I was expecting a baby, but I was also filled with guilt. I felt like I was betraying our friendship. I'm so sorry." Ashlyn looked at her with tear-filled eyes.

"You don't have to apologize," Cami told her friend, even though a second wave of tears threatened to fall. She didn't expect Ashlyn to not go on with her plans to start a family, but the fact that Ashlyn was pregnant was another painful reminder of Dallin's death. Once again, Cami felt as though her own personal progression had stopped when Dallin passed away. She recalled that after they got married neither she nor Dallin wanted to wait to start their family. But she hadn't gotten pregnant, and now it was too late. Cami realized that she would never have Dallin's child.

More tears fell.

She didn't want to take away from Ashlyn's happiness, but sometimes it was so hard to put aside her own pain to see someone else's joy.

* * *

Instead of going home, Cami took a long walk on the beach after she left Ashlyn's house. Just when her wounds seemed as though they were finally starting to heal, something else happened to open them back up, filling her with renewed pain and the remembrance of what she'd once had—and all that she'd lost.

In her moment of solace on the beach, surrounded by the call of seagulls, the crash and spray of surf on the shore, and the low-hanging clouds hugging the coastline, Cami dug deeper inside herself than she'd ever dug before. Somewhere in there she had a testimony of prayer, an absolute knowledge that God truly did love her and was aware of her. She'd believed that all of her life. She'd never had any reason to doubt.

But lately her prayers never seemed to get further than the ceiling, and while her scripture study had brought some peace to her soul, it hadn't revealed the secrets of the universe or answers to her questions as she'd hoped. She didn't make it to the temple as often as she wanted to. She just didn't seem to possess the determination to make herself do anything anymore.

Standing on the shore, Cami looked upward to the gray, churning clouds, feeling the stiff breeze in her hair and the spray of the crashing waves on her face.

A sudden rush of chills tore up her spine. She spun around, expecting to find someone standing nearby, but saw no one. Still, she was positive she had felt someone's eyes on her.

With a weary sigh and a thought that maybe her discouragement was turning into some grief-induced dementia, Cami hugged her arms around herself and shivered in the chilling gust sweeping off the surf.

"Heavenly Father," she said into the wind, "I feel so alone. I know I need to help myself, but I just can't seem to get my act together. Please help me to be strong so I can follow the path set before me."

The clouds dropped lower, and the waves grew bigger. Cami took several steps back so her feet wouldn't get wet. She closed her eyes and took some deep breaths. "Please, Father." Her voice was a pain-filled whisper. "Help me."

Then, an image came to her mind. A face. And along with that image came a warmth to her soul.

Josh's face.

She quickly opened her eyes and began walking, trying to force the picture from her mind.

But she couldn't. His smile, his eyes, his laugh filled her head.

"Okay!" she said out loud, stamping her foot on the hard sand. "So, what about Josh?"

Why had he all of a sudden popped into her head?

She looked up into the heavens, as if demanding them to tell her. "Tell me, Father. What about Josh?"

Admitting to herself the fact that she did have tender feelings for Josh was a big step. It wasn't quite love—she knew she wasn't ready for that just yet. But his kindness and his tender, gentle ways had shown her that she could open her heart to another man.

Again, and much softer, she asked, "What about Josh?"

She fell onto her knees and buried her face in her hands.

She was confused. She couldn't understand why Heavenly Father would help nurture feelings toward Josh when Josh was apparently quite involved with Jane.

Just like the clouds overhead that blocked the warm, illuminating rays from the sun, the clouds of confusion in her mind blocked her vision and, it seemed, her ability to receive inspiration from the Spirit.

Sinking down into the sand, Cami pulled her knees up to her chest and wrapped her arms around them. Then, as raindrops from the sky began to fall, tears of pain and loneliness trickled onto her cheeks.

CHAPTER 17

On Jane's last night at the inn, Pearl made linguini with shrimp, scallops, and crab in a buttery Alfredo cream sauce for dinner. The meal prompted a few words of Italian from Jane, which led to some from Josh. Grandpa and Pearl also knew a few words in Italian, and Cami quickly found herself lost in their display of foreign language skills, skills she sorely lacked. She smiled pleasantly at their continental bantering, but found herself wanting to tell all of them to just shut up already.

She was grateful to have the task of cleaning up the dishes. In the privacy of the kitchen, she went through the motions of loading the dishwasher and putting away leftovers. She heard Jane's cheerful laughter above everyone else's in the other room.

Cami rolled her eyes as she rinsed several pots in the sink before placing them on the racks in the dishwasher. She was glad Jane was leaving and that Josh was staying. Something inside of her felt like she had won, at least for the time being.

Jane's laughter, followed by Josh's deep chuckle, sounded again.

Cami clenched her eyes and prayed for strength.

Josh would leave, then Ashlyn would have her baby and be involved in that, and then who would Cami have? Pearl and her grandfather, yes, but they wouldn't be around forever. She was going to end up alone.

And the thought scared her.

* * *

Friday morning, Cami peeked out the window as Josh walked Jane to her car. They talked for a moment and laughed about something. Then, as they embraced and kissed, Cami let the curtains fall back into place.

Deciding she would never have love again, Cami wished that somehow she could turn off her heart so she wouldn't have to feel the pain and loneliness that seemed to exist in the absence of love. Feeling nothing would be a better feeling than this.

With a list of errands and plans to go to school to prepare for upcoming finals, Cami walked out the side door to her car and got inside. Waiting until she heard the sound of Jane's engine fade away, she started the engine in her own car and headed for town.

* * *

It was evening before Cami arrived home. Dinner was over, and the mansion was quiet except for muffled voices coming from the direction of the office.

Going straight to her room, Cami tossed her purse into a chair, then kicked off her shoes and collapsed onto the bed. She was exhausted. After completing all of her errands in town, she'd gone to the high school and ended up volunteering to help set up the stage for the final performance of the school choir and orchestra. Since the performance was going to be held in the gymnasium, it took quite a bit of work to create an atmosphere more suited to a concert instead of a basketball game.

Her stomach grumbled. Except for a cookie she'd grabbed while in the grocery store, she hadn't had anything to eat since breakfast. In the kitchen she sliced a cinnamon raisin bagel and smeared it with cream cheese. Taking a bottle of grapefruit juice from the fridge, Cami made her way to the office to see what was going on.

Grandpa Willy and Pearl didn't hear or see Cami at the doorway. They were busy going through pictures and writing down notes and information about places and events depicted in the photographs. They got into a disagreement about which Hawaiian Island Waimea Canyon, the "Grand Canyon" of the Hawaiian Islands, was on. Pearl was certain it was Kauai, but Grandpa Willy was convinced it was on the island of Lanai. Cami held her tongue, deciding to watch a minute longer before she let her grandfather know that Pearl was right.

"Alright, alright, dad-blast it!" Grandpa Willy exclaimed. "Since you're such an encyclopedia, tell me where this picture is." Another rousing discussion ensued, with Pearl taking a few guesses, then finally giving up, claiming that the picture didn't even look familiar to her. "That's because it's one of mine," he told her. He explained that it was the Mozambique Channel just off the island of Madagascar.

Instead of challenging him or trying to outdo him with an even better picture, Pearl looked as if she was thoroughly fascinated with the picture and asked him to tell her all about it. Cami listened as Grandpa Willy told her about a harrowing storm he'd weathered coming around the southern tip of Africa. Pearl leaned in toward him, her eyes glued to his face, her attention completely focused on his story.

It was then that Cami realized something was going on between Pearl and her grandfather. Whether either of them knew it or not, their casual relationship had become more comfortable—and more intimate.

Pearl scooted a little closer to Grandpa Willy as he pointed out some other landmarks and points of interest. Pearl oohed and ahhed at all the appropriate places and praised Grandpa Willy for his courage and heroic deeds. In turn, Grandpa Willy puffed out his chest and added even more drama to his story.

Cami had to smile. *I'll be darned,* she thought. *Pearl and Grandpa Willy.* The thought struck her funny at first, but the more she thought about it, the more she wondered . . . *why not?*

Even though they were eleven years apart, they had a lot of the same interests. And as much as they argued, Cami knew most of the heat simply came from all the hot air each of them blew as they compared daring adventures and exciting world travels. And they were both alone.

Again she thought . . . *why not?*

She didn't want to interrupt their cozy twosome, so she took her bagel out onto the back porch to catch the last rays of the setting sun. The clouds were ablaze with the final display of color. She never tired of the sunsets. Many evenings she and Dallin had watched the setting sun, arm in arm, in awestruck silence. Was he watching this one now? Were the sunsets in heaven even more amazing than the ones on earth?

"Hey there," a voice said. "I've been looking for you."

Josh approached from the pathway around the corner of the house. "Mind if I sit?"

She shook her head and scooted over on the bench swing so he could join her.

They rocked back and forth in silence, watching the crimson red of the sky turn to pink, then fade to gray.

"Busy day?" he asked.

Cami nodded.

Again, more silence.

"I just talked to Jane," he told her. "She called to let me know she'd made it home safely."

"That's good," Cami replied.

"She wanted me to thank you again. She loved the mansion and had a really great time while she was here."

"That's nice." Cami pushed the swing with her foot. Then she turned and looked at him. "She's a neat girl, Josh."

"Thanks," he answered. "She really is something."

Cami hoped he wouldn't sit and list all of the things he loved about Jane.

"I was really surprised to see her here on my birthday," he confessed. Then he looked Cami straight in the eye. "I didn't ask her to come."

Cami looked at him with curiosity, unsure of why he felt he needed to tell her that.

"She must care about you a lot to go to so much trouble," Cami stated.

He released a heavy sigh and relaxed back into his chair. "I suppose so."

Studying his blank expression, Cami tried to read the meaning between his words. "Is everything okay?" she asked.

He gave her a weary half smile. "Yeah," he replied, "everything's fine. I guess I'm still trying to figure out what my next move is."

"With Jane?" she asked, surprised at her own audacity.

"With Jane, with my teaching position, with my life," he answered, looking out at the sky that was turning into an inky blue. "I've gained a different perspective since I've been here, and I've certainly gotten a lot of answers, thanks to all of you," he answered. "I just don't know exactly how everything's supposed to change because of it."

"Do things have to change?" she asked, hoping to give him a springboard to help him sort out his thoughts.

"Well," he pondered her question for a moment, "yes. First of all, I've discovered that I'm interested in finding out more about the religion my mother and father practiced when I was young. My mother's death devastated my father. His marriage to my stepmother made it nearly impossible to practice his beliefs, since she basically made him choose between her and going to church. Now that I'm older, I can see that it was important to him to make his marriage work, and he must've felt that he owed it to my stepmother to make such a sacrifice for her. She was a selfish woman though, and no amount of effort or sacrifice he made ever seemed to be enough for her."

"I'm sorry," Cami said, wishing she knew what to say.

"Nothing to be sorry about," Josh answered. "That's just the way life sometimes is. I'm just glad I was led here so I could learn about my parents' church. The gospel has been the only thing since my father died that has answered any of my questions, the only thing that's really made much sense."

Even though Cami couldn't deny she had doubts about some of Josh's actions, she honestly felt in her heart that he was being sincere with her.

"I think that's why I've been drawn to history all my life," he continued. "It's fact, it's reliable, it doesn't change. You know you can count on history because it really happened and nothing can alter it. I think the gospel is like that. It's solid and reliable. I'm learning that when life gets hard, you can depend on the Lord and His teachings to help you through, to give you answers."

Cami knew that her family, but more importantly, her testimony and faith in God were the only things that had gotten her through the last year.

"I've been thinking about the things we've talked about a lot," he said. "I've decided that even though we have no control over the things that happen to us, we can control how we deal with them, how we let those experiences affect us. We can learn and grow and become stronger, better people because of them, or we can let them make us angry and bitter, mad at the world and even at God. I think that's what I was doing," he said.

"What do you mean?" she asked.

"I was blaming God for my problems. I was mad at Him for the challenges in life—for taking my mother when I was so young and then for taking my father. Now I have no one. But, it's not just that," he said, hesitating. "There's so much more, but . . ." He paused and looked at her, as if trying to decide whether to share more or not. "I guess the important thing is that what I'm learning is giving me a new perspective on all of life's experiences. Instead of the tunnel vision I used to have, I can finally see the whole picture."

Cami thought about his words. She knew that was why she'd had such a hard time letting go of the pain of Dallin's death. Instead of accepting it as part of "life's experiences" and "God's plan," she had refused to believe there was a purpose to all this pain and grief. But with a gospel perspective, she could see that there was a purpose and a reason for each trial and heartache she had experienced. Somehow seeing all this through Josh's eyes helped her to understand it better herself.

She pursed her lips as gratitude filled her heart. After taking a moment to calm herself, she said, "Thank you . . . for helping me understand what I already knew."

His eyebrows rose. "I did that?"

She nodded and smiled.

"Well," he chuckled, "whatever I did to help, I'm certainly glad I did it," he told her.

"Me too," she replied.

Then Josh stopped the swing and looked her in the eye. "I'm the one who should be thanking you though. Being here has changed my life," he said. "You and your grandfather and Pearl have come to mean so much to me."

He reached for her and pulled her into a hug, holding her close to him.

Cami rested her head on his shoulder and shut her eyes. Why, she wanted to know, when she had doubts and misgivings about this man, when she knew he had a girlfriend, and when she herself still wasn't over her husband's death, did she still feel attracted to him?

She didn't know the answer. All she knew was that there was strength and security in his arms. And for a moment, she let herself relax and relish the feel of warmth and comfort she felt from him.

Pearl's laughter from inside the house drifted out through an open window, breaking the tender moment between Cami and Josh.

"Well." Cami straightened, pulling herself away, but Josh held her for a moment longer. He moved his head back and in the process, brushed her forehead with his lips.

Cami's heart raced so fast she had to shut her eyes again and take a deep breath.

"Cami," he whispered.

She opened her eyes to see him looking her in the face.

She swallowed. "Yes?"

He opened his mouth to say more, but Pearl's voice rang through the night air. "Cami! Josh!" Then she said aloud, "Where are those two?"

Grandpa Willy hollered, "How in the tarnation am I supposed to know?"

Footsteps came their way, and with an abrupt jerk Cami and Josh both slid back to opposite corners of the bench swing.

Pearl threw the screen door open and looked outside, spying them. "There you are. I've been looking all over for you two." Pearl turned and hollered to Grandpa Willy that she'd found them.

"William and I are in the mood to make popcorn and watch a good movie. You two want to join us?"

Cami wasn't really in the mood, but figured a movie was better than being left alone with her befuddled thoughts.

"Sure," she said without much enthusiasm.

"I'm game," Josh added.

They relaxed in the back parlor, where a big-screen television and DVD player were hidden discreetly inside an antique bookcase. With the bookcase doors closed, the room appeared true to its Victorian decor, but inside the cabinet was a state-of-the-art in-home theater, complete with subwoofer and surround sound.

They decided on the classic musical *South Pacific,* since Pearl and William had been talking earlier about Hawaii and the film had been shot on the island of Kauai.

Cami had a hard time concentrating on the movie. Somehow she and Josh ended up sitting on the loveseat together with a bowl of popcorn between them. There was a large footstool for them to share, and occasionally one of them would bump the other one's foot, sending sparks of electricity up Cami's leg.

Pearl and William pointed out places they recognized in the movie and shared memories about the "good old days" when Hollywood made movies worth watching. Those memories spurred on more recollections of their past, which captured Josh's complete attention. He absorbed every word they said, apparently eager to hear firsthand accounts of life in decades from the past. For him, history had come alive.

After the movie ended, Josh continued asking questions, and soon the conversation took on a more serious note. Josh was curious as to how a fascinating and beautiful woman like Pearl had managed to stay single all her life.

As she spoke, Pearl's simple answer grew more emotional. Like peeling away layers of an onion, Pearl began to expose some of her most tender thoughts and feelings. Josh's kind and caring manner seemed to open Pearl's heart, and Cami found herself amazed at how much of Pearl's personal and private past she was willing to share.

Pearl told Josh about meeting Frederick, the love of her life, the man of her dreams. She detailed how they gave up their whirlwind careers full of travel and adventure so they could get married. They wanted to settle in Seamist. But Frederick, whose biggest vice was his love for gambling, decided to go to the tables one last time in hopes of making a fortune to provide them with enough money to start out their marriage.

Fighting back tears, Pearl told them how she'd begged and pleaded with him not to go back to San Francisco, claiming she didn't have a good feeling about it and she didn't care if they were poor, saying as long as they had each other they would be fine. But Frederick had insisted, and Pearl watched him leave with an unexplainable heaviness and dread in her heart. She told them tearfully that he'd been shot to death in a game of cards, accused of cheating.

"Did they ever find the man who did it?" Josh asked Pearl, who was wiping tears from her eyes.

She shook her head. "I couldn't get much cooperation from the police," she told him. "Because they were dealing with illegal activities, they considered Frederick a criminal and therefore deserving of what he got. For the sake of propriety, they conducted an investigation, but nothing came of it. I'm sure they didn't try very hard to find his murderer."

Josh shook his head. "That must have been so awful for you."

"I don't know how I made it through. Of course, there were other things going on in my life at that time that made it even harder," Pearl said with a faraway look in her eyes.

Josh waited for her to continue, but when she didn't, Cami was grateful he was kind enough not to question her further.

"Some things are best left in the past where they belong," Pearl managed to tell him.

Grandpa Willy, who'd sat back and listened to the conversation in silence, finally moved out of his chair. "It's late. I'm turning in."

"I think I'll do the same," Pearl said.

"I'll clean up," Cami told them.

Pearl thanked her and bid them good night.

Cami and Josh sat in awkward silence for a moment until Josh said, "I hope I didn't upset her. I didn't mean to pry."

"Pearl carries a lot in her heart. She's lived a very full and exciting life, but she's also dealt with a lot of heartache," Cami told him.

"Wasn't there ever anyone else in her life?"

"I think there were a lot of men who were interested in her, but she had sealed her heart. Frederick was the only one for her," Cami explained. "Her work became her life after him."

"Yet I get the feeling she has still had a lot of loneliness in her life."

"I think you're right," Cami agreed.

"Do you think she regrets not finding someone else? I mean, does she really think that Frederick expected her to never love again?" Josh asked.

Cami knew his question was about Pearl, but for some reason she turned the question toward herself. Did Dallin really expect her to never love again?

She'd talked about this with Josh before, and she thought she'd
had the answer, but her head and her heart hadn't been completely in
agreement. Now, because of her feelings for Josh, she could see how
sealed hearts could heal and open themselves up to care for someone
again.

"Cami, are you falling asleep on me?" Josh asked.

She blinked a few times and looked at him. Then one side of her
mouth lifted in a smile. "Sorry, I was thinking about something else."

"I don't mean to keep digging, but there just seems to be more to
Pearl's story than I'm hearing. I understand how tragic Frederick's
death was and how devastated she was after it. I'm amazed at what a
fascinating career she had too. But from some of the things she's said,
it's almost as if she's wanted to say more but just can't bring herself to
say it. It makes me think there's something more."

Cami had to hand it to him—Josh was insightful. He'd been able
to tell that Pearl wasn't giving him the full story. Feeling in her heart
that it was the right thing to do, and knowing that Pearl wouldn't
object to it, Cami decided to tell him the one thing in Pearl's life that
she just couldn't let go of, something even worse than Frederick's
death because it would never have closure.

CHAPTER 18

"There is something else," Cami told him. "But it is something so private for Pearl and so painful for her to remember she can't even talk about it."

Josh's gaze narrowed, his brows lowered in complete concentration. "What?"

"She was pregnant when Frederick died," Cami said.

Josh shut his eyes, squeezing them tight as if, for a moment, he felt Pearl's pain. When he opened them he said, "How sad for Pearl. No wonder Frederick's death was so hard." Then another thought struck him. "What happened to her child?"

Cami sighed. "Her parents were ashamed of her for getting pregnant, and her bishop counseled her to give the baby away. She had no support or help, so she decided to put her baby up for adoption. Even though she felt it was the right thing to do, it was still the hardest thing she's ever done. She wonders about her child often—what kind of family the baby had, if the parents were loving and kind—"

Josh's expression became anxious, and his breathing became hard, as if he'd been slugged in the chest.

"That's another reason she quit going to church," Cami continued to explain. "She was in such agony over losing Frederick and then having to give away her baby, she just couldn't handle it. What makes it even worse is that Frederick never even knew she was pregnant. She didn't find out until it was too late.

"It's only been during the last couple of years that she's started going to church again. It took her a long time to get past the pain and forgive herself for getting pregnant. But even harder," Cami swallowed, "is worrying about what kind of life her baby had."

Josh's expression looked strained, and in his eyes she saw pain and sadness.

"Josh?" Cami became alarmed. "Are you okay?"

The man swallowed hard, then pulled in several long, deep breaths.

"Josh?" she asked again. "What is it? Are you sick?"

After a moment, he spoke. "I'm fine. I guess I just . . ." He stopped and shook his head. ". . . I just feel so bad for her."

"To Pearl, that baby was a piece of Frederick," Cami said. "But back then, having a baby out of wedlock, especially in a small town, was one of the most humiliating things a young girl could endure. Her parents couldn't bear the humiliation and public ridicule they were certain would follow if she had that baby. They did things a lot differently back then. She didn't even get to see the baby, didn't even get to find out if it was a boy or a girl," Cami explained. "When she thinks about the whole experience, she struggles to remember that she's mended things with the Lord. It's something that she keeps buried deep in her heart. I think that's the only way she can deal with it. I would never bring it up to her because I wouldn't want to cause her that much pain."

Josh nodded, understanding Cami's reasoning.

For a moment they didn't speak. Then, noticing the time, Cami realized they'd been talking for quite a while.

"It's getting late," she said, getting to her feet. She checked the television and sound system to make sure everything was turned off.

"I'll help you clean up," Josh said. They gathered up popcorn bowls and glasses of melting ice and carried them to the kitchen.

Cami noticed Josh was walking funny and asked him why.

"My back is a little stiff from laying the flagstone. I'm not used to so much physical exercise."

"Can I get you anything for it?"

"No, I'll be fine after a good night's sleep," he said.

"Let me know if you need anything for it," Cami offered, dumping unpopped kernels into the already-full garbage can.

"I enjoyed tonight," Josh said. "Pearl and your grandpa are so great to talk to."

"They enjoy sharing their stories."

Their gazes connected for a moment, and Cami couldn't deny that there seemed to be some kind of chemistry between them, something that stopped her breath but sped up her heart. Did he feel it too? And if he did, what did it mean? Did it even matter?

"Well," Josh said, "I'll see you in the morning."

Cami told him good night, then placed the rest of the glasses in the dishwasher.

She worked slowly as her thoughts tumbled and bumped around in her brain. Unable to understand what had just happened, she felt her head grow thick with confusion.

Lifting the bag out of the garbage, she tied the top and carried it outside. The garbage cans were down the driveway and out of the way so they weren't visible to visitors and guests.

Heaving the bag into the receptacle, she let the lid drop with a bang and rubbed her arms to warm them against the chilling wind. The scent of rain was in the air, and she knew it wouldn't be long until another storm hit.

Flashes of lightning flickered in the distance, highlighting the dark, churning clouds. Filling her lungs one last time, Cami turned toward the house and heard the crunch of gravel behind her.

Flipping around, she didn't even have time to scream. Someone attacked her from behind and twisted her left arm up behind her, then grabbed her in a tight choke hold around her neck.

Terror struck her with paralyzing force. For a moment she couldn't think, she couldn't move, she couldn't breathe. Horrible visions passed through her mind. Judging by his size and strength, she knew the person holding her was a man. But the questions screaming through her mind was . . . what was he going to do to her?

With backbreaking force, he dragged her to the bushes and thrust her to her knees.

Cami cried out, causing him to wrench her arm so far up her back she expected her shoulder joint to pop any minute.

She struggled against his hold, but that only caused her more pain. The man didn't speak, which frightened her even more. Questions continued to fly through her mind. What did he want? Why was he doing this?

Please, God, she prayed. *Help me!*

The man leaned close, his breath heavy on her neck. Cami steeled herself for what was about to happen next, all the while praying for help from above, pleading for God to intervene, to save her.

Just then the sound of a door slamming brought them both up short. The man clamped his hand over her mouth and held her head against his chest so she wouldn't scream. She squirmed to get loose, but he gripped tighter, cutting off her oxygen.

Knowing if she didn't do something fast she would die, Cami pushed her fears aside, taken over by a driving instinct to survive. If she was going to die, she would die fighting.

With a rush of adrenaline coursing through her veins, she swung her right hand up, then reached behind and grabbed at the man, digging her fingernails into his neck. She felt the edge of a stocking cap over his face and tried to grab it, but he twisted free from her clawing grip and threw her facedown into the ground, knocking the wind out of her.

She struggled for air, gasping as oxygen finally refilled her lungs. Then, without pause, she screamed at the top of her lungs, "Help!"

The man drove his knee into her back with excruciating force. She cried out in pain but kept her focus, hoping that someone from the mansion had come outside. He held her head down on the ground, his hand so large it covered her entire skull. His entire weight seemed to press down on her, and she knew she was no physical match for him, so she had to stay alert and be ready for any opportunity to break free.

Please, God, she prayed. *Don't let my life end like this.*

From a distance, Cami heard someone call her name. She struggled, but the man held her firm. Just when she thought her lungs would collapse, a yellow beam of light split the darkness.

The man reared back and momentarily released his hold.

"Josh!" Cami screamed.

Instead of confronting Josh as Cami had expected, the man scrambled to his feet and bolted in the opposite direction. Josh dropped the flashlight and lunged for him, tackling him to the ground. They tangled and punched, grunting and groaning with each blow.

Cami dragged herself toward the flashlight so she could see who the attacker was. Just as she gripped the metal cylinder, she heard one last dull punch followed by an agonizing groan.

Shining the light, she illuminated the back of the man as he disappeared into the woods. Try as she might, she couldn't get to her feet to run after him. Then panic set in. Was Josh okay?

"Josh!" she cried, struggling to get to his side.

A gash on his cheekbone bled freely. He lay still, lifeless.

She said his name again, grabbed his hand and patted it several times, then shook his shoulders slightly, trying to rouse him.

His eyes fluttered open, and he attempted to lift his head. Their gazes connected for just a moment. Then his body went limp as he passed out again.

* * *

"You are not to leave this house alone." Grandpa Willy stared Cami in the eye. "Understand?" He looked at Pearl. "And you either! First thing in the morning I'm having an alarm system installed."

Both of the women nodded while Grandpa Willy huffed with anxiety as he paced the floor in front of them.

Pearl glanced over at Cami. "You don't look well. Are you okay?"

"I'm just exhausted. The doctor said the mild sedative he gave me would help me sleep." She yawned. "I think it's starting to work."

After help had finally arrived, Cami and Josh had both been taken to the emergency room. Cami hadn't sustained any injuries beyond bruises and scrapes, but Josh had a bruised rib and received five stitches in his cheek for the gash.

The police got a full report and searched the grounds extensively for evidence. They promised to return again in the morning to search in daylight.

Cami shuddered each time she thought about the man grabbing her and forcing her to the ground. She dreaded to think what could have happened had Josh not arrived when he did.

"I think I'll check on Josh one more time, then go to bed," she said.

"I'll walk Pearl home then," Grandpa Willy said. "I'll be right back."

Cami limped up the stairs to Josh's room. Her knee was tender and swollen.

Even with all the lights on, she felt jumpy, but she was determined not to let herself be consumed with fear. She'd been blessed and protected, and she knew God would continue to watch over her.

Tapping lightly on his door, she heard Josh tell her to come in.

She poked her head inside and said, "Hey there. How're you doing?"

"Hi," he answered, pushing himself up higher on his pillow. "I'm great. How about you?"

She sat in a chair next to his bed. "I'll be fine. I'm still a little shook up, but . . ." A sudden, unwelcome knot of emotion caught in her throat.

Josh took one of her hands in his.

"I . . ." She tried to talk again, but couldn't.

"It's okay," he tried to soothe her.

Tears trickled down her cheeks.

Josh pulled her into a hug and there, on his shoulder, she wept, releasing the turmoil of emotions she felt inside. Finally, when her tears dried and her voice steadied, she sat up, wiped her eyes and nose, and said, "You risked your life for me. Thank you."

He hugged her again and held her close.

"How did you know to come and look for me?" she asked when she had herself under control.

"I came back to the kitchen to see if you had some ibuprofen after all. When I noticed you weren't there and the garbage can was empty, I figured you'd taken out the trash. I was worried because it was late, so I went out to see if you needed any help. I thought I heard you yell for help, but I wasn't sure. I thought maybe it was the wind. Something told me to search anyway."

"You came at just the right time," she said. "Who knows what he would've done if you hadn't . . ." She had to force the images from her mind.

"I know," he replied. "I know."

She licked her lips and swallowed. She would always be in Josh's debt.

"How do your stitches feel?" she asked, noticing the patch of red staining the bandage on his cheek.

"They're fine. They don't even hurt."

"They're bleeding. I think I ought to change the dressing."

"There's stuff over there on top of the dresser."

Cami gathered the supplies and sat on the other side of the bed as she gently removed the old gauze bandage and applied antibiotic ointment to another pad.

"I'll try to be gentle," she said as she placed the gauze over the spiderlike stitches in his flesh. She leaned in closely to make sure the wound was covered.

Satisfied, she reached for the tape, but noticed Josh had his eyes shut.

"Josh, are you in pain?" She leaned in closely, worried that he'd passed out again.

He opened his eyes and smiled. "No, I'm fine. I was just . . . ," he paused for a moment, "I was just enjoying your perfume."

Their faces were only inches apart.

"Oh." Cami smiled. "Thanks."

Their gazes locked, and Cami's heart fluttered faster than a bird's wings in flight. Josh reached up and brushed her cheek with his thumb. "You sure you're okay? That guy was pretty rough with you."

"I'm fine. A few scrapes and bruises is all."

"I've never been so angry or frightened than I was when I saw that man attacking you," he confessed. His forehead furrowed with lines of worry. "I completely lost it when I saw you pinned to the ground."

"I was so glad to see you." She gave him a brave smile. "But it's over now. The police are combing the whole area for him. They'll find the guy who did it." She wondered if she sounded convincing, because even though she said the words, she didn't feel convinced herself.

"Well, until then, I plan on being your personal bodyguard."

"Oh, really?" She liked the idea of having a protector. "Are you sure you want the job? I hear the pay isn't that great."

"Yeah," he said, his voice husky with the effects of the sleep aid the doctor had also given him. "But I hear the perks are worth it."

She smiled dreamily at his words.

They continued gazing into each other's eyes, the space between them getting smaller and smaller.

"I'll never let anything happen to you, Cami," Josh said, reaching up and sliding his fingers through her hair.

She rested her head against the palm of his hand. "Thanks. That means a lot to me."

"You're welcome," he said, pulling her towards him.

Their lips met in a blissfully warm kiss. Then Cami slowly floated away to her room on the memory of his kiss.

* * *

It was noon before Cami finally woke up. The medication had afforded her a peaceful night's sleep, and she was grateful for the rest. Her elbows and knees were stiff and tender, and there were scratches on her face, but that was all that remained of the attack the night before. There would be no lasting physical scars, but she knew her sense of security and safety had been violated. The emotional scars would remain, to some degree, forever.

She got cleaned up, dressed, and then she walked toward the kitchen, where she heard Grandpa Willy's and Pearl's voices.

"I'm afraid if we tell her it will only make her more scared," Pearl said. "But she's going to find out anyway."

"Can't we let her recover for a few days before we break the news?" Grandpa Willy insisted.

"Maybe you're right. The poor thing—she's been through enough already."

"Then we'll wait to tell her," Grandpa Willy said.

Cami chose that moment to join them.

"Tell me what?" Cami said.

Grandpa Willy and Pearl looked at each other. "Nothing," they both said together.

"I don't believe you. What's going on?" Cami took a seat at the table and gave them both a level look.

"Why wouldn't you believe us?" Pearl exclaimed.

"Because I overheard you talking."

"Cami—"

"No, Grandpa. If something's going on, I need to know about it. Please."

With a sigh, Grandpa Willy said, "Alright. Yesterday afternoon they released the man they took in for questioning on the lighthouse murder."

"They let him go?!"

Grandpa nodded.

The reality of the situation settled in. "What are you saying? You don't think . . ."

"We don't know," Pearl said, taking Cami's hand in hers. "The authorities are looking into every possibility."

"But why here? What would he want with us? We're not a lighthouse. We don't have a treasure."

Grandpa Willy's eyebrows narrowed.

"Do we, Grandpa?"

"Of course not!" Grandpa snapped. "This whole treasure thing is ridicu—" Grandpa stopped, looking at the kitchen doorway.

It was Josh.

"Good morning, Josh." Pearl jumped up to greet him. "How are you this morning?"

"I'm fine, Pearl."

She fussed over him, making him take a seat and getting a plate of food for him. "Here, I saved you some breakfast," she said. "You must be starving. Would you like some orange juice to drink? Or would you like some lunch, instead? It is lunchtime."

"This is great," Josh said. "Thank you."

Pearl got him a drink and then finished straightening the kitchen. "I've got a load of linens to hang on the line. I better get to work." She hung the bedsheets and pillowcases outside to dry as often as she could, claiming that nothing smelled better than line-dried sheets.

"And I think I'll go down to the police station and see what's going on there. Maybe they'll have some good news for us. They spent enough time tromping around the yard, you'd think they would have discovered something," Grandpa Willy said, rising from his chair.

He and Pearl left, leaving Josh and Cami to themselves.

"I guess you heard?" she asked.

"Heard what?"

"They let the suspect in the lighthouse murder go."

Josh pushed a piece of bacon around his plate with his fork, then asked, "Do they think the guy last night had anything to do with the murder?"

"They don't know," she told him. "They think it's a strong possibility, though."

"How are you?"

"I'm fine. But the thought of that man possibly being the murderer really creeps me out. I don't think it's fully hit me yet—what might have happened had you not come along when you did."

"I couldn't bear the thought of something happening to you, Cami."

"I know. I'm sorry about your cheek."

He shrugged. "No big deal."

She shook her head. "No, Josh. It is a big deal. I'll never forget it. There's something else I'll never forget."

"What's that?" he said, pushing his plate away.

"Well, either it was my imagination, or I was hallucinating from the medication the doctor gave me, but I seem to remember us . . ." She stopped and smiled, feeling a sudden onset of shyness.

". . . kissing?" he finished for her.

She couldn't help smiling. "Yeah, kissing."

"I was wondering myself if it was a dream," he said, "because it seemed too good to be true."

"Really?"

He returned her smile. "Really."

Grandpa Willy pushed through the back door just then. He brightened when he saw them. "Glad you're still here, Josh," he said. "I wanted to thank you for digging all those postholes. When did you find time to do that?"

"Early in the morning," he said. "I was afraid you wouldn't let me do it if I asked."

Grandpa Willy placed a hand on Josh's shoulder. "Thank you, son. You're right, I wouldn't have wanted you to do all that work, but it was mighty kind of you. And mighty helpful."

Cami must've had a surprised look on her face because Josh noticed her expression and asked her if something was wrong.

"No," she said. "Nothing's wrong. But now I know what you were doing up so early the other morning, carrying a shovel around."

"You saw me?"

"Yeah," Cami said with a laugh. "I was wondering what you were doing. I thought you might be digging for buried—"

"Treasure?" Josh finished, his voice lacking any amusement at all.

Cami's laughter died in a hurry. There was nothing funny about what she'd thought. She couldn't tell him she had seriously wondered about him, that she'd questioned his motive for being at the inn.

"I'm sorry," she said. "I didn't mean to imply that you were the murderer."

"But whoever is after the treasure is the person who killed that fisherman," he said.

"Josh, I really didn't believe you were the one."

"Not even for a minute?" he asked. "You never wondered if I was the guy they were looking for?"

Cami shut her eyes, feeling a daggerlike pain in her chest.

"Cami?" Grandpa Willy asked, full of disbelief. "You didn't think Josh would do something like that, did you?"

"You said yourself that you wanted to search for buried treasures," Cami said. "And I saw you with the shovel, and . . ." As she said it, it all sounded so ridiculous, so impossible, that she wondered how she could ever even think such a thing. "With all that's been going on, I just jumped to conclusions I shouldn't have."

The hurt expression on Josh's face struck deep in her heart, piercing her soul. "Josh," she pleaded. "I'm sorry."

"That's okay," Josh said flatly, keeping his head turned away from her.

"It has been crazy around here," Grandpa Willy said in Cami's defense. "Everyone's suspicious about everyone else. Cami's been jumpy. We all have."

"It's okay, Willy," Josh said firmly, getting to his feet. "I need to go make a phone call."

When he left the room, Cami broke down. Her grandfather gathered her in his arms and held her as she cried.

* * *

"Cami, you haven't seen the silver candlestick holders, have you?" Pearl asked Cami when she came in the kitchen for breakfast.

Cami plopped down on a kitchen chair and winced at the throbbing ache in her head. She hadn't seen Josh since he'd walked away yesterday, and she felt terrible. She hadn't eaten or slept since their talk, and she knew she would go crazy if she didn't get a chance to apologize. She had to make him understand she was sorry.

"The ones on the mantle in the front parlor?" Cami asked, going to the cabinet for a pain reliever.

"Yes. I can't seem to find them anywhere, and I was going to put them on the dinner table tonight." Pearl examined the contents of several cupboards, then shut the doors with a frustrated bang.

"Why would anybody move them?" Cami asked as she found the medication and took two of the tablets.

"Move what?" Grandpa Willy grumbled as he shuffled into the kitchen, scratching his stomach and stifling a yawn.

"The silver candlestick holders," Pearl told him. "You haven't seen them, have you, William?"

"Nope," Grandpa Willy answered, plopping himself down at the table. "But they were there not too long ago. I remember because Mrs. Rothchild asked about them."

Pearl shook her head. "I'm sure they're here somewhere."

"I'll help you look," Cami offered. "Have you seen Josh yet this morning?" she asked her grandfather, the strain of worry beginning to throb in her neck. She prayed the pain reliever would kick in soon.

"Not yet," Pearl said. "Maybe he's still asleep."

"He's not sleeping," Grandpa Willy replied. "His car's not outside."

Pearl peeked out the kitchen window to the driveway where Josh's car had been parked. "That's strange. Now that you mention it, I don't recall seeing his car when I came over around seven this morning."

"I'll go check his room," Cami said.

"And I'll go look for the candlesticks. William, why don't you help me?" Pearl asked.

Cami stood outside his room for a moment before she tapped on his door. "Josh?" she called. "It's Cami."

No answer came, so she tapped again.

Wondering what was going on, she turned the knob and peeked inside. His room was immaculate, and all of his things were gone.

And propped on top of the pillows on the bed was an envelope with *Cami* written on the front.

Her heart stopped. Without even knowing what was in the letter, Cami got a sinking feeling in her stomach.

Forcing herself to pick up the envelope, Cami held it in her hand, turning it over and over several times. She couldn't make herself open it though. Something told her she didn't want to know what was inside.

"What's that?" Pearl's voice made Cami jump.

"Oh!" Cami exclaimed, placing a hand on her chest. "You startled me." She showed Pearl the envelope. "It's from Josh."

"Josh? Why would he be writing a letter? Where is he anyway?" She looked around the room. "Where's all of his stuff?"

"I think there's only one way to find out," Cami said. She slid a letter opener beneath the flap and sliced the envelope open.

She pulled out a check and a folded sheet of paper.

Opening the letter, she read:

> *Dear Cami, Pearl, and Willy,*
> *I didn't want to wake you this morning when I left, but something urgent came up and I had to return to Pennsylvania. I hope the check I left will cover the cost of my extended stay at your lovely inn.*

Cami looked at the amount of the check, and found that it was far more money than they'd agreed upon.

> *Please send me a bill for any difference, and I will happily cover the rest of the expense.*
> *I apologize for my hasty departure and hope that you'll forgive me. This wasn't the way I wanted to leave, but I was left with no choice.*
> *The time spent with you at your inn will always be thought of with great fondness—not only for the friendships that I developed while I was there, but for the healing and understanding I gained. I am leaving with much more than I brought with me, and I owe that to the three of you.*

Please tell Pearl that I will be in contact with her about her book. I want to help out with it any way I can.

I hope I didn't wear out my welcome while I was there, because I hope to return again someday. Until that time, know that I leave with you all my best wishes.

With love,

Josh

"Cami, what does it say?" Pearl demanded.

Cami couldn't talk. She just handed the letter to her and collapsed into a chair. He was gone. She'd driven him away, and she didn't know if she'd ever see him again.

"Well," Pearl said with disgust as she dropped the letter onto the table, then slapped it with her hand. "How about that? No good-bye, no explanation, nothing!"

Cami fought a losing battle with her emotions. She knew if she didn't get out of there, she was going to break down in front of Pearl.

"Excuse me," Cami said, and rushed from his room to the privacy of her own bedroom, where she fell onto her bed and let her tears flood freely.

She didn't hear Pearl follow her inside, but felt her weight as she sat down on the edge of her bed. "There, there," Pearl stroked Cami's hair softly. "Let it out."

Cami cried several minutes longer, letting her frustration, sadness, and hurt rise to the surface and spill over with her tears.

"It's all my fault," she sobbed.

Pearl gathered Cami into her arms and held her as the last of her tears ran dry, wiping at her own wet cheeks.

"He must've had a good reason to leave so suddenly," Pearl said in his defense. "Don't fret, deary. We haven't heard the last of Mr. Drake—I'm sure of it."

"No, you don't understand. I drove him away." Cami explained to Pearl what had happened and how she'd suspected him and questioned his actions. He'd come to them for help and answers, and she felt she had ruined everything.

"There, there," Pearl soothed. "Everything will work out. Maybe some distance is just what he needs right now."

Pearl held Cami until sleep overcame her and she escaped to a carefree world of dreams. At least in sleep she found peace.

* * *

Pearl, Grandpa Willy, and Cami ate in silence that night. It had been a long, busy day, and everyone was exhausted. The inn had been overhauled with a high-tech alarm system. Though none of them wanted to believe it was necessary in their small, safe little town, they couldn't deny the need for it any longer.

Their guests at the inn had gone out for the evening, so the mansion was quiet except for the ticking of the grandfather clock in the hall and the wind chimes tinkling on the back porch.

After the meal was cleaned up and put away, Grandpa Willy and Pearl retired to the office to plow through more pictures, but Cami needed a breath of fresh air. Grandpa Willy gave her permission to go out onto the porch, but only as far as the swing. The office window was right behind it, and he figured he could keep an eye on her that way.

Rocking the swing gently back and forth, Cami watched as the sky lost its last pink tinge of sunset.

She missed Josh. They all missed Josh. In such a short period of time he'd come to mean a lot to each of them. Perhaps they had wanted to take him under their wing because he was so vulnerable and needy. Or perhaps it was because he was so charming and handsome, and so very sweet. Maybe it was his teasing smile, his quick wit, or contagious enthusiasm. For Cami it was all of that and more. She appreciated the way he listened with such focus and understanding, as if what she said was the most important thing in the world to him. And most of all, it was the way she felt when she was around him— comfortable, safe, accepted, and happy.

But she'd ruined it all.

She rested her head back against the swing and groaned. She would do anything to make it up to him. Anything.

Tears leaked out of the corners of her eyes, running into her ears.

She berated herself for being stupid, suspicious, and inconsiderate. He'd simply kept some things to himself—private, personal things. And she'd jumped completely to the worst conclusion possible. How did she expect him to react—with joy?

"I'm such an idiot," she said out loud, smacking the palm of her hand onto her forehead.

He'd kissed her. Obviously she meant something to him, or at least, she *had* meant something to him. And, even more surprising, she'd enjoyed his kiss. That had been an enormous hurdle for her to get past, but she'd done it. She'd opened up her heart to new possibilities.

And then she'd ruined it all.

She couldn't sleep that night. Her bedcovers felt like chains, her room like a stifling cave with the walls closing in. Night sounds such as floorboards squeaking as the house settled for the night, branches scratching against the siding, and the echoes of emptiness in her heart were more than she could handle.

Throwing off her covers, Cami shoved her feet into her slippers and padded to the office, where she shut the door and turned on the light. She glanced at the secret door that led to the inner passageways of the house, remembering that Josh was going to help Grandpa Willy seal all those doors before he went home. The doors now served as a painful reminder that he'd left unfinished business in his haste to return to Pennsylvania.

She looked around at the stacks of pictures that were beginning to take on the appearance of an organized mess. There were still plenty of photographs to go through, but with Grandpa Willy's constant help and Pearl's determination and passion for the book, they had made a lot of progress, not only with the book, Cami mused, but perhaps even toward a relationship of their own. Although they seemed to butt heads more often than two stubborn old goats, there was something charming and endearing about their playful bickering. Their tones weren't at all condescending or serious, but teasing and even flirtatious.

Yes, she thought, whether they knew it or not, Grandpa Willy and Pearl had developed feelings for each other. And Cami couldn't have been happier for them.

The clock in the entryway chimed the hour—midnight.

Another day. She and Josh had planned on going whale watching. And on going to church one more time.

She wondered if he would attend his ward back in Pennsylvania. Would he continue to grow in the gospel? Would Jane let him? Would she eventually join the Church? Perhaps they would get married in the temple and start their own eternal family.

Cami shook her head and scattered her foolish thoughts. Her imagination seemed to be in constant motion lately—wild and unrealistic. And now she was filled with regret.

Looking around the room, her gaze landed on the shoe box she'd found in the attic. She'd been meaning to look through it for weeks, and she decided now was as good a time as any to finally see what was inside.

It took a moment to find a pair of scissors to cut the twine binding the box, but finally she managed to lift the lid and expose the contents. When she did, her breath caught in her throat.

A journal. Right on top of everything was a journal. And on the inside cover, written in beautiful handwriting was her mother's name—Grace Olivia Davenport.

Was it possible? Had she actually found her mother's journal?

She opened the book to the first entry.

June 12, 1969

Happy Birthday to me. I'm sixteen today. Sweet sixteen and never been kissed. Darn it! I actually thought Eddie would finally get up enough guts tonight at my party to kiss me, but he chickened out. It was so perfect too. Mom and Dad let me invite a bunch of friends over for a barbecue and volleyball on the beach. We even built a campfire and sang songs and roasted marshmallows. It was soooooooo much fun. My best friend, Kandis, finally got together with Donnie, the boy she's liked since ninth grade. They held hands and made goo-goo eyes at each other all night.

Anyway, Eddie asked me if I wanted to walk down the beach with him, and of course I said yes, and he held my hand and everything. He was so close to kissing me, I mean, I actually had my lips puckered and my eyes shut, when he said, "Hey, did you hear about Coach Everett eloping with Miss Johnson?" Miss Johnson is our home ec teacher.

Of course I'd heard all about it and wasn't interested in discussing someone else's love life when I was busy trying to get a love life of my own going.

Cami chuckled at her mother's aggressive style, realizing how much like that she, herself, used to be.

Well, of course by then he'd missed his chance because everyone had decided it was time to break up the party and go home. I wanted to bury him in the sand for being such a coward, but then he flashed me that gorgeous smile of his and asked me out for Friday night. Guess it wasn't a complete loss. But Friday night, one way or the other, I'm kissing Eddie Grant!

Cami smiled and closed the book, anxious to read on but curious to find out what else was in her mother's special box.

There were some stacks of pictures with names written on the back. Some of the people Cami remembered, some were people who still lived in Seamist, but others she didn't recognize. She was happy to find a picture of Eddie Grant with thick, black-rimmed glasses and a flattop haircut.

"Oh, Mother, you had to have had better taste than that!" Eddie looked more nerdy than anything, but Cami figured if her mother had been so hooked on the guy, he must have had some redeeming qualities.

Cami found a charm bracelet with a pair of ballet shoes, a cheer-leading megaphone, a sailboat, a dog, a miniature lighthouse, and a tiny crown hanging from the links. Grandpa had always called Cami's mom "Princess," which probably explained the crown.

There was also a first-place 4-H ribbon for something her mother had entered in the county fair, as well as birthday cards from her friends and her parents, some jewelry that had tarnished over the years, a wilted and crumbling corsage, some movie ticket stubs, a strand of hair—her mother's, she guessed—and a small velvet pouch.

Cami lifted the velvet pouch and gently shook it.

Loosening the strings, she opened the pouch and poured the contents into her hand. Then she gasped. It was a solid gold coin. With something that looked like Spanish writing on it.

CHAPTER 19

Cami dropped the coin as though it was going to bite her. She looked at the coin suspiciously, then examined it closely. It couldn't be what she thought it was . . . could it?

"There's no way," Cami said out loud, picking up the coin and turning it over several times in her hand. Could this really be one of the coins from the Spanish gold presumably buried somewhere along the coastline? One of the coins that had caused so much commotion? There was no doubt the writing was Spanish, but she couldn't make out any kind of date on the surface.

What if it were indeed part of the buried gold? What would happen then? It would validate all the legends that had floated around the area for years, bringing all sorts of crazy people—gold diggers and con artists alike—to the area.

But what she really wanted to know was why in heaven's name her mother had one of the coins in the box. She looked at the journal and wondered if there was some mention of the coin in it. Maybe her mother knew something about the Spanish gold and had recorded it in her journal.

Opening the journal, Cami relished every word written by her mother, every feeling recorded, every private thought shared. Hoping for some mention of the gold, she read until she fell into an exhausted sleep.

* * *

"There you are," Grandpa Willy announced when he entered the room early the next morning and found Cami asleep, her head resting on her folded arms on her desk.

Cami awoke with a start. "What . . . who . . ." she stammered, then squinted her eyes while her vision became focused on her grandfather standing in the doorway.

"I've been looking all over for you. Church is in half an hour. What in the blazes are you doing in here anyway?"

Cami knew her news would give her grandfather a shock. He'd adamantly denied any knowledge about a buried treasure. How was he going to react to this?

"Aren't you going to church?" he asked, giving her a quizzical look.

"I was planning on it," she told him, "but there's something I need to show you first."

He let out a flustered puff of air. "Cami, at this rate, you'll never be ready."

"Grandpa, you're going to want to see this." She lifted the box toward him. "I found this. It was my mother's."

"This was Gracie's?" he exclaimed. Grabbing the box from her, he sifted through the contents, pausing upon seeing several items, a smile spreading on his face as he reflected on memories of his only child.

"This was inside," Cami said, handing him the journal.

"Her journal," he said softly. "She was always writing in this thing. Have you read any of it?" he asked.

"Yes. It's wonderful," Cami exclaimed, feeling as though her mother had come back to life again. "It starts when she's sixteen. I'm up to the part where she graduates from high school," Cami told him. She didn't tell him that in the journal, her mother had just met the man she would eventually marry, Cami's father. A man who eventually became a drug addict and wife abuser.

Grandpa Willy shut his eyes, as if in reverence for his deceased daughter.

"Grandpa," Cami couldn't wait any longer to tell him, "I also found this."

She held her palm up toward his face, then slowly uncurled her fingers to expose the gold coin.

"Good gravy!" he exclaimed, jumping back. "What in the blue blazes have you got?"

He reached forward with slow, cautious movements. Carefully he picked up the coin and examined it. Then, after studying it, the reality of what the coin could possibly be hit him, and he sat weak-kneed on the edge of the desk.

"Do you realize what this is?" he asked Cami.

"A gold coin," she answered. "A Spanish gold coin."

"Spanish gold," he said in a whisper. Then he shook his head slowly. "This isn't good."

"I know."

"Cami-girl, if word about this gets out, the whole coastline is going to torn apart faster than gifts on Christmas morning. Every crackpot in the country—no, the world—will come digging for the rest of it. Not to mention the danger this thing will put us in. You've already been attacked once, and while I hate to say this, next time you may not be so lucky."

Cami knew that was true because Josh wouldn't be there to save her.

"Where do you think my mother found it?" Cami asked.

"I wish I knew," Grandpa Willy answered. "Maybe it got washed ashore."

"Are you saying you think it's still buried around here somewhere?" Cami asked, unable to hide the amazement from her voice.

Grandpa Willy released a frustrated sigh. "It's true that a Naval survey schooner called the *Shark* wrecked somewhere along this very coastline. Part of the deck and the small iron cannon drifted ashore just north of here. That's how—"

"Cannon Beach got it's name," Cami exclaimed with excitement. "So it *is* true."

"Listen, Cami," he spoke in hushed tones, "I don't want anyone else to know this coin even exists. Not right now anyway. Your mother didn't say anything about it in her journal, did she?"

"I only got about halfway through. I'm reading very closely though."

Grandpa Willy handed the coin back to her. "We need to find a place for this coin—a safe place. And no one—I mean, not one single soul—can know about it until we decide how to handle this. Agreed?"

"Agreed," Cami said, her stomach turning. She felt as though she was holding a time bomb in her hand and couldn't wait to have it tucked away somewhere safe. First thing tomorrow she'd head to the bank and put the coin in her safety deposit box. Until then, she'd tape it underneath one of her dresser drawers.

Buried treasure. Spanish gold.

It really did exist!

* * *

After church and dinner were out of the way, Cami felt restless and unsettled. A walk outside would have been perfect, but it was getting too dark to be safe. She'd have to find something else to do.

Wandering into the office, she thought about organizing the mess on her desk but couldn't make herself sit down and tackle all the stacks of papers.

The door to the passageway caught her eye. There was still enough light she could go inside and scout around—look for clues and hopefully figure out what was going on with this whole buried treasure.

Why not? she thought. She borrowed a flashlight from her grandfather's room and shut the door to the office so he and Pearl would think she was busy and not interrupt her. Climbing through the opening, she stepped into the shadowy confines and forced herself to take in slow, deep breaths. Even though there was plenty of space to move around, she still felt smothered by the narrow passageway.

"You can do this," she told herself. "Just stay focused."

With the flashlight beaming brightly before her, she made her way along the wooden corridor, examining every detail along the way.

Shuddering as her cheek brushed against a spiderweb, she forced herself to continue, keeping watch for her earring as well as anything else unusual.

She neared the spiral staircase leading to the second floor and scoured every inch of space. Then something caught her eye. She'd thought at first that it was just a doorway to another part of the house, but upon closer inspection, she realized it was an outside entrance.

Testing the door, she found it not only tightly locked but immovable because of a wooden plank fastened across it and nailed to the wall. She made a mental note to go outside and check the entrance just to make sure it was secure.

She jumped when she heard a clamoring of footsteps and her grandfather's voice calling her name. *He'll kill me if he finds me in here,* she thought as she scurried through the passageway, feeling like a rat in a maze.

She made it out through the doorway just as her grandfather knocked on the office door. "Cami, are you in there?"

"I'm here," she answered.

"Come outside. There's something you need to see."

Cami followed right behind her grandfather to the backyard, where Pearl stood with a handful of wildflowers and a frightened look on her face.

"Right there." Grandpa Willy pointed at the flower bed.

Cami looked closely in the fading sunlight and saw the outline of footprints in the rich, black dirt. All along the side of the house where the wildflowers grew were big, deep footprints.

"The person who made those was big, maybe six-five or six-six," Grandpa Willy guessed. "Weighs 225 or so, I'll bet."

"You don't suppose they're Josh's, do you?" Cami asked.

Pearl shook her head. "They're too big to be Josh's," she said. "He wears a size ten shoe."

"How in tarnation do you know that?" Grandpa Willy asked.

"I asked him when I was trying to outfit him with waders when we went clamming that one time," she replied.

Cami's mind rejected the possibility that someone could know about the gold coin in the house, but the legend of the buried treasure was well-known along the coast. And, as her grandfather had said, the gold would only bring trouble. That was something they definitely didn't need.

Cami tried to put the image of a stranger peeking through their windows out of her mind, but she couldn't. The thought of her every move being watched was eerie.

"I better go call and get someone over here to take a look. Someone must think we have some gold here—or at least something to do with that blasted treasure. A lot of good our alarm system did."

Cami swallowed, wondering how much danger they really were in.

"I'm going to see if we can have a squad car patrol the area on a regular basis for the next little while and get some more motion sensor lights put in. I'll get this place as secure as Fort Knox if I have to."

"Let's just hope they find the guy who's doing all of this soon," Pearl commented.

Grandpa Willy rushed off to make the call, and Pearl went inside to put the flowers in water. Before she forgot, Cami located the outside entrance to the passageway and saw that not only was it completely covered by an overgrown lilac bush, it was boarded up tightly. The door couldn't be more secure.

Feeling somewhat relieved, she went to see what her grandfather found out, wondering what could possibly happen next.

* * *

Grandpa Willy and Pearl spent their spare moments sorting through pictures and working on Pearl's book. They'd made a lot of headway and were down to the very last box, which contained pictures that weren't related to events or places.

Cami couldn't concentrate on much of anything. She finally took out her mother's journal, curled up with a cup of hot chocolate and a bowl of popcorn, and began to read. The older her mother got in the journal, the less she wrote. Still, Cami became lost in another world, in a place and time when her mother was young, alive, and happy.

Joey and I have been married now for a year. We went through the temple together, but I sometimes wonder if Joey was worthy. I love him with all my heart, but there's a side of him that I find frightening. He doesn't go to church anymore with me. Every week he promises to go with me, but each Sunday when I mention it, he gets angry with me. He says it's because he didn't go to church much as a child and isn't used to going every Sunday. But I wonder if there's more. I know he didn't have a very happy childhood—I've known that since we met—but I'm beginning to wonder now if maybe some of the things that happened to him when he was young are beginning to affect him now.

Instead of spending our anniversary with me, Joey went out with some of his buddies from work. He can be so sweet and sensitive sometimes. But then there are times when his personality completely changes. These are times when he seems angry and unhappy, like he hates the whole world, including me. I find that the best thing to do when he's like this is to just stay out of his way. These dark moods scare me.

Cami's heart ached for her mother. Her parents had been married over twelve years before her father finally left. How had her mother stood all the mental, emotional, and physical abuse all those years?

Joey came home drunk last night. But I don't think that was all. His eyes were glazed. He looked at me as if he didn't even know me. When I questioned him about where he'd been and who he'd been with, he flew into a rage. I'm used to his outbursts and knew I just needed to get out of his way, but when I tried to leave, he grabbed my arm, and . . .

Cami turned the page to an entry made almost a month later.

I can barely bring myself to even write these things, but part of me wants to record them just in case something happens to me. At least someone will know the truth.

The most wonderful thing happened. Yet something that was so truly wonderful turned into something so horrible I can barely see through my tears to write.

I'm pregnant. I've wanted a baby for so long, and now, finally, I'm expecting. I was so excited to tell Joey, and I prayed that maybe this would be the one thing that would turn him around. Maybe having a child would help him see that he needed to quit hanging around with his "friends" and stop drinking and wasting all our money on drugs. I know he has a terrible drug problem. I've known it for a long time, but every time I bring it up, he gets angry and then he hurts me. I have to hide the bruises and cuts and lie to my parents. They wouldn't tolerate his abuse for even a minute. There's a constant pain in my neck and shoulder where he threw me against the wall. But the ache in my heart is the worst.

I was so excited to tell Joey. I hoped maybe this would finally turn him around, help him have the strength to change. I made a special dinner for him and borrowed candles from my mother and her good china, since we had to sell ours to make our rent payment. At first, Joey liked the special meal and seemed to appreciate all my efforts, but when I told him my news, he exploded. This was the first time I thought for sure he was going to kill me. I was so frightened. I knew I had to get away before he got his hands on me. If he caught me, I knew he would try to kill my baby.

Cami was crying now. Tears streamed down her face as she thought of her mother—young, frightened, and pregnant—being attacked by her husband, the father of her child.

I ran up the stairs, then stopped suddenly and turned, catching him off guard. When he got close to me, I kicked him hard in the chest, then pushed him with all my might. I didn't even stop to think I could have killed him, but I had to do something drastic or I knew either my baby or I could possibly die.

As soon as he began to fall down the stairs, I ran to our bedroom, out to the balcony, and climbed down the fire escape. I ran all the way to my mother's house. I finally told her everything. I thought my father was going to go over to my apartment and find Joey and kill him (if he wasn't already dead), but we calmed him down. My father is very protective of me. He wasn't going to let anyone get away with hurting me. For now, the baby and I are safe.

Cami's heart literally ached for her mother.

> *My marriage is over. I told Joey I was filing for divorce. My parents were with me. I was afraid he would come after me when I told him, but he didn't. He actually cried. He confessed that he had a drug problem, and that all his behavior was because of the drugs and that he wanted to get help. He wants us to be a family. He's even promised to go talk to our bishop and get his life together.*
>
> *I know it sounds ridiculous, but I believe him. He looked like a lost child, so frightened and scared. He apologized at least a dozen times. He promised me the sun, moon, and stars if I would just give him a second chance. We're going to see a therapist and get him into a program. All I can do at this point is pray.*

The journal entry broke Cami's heart. She knew the outcome. She knew the hell that still lay ahead for her mother. Taking her father to therapy, giving him a second chance, had been the moment of decision for her mother. It was almost torturous to think how different things would have been if her mother would have stood her ground and not fallen into the manipulations of her father. Cami knew had her mother gone through with the divorce, she might still be alive today.

Cami bore no resentment toward her father. He'd had a horrible childhood and had never had anyone in his life who loved him except Cami's mother. He just didn't know to how handle that love and how to treat other people. But Cami wished that even though his life was on the path of destruction, he wouldn't have had to destroy her mother along with himself.

* * *

Cami was grateful to have a class to teach that next morning. She was glad to have something to get her mind off the gold and Josh for a while. She'd also grown fond of the girls in her class and enjoyed sharing her knowledge of interior design with them. It made all those years at school and all those projects she'd labored over finally worth it.

Even though her body was present in the classroom that day, her thoughts were somewhere else. Twice she couldn't find her pen only to be reminded by the girls that it was behind her ear. The first time had been funny; the second time, embarrassing.

Later that day, she and Pearl did some light housework together around the mansion.

"I miss Josh," Pearl said as she and Cami changed sheets and cleaned guest rooms. The inn had been busy, and Cami had gone through her duties robotically, her mind on everything but their guests.

"Me too," Cami said, her heart twisting as she spoke. She missed Josh more than she'd dreamed possible.

"It seems empty without him here," Pearl added. She shook the corner of the sheet and laid it out on the mattress. On the other side of the bed, Cami tucked in the edges of the crisp, fresh-smelling sheet. "I know he's upset, but he could at least call and let us know he made it home safely. I'd like to know how he's doing." Pearl shook pillows into their cases while she talked.

"I'm sure he's busy. He was gone for such a long time, he's probably had a lot to take care of since he's been home." But to Cami, the real reason he didn't call was all her fault. She missed him terribly, and her heart ached because she knew he was gone because of her.

Now he was home with his job and with Jane. She'd known his stay at the inn was only temporary. She'd known all along he would eventually leave. But that hadn't stopped her heart from caring when he was there, and aching now that he was gone.

CHAPTER 20

The pictures and text for Pearl's book were coming together quickly. While Grandpa Willy and Pearl dug through the last box of photographs, Cami converted Pearl's written notes onto the computer. Each account fascinated her; each world event that Pearl had been an eyewitness to left her in awe—coverage of Watergate and President Nixon's resignation in 1974, the shocking horrors of the Vietnam War, the global popularity of disco, the eruption of Mount St. Helens, and the assassination of John Lennon in 1980. The pictures spanned from her years of working at the newspaper in Portland in the 1960s to her job as a freelance photographer and regular contributor to *National Geographic, Time,* and *Life* magazines, which took her across the United States and all over the world.

While Cami typed, she kept one ear trained on Pearl and Grandpa Willy's playful bantering with each other. They went from teasing and arguing to laughing at old memories—the days of black and white television, styles and values of decades past when life in many ways was simpler, when fathers went to work and mothers stayed home with the children.

There was an entire section reserved in the book for pictures of some of the old vintage automobiles Pearl had. She'd always owned the latest and trendiest cars when she was younger, opting for sporty race cars over family wagons.

"What I'd give to have some of those old cars back," Pearl said, looking wistfully at a picture of an old Aston Martin DB5, similar to the one James Bond drove in the movie *Goldfinger.*

"It'd be worth a fortune today," Grandpa Willy said.

"It was worth a fortune then," Pearl said. "It was a gift."

"A gift!" Cami exclaimed, unable to hold in her remark. "Who in the world gives cars like that away?"

"I met a sheik from the Middle East while I was in Egypt," Pearl answered as she continued to sort pictures.

"And?" Cami prodded.

"And nothing. I interviewed him for a piece I was doing for *Time* magazine, and for some reason, he took a fancy to me. He sent roses to my hotel, then diamonds, then fur. When I continued to refuse his offer for dinner, he sent the car. I'd told him that I'd recently seen the movie *Goldfinger* and how much I liked the car."

"So he bought you one?" Cami exclaimed with disbelief.

"The man owned half the oil in the world—it was nothing to him. But he knew it was a big deal to me," Pearl told her.

"Did you go out to dinner with him?" Grandpa Willy asked.

"Of course I did. Dinner for a free car. I may be stubborn, but I'm not stupid," Pearl told him matter-of-factly.

"What happened?" Cami asked with amazement.

"We actually had an enjoyable time at dinner. He was an older man, twenty years older than I was, but very charming and handsome in an Omar Shariff sort of way."

Cami remembered Omar Shariff from the old movie classic *Dr. Zhivago.* She nodded in approval.

"Ha!" Grandpa Willy said with disdain. "Stick a mustache on anyone and they suddenly become handsome and mysterious."

Pearl and Cami looked at each other and laughed.

"So, what happened?" Cami had to know the rest of the story.

"The man was relentless. He continued to pursue me—heaven knows why—and I continued to let him. I mean," Pearl finally put down the pictures in her hand, "the man flew me to Paris for lunch and an afternoon at the Louvre because I'd never been there before. He also offered to buy me a chalet in the Swiss Alps."

Cami shook her head with amazement.

"He swept me off my feet. That is, until I learned of his seventeen other wives and countless concubines," Pearl said with a smirk. "Can you believe that?!"

"Ha!" Grandpa Willy said again. "Can't trust a man with a mustache, I always say."

"Grandpa!" Cami scolded. Then she turned to Pearl. "Seventeen wives, really?"

"He was proud of it, too, when I finally asked him about it. He said he liked me because I was different and funny. And intelligent."

"How flattering," Cami said flatly.

"That's what I thought," Pearl agreed. "When I told him I wouldn't marry him he said, 'Who's talking about marriage? I don't need another wife.'"

"No!" Cami stared at her, dumbfounded.

"It's true. He just wanted a mistress. He liked the fact that my job took me all over the world and that I had been to so many exotic places."

By now Cami was sucked into the story and pumped Pearl for more and more information. Grandpa Willy excused himself to go and make a sandwich for lunch, leaving the two women to talk about the many relationships and marriage proposals Pearl had received in her lifetime.

As they talked, Cami shuffled through several stacks of photographs that hadn't been sorted when she suddenly stopped.

She blinked several times, then held the picture closer to get a better look. The man in the picture could have been a twin of Josh. Same hair, same build, same profile.

But it couldn't have been Josh. The picture was probably thirty years old.

Pearl had been good to write dates and names of people and places on the back of most of the pictures. Slowly Cami turned the picture over and read the back.

Frederick at Fourth of July picnic.

Frederick? The man in the picture was the love of Pearl's life?

She looked at the picture again. At first glance it was as if Josh were in the picture, but as she looked closer, she could tell it wasn't. Still, the resemblance puzzled her. It was uncanny. It was impossible. It was just coincidental.

Or was it?

A thought struck her with force so strong she wondered if Pearl had noticed. But Pearl was labeling a manila folder of pictures and placing it chronologically in a file box.

With the possibility still in Cami's mind, she looked at Pearl through different eyes. Then she saw it. The resemblance—Pearl's eyes and the shape of her mouth and chin.

Cami's heartbeat raced out of control because it all made sense. That was why Josh had spent all that time at the mansion. That was why he asked so many questions about Pearl—personal questions about her past, about her when she was younger. Cami had wondered why he was so interested in Pearl.

No. She chided herself for being silly. *It isn't possible.*

Yet when she glanced at the picture again, then back at Pearl, the thought that crossed her mind gave Cami tingles of excitement.

The resemblance was undeniable. She'd stake her life on it. Yet it was preposterous. There was no way Josh could be Pearl's son.

Could he?

And if he were, why hadn't he said anything? What was going on?

* * *

"I sent some cinnamon rolls to Josh," Pearl told Cami the next day. "I know how much he loved them. Do you think that was silly of me?"

Cami's mind was going a million different directions. First her mother's journal and now the outrageous notion that had her mind (which she was clearly losing) seriously entertaining the thought that Josh could possibly be Pearl's son, the one she had given up for adoption thirty-something years ago.

"I said," Pearl's voice came louder, "do you think that was silly of me?"

"Cinnamon rolls?" Cami said, focusing in on the fact that Pearl was talking to her.

"In the mail. I sent some to Josh," Pearl said.

"He'll love that," Cami replied. "I think that was really nice of you." Cami looked long and hard at Pearl, searching for clues or features that belonged to Josh. The thought that Josh, of all people—someone Pearl had already grown fond of—could actually be her son sent tingles up Cami's spine. But she was apprehensive about sharing her hypothesis with Pearl—or anyone for that matter. How would Pearl react?

"So," Cami said, changing the subject, "what do you want to do for your birthday?"

"My birthday!" Pearl exclaimed. "Who said anything about my birthday?"

"I did," Cami answered with a mischievous smile. "You didn't think I'd remember, did you?"

"Actually, I was hoping you'd forget." Pearl rolled her eyes and tied her apron around her waist. "I would prefer that you do nothing. I plan on ignoring the fact that I'm turning another year older. I would like you to do the same."

"Okay, Pearl," Cami said, fighting a smile. There was no way she would ever forget Pearl's birthday. Nor would Grandpa Willy. They'd already thought of taking a picnic out on the ocean and watching the sun set. That was, if the weather was good. Otherwise they would take Pearl out to dinner and try and make her night a memorable one. Cami loved her like family, and she had a hunch so did her grandfather.

"Now, don't you have something you need to do?" Pearl said to Cami, obviously not wanting to continue the topic of her birthday.

Cami found her grandfather outside tinkering around in his toolshed.

"Grandpa," she said.

"Yes, Cami-girl?" He wiped at his brow, leaving a streak of grease on his forehead.

"What can we do to make Pearl's birthday special? She's done so much for us, I just feel like we should really fuss over her," Cami said.

"I agree, but she's so blasted stubborn she won't let us do anything for her."

"That doesn't mean we can't," Cami replied.

"Well, we could have a barbecue like we did with Josh's birthday. That turned out nicely," Grandpa suggested.

Yeah, except that Jane was here, Cami thought to herself.

"I thought about a barbecue, but I can't make all that great food Pearl did without her noticing. I guess I could see if Ashlyn will let me cook the food at her house. It's just that I really want to do something big for her."

"We can still go sailing. I think she'd like that," Grandpa Willy said.

Cami walked away, mulling ideas over in her head. Sailing at sunset with a picnic dinner would be wonderful, but somehow not enough.

Then an idea struck her. There was something she could do to make the night a memorable one. But did she actually dare go through with it? It would take all the courage she could muster, but for Pearl, it would be the one thing to make this birthday special.

Hurrying into the house before she lost her nerve, she secluded herself in the office and picked up the phone. The muscles in her stomach bunched. Josh just had to be home.

After several rings, the answering machine clicked on. Her hopes fell, and she almost hung up, but she decided to leave a message anyway.

"Hi, Josh, this is Cami from the Sea Rose Bed and Breakfast." *He knows that, silly,* she told herself. "Anyway, I just wondered how everything was going, and I wondered if you wouldn't mind giving me a call. There's something I'd like to talk to you about." *Like, if you're Pearl's son, for starters.* "So," she paused, trying to think of something else to say, but not knowing what, "I guess that's all. I hope to hear from you soon. We sure miss you around here," she said. Then without thinking, she added, "I'm sorry for what happened."

Panic struck her when she hung up the phone. Why did she have to go and say that? She wished there was some way to call back and change her message.

That was so stupid, she scolded herself. *What were you thinking?*

But she realized that was the problem. She wasn't thinking. She'd been nervous, and her heart had gotten in the way of her mouth.

Oh well, there was nothing she could do about it now. All she could do was wait for his phone call.

CHAPTER 22

My precious daughter was born yesterday. She's perfect. Already I can tell she's got my legs and toes. I don't see much of Joey in her. His skin, eyes, and hair color are so dark, and Camryn is fair skinned. Her peach-fuzz hair is almost white, and her eyes will be blue. They say you can't tell, but I know they will be.

When I held my baby in my arms for the first time, I realized that she was the most important thing in the world to me and I would guard her with my life if I had to. I love the way her mouth puckers like a little bird's when she's about to cry. I love how warm she is to hold and how good she smells. This is the greatest experience of my life. I will never be able to repay God for sending me such a precious angel.

Cami felt warm and tingly inside as she thought about her mother's love for her. A sense of gratitude filled her to have these words written by her mother's hand from her heart. To know her mother loved her so completely filled her with joy.

It's difficult living with my parents, but since Joey can't find a job, we can't afford our own place. It's not that my parents aren't wonderful and don't help every way that they can. They do help so much—they couldn't be better. But Joey, well, he's difficult to live with. He's moody and has such a temper.

After the baby was first born, things were so good. But Joey doesn't have much patience with her when she cries. I try and keep her as happy as I can when he's around so he can enjoy her.

I don't know what it is, but he can't seem to hold a job longer than a week. Because our town is so small, he's having to drive to other towns to find work. Part of the problem is that he's started drinking again and who knows what else. He stays out late with his buddies, and if I even bring it up, he flies into a rage. It upsets my parents when we fight, so I don't say anything, but I don't know how much longer I can take it.

I used to be able to look past his flaws and see his good qualities. I loved him so much. But I can't see the good in him anymore. There's a darkness in his eyes, in his soul. My feelings for him have changed, especially now that we have Camryn. I want her to have a happy home with loving parents. Sometimes when Joey leaves I wish he'd never come home. It would be easier if he were gone.

He tells me things would be better if he could just make some money, but I know if he did have money he would just blow it all on alcohol and drugs. He wants me to get a job, but I don't want to leave the baby. We fight about it constantly.

He would die if he knew about the coins I found, but I will never tell him about it. Never. He would spend it all on drugs. I haven't even told my parents yet. But I will soon.

Coins! Cami's eyes opened wide. Her mother had known where the coins were!

She got chills. *Buried treasure.* The thought was mystifying and exciting.

And completely frightening. Where there was treasure there was sure to also be trouble. They'd already learned that those desperate enough to find the treasure would go to extremes to get it.

Maybe right now the treasure was better where it was. Safe and sound.

Cami knew she had to wait for the right time to tell Grandpa about her mother's journal entry, but she knew it would have to be soon.

* * *

In the middle of paying bills, the phone rang. Grandpa Willy was taking a bunch of tourists on a harbor tour, and Pearl had gone to town for groceries, so Cami answered the phone.

"Cami?" the voice said.

She immediately recognized the caller and felt her heart jump in her chest. She'd been staying as busy as possible to keep her mind off Josh, but it hadn't been easy. She'd hoped that the longer Josh was gone, the less she would miss him. But Josh had found a way to her heart, and hearing his voice again reminded her of that. She'd never dreamed she would have any more room in there for someone else, but she did.

"Yes," she answered.

"This is Josh Drake. How are you?" His tone was friendly but formal, not the same as it had been before.

Immediately tears sprang to her eyes. She clutched the phone tightly in her hand and pulled in a calming breath. She told him how everyone was doing, then returned the question to him. He told her he was back at work, teaching summer school. She told him that her own classes had ended, and that she'd accepted an offer to teach again in the fall.

Then they both fell silent.

Cami shut her eyes and prayed. She'd been so anxious to talk to him but seemed to be at a loss for words now that he was on the phone.

Apparently he was also at a loss for words.

Finally she couldn't stand the silence.

"So," she said the first thing that came to her mind, "how's Jane?" She wanted to kick herself. Why had she asked about Jane?

"Um, she's good," he answered. "She's not teaching this summer. She's doing some research and traveling. She's in England with her parents right now."

"That's nice," Cami said. An awkward silence fell between them.

"So, your message said you had something you wanted to talk to me about," he questioned.

"I do," she answered, wondering why she'd thought this such a good idea in the first place. It was a lot to ask to have him come clear out there again, and seeing him again would only make it harder to get him out of her system.

"What is it?" he asked when she didn't continue.

"I was wondering, I mean, Grandpa and I were wondering, that is . . ." She was really making a mess out of this.

"Yes?"

"I know how upset you probably are with me. But, you see, Josh, Pearl's birthday is coming up and we were wondering—"

"You want me to be there for it?" he cut her off.

She couldn't tell by the tone of his voice if he was upset by her request or not.

Her hopes fell. She'd made a mistake even asking. "I'm sorry. I realize now that's a lot to—"

"When is it?" he asked.

She could barely get out the words. "On Saturday," she finally managed. "We're taking a picnic out on the boat and watching the sun set over the ocean. That is, if the weather's good. If not, we'll do something here at the house," she explained. "I know it's a lot to ask, and I know how busy you are and that you've—"

"I'll be there," he blurted out.

She stopped to process his words. Her heart jumped inside her chest. "You will?" she whispered with disbelief.

"I can be there Friday night. Unless you want me to wait until Saturday."

"No, no. Friday would be great." She didn't dare get her hopes up. He was coming for Pearl. But she couldn't ignore the fact that him even considering coming was a good sign. "You're sure this isn't going to be a problem for you to leave again so soon?"

"It will be fine," he assured her. Then the tone in his voice grew warmer, softer, more like himself. "To be honest, my body's been here, but my mind hasn't."

She waited for him to explain.

"I've had a hard time concentrating since I got back. I feel so distracted, and I can't focus," he told her. "I think I left my mind back there with you guys."

Cami laughed. "Well, if I find it, I'll put it in a safe place until you come back and get it."

"Thanks." He chuckled along with her. Their laughter seemed to break the ice.

"I bet you'll never guess what I did Sunday."

"I can't imagine," she answered.

"I went to church," he said proudly.

"You did? Which one?"

"The Quaker Church," he joked. "No, I went to the LDS ward here."

"How was it? I mean, did you enjoy it? Were the people nice?" She prayed in her heart that they were, that they'd welcomed him with open arms, embraced him, and helped him feel a part of them.

"I enjoyed it. And I met the missionaries. They wondered if I was a nonmember investigating the Church. I told them that I was a member investigating the Church, which really confused them."

Cami laughed.

"I explained my situation to them, and they offered to come and teach me the lessons. Even though I got baptized, there's so much about the Church I don't even know. This seemed like the best place to start. They came over last night, and I'm having them again tonight and tomorrow night."

"Josh, that's wonderful." Cami couldn't have been more happy for him.

"I'm so amazed at how much I feel like I already know, but there's still so much I have to learn. Still, it's like I said before, it feels so right, like something I've always known. I mean, I've always agreed with the principles of the Word of Wisdom and with tithing. But I think my favorite thing to talk about is the plan of salvation and the idea of eternal families. I never get tired of hearing about that."

"Does Jane know you're meeting with the missionaries?" she asked, unable to quell her curiosity.

"Yes, she knows. I don't think she's very happy about it," he said. "Why?"

"She was raised Catholic, and even though she doesn't go to church that much, her religious traditions go pretty deep. She thinks members of the LDS Church are a bunch of loony extremists who are trying to take over the world."

"What?" Cami exclaimed. "Where did she come up with that?"

"Beats me. But it doesn't matter. I have to do this. Not only for myself, but for my father and my mother. I feel a duty to learn about the Church for them. Had things worked out differently, they would have raised me in the Church. I think they would want me to do this because I know it was important to them."

Cami was proud of him and very happy for him.

"We'll have a lot to talk about when I get there," he said.

Cami remembered about his resemblance to Pearl's beloved Frederick and said, "You're right. We do have a lot to talk about."

"This will also give me a chance to see how the book is coming along."

"We've been through all the pictures," she told him. "Pearl's starting to write the text that goes with each group."

"Good, good. I knew she'd run with this. She's a great lady," he said.

Just like her son, she thought.

"Having you here is going to make her birthday unforgettable, Josh. She's really missed you." Cami wanted to say she had too, but didn't. "Thanks for agreeing to do this."

"I'm glad you called."

Cami's heart soared.

"So am I. And Josh? I'm really sorry."

"I know," he said quickly. Then, in a more gentle tone, he said, "We'll talk when I get there."

They said their good-byes, and Cami hung up the phone feeling as if she could float on air. Josh was coming back. She was going to see him. Friday!

* * *

By Friday afternoon, Cami was going crazy with anticipation. She seemed to feel the tick of every second. Pearl needed an errand run in town, and Cami quickly volunteered to do it. She was willing to do anything to make the time pass more quickly.

She ran into Bradford Hardware to pick up something her grandfather had ordered for his workbench. Mitch was working, so they chatted about the excitement of the baby and about Pearl's birthday party. She kept Josh's arrival a secret, wanting it to be a surprise for everyone.

Running next door to Gardner's Groceries, Cami picked up the food she needed for the party. Her in-laws owned the grocery store and were always so happy to see her whenever she stopped by. She knew she needed to visit them more often at home, but visiting them always left her depressed because all they talked about was Dallin. Not that she didn't want to talk about Dallin, but every memory, every reminder they brought up only renewed the pain that had slowly, finally, begun to heal.

"Cami!" a voice called from the front of the store as she stopped to choose some fresh fruits and vegetables. It was her father-in-law, Chip Gardner. His real name was Charles, but Chip seemed to fit him better. He rushed to the produce section and greeted her with a warm hug.

"We haven't seen you around the house for a while. Laurene was going to call and invite you to dinner," he said.

"Dinner would be nice," she replied.

He helped her choose some of the best produce for Pearl's party and then accompanied her to the check-out stand. While he rang up her purchases, they shared small talk about the inn and Grandpa Willy's arm, which was feeling better. She told him about Pearl's book and how much she'd enjoyed substitute teaching at the high school and that she was going teach again in the fall.

"That's just wonderful, Cami," Chip said, bagging her purchases. "Dallin would be so proud of you."

Cami smiled and nodded. "I think so too." She knew this was the best time to make her exit and began looping her fingers through the handles on the plastic grocery bags to make a quick getaway.

"Want this on your account?" he asked.

"That would be fine," she said, looking up as a couple of older women came through the door. Cami knew both of them and felt her heart sink.

"Cami!" one of the women exclaimed when they saw her. "How are you, dear?"

Cami smiled and said, "I'm doing fine, Mrs. Dawson. How are you?"

While Mrs. Dawson reported about her recent hip-replacement surgery, Cami felt the circulation in her fingers get cut off from the heavy grocery bags.

"Well," the woman finally concluded her story, "it's wonderful to see you, dear. You look like you've got a little color in your cheeks finally. You just need to put some meat on those bones, doesn't she, Iris?"

The other woman kindly said, "I think she looks just fine, Ada. You look wonderful, Cami."

"Thank you," Cami told the other woman.

"Tsk, tsk," Mrs. Dawson said, shaking her head. "You're such a pretty thing to be all alone at such a young age."

"Such a shame," the other woman agreed. "But you're so devoted to your sweetheart. Just like we are to ours. Isn't it wonderful how devoted she is to your son, Mr. Gardner?"

"Yes, Iris, it certainly is. Cami's just like a daughter to us," Mr. Gardner replied.

Cami's fingers were numb.

A break in the conversation came just when she needed it to. "I guess I better get these groceries home. It was wonderful to see you both," she told the women.

"I'll get the door." Mr. Gardner hurried around the side of the counter and opened it for her. He gave her a kiss on the cheek and reminded her that she'd hear from her mother-in-law soon.

Hurrying out the door, Cami heard the "tsk, tsk-ing" behind her as she left.

Rolling her eyes, she escaped to her car and stowed the grocery bags in the trunk. A car pulled in next to her with an Avis Rental sticker in the window.

Cami glanced over at the car as a tall, black-haired man with a thick black mustache walked around to the passenger side of the car and opened the door for a petite woman with curly, platinum-blonde hair, wearing tan suede pants and a matching jacket. The couple was very stylish, very chic.

The man closed the woman's door for her, then turned and looked at Cami. Their eyes connected, and in that split second of time, Cami had a sense of recognition. Yet she knew these people were tourists and that she'd never met this man in her life. She had a good memory for the people who had stayed at the inn, and these people had never been there before.

The couple went into the grocery store, and Cami shrugged off the strange feeling and got in her car. Scanning her memory one last time, she came up with nothing.

Pushing the occurrence to the back of her mind, she started up the car and headed to Ashlyn's. Right now there were more important matters to attend to.

* * *

"Will you settle down, Cami?" Ashlyn said firmly. "You're not an old bag."

"I might as well be," Cami answered. "Ada Dawson and Iris Lowell have adopted me into their little 'widows' circle.' How much worse can my life get?"

"Don't let them get to you." Ashlyn found a spot for the pineapple and watermelon on her counter. The rest of the groceries she put in the fridge. "You have the rest of your life ahead of you."

"You know, I honestly think they expect me to stay single the rest of my life."

"Of course they don't," Ashlyn said.

"They do. They're talking about how *devoted* I am to Dallin and how much I'm like them now." Cami groaned with frustration. "Sometimes this town drives me crazy."

"Cami, you don't have to live your life to please everyone," Ashlyn counseled.

"That shows how long you've lived here," Cami replied. "Everyone in this town knows your business and sits in judgment of every action you make."

Ashlyn looked at her evenly. "Wait a minute. Are you upset because you're interested in someone? Is that it?"

Cami's mouth dropped open in pure shock. "Interested in someone? Me?"

A smile grew on Ashlyn's face, and she nodded slowly, like she knew something. "You *are* interested in someone. And I think I know who it is. Josh Drake!" she exclaimed.

"Josh!" Cami shot back. "Don't be ridiculous. He's got a girl-friend. He lives on the other side of the country. And besides, even if I were interested, I pretty much ruined any chance of anything happening between us anyway."

Ashlyn's telephone rang. "That was all a misunderstanding. You two just need to talk," she said as she walked to the phone. She answered it, then told the caller to hold on a moment. "It's for you," she said.

"It is?" she asked. "Who is it?"

"Josh," Ashlyn said, a deadpan expression on her face.

* * *

"How do I look?" Cami asked Ashlyn for the thirteenth time.

Ashlyn rolled her eyes. "If you ask me that again, I'm going to scream."

"But—"

"Cami! You look wonderful. Your hair, your makeup, your outfit—it's all perfect. Now stop worrying."

With her hand on her stomach, Cami turned from the mirror to face her friend. "I'm just so nervous. He was so upset with me before he left."

"I know you think I've been so morning sick that I haven't noticed something going on between you and Josh, but it wasn't hard to tell that you two hit it off. He's wonderful, and you two are perfect for each other," Ashlyn told her.

"You didn't see how badly I hurt him."

"He's coming all this way to see you, isn't he? I think that says something," Ashlyn told her.

"He's coming for Pearl's birthday party tomorrow, not to see me," Cami reminded her.

"The party's part of the reason. But he's also coming because he missed you. I know that's it."

A car pulled up in the driveway. Josh had called Cami to tell her he was on his way from the airport, and she'd told him to meet her at Ashlyn's so they could surprise Pearl.

"It's him!" Cami nearly hyperventilated saying the words.

"Let me answer the door. You just stand there by the fireplace and look alluring," Ashlyn told her.

"I don't know how to look alluring!" Cami hissed as Ashlyn put her hand on the doorknob.

"Then try looking normal instead of like you're about to jump out of your skin or something," Ashlyn said. Cami just stared at her. "Cami, breathe!" Ashlyn ordered.

Cami let out a breath she'd been holding and took in a long draw of air, trying to calm down.

Before Josh had a chance to knock, Ashlyn opened the door. "Hi, Josh. Come in."

Josh walked through the door, looked up, and saw Cami.

She didn't know what to do. Inside she was all aflutter.

Their eyes met, and Cami felt as if she were going to throw up. It was so good to see him, but she was so nervous.

Then a smile appeared on his face. "Cami," he said, walking straight toward her.

Magnetically, she walked into his outstretched arms. They didn't speak, they just held each other. Cami struggled to keep her tears in check. She didn't want to cry, but it felt so good to have his arms around her.

He held her for a moment longer before finally letting go. Stepping back, he looked into her eyes. "You look great. How have you been?"

Her heart thumped so hard she thought it was going to jump out of her chest.

"I've been well. How about you?"

"Good," he said with a nod, still not taking his eyes off her face. "Tell me what's been going on around here." He took her hand and pulled her to the couch. Cami didn't know when, but Ashlyn had left them alone in the room.

Cami filled him in on some of the happenings at the mansion, leaving out the discovery of her mother's journal, the gold coin, and Frederick's picture. She wanted to tell him about those things when the time was right.

"Thank you so much for coming, Josh," she said.

"I'm glad you called," he confessed. "I'd been trying to find a reason to come back."

"I feel so bad about—"

"I know. I feel bad about how I left. We need to talk."

They did indeed, but Cami felt encouraged by the gentle sound of his voice.

"Come on," he said. "Let's go surprise Pearl."

* * *

"Pearl!" Cami called when she entered the mansion. Josh followed behind her, waiting to surprise Pearl.

"In the kitchen," Pearl answered. "We had a couple of messages while you were gone. Some people wanting to make reservations." Cami and Josh crept toward the kitchen, pausing just outside the door. "I told them you'd get back to them." Cami peeked in and saw Pearl had her back to them, kneading dough on the counter.

Cami stepped inside, and Pearl turned. "I left their numbers by the phone out front."

Cami didn't answer, she just smiled.

Pearl's eyebrows narrowed with curiosity. "What is going on with you today?" Pearl asked. "I've never seen you act so strangely. I swear you'd think—"

Josh stepped through the doorway.

Pearl gasped. Her mouth dropped open. Then a smile grew. "Josh! Oh, my goodness!" She rushed over to him. "I can't believe it! What a wonderful surprise. What are you doing here?"

Josh gave her a squeeze and a peck on the cheek. "How's my favorite girl?" he asked.

Pearl giggled and turned a bright shade of red.

"I just happened to be in the neighborhood and thought I'd drop by," he teased. "Hope you don't mind."

"Mind!" she exclaimed. "You know you're welcome here anytime."

"Good, because I ran out of cinnamon rolls a few days ago and I'm going through withdrawal."

"I was just making a batch right now." Pearl pointed to the lump of dough on the kitchen counter.

"I also understand that the book is coming along well. May I take a look at what you've gotten done?" he asked.

"Of course," Pearl said. "It's all very rough, and I'm not sure it's what you want—"

"It's going to be great, Pearl," Josh interrupted. "I haven't got a doubt about it."

Cami watched the two interact and knew that if in fact they were related, she couldn't think of two people who needed each other right now more than they did. Pearl had worried and wondered about the child she had given away, and Josh was full of grief and loneliness having both of his parents dead. It was a time for all of them to heal in their own way. Cami prayed with all her heart that God would help them open their hearts to forgive, forget, and move on.

In the office, Cami showed Josh the pictures, which were neatly separated and filed chronologically. Pearl had recorded her thoughts and feelings about each incident, as well as its time and place, details that made the photographs come alive. Not only were the pictures amazing—some unique, some breathtaking, some disturbing—but Pearl's narrative to go along with them managed to take something from the past and make it jump right to the present.

Josh read several of Pearl's recollections, and then looked up at Cami with a serious expression on his face.

"What's wrong?" she asked.

"This is much bigger than I thought," he said.

"Bigger? What do you mean?"

"Not only is there enough material here for two or three volumes, but what she's written here is powerful." He glanced at the boxes of filed photos around him. "We've got a best-seller on our hands."

"Josh," Cami said breathlessly. "You really think so?"

He nodded. "I do. I don't know if Pearl's ready for it, but she's going to get a lot of attention when this book comes out."

Cami got goose bumps.

"I'm going to give Max a call first thing in the morning. She's got enough here to send him so he can get an idea of what he's dealing with. This is going to be huge."

Cami glanced over at the small envelope she'd set aside containing pictures of Frederick. Was this the best time to show them to Josh? She didn't know if there would ever be a perfect time. They were alone, and they were already in the room, looking at the pictures.

I might as well do it, she thought.

"Would you like to see some pictures of Pearl's fiancé, Frederick?" Cami asked.

"You have pictures of her fiancé?" he answered, his eyes full of anticipation. "I'd love to see them."

Taking the photographs out of the envelope Cami handed them to Josh, then waited for his reaction.

CHAPTER 23

Josh gazed long and hard at the picture. He said nothing, but judging by the look of deep longing on his face and his intense studying of the man in the photograph, Cami knew the connection was there.

Slowly lowering the picture, Josh lifted his chin and looked at Cami.

"Is there something you'd like to tell me?" she asked him.

Raking his fingers through his hair, Josh sighed. "Has Pearl seen this?" he asked.

"Not this particular picture, no," Cami told him.

Josh looked at the picture again.

"What's going on, Josh?" Cami persisted.

His gaze met hers. "What do you think is going on?"

"I think you're a dead ringer for Frederick, if that's what you're asking. I don't know how Pearl missed the resemblance, but you couldn't look more like the man if you were him in the flesh," Cami told him.

"It's true then," Josh said with a nod of his head. He gazed at the picture again for a moment. "The main reason I came here was to find her." He drew in a breath, then released it slowly. "I still can't believe that I did."

Cami thought of the time, effort, and distance he'd come in search of his mother. She was happy that he'd finally gotten the answer he'd needed. She knew that the news would also bring Pearl great joy

"You understand why I didn't want to tell her right off, don't you?" he asked her, his voice filled with concern.

"Of course I do," she answered. "It would be cruel to say something to Pearl unless you knew for certain. But you have to understand, that's what added to my confusion."

Josh nodded.

"I knew there was something you were keeping from me. I felt it when we talked. Like you had a secret, or," she shrugged, "I don't know. I added up everything and came to the wrong conclusion. I've never really been good at math."

"So many times I wanted to talk to you, but I just didn't want to say anything until I was sure."

"But I was wrong, and I hurt you," Cami said. "I never meant to do that."

"I know. I should've stayed and talked it out."

"I'm sorry. Can you ever forgive me?"

He gave her a lopsided smile and leaned toward her. Cami's pulse quickened. Their kiss said more than words ever could.

Cami blinked to clear the moisture in her eyes.

"Hey," he said, cupping her chin in his hand, "everything's okay, right?"

She nodded. "I missed you."

"I missed you too."

He kissed her again, and she realized she could get used to this.

"So," he said, "what do you think Pearl is going to say when I tell her?"

"Josh," Cami looked him square in the eye, "Pearl has struggled to find closure with giving up her baby," she stopped and restated her words, "giving *you* up for adoption." She paused again. "Omigosh, Josh. It just hit me. You're Pearl's son." With her hand on her chest, she felt the pounding of her heart. "This is incredible."

Josh got up from his chair and paced across the floor. "Tell me, how do you think Pearl is going to react to this news?"

Cami tilted her head to look up at him. She reached her hand toward him, and he walked over to her and knelt down, looking her in the eye. "I'm sure it will come as a shock at first, but she already cares about you," Cami assured him. "I think finding out you're her son will bring her the greatest joy she's ever had."

"I hope you're right," he said. "I wouldn't want to cause her any pain." He continued holding Cami's hand, gently stroking her knuckles with his thumb. "When should I tell her?"

"Tomorrow night," Cami said. "After the party."

He nodded, then pushed himself up.

Placing Frederick's photograph inside an envelope, she put it inside her planner for safekeeping. Pearl would want to see it later— she was certain.

"Hey," Josh said, "have you been through that secret passageway again?"

"Yes, but I didn't find anything."

"Do you want to go in and try to find your earring?" he suggested.

Cami hadn't forgotten about the earring, but she had given up hope of ever finding it.

"Sure. If we hurry, we can be out before Grandpa gets home."

Stepping through the opening, they entered the passageway, which was dim and shadowy from sunlight filtering through the stained-glass windows.

"We were about here when I lost it, wouldn't you say?" she asked Josh when they got to the approximate spot where they'd been that night.

He agreed and bent down to look for the diamond.

Cami crawled around on the floor, not caring if her hands and knees got covered with dust if it meant finding the earring.

They looked long and hard, but still found no sign of the diamond.

"It's like it disappeared," she said.

Josh still hadn't given up, and said he was going over the spot for the fourth time, just in case.

Cami sat back and rested against a two-by-four. She appreciated his persistence, even though she doubted it would pay off.

She looked up the passageway one direction, then down the other direction, all the while praying for guidance to find the earring.

At the end of the passageway to her left, something caught her eye. It was some sort of writing on the two-by-four frames.

"Hey, Josh," she said, "look at this."

Hunched over, they crept to the end of the passageway and found chalk writing and pictures drawn on the floorboards and the framework.

"Look!" Cami exclaimed. There, written on the floor was *Grace loves Eddie,* with a large heart around it and the date, *May 12, 1970.* Next to it was another heart in which was written, *Kandis and Donnie Forever.*

"Grace," Cami said. "That's my mom. And Kandis was her friend. They must've written this when they were about fifteen or sixteen."

"Hey, what's this?" Josh pointed at more writing on a panel of sheetrock.

"It looks like a poem," Cami said, scooting over to get a closer look.

It's not just a penny, or even a dime,
To find the treasure, first find the time.

Cami read the poem out loud, then gasped. "My mother wrote this."

"What does she mean by *treasure?*" he asked.

"Josh," she whispered, "I think my mother knew where the treasure is. This is a clue."

"But your grandfather said the treasure doesn't exist," Josh said.

"Come with me," Cami whispered, her heartbeat kicking into a frantic pace. "I have to show you something."

She grabbed his hand and dragged him through the passageway to the opening.

"Cami, slow down," he said as he bumped his head on a low board. "Ow!"

"Sorry," she said, "but you're not going to believe this."

She continued hauling him behind her as she went from the office to her bedroom, where she pulled out one of her drawers, dumped out the contents, and flipped the drawer over. "Look!" She peeled off the tape and lifted the gold coin for him to see.

"What is that?" he asked, snatching the coin away from her. "Cami! Do you know—" He quickly lowered his voice to a whisper. "Do you know what this is?"

"It's a gold coin," she whispered.

He nodded, turning the coin over several times. "It's not just any gold coin. It's Spanish gold." He closed his hand tightly over the gold piece and looked at her with a somber expression. "Do you know what this could mean?"

She nodded. "If anyone finds out about this—"

"—there could be some serious trouble," he finished her sentence. "Who else knows about this?"

"Me, you, and Grandpa," she said. "Not even Pearl."

He nodded. "We need to get with your grandfather and have a discussion about this. I know what I think we should do, but he may not agree."

"We need to find the right time to tell my grandfather," Cami said. "When it comes to this treasure, he seems completely closed minded. Every time the subject comes up, he gets nervous and angry."

"Maybe we should wait until we know more," Josh suggested.

Cami agreed. "So, what's our next step?" Anxiety clutched her chest. "We need to find that gold!"

* * *

Saturday morning, Cami was busy getting ready for the outing on the ocean. She spent the morning at Ashlyn's preparing the food while Grandpa Willy and Josh went to the marina to get the boat ready. Pearl spent time working on her book. She was nearly finished and hoped to wrap it up before Josh went back home.

Cami was completely distracted while she sliced vegetables and arranged them on a tray. Every time Ashlyn spoke to her, it was as if Cami had to transport her mind back from a different dimension. Her thoughts and concentration were focused on Josh's news about being Pearl's son and the riddle about the treasure.

By midafternoon, they were ready to pack their picnic onto the boat and head out onto the ocean. With a steady wind at their backs and a clear sky overhead, the large white sails billowed, pulling the ship through the waves like a hot knife through butter.

Their main goal was to search for whales, but after looking for over an hour and not finding any, they gave up the search and opted for food instead.

Dropping anchor, they found a calm cove where they could pull out their picnic and eat. Gentle waves lapped gently against the ship's sides as the six passengers relaxed after a delicious meal. Even with everything going on, Cami found it difficult not to relax.

The sun sank lower as they talked and ate, snacking on leftovers and feeding pieces of sandwich rolls to the fish. Pearl told them about the time she went scuba diving off the Great Barrier Reef and saw several sharks.

"Is there anything you haven't done?" Josh asked Pearl.

"Well," she thought for a moment, "I haven't been in space . . . yet."

Everyone laughed.

"Guess we ought to get started back," Grandpa Willy said. "We don't want to get caught out here in the dark."

With Mitch and Josh working the sails and Grandpa Willy steering the ship, they were soon out on the wide open sea, heading back to Misty Harbor. As the sun sank lower on the horizon, they trimmed the sails and drifted near the cape just below the Sea Rose Bed and Breakfast.

"Look how beautiful the mansion looks!" Ashlyn exclaimed. The sun's rays spotlighted the Victorian structure, illuminating it above the tree line as if it were magically suspended in the air. This time Josh did have his camera with him. Even though he never saw any whales, he managed to get some beautiful shots of the ocean, the coastline, and the Sea Rose mansion reflecting the setting sun.

Silence settled in as everyone turned and watched the fiery display in the sky as the sun sank into the ocean. Ashlyn was relaxed in Mitch's arms, and Pearl and Grandpa sat next to each other on the bench seat. Cami looked at Josh sitting on the opposite side of the boat and found herself wishing she was next to him, feeling the warmth of his shoulder next to hers, letting him hold her small hand in his strong, capable one.

With the sun sufficiently set, Mitch and Josh raised the mainsail, which snapped taut in the steady breeze.

"Thank you for going to so much trouble," Pearl said to Grandpa Willy.

"Don't thank me," he grumbled. "Talk to Cami—she planned it all."

Pearl glanced over to Cami, who shook her head and pointed at her grandfather.

Smiling, Pearl surprised Grandpa Willy with a quick peck on the cheek.

Grandpa responded with a grouchy, "Hey!" but quickly softened as Pearl smiled sweetly at him. "Well, I guess I had a little something to do with it."

Pearl stayed close to Grandpa as he steered the ship back to shore. It was a heartwarming scene that Cami hoped to see often.

* * *

That night, gathering around a low, cozy fire in the fireplace, Grandpa Willy, Pearl, Josh, and Cami relaxed.

Cami caught Josh's eye and knew that the moment was right for his big news. Sending a prayer for him, Cami watched with anticipation as he leaned forward in his chair.

"Pearl," he said, "there's something I'd like to tell you."

"Yes, Josh?" Pearl answered, twisting slightly in her chair to face him better.

He took a deep breath and let it out slowly. "I didn't plan to tell you this on your birthday—it just kind of worked out that way— but . . ." He licked his lips and rubbed his palms on the knees of his denim pants.

Pearl tilted her head in curiosity.

Cami wished there was some way she could help him, but she knew the right words would come no easier for her.

"You see, it's like this," he said. "After my father died, I went through his things—you know, clothes, personal belongings, papers . . ."

Pearl nodded.

"I had always known something about myself, but when I found a document . . ." He paused again.

"Josh, what are you trying to tell me?" Pearl finally said.

"I was adopted. And . . . I think you're my birth mother," he blurted out. He froze and looked at Pearl, watching for her reaction.

Her forehead wrinkled as the words seemed to slowly sink in. She glanced over at Grandpa Willy, who stared dumbfoundedly at Josh.

She then looked at Cami, who nodded her confirmation of Josh's words. Her gaze traveled back to Josh.

"Pearl?" Josh said, scooting to the edge of his chair as if prepared to rush over and help her if she went into cardiac arrest or passed out from shock.

Lifting her hand, Pearl pointed her finger at him and opened her mouth, then slowly drew back her hand and placed it over her mouth. "I have a . . . you're my . . . my son!" The words came in a trembling whisper. "You?"

Josh nodded, smiled, then looked worried again. "Are you okay?" he asked.

Pearl brought her other hand up to her face and held both of them to her cheeks as tears glided down her fingers. "After all these years," she said. "I didn't think . . . I never expected . . ."

"To find me?" Josh said.

"Never." She shook her head. "Josh." A sob caught in her throat as she said his name. "Son." She held her hands toward him.

Hurrying to her, Josh gently pulled Pearl to her feet.

"Mom," Josh said.

The two fell into a hug, Josh's tall, sturdy frame gently holding Pearl's smaller, petite frame.

Tears streamed down Cami's own face, and even Grandpa Willy wiped at his eyes.

"Is it really true?" Pearl asked, when their hug ended. "Are you absolutely sure?"

"There was no father's name listed, but yours was on the adoption papers," he told her. "I hope it's good news, because I'm really your son."

Pearl hugged Josh again. "I've dreamed about this moment for over thirty years. I've wondered what you would look like, what type of person you would be," she said.

"And . . ." Josh said.

"You turned out even more wonderful than I even dreamed you would be," she answered, choking up again. "I have to say, though, I'm glad I had a chance to get to know you before you told me the news. I don't think my heart could have taken it."

Josh chuckled. "I'm glad you're not upset or mad at me."

"Mad at you? You've just made me the happiest woman in the world. How could I be mad at you?"

"I do want to ask you something," Josh said to his mom. "On my birthday, I noticed that a few times you got kind of distant and even looked a bit sad."

Pearl nodded.

"Were you thinking about the baby you gave away?" he asked.

"The entire day. It has haunted me all these years. My biggest fear was wondering if you went to a home where you were loved. Tell me, Josh, did your parents love you?"

"Yes," he told her. "Very much. I had a wonderful mother and father. They loved me and taught me wonderful things about life and the world. You would have liked them. And," he paused, giving her a smile, "they would have loved you."

Pearl dabbed at her eyes with the corner of her apron. "You don't know how happy it makes me to hear that."

"Even though I wasn't with you while I grew up, I am pretty amazed at how much I'm like you," Josh said. "The things you've done with your life, the excitement and adventure, is something I've lived for and dreamed of. I'm honored to be your son."

Smiling through her tears, Pearl said, "And I'm honored to be your mother."

* * *

Leaving Pearl and Josh alone, Cami and Grandpa Willy went on to bed. But Cami couldn't sleep. She was too wound up over Pearl's and Josh's reunion. The immediate love and bond between mother and son had been touching and tender. Cami would never forget the pure joy on both of their faces.

With her mother's journal in hand, Cami propped herself up in bed and opened the pages of the book to continue reading.

> *I thought things would be better with Joey gone. But I can't seem to snap out of this dark fog that seems to surround me. If I didn't need the money so desperately, I would gladly stay in bed all day. But I have to provide*

for myself and Camryn. She needs me. Thank goodness
she has her grandma and grandpa in her life who love
her. She is an adorable child with such a sweet disposi-
tion. I am blessed to have her.

I know I need to pull myself together and be the kind of
mother she deserves. I just don't know how to do that. I'm
going to the doctor tomorrow to get some help for my neck.
Maybe he'll be able to help me with my depression also.

Cami read page after page of her mother's journal, waiting for
further mention of the treasure and praying that she had the
strength to read the events leading up to her mother's death—
events and experiences seen through her mother's eyes and felt
through her mother's heart. Cami's newfound understanding of her
mother helped her gain insight and deeper compassion toward her
mother and her ultimate choice that changed everything. Cami
knew that her mother had developed a dependence on prescription
drugs. Instead of helping her mother find the root of her problems,
the doctor gave her amphetamines to chemically lift her mood and
barbiturates to help her sleep at night. Instead of leveling out her
moods and stabilizing her depression, the drugs only added to the
chemical imbalances in her body, imbalances that finally pushed
her too far.

I can't go on. I feel as though I've been digging a hole
to escape the hell my life has become only to dig my own
grave, a grave so deep, that I cannot escape from it.
Death would be a welcome relief. Sometimes I think my
daughter would be better off without me. I can't function
anymore. I don't know how to take care of her. In fact, I
feel as though I've become a child again myself. My
mother has to take care of me just like she would a child.
I used to be beautiful, intelligent, and funny. When I
look in the mirror, I see a nobody. I've lost my personality.
I have even lost my feelings. I don't care enough to keep
trying anymore. It's just too hard.

Cami stopped reading.

She shut her eyes and pictured her mother struggling to get through each day. And she realized that over the past year, she'd felt similar feelings of hopelessness and helplessness in her own life.

For some reason, Cami found comfort in the thought that her mother knew what she was going through in her life. There had been times that she'd felt her mother's presence close by. Nothing tangible, just a fleeting moment when her thoughts turned to her mother and a warmth filled her soul. There was a bond between them forged by the suffering and heartache of trials and challenges, a bond that helped Cami understand her mother's complete lack of hope.

Forcing herself to read the final entry, Cami turned the page and began.

> *Today has actually been a pretty good day. My father gave me a blessing, and I feel better, stronger somehow. I don't know what I would do without the blessings of the gospel in my life.*
>
> *I had a job interview with a woman named Pepper Nicholson in Tillamook who needs an assistant. She's a decorator, or interior designer, I guess you would say. She said if I was interested, she would be willing to train me on the job. This is a dream come true! I've always loved art and design, and I think I could actually make a career out of this.*
>
> *It's been a long time since I've been this excited. Finally I'll be able to make a new life for me and my sweet Camryn. I haven't told my parents yet, but I know they'll be excited.*
>
> *It's been a long day and I'm really keyed up, but I've got to get some sleep. Pepper wants to meet with me again tomorrow, and I want to be at my very best. My neck has been so painful I can barely sit up to drive without having to hold my head. I don't feel like the pain medication is even helping anymore. Instead of two, I take four. But tonight I'm going to take some extra so I won't wake up tomorrow with so much pain. I worry though.*

Between the antidepressants and the pain medication, I know I take too many pills. Mom worries about the combined effect of everything I take, but it's the only way I can get through each day. I have an appointment with a specialist in Portland next week, and I hope maybe he can help me.

Before the pills kick in, I think I'll go out on the balcony and watch the sunset, then go to bed. Tomorrow is the first day of my new life.

Cami turned the page, but there was nothing else written. She flipped back to the last entry and read the last line.

Tomorrow is the first day of my new life.

Those were not the words of a suicidal woman. All this time, all these years, she'd been told her mother had committed suicide. It wasn't something she discussed with her grandparents, but they had told her the details of her mother's death and had never said her death was an accident. They'd allowed her to assume it was a suicide, because judging by the circumstances, it probably seemed as though she'd tried to kill herself with the drugs and jumping into the ocean.

Cami now realized that, yes, her mother did die by her own hand, but it was an accident. A terrible, horrible accident. Her mother had probably been wobbly and unsteady as she stood on the balcony, then, perhaps she'd leaned over the edge, and . . .

Cami squeezed her eyes shut, unable to bear the image of her mother plunging to her death. But Cami drew strength from the fact that she knew the truth. She knew the state of her mother's heart. Her mother was excited about the future. She was ready to start a new life. Her mother's death had been an accident. And that, Cami thought, made all the difference.

A numbing emptiness washed over Cami as she read the words on the page one last time. Her vision blurred. There was still half a journal of empty pages left. Just like her mother's life. She'd still had so much life to live.

Flipping through the empty pages, Cami imagined just how different her life would have been had her mother been alive. Her mother would have been so proud to see her graduate from college. She would have cried at Cami and Dallin's wedding. She would have been there to help Cami through Dallin's death.

Cami turned the empty pages until she came to the last one, and as she flipped it over, she gasped with surprise.

A key—a tiny, brass key—was taped to the inside of the back cover.

And underneath it, all that was written was *Great-grandma's treasure.*

Her breath caught in her throat. *Treasure.* It actually said the word. Did this key go to the treasure chest?

But what treasure chest? And if there really was one, where was it?

Her tears dried as she removed the key from the journal and examined it closely. It was a curious little key, long and skinny with only two teeth on one end and a scrolled oval on the other end. The touch of the cold brass metal tingled the tips of her fingers. She had to find Josh and tell him.

In stockinged feet, she raced from her room, hoping Josh and Pearl were still in the parlor talking, but the house was dark and quiet. Everyone had already gone to bed.

"Great," Cami muttered. She would have to wait until morning.

Heaving a sigh of disappointment, she took a step toward her room and stopped.

A shadow, dark and still, appeared in the window.

CHAPTER 24

Cami froze, hoping whoever was out there couldn't see her. She didn't know what to do. She was too frightened to move, but too terrified to stay there.

Gripping the key tightly in her hand, she took a slow step backward.

The shadow moved, propelling Cami into flight. She found herself outside of Josh's bedroom door. A crack of light shone along the threshold.

With a rapid tap on the door, she whispered his name. "Josh." She tapped again. "Josh, it's me, Cami."

The knob turned, and to her relief, Josh opened the door.

She rushed into his arms.

"Cami!" he exclaimed. "What is it? What's wrong? You're shaking like a leaf."

"A man!" she whimpered. "Outside the window."

He thrust her away from him. "You saw a man outside?"

She nodded her head, then clung to his chest again.

"Just a minute," he said. "Let me grab my shoes."

He was back in a flash, and together they crept down the stairs.

"What in tarnation is going on?"

Josh and Cami both gave a startled yelp when Grandpa Willy spoke from the entryway.

"Grandpa!" Cami exclaimed. "You scared us to death."

"Well, all this sneaking around could do that to a person. What are you two doing?"

"Cami saw someone outside her bedroom window," Josh explained.

"Cami, are you sure?"

"I'm positive, Grandpa," Cami told him.

"Well, what are we doing standing around here? Let's go find the varmint and teach him a lesson." Grandpa swung open the entry closet and grabbed his .22 rifle from inside.

"Grandpa, you can't take that gun out there. What if you shoot someone?"

"I'm not shootin' anybody," he growled. "I just plan on scarin' the bejeebers out of whoever's out there. Now, you stay in here, Cami, while me and Josh go take a look."

"No way," Cami said. "I'm not staying in here all alone."

"Cami, I don't have time to argue with you. He might be gettin' away."

"I'm coming with you," she said again.

"Alright, fine. Let's get a move on," he grumbled. "Grab that flashlight there, Josh." Grandpa motioned to the flashlight at the top of the closet. "Let's go."

Sandwiched by her grandfather and Josh, Cami tiptoed through the darkness, her socks getting wet from the dewy, cold grass.

They nearly circled the entire house when Josh exclaimed, "Footprints!"

They turned the beam of light onto the ground and, sure enough, there in Pearl's flower beds were footprints.

"They look just like the other footprints that we found here, Grandpa," Cami said.

Grandpa nodded. "They do! Blast!" Grandpa spat. "He got away again."

"What do you think he was after?" Josh asked.

"Who knows with all the crazies out there? Could be anything. All I know is that first thing in the morning, I'm calling the sheriff," Grandpa declared.

"Let's take a look around the grounds," Josh suggested.

"Good idea, son," Grandpa Willy answered. But in spite of all their looking, the search was futile. There was nothing else to be found.

Josh offered to sleep on the couch in the parlor so Cami wouldn't be scared. With Grandpa and Josh both in rooms next to hers, she felt safe enough to go to bed. She doubted she would be able to sleep, but she crawled into bed, exhausted. It had been a very full day.

* * *

"You look awful," Pearl announced when she saw Cami the next morning. The older woman was flipping pancakes on the griddle while bacon sizzled in a pan and filled the room with a mouth-watering, hickory aroma.

"Thanks," Cami said, plopping onto one of the kitchen chairs. She didn't have enough energy to lift her glass and take a drink of orange juice. She hadn't slept well. In fact, she wasn't sure if she'd slept much at all.

"I heard about all the excitement last night," Pearl informed her. "Are you all right?"

"I'm fine, but I couldn't sleep last night. Every time I shut my eyes, I'd see that shadow there," she told her.

"How awful," Pearl said. "You poor thing."

"Where are Grandpa and Josh anyway?"

"They met with Sheriff Barton earlier and went with him down to the station. They said they'd be back in time for church."

"How are you feeling?" Cami asked her. "You had a pretty important day yesterday."

Pearl stopped getting plates out of the cupboard and said, "I'm still floating on air. All of my wondering has finally been put to rest. I think it's what therapists call 'closure.'" She nodded. "I finally have closure because I know it was the right decision."

Cami smiled at her dear friend. "I'm so glad," she said. "It's been long enough."

"That it has," Pearl said.

The bell on the front door sounded.

Pearl and Cami looked at each other, knowing that if Grandpa Willy and Josh had come home, they would enter through the side door.

"I wonder who that is." Cami pushed herself away from the table. They were expecting guests to arrive, but not until later.

Standing in the entry were a man and a woman, both in their midthirties. The man had long, wavy hair pulled into a ponytail that hung to the middle of his back, and he wore a crisp white dress shirt and jeans with boots. The woman wore jeans and a deep red leather jacket.

"Good morning," Cami addressed them. "Can I help you?"

"We're the Rogers, Graham and Lila," the man said. He had a touch of an accent from Texas or somewhere in the south. Cami wasn't sure.

"Welcome to the Sea Rose Bed and Breakfast. We weren't expecting you until this afternoon," Cami said, pulling their names up on the computer.

"I had an early appointment. Is it too early to check in?" he asked.

Cami remembered that Mr. Rogers was an artist who was coming to town to see about arranging an art show at one of the galleries in town. "Not at all. Your room is ready," she told them.

They signed the necessary papers, and she gave them the key to their room and showed them the way. They weren't the most talkative couple, so Cami filled them in on small details about the place and gave them some background on the area. She offered to help them if they needed any suggestions for sightseeing or things to do around Seamist. Mr. Rogers just absentmindedly grunted at her offer, and Mrs. Rogers thanked her and told her they were there on business and wouldn't have a lot of free time.

Leaving them on their own, Cami returned to the kitchen and gave Pearl a rundown on their new guests, wishing that Josh and her grandfather would hurry up and get home. She was dying to know what they'd found out, and she was anxious to talk to Josh about the key from her mother's diary.

They arrived just before it was time to leave for church.

"Where have you boys been all morning?" Pearl quizzed them. "We were beginning to wonder if something had happened."

"Something did happen," Grandpa Willy said. By the tone of his voice, whatever had happened was serious. "You know old Patrick McDougall over at the Misty Harbor Lighthouse?"

"Of course we know Patrick. He's been around here since . . . well, good heavens, I can't think of a time he wasn't around. Why?"

"He was found dead this morning," Grandpa Willy's voice cracked. Cami noticed that his eyes were puffy and red rimmed.

"Floating in the bay. He'd been shot in the back, then thrown into the ocean."

"Shot?" Cami exclaimed, aghast. "He was murdered?"

Pearl's eyes grew wide with fear. "Why would anyone murder Patrick?"

Grandpa Willy shook his head. "Good question. It's such a shame. Patrick was a good man."

"There's going to be an investigation. They want to come and talk to you, Cami, about the prowler last night," Josh told her.

"Obviously they think there's a connection," she said, feeling queasy in the middle.

"They do now," Josh told her, taking a step toward her. "Do you need to sit down? You're white as a sheet."

Cami swallowed and nodded. She did feel faint.

Josh helped her to a chair, where she took in several deep breaths.
"Better?" Josh asked her.

She pulled in another long breath. "I think so."

Josh took her hand and stroked it gently. "It's going to be okay," he assured her.

She hoped he was right.

* * *

After church, everyone was famished. Luckily Pearl had a delicious roast chicken in the oven. Their guests, the Rogers, had already eaten, so it was just the four of them: Grandpa Willy, Pearl, Josh, and Cami.

They avoided the subject of the prowler and Patrick McDougall's death, talking instead about Pearl's book. Josh had talked to his friend Mr. Simons in New York. Mr. Simons wanted Pearl to Fed Ex the package to him the next day.

"So," Grandpa Willy asked Josh, "how long can you stay with us?"

Pearl and Cami both listened anxiously.

"I need to be back Tuesday. I have to take the red-eye Monday night."

Cami and Pearl exchanged alarmed glances. Neither of them wanted him to leave so soon, and Cami couldn't help being concerned at the thought of him driving those winding mountain roads back to Portland at night.

Pearl began gathering the dishes and stacking them together to take into the kitchen. The way she clanked the stoneware and nearly broke it made it obvious she wasn't happy to have Josh leave so soon, just when she discovered he was her son.

Josh and Cami went to the parlor and sat on a floral divan next to the picture window overlooking the ocean.

"Pearl's upset," Josh said. "I feel terrible leaving, but I haven't got a choice. Not if I want to continue teaching. I have to get back."

"She understands," Cami said in Pearl's defense. "She's probably just wishing you two had more time to spend together. She'll be okay as long as she knows you'll be back soon." She was speaking in Pearl's behalf, but Cami was just as anxious for her own sake.

"I will." He nodded. "Every chance I get."

Their gazes connected, and Cami felt a tightening around her heart. She tried to ignore the feelings inside, deny that they meant anything, but she knew she couldn't fool herself any longer. Josh had gotten to her. And the way he looked at her, she felt as if he were able to read her thoughts, interpret her feelings.

"Josh, I need to tell you something," she said, grateful to have a way to shift the focus of their interaction.

His forehead wrinkled. "What is it?"

"I found something," she said, pulling a long string from around her neck and producing the key from her mother's journal.

He raised his eyebrows.

"This was in my mother's journal," she told him.

"What does it go to?" he asked.

She looked from one side to the other. "My great-great-grandmother's treasure," she answered.

"Your great-great-grandmother's treasure?" he asked. "She had a treasure?"

"I don't mean *her* treasure," Cami lowered her voice. "Remember the Spanish gold coin?"

Josh nodded. Then his eye grew wide. "That treasure?"

"Shhhhh." Cami panicked.

"But where's the chest?" he questioned.

She shook her head. "I don't know, but I think we'd better find out. I don't want another dead body around Seamist. Especially one of ours. With all that's been going on, I can't help but think we're somebody's prime target."

Floorboards in the entryway squeaked, and Cami glanced up to see Graham Rogers looking at them. She wondered where he had appeared from.

She jumped to her feet. "Mr. Rogers, is there something I can help you with?" She met him at the registration desk.

"We're having some trouble with one of the faucets upstairs. Is there someone who can come and look at it?" he asked.

Josh immediately piped up. "I'll be right up to take a look," he said.

Cami scowled at him. He was a guest at the inn. He didn't need to be fixing the plumbing.

"I'll wait for you upstairs," Mr. Rogers confirmed.

After the man left, Josh wouldn't listen to Cami's argument. "Your grandfather is busy, and I don't mind at all," he said. "It will only take a minute."

"Do you think he heard us talking?" Cami whispered.

Josh shook his head. "Not from that far away." He gave her a wink. "I'll be right back."

Cami didn't like the turn of events around their town and their inn. Things were usually so uneventful, bordering on boring, that this much excitement was hard to handle. No, she didn't like it. Not one bit. She worried about everything that had been going on at the mansion, and now sweet old Patrick McDougall was murdered. Was it all connected? And if it was, how would it affect all of them?

* * *

Cami was in the garden gathering flowers for an arrangement for the dinner table when Josh found her.

"We have to talk," he said.

She leaned over to gather some of the cut flowers so she could take them inside. "I'm almost—"

"Cami, this won't wait," Josh said grabbing her hand and pulling her toward the trees.

"What in the world are you doing?" She trotted alongside him as he continued pulling her to the wooden steps leading to the beach.

"We have to make sure we're completely alone," he said as he quickened his pace.

By the time they arrived on the beach, she was winded and nearly overcome with curiosity.

"Josh, what is going on?" she demanded when they finally stopped.

"Your guest is up to something," he told her.

"Mr. Rogers? He's an artist. What's he doing, painting one of the walls?"

Josh wasn't amused. "I saw inside one of their suitcases. It's full of high-tech electrical equipment—like something James Bond might keep in the trunk of his car."

"A lot of people bring laptops, digital cameras, and electronic devices on vacations. Some people do a lot of work—"

"I think he has a gun," Josh said.

Cami stopped talking, stunned.

"A gun? Are you sure? We need to tell the authorities!" she cried, moving toward the house. But Josh stopped her.

"Not until we know for sure. I caught a glimpse right before Mrs. Rogers shut the suitcase, but we can't do anything drastic until we're positive it's a gun."

"Then let's check in his room and find out for sure," Cami suggested.

"It's risky. We might get caught."

She thought for a moment. "I know—maybe we can peek into the room through the passageway door. We can sneak in next time they leave."

"Cami, I don't think that's such a good idea."

"I don't think it's a good idea that one of our guests has a gun, either," she stated.

"You're right," Josh agreed.

"Then we can tell the sheriff and have him run a check on the Rogers," Cami said, chewing her bottom lip as she worried about their safety.

"Cami." Josh took her by the shoulders and looked into her eyes. "Nothing's going to happen. I promise."

Her heart skipped several beats. Along with his warmth and caring, Josh's presence added an element of safety and security to her life and to the inn. He always seemed to know just what to do. He was so strong and capable.

And he was leaving soon.

The thought filled her with sadness.

"What's wrong?" he asked.

"Nothing." She looked away.

"Cami," he cradled her cheek in the palm of his hand, "talk to me."

She looked up into his eyes, wishing she could stop the tears that filled her own.

"Hey," he said, wrapping his arms around her and pulling her close. "I don't want you to worry."

"Okay," she said.

"There's something else though, isn't there?"

She blinked and pulled in a calming breath, but couldn't bring herself to say what was on her mind and in her heart.

"Cami?" He dipped his chin and looked at her with an unyielding gaze.

She buried her head into his shoulder, hating the confusion that swirled inside of her.

"Cami?" he asked. "Please tell me what's wrong."

She held her silence.

"Cami," he persisted.

"Alright, fine!" she said, her frustration mounting. She squared her shoulders and looked him straight in the eye. "You make me happy, okay? And I don't want you to leave again," she added. "I hate how it feels when you're gone. And . . . ," a sob caught in her throat, "I'm so confused."

Putting some distance between them, he looked into her face, but she turned away. "I make you happy?" he asked. "Is that what you said?"

"Yes, that's what I said," she replied.

"But, isn't that a good thing?" he asked.

"Yes," she said. "I mean, no!" She rested her head on his shoulder again, wishing he wouldn't press her for answers she didn't know herself.

He chuckled and rocked her gently, trying to soothe her.

After a moment she took a long, deep breath and let it out slowly.

"I'd like to tell you something," he said.

"What?" She looked up.

"You make me happy too." He stroked her cheek with his fingers. "And when you called asking me to come back for Pearl's birthday, it was all I could do not to hop on the plane right then and come out to you."

"Even though you were mad at me?" she said, finally looking at him.

"I wasn't mad. I was hurt. I couldn't believe you thought I was capable of—"

"I know, I know." She couldn't bear to hear him say it. "I think back now and realize how stupid I was."

"I couldn't really blame you for drawing the conclusion you did, especially with everything that's been going on. In fact," he admitted, "I was going to call you and talk to you about it. You just happened to call before I had a chance."

"I'm still sorry," she said.

"And I'm sorry I left in such a hurry. It wasn't all because I was upset."

"It wasn't?"

"No, I called to check in with the dean of our department, and he basically told me that if I didn't get back to my classes, he would replace me permanently. I should have explained everything when I left, but I was hurt and it took me a few days to put my pride aside."

"I understand," she said.

"Good, then let's put it behind us, okay?"

"I'd like that," she said, anxious to look forward to the future with anticipation rather than to the past with sorrow.

"Now, let's get back to what you said just a minute ago. You said I make you happy. Why isn't that a good thing?"

"It's just that," she searched for the right words, "I want to be happy because I'm happy, not because you make me happy."

His brow wrinkled as he thought about what she said.

"You see," she tried to explain, "when Dallin died, part of me died with him. And I realized it was because so much of my happiness depended on him. I can't do that again. I couldn't bear to give my heart to someone and have that person taken away from me. This time it would kill me for sure."

After Cami took several measured breaths, Josh let her continue, keeping his attention focused on her completely.

"I have to be strong and secure and happy as an individual before I can make another person happy. Does that make sense?" she asked.

He stared at her for several moments, then he leaned down and kissed her gently on the forehead. "Yes," he said, "it makes perfect sense."

"It does?" she asked, her voice quivering again. "Really?"

He nodded. "I understand what you're saying. And I also understand that you need time to get used to all of this. And that's okay, because I need time too."

His words relieved some of the pressure inside of her.

"So, where does Jane fit in?" she asked.

He cocked his head to the side and hunched up his shoulders, relaxing them with a sigh. "Jane is a wonderful person. She's on the ball, witty, charming, beautiful . . ."

Cami shrank with every adjective.

"But," he said, "she's not you."

Wide-eyed, Cami looked at him. "What are you saying?"

"I'm saying that even though I care a great deal for Jane, I'm not in love with her."

Cami waited for him to go on, her heart thumping loudly in her chest.

"Jane and I get along well and have a lot in common. But after my father's death, things between us changed."

"How?" Cami asked.

"She can't understand why I'm having such a hard time accepting his death. She thought I should grieve for a few weeks or so and then move on. I couldn't share my feelings with her or talk to her about how hard losing my father was. I began to pull away from her. And now Jane and I are in completely different places. So much has changed—I found my birth mother, I found a place that brings peace to my soul, and I found you."

Cami's heart melted.

And as Josh drew closer to her, she felt as if her insides would melt too.

There, with waves lapping against the shore, the call of gulls overhead, and the sea-kissed breeze rustling the trees, Josh kissed her, fanning a flame in her heart that she'd thought had long since burned out. His kiss left her light-headed and weak-kneed.

"So," he said, pulling her from a dreamlike state, "now that we have that out in the open, there's something else we need to talk about."

"What's that?" she asked, still swooning.

"The treasure. I think we better find it before anyone else does."

CHAPTER 25

"Excuse me," the man at the reception desk said as Cami walked in from the backyard. "I wondered if you had a room available for the night." The man was older, with a slight build and dressed in a suit and tie. "I'm in town on business, and someone recommended your inn," he continued.

"Actually I do," she told him. "Just for one night?"

He nodded and dug out his ID and a wad of cash.

The man, Mr. Richardson, wasn't much of a conversationalist, giving Cami one- or two-word answers to her questions, but she wasn't in much of a mood to chitchat anyway. She had more important things to attend to right now.

Getting his signature on the register, she showed Mr. Richardson to the Asian Room and made sure he had everything he needed, then hurried back to find Josh waiting for her.

"You ready?" he asked.

She nodded, checked to make the sure the coast was clear, and then quickly they ducked into the office and closed the door.

"Grandpa's right," Cami said to Josh as they stepped inside the passageway. "We need to seal off these passageways. They're starting to give me the creeps."

The eerie evening shadows illuminated the cobweb curtains and fine layer of dust inside.

Not wanting to alert anyone to their presence, they tiptoed along the corridor and up the stairs. Every once in a while, one of them would step on a loose floorboard, which would then complain with a loud creak, making them freeze in their tracks.

"There it is," Josh said as they finally approached the doorway to the Rogerses' room. "You're sure they're gone?"

"I'm positive. Pearl said they just left and aren't expected back until later this evening."

"I don't have a good feeling about this," he said.

"Josh, we have to know if he has a gun."

"You're right." He nodded with reluctance. "Let's just hurry and get it over with."

"Help me open the door."

Cami moved the latch, then together they pressed on the door. It wouldn't budge.

"Hey," Cami said. "Why won't it open?"

"Maybe they didn't want people coming into their room," he said flatly.

"Let's try again. Maybe the wood's swollen. It has been humid and warm." She tried to sound encouraging.

Putting their shoulders into it, they both gave another push. This time the door swung open, and they nearly fell inside the room.

"There it is." Josh pointed at the suitcase that was on the bed across the room.

"I'll go see." Cami started through the opening, but Josh grabbed her.

"You stay here. I don't want anything to happen to you. I'll go," Josh said.

Biting her bottom lip, Cami watched nervously as Josh stepped through the opening into the room and crept across the floor to the bed.

With each pop of the suitcase latch, Cami flinched. In the stillness of the room, they sounded like explosions of noise.

Josh was slowly lifting the lid when footsteps and voices sounded on the stairway.

He looked at her with alarm and quickly shut the lid, then started toward the passageway.

"Close the latches!" Cami hissed.

Josh's face registered alarm, and he turned and pushed the latches shut.

The voices were just outside the door, and the knob on the door rattled as a key was inserted.

Dropping to the floor, Josh scrambled underneath the bed and out of sight.

Cami pulled the passage door shut and began an earnest prayer.

"You said you had the car keys with you," a male voice said.

"I gave them to you. You put them in your pocket," a woman replied.

"I saw you put them in your purse," the man answered with annoyance.

"And I remember you putting them in the pocket of your jacket!" she exclaimed. "I've looked all over, and they aren't in my purse."

"Alright," he retorted, "keep your voice down. Did you get the blood off the sleeve of my shirt?" he said.

Cami's breath caught in her throat.

"It came out," the woman said. "It's still soaking in the sink."

Footsteps went toward the bathroom.

"I found them," the man called.

"Good," the woman answered. "Now let's get out of here. We need to make some appearances at the galleries downtown or people will start to suspect us."

"You're right," the man said. "I'm ready."

With a jingle of keys, the couple left the room, pulling the door shut behind them.

Cami remained frozen inside the passageway, unable to comprehend what she'd just heard.

She jumped when Josh tapped on the door.

Pushing it open, he lunged inside and pulled it shut behind him.

"Josh!" she whispered, feeling frantic but relieved that he was safe.

He held her close and said, "That was too close. Are you okay?"

"I'm fine, but I was so scared."

"That makes two of us. I can't believe they came back," he said.

"I can't believe what they said," she added. "It's them. They killed Patrick McDougall."

"Cami, we don't know that for sure."

"It sure seems obvious, though. They show up the morning after the murder, they have a gun, and there's blood on the sleeve of his shirt. What else do we need?"

"We need to find that treasure before they do."

Cami knew he was right.

"Let's go back to the riddle and see if we can find any other clues," Josh suggested.

They found the riddle written with chalk on the wall, and Cami read it out loud again.

It's not just a penny, or even a dime,
To find the treasure, first find the time.

"Any ideas?" Josh asked her.

"Well, the legend says the treasure is somewhere along the coastline. Maybe 'time' has something to do with the tide. Maybe the spot can only be found during low tide or something," she offered.

Josh nodded, obviously impressed. "I'd buy that. That sounds like a perfect explanation. There's just one problem," he stated. "How many miles of beach do we have to dig up to find it?"

Cami pulled a face. "Yeah, you're right. There's got to be more to this."

Josh knelt down and read it again.

"We better figure this out before it gets dark," she told Josh. "I don't want to be in here too late. Not with everything that's going on."

"As soon as we get out of here, we better contact Officer Spencer. Hopefully he'll have something on Mr. Rogers," Josh said.

"I'm starting to feel as skittish as a long-tailed cat in a scissor factory," Cami said.

Josh looked at her, then burst out laughing. "Where'd you get that saying?"

"It's one of Pearl's."

"Sounds like her, doesn't it?" Josh said, chuckling again. He shook his head. "I'm looking forward to getting to know her even better. It's strange how she's everything I always wanted to be when I grew up—an explorer, a traveler, an adventurer. I was pretty lucky to have three incredible parents."

"I'd say you were very lucky," she answered.

Her comment made him smile with pleasure. "I really can't call it luck, though, can I? It's all been in the Lord's hands. I wasn't ready to meet Pearl before now. And I know that He led me here to find her and to find you. There's absolutely no doubt in my mind."

Cami allowed herself to bask in his gaze. When he looked at her, it was as if nothing else seemed to exist.

The shadows deepened, and suddenly they heard the chime of the grandfather clock downstairs.

"What time is it, anyway?" Cami asked.

Josh checked his watch. "Six o'clock," he answered.

"It's amazing how well you can hear the clock in here," Cami observed as it finished chiming its hourly tune before donging out the time of day.

"It sounds like it's coming up through that vent in the floorboards over there," he said.

Cami looked over at the vent, and then a thought struck her. "Find the time," she said.

Josh's eyes opened wide. "Do you think?"

They both scrambled to the corner of the passageway where the sound of the clock chiming six bells could be heard best.

They searched the area but found nothing obvious indicating a chest or box of any sort. But on closer inspection, Josh noticed a board strategically placed across some ductwork, concealing space between the floor joists.

"We need something to pry up this board," Josh said, looking around. "I know. Give me your belt."

"My what?"

"Your belt. I can use the buckle," he told her.

She pulled off the belt and handed it to him. The buckle was rectangular and flat, and made out of metal.

"I'll try not to bend it," he said as he began to work the buckle into the cracks in the board.

It took some doing, and he succeeded in completely mangling the buckle in the process, but Josh managed to wedge the board up enough to get his fingers under it. After considerable effort, he pulled, the nails squeaking and groaning as they came loose.

Then, with one last try, Josh pulled with all his might, the board came loose, and he went flying backward into the wall.

"Ugh!" He landed with a thud.

"Josh!" Cami cried, lunging for him. "Are you okay?"

He moved slowly as he tried to sit up, then after realizing nothing was broken, he nodded. "I'm fine. How's the wall?"

"It fared better than you did," she told him.

He got back on his feet and held up the board with prongs of nails sticking through it. "We did it," he declared. "Sorry about your belt."

She waved his words away. "No problem. C'mon." She grabbed his free hand. "Let's take a look."

Kneeling down next to the opening, where shining tubes of duct-work ran the length and width of the house, Josh and Cami peered inside. Cami's heart nearly stopped in her chest when she saw a cigar box tucked into the corner.

"Omigosh!" she whispered. "There's something there."

"Doesn't look much like a treasure box," Josh remarked.

"Can you reach it?" she asked.

He stretched his arm inside and grabbed hold of the box. Pulling it from its hiding spot, he handed it to Cami.

She shook it, but instead of hearing a jingling noise like gold coins would make, it didn't make a sound.

"Is it empty?" Cami asked.

"There's only one way to find out," he said.

With a deep breath, Cami slowly opened the lid. Inside was an envelope, yellowed from the passage of time.

They looked at each other, then back at the contents. Josh shrugged. Carefully he took the envelope from the box and removed a letter inside.

With great care, he unfolded the piece of paper, and both of them gasped at the same time.

"A treasure map!" Cami exclaimed.

"That's what it looks like," Josh said.

On the paper was a sketch of the Misty Harbor, the south shore around the point where the Sea Rose Bed and Breakfast stood, and two hundred feet of coastline.

Following the path with her finger, Cami noticed how a dotted line of the map led from the mansion, down the side of the cliff, and northward around the Misty Harbor Bay. The path stopped at the cape where the Misty Harbor Lighthouse stood.

"Where does it go?" she asked.

Josh pointed to a darkened half circle at the edge of the cape. "Cami," he looked at the map again, "it leads to the lighthouse."

"The lighthouse!" she exclaimed. Then her breath caught in her throat. "Patrick McDougall." She suddenly realized that the person after the treasure wasn't going to let anything stand in their way. "Josh, this is getting scary."

"We'll be okay. As far as anyone's concerned, we don't know anything. We just have to be careful."

"What do we do now?" she asked him.

"You feel like getting up early?" he asked.

"Are you sure we should do this?"

"If we find the gold, we can turn it over to the authorities. I doubt anyone else who's looking for it is after it for its historical significance," he said.

She agreed, and it was decided. Early Monday morning they would sneak up to the lighthouse and find the treasure.

* * *

Well before the sun came up, Josh and Cami donned jackets and gloves and silently left the house. Cami had been too nervous to sleep, jumping at every creak or sound from inside or outside the house, so Josh offered to stay up with her and keep her company.

They'd watched television, then looked at photo albums of Cami as a young girl growing up and some of her and Dallin. She appreciated Josh's understanding and patience with her need to talk about Dallin. He fully accepted Dallin's place in Cami's heart and in her life, which, to her surprise, made letting go and moving on that much easier.

She also found that the more she talked about Dallin, the more she appreciated Josh. He was giving and caring in a completely unselfish way. And with each passing moment they spent together, they grew closer together, as if their souls already knew each other.

And now, here they were, walking through pitch-black darkness along the trail to the lighthouse, looking for a buried treasure. The adventure was daunting, and Cami's nerves were on edge, but she felt safe with Josh.

"I can't believe we're really doing this," she said to Josh as he grabbed her hand and led her along the fern-lined path through thick Douglas firs.

"I've lived all my life for a moment like this," Josh said.

"How do we know it's *inside* the lighthouse and not buried somewhere *outside* the lighthouse?" she asked.

"We don't. But why would they bother putting the treasure up here if it weren't in the lighthouse? There's nowhere else to put it. The ground is too rocky to dig a hole to bury the treasure. No," he said with conviction, "I'm positive it's somewhere inside of there. Too bad . . ."

He didn't finish.

"Too bad, what?" Cami asked.

"Too bad Mr. McDougall isn't around to ask."

The same thought had occurred to Cami more than once.

Keeping their flashlights off until they got inside, they squinted through the darkness as they neared the lighthouse.

"The police have cordoned off Patrick's house." Cami spoke in hushed tones. "Do you think it's okay to go into the lighthouse?"

"I don't see a barrier. I think we're okay," Josh assured her, his voice also lowered. "We'll go in, look around, and get out."

"That fast?" she asked.

"That fast," he promised.

"How are we going to get in?" she asked. "I'm sure the place is locked up and secure."

"I brought plenty of tools," Josh answered. "What do you think's in this backpack?" he asked.

"I was hoping breakfast."

Josh laughed. "We'll stop at the Bayside Diner for breakfast. My treat."

They stopped conversing as they emerged from the covering of trees. The windswept clearing seemed like miles across before they got to the conical structure. Cami felt like she and Josh were sitting ducks out in the open, even though it was still completely dark.

"Ready?" Josh said in a soft whisper, reaching for her hand.

Cami nodded, and together they crept to the lighthouse.

"This chest better be loaded with gold," Cami whispered.

Josh chuckled. "It will be. You brought the key, didn't you?"

"It's still around my neck."

Standing directly in front of the lighthouse entrance, Josh removed his backpack. He pulled a crowbar from inside and wedged it between the doorjamb and the door. With one quick movement, the door gave an earsplitting squeak and swung open.

There was no turning back. They were inside now.

"Where first?" Cami asked, feeling the hair on her neck stand on end. If it hadn't been for Josh's perseverance, she would have high-tailed it back home by now.

Josh led the way up the winding staircase to the top of the light-house.

"I'm scared," she said.

"We'll be fine," he said, giving her a quick kiss for luck. "We just have to hurry before it gets light."

They secured dark cloths over their flashlights with rubber bands to prevent the glaring light from drawing attention, and searched by the dim glow for any possible hiding spot for the chest. Finding nothing, they descended the stairs and searched the main floor of the structure for some type of hiding spot where a treasure could be deposited.

"Maybe there are some loose bricks," Cami said, running her hand along the smooth, painted brick wall. But search as she might, she found nothing. Josh checked the floor, the furniture, everywhere possible, but nothing turned up.

A small souvenir shop was attached to the main structure. They searched every inch but found nothing even remotely possible as a hiding spot.

"It's just not here," Cami remarked, noticing that she could see the details of Josh's face. The sky grew lighter. "Unless this place has a basement, I just don't think it's in here!"

Josh's eyes grew wide. He grabbed her by the arms and smiled. "You're brilliant!"

"I am?"

"The storm cellar. Patrick showed me the entrance when he gave me the tour. Not many people even know about it. Come on." Josh grabbed her hand and led her to a storage room, which was the size of a closet, where a set of stairs was located.

"I didn't know these were here," she said, thinking back on the many times she'd been to the lighthouse.

"Patrick didn't tell many about them. He said there are some things about the lighthouse's history that are best left in the past."

"Like what? Buried treasures? Spanish gold?" she asked.

"Ghosts and spirits too," Josh added, leading the way down the stairs. "We can pull the cloth off the flashlights now. No one can see the light down here."

At the bottom of the stairs, they found nothing more than a narrow landing and a small door barely four feet tall.

"The room behind this door was destroyed when the first lighthouse collapsed in the storm. Patrick said it was easier just to seal off the cellar than to rebuild," Josh said. Grabbing his crowbar again, he worked at prying the door open. Once he'd loosened the door around each side, he took a few steps back and with several mighty kicks, he broke down the door.

"I hope the police don't care that we're doing this," she said, looking at the shattered door.

"They'll thank us when we turn the treasure over to them," Josh said. He directed his light inside the room, and together they bent close and peered inside. The damp, moldy stench of the air assaulted their nostrils.

"Smells like something died in here," Josh remarked.

Cami's eyes opened wide at the thought.

"I didn't mean that," he said quickly.

"I can't go in there," Cami told him.

"Cami, it's fine."

"No, you don't understand. I'm claustrophobic, remember? Small spaces, especially in the dark, freak me out."

"Listen, I'll go in first and check it out, okay?"

Cami agreed and stood outside the door, wishing they hadn't come. She would never forgive herself if anything happened to them, especially to Josh.

"Josh?" she called, suddenly anxious to know if he was safe.

"I'm here. Cami, come on in, it's not as small inside as it looks on the outside. It's quite big, but it is dirty and in shambles."

Dreading the thought of going into that room but curious to see what was inside, Cami finally ducked under the door and stepped into the room.

"Wow, it looks like half of the debris from the old structure came inside," she remarked, stepping over piles of bricks and stones, all covered with a thick layer of crusted dirt.

"How are we ever going to find it in here?" Josh wondered out loud.

Cami felt as bewildered as Josh sounded. She scanned their surroundings, not knowing where to begin. Then her gaze landed on a large, box-shaped item against the far wall.

"Josh," she said, "is that a trunk?"

"Where?" he asked, then turned and saw what she was pointing at. "That's certainly what it looks like."

Climbing over debris, they got to the large trunk and, after searching the exterior, found handles practically cemented in mud. Kicking loose the crusted dirt, they grabbed the handles and moved it away from the wall so they could open the lid.

"It's not even locked," Josh said, pointing at the latch in front. He banged the lid several times to loosen it, then together they opened it wide.

Holding their breath, they shined the lights inside and found a pair of old leather boots, a rope, a moth-eaten wool blanket, and a tarnished old trumpet.

"Any gold coins at the bottom?" Cami asked.

"Not that I can see."

Shutting the lid with a bang, they sat down on it and looked at the mess inside the room.

"We need a forklift," Cami said.

Josh gave an exasperated sigh, then he jumped up. "I just found the next best thing."

Leaning against the wall near a bank of broken shelves were several shovels and a pitchfork.

"Take your pick," Josh said, holding up one of each.

"I'll take a shovel," Cami said.

Josh brought it to her.

"Sure hope these flashlights hold out," she said as she looked at the piles in front of her.

"I'll turn mine off and we can save it in case your battery runs out." Josh placed the light in his backpack and slung it over his shoulder. "Ready?" he asked.

She nodded.

"Let's dig in."

* * *

Cami didn't know how long they dug. It seemed like hours, but Josh assured her it had been thirty minutes at the most.

"This is so unreal," Josh said as he cleared away stones and bricks. He'd turned in the pitchfork for a shovel. "I mean, a buried treasure. When I was a kid," he lifted a shovelful of dirt and tossed it off to the side, "I used to pretend like I was an explorer looking for treasures. Who would have thought that one day I would actually be digging for Spanish gold?"

Cami smiled at Josh, his excitement giving her added energy to dig quickly and tirelessly. Like a machine, Josh's shovel flashed as he dug and flung load after load of heavy sand.

Then suddenly, with a resounding thud, the shovel struck something hard.

Cami froze, then slowly turned her head. They looked excitedly at each other, and smiled.

Kneeling down, Josh cleared sand away with his hand to expose the object.

"I hope it's not just a rock," Cami said, trying to look down into the hole.

Josh froze, then he looked up at Cami. "It's not a rock."

"Is it the treasure box?" she asked anxiously. "Did you find it?"

Instead of answering, Josh pulled out several objects for her to see.

They were the skeletal remains of a human hand and forearm.

CHAPTER 26

Bile rose in Cami's throat. A sense of dread filled her. Suddenly the cellar seemed to close in, and the air became stifling. She turned her head, closed her eyes, and pulled in several long, deep breaths, hoping to calm the panic rising inside of her.

"Cami?" Josh questioned.

"I'm okay," she answered quickly. "I just . . . need to . . ." She shuddered, picturing the remains of a decayed body beneath her.

"Breathe?" he finished her sentence for her.

She nodded.

"I have a feeling we're close to the chest," Josh said. "We have to keep digging."

Cami nodded as her nerves began to settle.

"Are you all right?" he asked.

She pulled in a long breath and let it out slowly. Finally she opened her eyes and looked at him. "I'm better now. I just didn't expect to find . . . that," she said, and shuddered again.

"Poor guy. He was probably one of the guys who got buried in the storm."

Joining Josh, Cami helped clear away mud and debris, afraid that every brick she lifted would expose another body part.

They worked furiously, clearing away shovelfuls of mud, widening the hole until Josh's shovel struck something else hard with a resounding thud.

"That better not be a skull," Cami said, not bearing to look down.

Josh chuckled and asked her to shine the flashlight on the spot for him while he investigated.

After a few seconds, Cami couldn't bear the suspense. "What is it?" she asked.

Josh looked up, wide-eyed. "This is too easy," he said.

"What's too easy?" she asked, not liking the strange expression on his face. "What are you talking about?"

"Cami," he said her name with trepidation, "we found the treasure box."

"That's great!" she exclaimed.

But he didn't move.

"Josh?"

"I just got a very uneasy feeling," he said.

A streak of cold chills ran up her spine.

"I think we should get out of here and go get help," he told her.

The idea sounded great to her. She was about to drop her shovel and leave when a movement at the entrance of the cellar made both of them jump.

Suddenly the room was illuminated with the light from a battery-powered lantern.

Cami and Josh barely had time to look at each other before a man, a stranger, ducked in through the hole. Cami gasped, somehow knowing he wasn't on the right side of the law. When he straightened, he stood as tall as the room, and was broad shouldered and bald.

"Good work," he said. "You found it."

Cami looked at the stranger, feeling that he was no stranger at all. She knew she'd seen him or met him somewhere.

"Who are you?" Josh challenged, lifting his shovel.

"It doesn't matter who I am," the man answered tersely.

The man was foreign—German maybe. He was older, perhaps in his fifties, but he had the physique of a man much younger.

His steel-gray eyes bore into her.

"What do you want?" Cami asked.

"The same thing you want," he said. "I knew it was only a matter of time before you led me here."

Where have I seen him? Cami scanned the recesses of her memory but came up empty.

"So." The man slid his hand into the front flap of his jacket. When he pulled it out, he held a small revolver. "I'll take it from here."

Josh moved quickly to Cami's side.

"Rita!" the man hollered, the echo of his voice bouncing off every side of the earthen walls. "Come!"

The scrape of movement against the low rock entryway announced the arrival of the person called Rita. The woman entered, also wielding a pistol.

It only took one short glance and Cami finally recognized the people standing in front of her. The woman's hair was a fiery shade of red instead of honey colored like it was before, but Cami was positive she knew these people.

The Rothchilds.

"You!" Cami exclaimed, suddenly thinking of every synonym for *weasel* she could. They'd obviously come to the bed-and-breakfast in disguise. Grandpa Willy hadn't felt good about them. Now Cami knew why.

"Keep them out of my way, Rita," the man's voice boomed.

"Back against that rock," Rita commanded, waving her gun in the direction she wanted them to move. "Come on," she ordered. "Move it!"

She too had a German accent.

"Josh, it's the Rothchilds from the inn," Cami told him.

"How can you be sure?" the man tested her, his tone mocking.

Cami didn't know how to answer, afraid of how he'd react to what she said.

"Perhaps you've seen us around town?"

"I would remember you if I'd seen you," Cami said.

"Would you now?" His gaze bore into her.

She nodded.

"We've crossed paths many times," he said.

"I don't believe you."

"There was actually one time when I thought you did recognize me." His taunting made her on edge. Perspiration formed on her brow. Why was he doing this?

"All those years in theater paid off, didn't they, Rita? The costumes, the makeup. All preparing us for this—the greatest discovery of buried treasure in North America."

"Let's just get out of here," the woman pled.

"Silence!" the man exploded. He stepped over the piles of rubbish and looked down into the hole, apparently finished with his game.

Cami's mind whirled. How long had they been hanging around Seamist without anyone noticing? Which strangers, which tourists, had she actually walked past, bumped into, even smiled at, who in reality were this creep and Rita?

"Is it there, Wolfgang?" Rita asked.

"Ya, it's here," Wolfgang answered. He looked at Josh and Cami. "Well done. It's taken me years to locate this chest. Unfortunately, we went to the wrong lighthouse first."

Cami's mouth dropped open. She looked at Josh, who also had a stunned expression on his face.

"I told you we had the wrong lighthouse before," Rita murmured.

Wolfgang's anger flared. He whirled and shot his gun over Rita's head, sending a shower of plaster to the ground. The woman didn't even flinch.

Cami knew they were dealing with a madman who was willing to do anything to anyone if it served his purpose.

"Es macht nichts!" he yelled at the woman. "What matters is that we have the right one now."

"How did you—"

"Find out where you were digging?" Wolfgang finished Cami's sentence.

She nodded.

"Easy," he said. "There are bugs in every room of your inn."

Cami's mouth dropped open.

"Yes," Wolfgang said with a laugh. "Your conversations have proven . . . most entertaining." His tone was mocking and irreverent.

Anger flared up inside of her. How dare they bug the mansion, eavesdropping on private conversations!

"You have no right to this treasure," Josh informed the man.

"Ha!" Wolfgang's voice boomed. "And you do? This treasure belongs to whoever is willing to fight for it. However, I," he looked at them with an evil, squint-eyed glare, "am willing to kill for it."

Cami shrank back, leaning against Josh for support.

"Enough talking!" Rita announced. "We don't have much time."

Wolfgang set to work extracting the chest from its grave.

Slowly he stood, placing the chest on a mound of bricks.

The chest was much smaller than Cami had expected, no bigger than Pearl's bread box.

"Now," he turned to Cami, "the key."

Cami tensed. Josh stretched his arm across her for protection.

"It's no use," Wolfgang told Josh. "I know she has it around her neck." Then he spoke to Cami. "But it's your choice. You can cooperate and stay alive, or I can kill you . . . just like the fisherman who claimed to know the location of a buried treasure."

Cami swallowed, knowing Wolfgang wasn't kidding.

"Too bad for him he didn't have all of the information we needed." Then Wolfgang laughed. "Actually, even if he would have been correct about the treasure, we still would have killed him, right *liebling?*" he said to Rita.

Rita laughed along with Wolfgang, as though the whole thing was just some amusing game to them. "Just like the keeper here," she said.

"Ya, that's right. He told us everything we wanted to know, and we still killed him."

Rita laughed again.

"So, here we finally are, and here is the item we've searched many months for." He gazed down at the chest. Without looking up, he reached his hand toward Cami. "Give me the key."

Cami shrank back.

His head snapped up, malevolence sparking his eyes. "Now!" he barked.

"Give it to him," Josh said gently.

With trembling fingers, Cami removed the string from around her neck. Wolfgang quickly snatched it out of her hand and inserted the key into the mud-encrusted lock.

Cami held her breath, waiting to hear the click of the lock.

But there was no click.

"Was ist los, Wolfgang?" Rita asked.

"The lock is either rusted, or this isn't the right key," he said, thrusting the key into the lock again and turning it with a grunt.

Still, the lock didn't give.

Suddenly he turned. "Where is it?" he bellowed, throwing the key at Cami's feet. "Where is the right key?"

Cowering, Cami answered, "That's the only key I have, I swear it!"

Wolfgang let loose a string of angry German expletives. Then, without warning, he turned, aimed his gun at the chest, and fired.

Josh and Cami ducked, covering their heads with their arms, the deafening sound of the bullet blasting in their ears.

This time Rita jumped, and from the tone of her voice, it was obvious she was giving Wolfgang a good scolding for not warning her.

"Silence!" he yelled. Then he bent down and reached for the lid.

Josh, Cami, and Rita leaned in to watch as he slowly opened the chest.

And when he did, he erupted like Mount Vesuvius.

"Empty!" He stood and kicked the chest with his foot, sending the small box crashing into the wall. "What is the meaning of this?" he said, charging at them, coming to a halt just inches away from them.

"We didn't know," Cami confessed. "Please."

Wolfgang hurled angry words at them they didn't understand. Cami trembled with fear, wondering if he would shoot them on the spot.

"They know nothing," Rita told him. "We're wasting our time here. We have to get out!" She spoke intensely. "Now!"

"Tie them up," Wolfgang commanded.

Cami's throat constricted. Her gaze connected with Josh's frightened one.

The woman removed the loops of nylon rope slung over her shoulder and tied each of their hands together behind them, then had them sit back-to-back so she could wind the rope around their bodies, lashing them together. She tied Cami's feet firmly together and did the same to Josh's.

When she was finished, Wolfgang drew from a bag an object that was about four inches long, five inches wide, and had a tangle of wire and fuses, all of which was wrapped in duct tape. This he placed just inside the cellar door. Then he adjusted something and stood.

"That should give us plenty of time to get away before this explodes," Wolfgang said.

Fear struck Cami's heart. She felt Josh's hands clench, and then he looped his thumb over hers. It was all Cami could do not to cry out, beg for mercy, plead for their lives. But she didn't.

"You won't get away with this," Josh said to them.

"Ha!" The man laughed. "We already have."

Both Wolfgang and Rita laughed as they left the cellar, their voices echoing against the rock walls, then disappearing. All that was left was the faint ticking of the device at the entrance of the cellar.

"Cami," Josh's voice came. "Are you okay?"

"No," Cami whimpered.

"We need to get loose." He struggled against the ropes, and the movement caused them to cut into Cami's skin. She couldn't help crying out.

"There's got to be a way to get these off," Josh said.

"Wait," Cami said. "The treasure chest. The metal edges are sharp where the bullet hit. Maybe they would cut through this rope."

Josh thought the idea was worth a try, so they scooted toward the chest, and Josh lifted his legs and worked the rope around his feet along the sharp-edged metal of the chest. "Come on," he said. "Come on!" He moved his legs along the side of the chest until the rope was severed in two. "It worked!" he exclaimed.

Cami freed her feet next.

"Hurry!" Josh exclaimed. "We have to do our hands."

"I'm trying," Cami struggled. It was difficult keeping her legs elevated and her feet moving back and forth. She didn't know how long they had until the bomb exploded, but every second was precious time wasted.

"There!" she exclaimed as the bands fell loose.

They knelt next to the mangled chest and, using a piece of the sharp, metal edge, began sawing away at the rope.

"Ouch!" Josh flinched and cried out.

"What happened?"

"I just cut my wrist. Can you lean over farther?"

Cami did her best to lean without falling over.

"I feel it loosening," Josh said. "We've about got it."

Sure enough, the tightly wrapped rope slackened, and their hands came free.

Sliding the rope from off around their shoulders was simple, and in seconds they were free.

Cami saw a rivulet of blood dripping down Josh's hand.

"Josh! Your hand!" she exclaimed.

"It's okay," he answered anxiously. "We've got to get out of here."

They took one step closer to the device and stopped.

"Is it ticking louder, or is it my imagination?" Cami asked.

"I don't know, but we better not go out the front door," Josh said. "Wolfgang and Rita might be waiting."

"Then where do we go?" Cami cried.

Josh began frantically pulling shelves away from the walls, tipping them over with their contents. "Somewhere in here is an opening to a passageway that leads to the caretaker's house, an underground tunnel that was sealed off after the collapse of the first lighthouse. If we can just . . ."

He tipped over another bank of shelves.

"Look!" Cami cried when the door was exposed.

"This is it!" he exclaimed.

Cami helped him clear a space by the door. Josh tested the door, yanking and pulling with all his might. "It won't budge," he said in defeat.

"Wait a minute." Cami peered at the door, taking a closer look.

"What?" Josh asked with urgency.

"Try pushing," she said.

Josh got down on one knee, turned the knob, and drove his entire body into the wooden door. Weakened with age, the door splintered apart against the force, and Josh tumbled inside.

"Josh!" Cami cried. "Are you okay?"

"I'm fine," he replied. "Let's go before that thing blows."

Cami stepped back. "I can't."

"You don't have a choice, Cami." Josh scrambled from the tunnel, reached for her hand, and tugged.

"Why didn't we listen to Grandpa?" Cami whimpered as she fell to her knees.

Crawling headfirst into the hole, Cami shuddered as a curtain of cobwebs brushed across her face and clung to her hair and clothes.

"Go!" Josh hollered.

Cami flashed the light ahead of her and saw that there was room to stand. Scrambling to her feet, she hurried along the tunnel with Josh right behind her.

Moments later, a deafening blast shook the ground, throwing Cami and Josh to the ground as dirt and rocks showered down on them.

CHAPTER 27

"Cami?" Josh's urgent voice came in the darkness. "Cami!" he cried.

There was still ringing in her ears, but Cami heard Josh's call. She opened her mouth to answer, but a cloud of smoke and dust enveloped them.

She coughed to clear her throat. "Are we dead?"

"I don't think so," he said, also coughing. "Are you okay?"

She did a quick mental check to make sure she had both her arms and legs. "Yes," she answered. "Are you?"

"I'm fine. I just wish we could see."

The tunnel was pitch-black. "I can't find my flashlight!" Cami cried.

"I've got mine in my backpack," he told her.

He rummaged through his pack, found the light, and flicked it on. A wall of dirt and rock had fallen behind them. Farther down the tunnel was another mound of dirt from the explosion.

"So, Dakota Drake, now what do we do?" she asked, fighting the urge to panic.

He looked behind them and then forward again. "We need to get out of here before the rest of the tunnel caves in."

Cami whimpered. "You think it will?"

"I'm sure of it," he said. "Let me go in front of you, and I'll try to dig out an opening."

Pressing herself against the side of the tunnel, Cami created space for Josh to get by. She pulled in slow, steady breaths, forcing herself to remain calm and keep her mind off the tunnel.

Digging with his hands, Josh worked feverishly to make an opening for them to crawl through.

Cami couldn't do much more than force herself to breathe and not freak out. Getting confined in a small, dark space like this was truly her worst nightmare come true. She was buried alive.

"Cami," Josh called back, "I think we can make it through."

Cami had her eyes shut, and she consciously pulled in a deep breath, then exhaled slowly. She was on the edge of a full-blown panic attack.

"Cami?" Josh called.

"I'm here," she said, keeping her eyes closed.

"We're going to make it," he told her. "There's only about three feet where the wall collapsed, then it looks clear the rest of the way."

"Three feet?" she asked.

"That's all," he said. "I'll be there for you every inch of the way. I promise I won't let anything happen to you."

"I'm going to hold you to that promise," she said.

"What's this?" he asked, looking down at her clenched right fist.

She smiled and opened her hand. "I grabbed the key," she said. "I know it didn't work, but it was still my great-great-grandmother's."

He gave her a smile. "Are you ready?"

She slipped the key around her neck. "I'm ready."

Letting Cami go first, Josh followed behind, shining the light for her to see her way.

"Do you think anyone heard the blast?" she asked.

"I'm sure of it. Somebody is probably out there right now trying to figure out what happened."

"If only we'd told Grandpa and Pearl where we were going, they'd know to look for us in here," Cami said with regret. But then she realized her grandfather would never have let them come in the first place. He would have told them it was too dangerous, and he would have been right.

She dragged herself army style along the small space, praying every inch of the way.

"Willy was right about the Rothchilds all along," Josh said as he crawled behind her.

Cami slid down to the floor of the tunnel on the other side, landing on her back. Her stomach and thighs were raw from the gouging rocks, her palms scraped and bleeding.

Josh slid down, bumping into her. "Sorry."

Cami assured him she was fine. She was just glad to get that obstacle out of their way.

"Your grandfather never trusted them," Josh reminded her.

Cami nodded. "He's always had this uncanny ability to know if people are honest or not." She remembered that her grandfather had remarked that Josh had a "good heart." The thought warmed her.

"We better get out of here." Josh pushed himself up and offered a hand to help Cami to her feet. "No telling when this tunnel will collapse."

Keeping ahold of her hand, Josh led the way to the end of the tunnel, where they found another door that most likely led to the caretaker's house.

The door was locked.

"You don't have an extra crowbar in your pack, do you?" Cami asked, looking back at the dark tunnel, picturing in her mind's eye how frightening it would have been to have the whole thing come crashing down in front of them.

"No crowbar," he said, "but I do have a pocketknife. Maybe we can pick the lock."

Cami held the flashlight for him while he picked at the lock. Josh kept trying, but couldn't seem to open the door.

Behind them, sand sifted into the open tunnel, and rocks clattered to the floor.

Panic struck Cami's heart. "Josh, hurry! I think the tunnel's caving in!"

"I'm trying," Josh said, digging at the lock. "This thing's as solid as a rock."

Cami felt a tremor under her feet. "Did you feel that?!"

"Yes!" Josh replied, pounding the door.

They were going to get buried alive, Cami just knew it.

"Wait," Cami said, getting an idea. "Why can't we just pull out the hinge pins? Then we can pry the door open from the other side."

Josh gave her an appreciative smile, then without warning, he kissed her. "You really are brilliant!" he exclaimed. The rusted pins were lodged tightly, but Josh had both of them out within minutes.

Just as he wedged the knife blade in the crack of the door to pry it open, the earth beneath them shuddered.

"Hurry!" Cami cried. Josh managed to open the door wide enough with the blade to grab hold with his hands. Dirt and rocks began to sprinkle from the sides of the tunnel.

"It's caving in!" Cami told him.

With a labored groan, Josh pulled with everything he had. The lock snapped, and the door flew open. "We're in!" he yelled.

They were barely inside the door when the tunnel crashed down behind them. A cloud of dust followed them inside the caretaker's house. But finally they were safe.

* * *

Josh and Cami were exhausted by the time the news reporters, police, and interested townspeople left the hospital where they had both received medical attention. It took seven stitches to close the gash in Josh's left wrist, but aside from being frightened and dirty, Josh and Cami were fine.

The lighthouse had received extensive damage and looked like the Leaning Tower of Pisa. The authorities set up barricades and posted a twenty-four-hour watch to keep the area secure. Everyone prayed that the weather would stay calm, knowing that one big wind might topple it. The place had been condemned, and it would need to be rebuilt. Again.

By the time she and Josh arrived home, it took all of Cami's strength to get from the car to the house. The police had also spent countless hours searching the inn, removing the listening devices planted there by Rita and Wolfgang, and gathering any other evidence for the case.

While Josh called the airline to cancel his flight, Cami noticed that her grandfather had been unusually quiet during the rescue and the police questioning, and she could tell by the look on his face that he was ready to explode.

"Grandpa?" she said when they got inside and sat at the kitchen table while Pearl threw some turkey sandwiches together. "What's wrong?"

She prepared herself for the biggest lecture of her life, knowing her grandfather was liable to go through the roof on this one.

Instead, his eyes teared up and his bottom lip quivered. "I nearly lost you," he said, clearing his throat. "I just couldn't bear it if I lost you too."

Cami walked over to the sweet old man and gave him a giant hug. "I'm so sorry I put you through this. You were right all along. I should have listened to you."

"Yes," he said, patting her on the back. "You should have."

"I'll never doubt your word again," Cami said, giving her grandfather a peck on the cheek.

"And I'm sorry, sir, to put your granddaughter in danger," Josh said with great sincerity. "I would never do anything to harm her."

"I know that, son," Grandpa Willy told him.

"I still can't believe the Rothchilds were capable of this!" Pearl exclaimed.

"I should have seen all of this coming," Cami said. "I saw them at the diner dressed as bikers, then again at the market. I knew there was something familiar about that man."

"You couldn't have known they were in disguise and that they would do something like this," Josh told her.

"Of course not!" Grandpa Willy remarked. "Those shifty-eyed buggers were professionals. It would've taken an expert to catch them. I just hope the police find them before they get away."

"We'll probably never get another guest here with all that's happened," Cami said, worry in her voice.

"Maybe it will boost interest," Josh said.

"We already lost one guest," Pearl said.

"What do you mean, 'lost' a guest?" Grandpa Willy asked.

"Mr. Richardson has disappeared. I don't even think he slept in his bed last night. I went up to check on him, and when I didn't get an answer, I got worried. I know we have a privacy policy, but I really thought something might have happened to him."

"Did you go into his room?" Cami asked.

"Yes, and it was very puzzling because I found this." She pulled a folded paper towel out of her pocket and opened it up. Inside was a hairy black strip about three inches long.

"What in the blue blazes is that?!" Grandpa Willy exclaimed, rolling up a newspaper, ready to kill the thing if it moved.

Cami knew exactly what it was. "It's his mustache. Actually I should say *her* mustache."

"Her?" Grandpa Willy asked.

Josh looked at Cami with sudden understanding. "Rita?"

Cami nodded. "I'm sure of it."

Josh explained. "The woman with Wolfgang—it had to be her."

"Excuse me," a man's voice came from the doorway.

Everyone turned to see Mr. Rogers and his wife.

Cami's blood ran cold. After all that had happened, she wasn't sure she could ever trust any of their guests again.

"Yes?" Grandpa Willy answered, his tone curt and unfriendly. He obviously felt the same way Cami did.

"I'd like to have a word with all of you if I might." Mr. Rogers's accent was gone, and he spoke with an air of authority.

What was going on? Cami wondered as her stomach turned. It wasn't possible for the Rogers to be involved with the Germans, was it?

He pulled something from his shirt pocket. Cami jumped to her feet, sending her chair clattering to the ground. Was it a gun? Another bomb?

"I'm Agent Bentley," he said quickly, flashing his badge. "I'm with the FBI."

"FBI?" Cami said, making sure she'd heard him correctly.

"Yes, and this is my partner, Agent Emerson. We have some questions for you about what happened today."

* * *

"At first we thought you were the ones who killed Patrick," Cami confessed.

"Us?" Agent Emerson exclaimed. "How did you arrive at that conclusion?"

"We noticed your gun," Josh said.

"And Agent Bentley had blood on the sleeve of his shirt," Cami told them.

Agent Emerson chuckled, which caused Agent Bentley's face to turn red with obvious displeasure.

"I told him to let me change the flat tire," Agent Emerson said. "But he wouldn't listen."

"That's enough, Emerson," Agent Bentley said.

"He nearly sliced off his finger," she said. "But it served him right." She glanced at her partner. "I'm the one with extensive auto mechanics training. Still, he had to be a man—"

"I said that's enough," Agent Bentley snapped.

Agent Emerson pursed her lips together and rolled her eyes, apparently not intimidated by her partner's temper.

"If you would please start from the beginning," Agent Bentley addressed Cami and Josh. "Emerson, make sure you get all of this down."

Cami and Josh told them everything that happened starting back when the Rothchilds had first stayed at the inn and had asked questions about the buried treasure.

Agent Emerson scribbled down notes and nodded her head from time to time.

"We've been after these two for years," Agent Bentley told them. He pulled a picture from his pocket. "Look familiar?"

In the picture was a tall man wearing a thick fur hat and down-filled ski parka. He was, without a doubt, Wolfgang. The woman standing next to him, also in a ski parka, had shoulder-length black hair. At first Cami wasn't sure, but upon closer inspection both she and Josh agreed it was Rita.

"Who are they, anyway?" Cami asked.

"Wolfgang and Ritagne Drago. They were both in the theater in Europe. He's German, she's actually Russian. He helped her defect, and they came to the United States. Because of his work, he has developed many connections with some of the world's most wealthy and famous people. Of course, there's not a great deal of money in theater, especially for an aging actor, so Wolfgang and Rita decided to supplement their incomes. At first they started out with small crimes—mostly jewel theft—but he soon moved to bigger robberies and even got involved in embezzling money. Not only that, Wolfgang is wanted for the murder of a casino owner in Monte Carlo. He's now on Interpol's Top Ten Most Wanted list. He and his wife are both masters of disguise."

"We're well aware of that," Cami told him. "Wolfgang told us himself. And now that I've had time to review the last few months, I can think of several occasions I might have seen him."

"They've got quite a cast of characters between them. They've masqueraded as bikers, hippies, homeless people . . . We've tracked them throughout Europe, Asia, and now in the U.S."

"So how did you know he'd come looking for this buried treasure?" Josh asked.

"Not too difficult. We intercepted several phone calls and overheard the plans. He's obsessed with finding a treasure chest of gold that is buried around here, and he's been acquiring historical documents attesting to its existence. Drago seems to think he's the one who should dig it up."

Cami saw her grandfather bristle at the mere mention of the word *treasure*.

"Back in the mid-1800s, Spanish gold accounted for nearly half of the coins used in America. Some of the bankers recognized the potential worth of the coins, or doubloons, as they were called. A banker in Astoria collected the gold and sent deposits by courier to San Francisco. His last deposit was sent on a United States Naval Survey schooner, called the *Shark,* which wrecked just off the shore north of here in 1846. There's a rumor that the men carrying the gold made it to shore during the storm and sought refuge at the lighthouse, but they were buried underneath when it collapsed."

"Is that who we found down there?" Cami asked Josh.

"What do you mean?" Agent Emerson questioned.

"We found bones of a skeleton at the exact spot where the chest was buried," Josh explained. "It would be nearly impossible to get to it now underneath all that dirt."

"Tragic," Agent Bentley said. "Finding that gold and identifying the remains of that skeleton would finally put the story to rest."

"What about finding Rita and Wolfgang?" Pearl asked.

"Somehow they manage to elude us every time. It's almost as if they vanish into thin air," Bentley explained. "But we have our best agents on it. Maybe this time we'll find them."

"Until then?" Grandpa Willy asked.

Bentley shrugged. "You're safe. They never strike in the same place twice. Now that they know the treasure doesn't exist, they could be halfway across the country."

Cami jumped when the front door opened, and Grandpa Willy rushed to greet whoever it was.

"Afternoon, Willy," Sheriff Barton said. "Just wanted to give you folks an update. We ran a check on your Mr. Rogers. You'll be interested to know—"

"He's FBI," Grandpa Willy answered him, stepping aside so Sheriff Barton could see into the front parlor.

Sheriff Barton nodded. "I see. Well, I just wanted to pass that along. We'll keep you posted if anything turns up."

"Any chance some of your men could drive by the mansion throughout the night?" Grandpa Willy asked. "You know, just in case Drago decides he's not ready to give up."

"You can count on it," the sheriff replied. "Afternoon, folks," he said to the group in the parlor.

Agents Bentley and Emerson said they needed to report back to their headquarters, but they, too, promised to stay in touch about the case.

Cami didn't know why, but even though the local law enforcement agency and the FBI were all working on the case, she was still uneasy.

One thing she did know: she was ready to take a shower and get rid of all of that dirt.

CHAPTER 28

That night Cami lay in bed, trying to fall asleep, but sleep didn't come. She was still wound up from the events of the day.

Fingering the key she still had around her neck, she marveled that just that morning she and Josh had dug up an empty treasure, survived an explosion, and escaped getting buried alive in a cave-in. With all that going through her mind, how was she supposed to sleep?

Finally, as the clock in the hallway struck midnight, she got up to make herself some hot chocolate. Taking the steaming mug to the back parlor, she sat in a chair, looking out into the inky black sky. Sipping the smooth, creamy cocoa, Cami relaxed into the soft cushiness of the overstuffed chintz chair and tried to clear her thoughts. Her body was exhausted, but she just couldn't get her mind to shut off.

She heard a bump and sat up with a start, straining her ears to listen for the noise to come again. After a minute of silence, she realized that it was probably just the wind outside. A storm was blowing in. She hoped the lighthouse was secure. It would break her heart if it were destroyed.

Draining the last chocolatey drops of liquid from the mug, she paused before going back to bed. There was something else on her mind, something she could neither ignore nor wanted to ignore. Josh.

Her heart fluttered as she thought about him, and a picture in her mind replayed the events of the day. She'd felt safe with him. He'd been a source of strength and protection for her. And a source of comfort.

She felt alive and happy again. She knew she would always love and miss Dallin. She would still have moments of heartache and sadness because he was gone. But she had realized that even though a part of her heart would always be locked with devotion to Dallin, there was room for another. There was room for Josh.

She loved him. She loved everything about him.

Shutting her eyes, she drew in a deep breath. Inside her heart and mind she turned her thoughts to Dallin. *It's time for me to move on,* she thought. *I'm finally ready. You know how hard things have been for me since you left. I've missed you and felt so empty without you. But I don't feel empty anymore. I finally feel happy again. I've met someone. You're probably already aware of that.* She smiled to herself, thinking he probably knew everything she was feeling and saying without her expressing it. Still, she needed to share what was in her heart. *You know what? I think you'd like him. I know he'd like you.*

He's a good man. In fact, he's Pearl's son. She smiled again. *You probably already know that too. Anyway, even Grandpa likes him, and that says a lot.*

So I guess what I'm saying is, I'd like your blessing to let me move ahead. I love Josh. She opened her eyes, a little shocked that she'd admitted it so easily to Dallin. *That doesn't mean I won't always love you. But I love Josh too. He can never take your place, but I have room in my heart to love him too.*

If there's any way you can show me, please let me know it's okay. I know you want me to be happy, and being with Josh makes me very happy.

"I love you, Dallin," she whispered. "Good-bye."

It was one thing to say it. It was another to remove his ring from her finger in a final act of closure. A twinge of pain edged her heart but was soon replaced by a calming warmth. And she knew all was well.

Breaking her moment of peace, she heard the bump again, this time coming from overhead.

"What in the world . . ." she said, getting to her feet.

Surprised at her own bravery, she climbed the stairs to search for whatever was making the noise. She thought perhaps it was one of the shutters blowing in the wind or a branch hitting against the house.

She tiptoed through all three bedrooms upstairs, looking and listening for the bump to sound again, but everything was still. Before she went back downstairs, she stopped outside of Josh's door. All was quiet inside. She lingered for a moment as she thought about how badly she wanted to tell Josh she loved him, but she knew she had to wait until morning.

With no success in locating the noise, she went back to her bedroom and climbed into her bed. Her eyelids grew heavy as she listened to the rustle of leaves outside, of branches creaking in the wind, and the rhythmic pounding of raindrops against the window pulling her into the foggy realms of sleep.

* * *

Cami sat up with a start. Rubbing the sleep from her eyes, she checked the clock on the nightstand. It was 3:17 A.M. She'd only been asleep for two hours.

A sudden chill rushed over her. Her nerves spiked with fear.

She wasn't alone in the room.

Her eyes shifted to her door. She always slept with it locked. It was still closed, yet she felt an undeniable presence in the room with her.

"Grandfather," she asked out loud, surprised that he had awakened since he mentioned he was going to take a strong sleeping aid in order to get to sleep after the day's events.

Then, a flash of lightning split the sky, illuminating the outline of a figure near the window. Cami opened her mouth to scream, but the figure rushed toward her and clapped a hand over her mouth and nose.

She kicked her legs and thrashed her arms, but the person holding her had a viselike grip and the strength of steel.

"Where is it?" a voiced hissed in her ear.

Cami tried to turn her head to look at her attacker, but he snapped her head forward so fast she felt her neck crack.

"I know you've got it. Show me or this time I'll kill you myself."

Immediately Cami knew who was holding her hostage. Wolfgang Drago. How he got in she didn't know. But one thing she knew for certain—he meant every word he said.

He clicked on the light beside her bed. He wore a black stocking cap over his head with a miner's light strapped on. She remembered the cap well.

"How did you get in here?" She knew the alarm system was set, the doors were double- and triple-locked, the windows had sensors, and the police were patrolling the area constantly.

"I had a little help from the inside."

Cami's forehead wrinkled with confusion. "From the inside?"

"You've made finding this treasure quite a challenge," he said. "And I *love* a challenge."

"But how—"

"It was simple. Rita paid you a little visit. She opened the outside entrance to the passageway."

"Mr. Richardson!"

"Is that the name she used?"

Cami nodded. Why hadn't she seen through the disguise?

"But enough of this," Wolfgang barked. Taking a gun from inside his coat, he held the barrel to her head and said, "This is your last chance. Where is it?"

"What?" she asked.

"The gold," he hissed. "You've got it hidden here somewhere."

Cami's eyes darted around the room. What was she going to do?

Then she got an idea, and she knew it was her only chance.

"We have to go back through the passageway."

He grabbed her elbow and forced her to her feet. "Let's go."

Keeping a bruising grip on her arm, he led her to the passageway door in the office and shoved her inside. Her injured knee gave out, and she stumbled to the floor, creating a loud racket.

Separating a pair of her ribs with the gun barrel, he yanked her to her feet and said, "Another move like that and you're dead."

Cami gave a muffled groan and took a step forward to get away from the gun.

He clenched her arm tightly and stopped her from moving, then spoke a string of German into a two-way radio. A crackle sounded, then a woman's voice replied in German. Rita's voice.

Drago replied and stuffed the radio into his back pocket, then nudged Cami forward with the gun. "You better not be playing games with me," he growled. "I'll kill your entire family if I have to, to find this treasure."

She knew if she tried to communicate that the treasure didn't exist, she wouldn't succeed. He was convinced she knew where it was.

Her biggest concern was the fact that what she was about to do would put Josh in danger. But he was her only hope.

She climbed the inner stairwell up to the second floor, where she negotiated the floor joists and framework structuring of the mansion. Drago remained a hair's distance behind, keeping the nose of the gun firm against her spine.

Her steps slowed as she neared the doorway to Josh's room. Her plan had to work. It just had to.

Using every fiber of courage she possessed and exercising all of the faith in her soul, she prayed for help from above and drew in a deep breath.

Placing her hands on the door, which she knew was like the others and very difficult to open, she gave a push. The door didn't yield. Trying again, she strained with the effort but just couldn't budge it. Cami knew if she pushed hard enough she could get it open, but that wasn't part of her plan.

"Here," Drago said in a growled whisper. "Out of my way!"

Keeping the gun trained on her, he wedged his shoulder against the door, just as Cami had hoped he would. As he gave a mighty shove, Cami took aim, bolstered her courage, and kicked at his hand holding the gun.

The gun went flying, clattering into the dark passageway just as Drago crashed through the passageway door onto the floor in Josh's room.

Leaping over Drago, Cami scrambled into the room.

"Josh!" she called. "Josh!"

"Cami?" Josh's voice came in the darkness.

"Josh!" she cried. "We have to get out! Drago's in here!"

Josh flipped on the lamp and scrambled from the bed to face a frightened Cami and an angry Wolfgang Drago.

Drago's two-way crackled and sounded. "Wolfgang?"

He ignored the radio and eyed Cami, then Josh, then glared at Cami again.

Instinctively Cami jumped behind a wing-back chair just as Wolfgang made a move for her.

The man swore and turned as Josh tackled him, ramming him into the dresser. The dresser mirror tipped and slammed down on Wolfgang's head. He cried out, but his pain only seemed to heighten his anger.

Like a mad bull, Wolfgang reacted, turning on Josh and crouching low, as if ready to butt him through the wall. Josh moved cautiously sideways, keeping constant eye contact with Wolfgang.

Cami watched the two men, wondering what to do. Wolfgang had Josh by five inches and fifty pounds. Josh was quick and strong, but Wolfgang was so incensed he looked like he could bend metal with his bare hands.

Tension sparked between the two men like bolts of lightning. Eyeing the door, Cami knew what she had to do.

With every nerve on edge, ready to spring when they did, Cami watched, shifting her gaze from Josh to Wolfgang and back again.

Then, with a sudden lunge and menacing yell, Wolfgang attacked Josh. Cami flew to the door and threw it open. Holding Josh by the neck, Wolfgang looked up at her with pure murder in his eyes.

Josh wrenched himself free and let his fist fly with a deflating blow to Wolfgang's midsection. The man doubled over, and Josh and Cami took flight. But they didn't get far. The next thing Cami knew, Wolfgang tackled Josh as he came through the door, and both of them landed on top of her, knocking the wind right out of her.

With panicked gasps, Cami fought for air, managing to roll to her side as Josh and Wolfgang tangled again. Dragging herself by her elbows, she crawled to the wall, turning just in time to see Wolfgang pin Josh's arms behind him and slam him into the ground, then grind a knee into Josh's back.

"Stop!" she cried. "You're going to kill him!"

Wolfgang's wicked laugh made her heart race with terror.

She had to do something now.

Without a thought for her own safety, she got to her feet, crouched low, grabbed the nearest object, and charged.

Cami swung the crystal vase in her hands and brought it down at the base of Wolfgang's skull with a loud *crack!* The vase shattered in her hands, sifting through her fingers like shards of ice. Blood trickled from the gash in the back of his skull but didn't stop him. Wolfgang turned, reached, and grabbed her nightdress. Cami let out a high-pitched scream. He had her.

Reflexively, she brought her knee up with a mighty snap, striking him underneath the chin. Wolfgang's eyes rolled to the back of his head and he collapsed to the floor.

Cami eyed Wolfgang, her leg poised and ready to strike again if she had to.

Josh scrambled to his feet.

"You're bleeding." Cami noticed the slash across his eyebrow.

"I'm fine," he said.

Cami looked back at Wolfgang, watching closely for any sign of consciousness or movement.

"Cami, he's out cold."

"No, he's not," she replied. "I know how it works. He's pretending he's out just to fool us."

"That's only in the movies," Josh told her.

Cami shook her head. "I'm not taking any chances. Grab the phone over there and call the police. I'll keep an eye on him."

Josh wiped at the trickle of blood trailing down the side of his face as he went for the phone not ten steps away from her.

Cami listened as Josh placed the call, relieved to know that help would arrive within several minutes. She breathed easier. It was almost over.

"Thanks, Sheriff," Josh said into the receiver. "We'll have the front door open. We're upstairs." He paused. "Yes," Josh answered, "I think he's still alive." He looked at Cami, who nodded. Then a sick feeling washed over her. He *was* alive, wasn't he?

Cami peered closer at the man lying facedown on the floor. *Oh no,* she wondered. *What if I killed him?*

Leaning in, she watched for a sign that the man was still breathing, praying that the pool of blood from his head didn't mean he was dead.

His eyelid flickered, bringing relief to Cami's soul. He was still alive.

She didn't see it coming.

MICHELE ASHMAN BELL

Wolfgang roared to life, grabbing Cami and pulling her down, his left arm wrapping around her neck and squeezing like a giant python.

She couldn't breathe. White spots sparked in front of her eyes. In a distant fog, she heard Josh yell, but she couldn't focus. Her neck was being bent so far back she knew it was only a matter of seconds before it snapped.

Then, as if a locomotive hit them, Cami felt herself flying, and then slamming into the wall, causing the picture hanging above her to come crashing down on top of her.

Gulping in deep breaths of air, Cami felt a sob competing for space in her throat, but she fought it back. She had to keep her wits about her or they'd both be dead for sure.

Flinging the picture off of her, she saw Josh and Wolfgang tangled on the floor, rolling and colliding with furniture and plant stands. Using the wall for support, she dragged herself to her feet and stumbled toward the stairs. She had to open the door. The sheriff would be there any second.

Then suddenly, the scuffling behind her stopped.

Please no, she prayed.

She forced herself to turn around just in time to see Wolfgang stagger to his feet and tromp toward her like a demonic monster.

In a millisecond, she scanned her surroundings and grabbed for the nearest object. Holding the African spear in front of her, she crouched low and knew it was down to her or him. Seething with anger that this man had disrupted their lives, intruded on their peace, and injured Josh, she took aim. She'd been afraid once that she might have killed him. Now she was more afraid for her own life.

Wolfgang looked at her warily as he walked with his arms outstretched in front of him, ready to grab her. A wicked smile grew on his face with each footstep, then he began laughing.

Run! Cami told herself. But her feet wouldn't move.

Gripping the spear like a lifeline, she steeled herself, praying that help would be there any second.

"It's over for you," Wolfgang threatened. His collar was saturated with blood, but he didn't even seem to notice.

Cami aimed the tip of the spear at his chest, ready to strike if he got any closer.

He continued to smile like the devil himself, which fueled Cami's anger. Thoughts of fear or doubt vanished. She was ready for whatever happened.

"Tell me where the gold is," Wolfgang said. "I will spare your life."

She knew his words were lies.

She didn't answer.

"Tell me," his voice grew louder.

Cami focused on her target. Even if she did know, she wouldn't tell him.

"Tell me!" he yelled, his voice echoing in the hallway.

"Over my dead body," she said.

Wolfgang charged.

Cami drew back the spear, ready to thrust, when to her surprise Wolfgang began falling forward. With a quick glance she saw that Josh had grabbed ahold of his foot.

It all happened so quickly even Cami was shocked when he fell into the spear, the point piercing his shoulder, the wooden shaft splintering beneath the weight of his body. Cami jumped aside just as he landed with a groan at her feet.

Behind her at the bottom of the stairs, the front door burst open and in charged the sheriff with Mitch.

CHAPTER 29

The sun sank below the line of evergreen trees, casting a golden veil of light over the ocean.

"It feels so good to relax," Cami said as she sank deeper into the cushion of her chair.

"Those reporters couldn't get enough, could they?" Pearl commented.

"This was great exposure for the inn, though," Josh observed. "And for your book, Pearl. Do you realize how many people read *People* magazine?"

"Well, I for one could do without all of this foo-for-rah!" Grandpa Willy stated. "I liked things how they used to be—dull, boring, and predictable. I've had enough excitement to last the rest of my life. And if one more reporter asks me if I know where the treasure is, I swear I'm going to—"

"Now, Grandpa," Cami stopped him. "It's all over. Don't get yourself so worked up."

Josh chuckled. "Those two FBI agents, Bentley and Emerson, sure didn't appreciate us solving the crime without them, did they?"

Cami laughed with him.

"But we have to give them some credit," she said. "They were the ones who found Rita, even if she was dressed like a nun."

Josh nodded in agreement, then said, "Did you notice how impressed they were that *you* were the one who finally brought Wolfgang down?"

"Who would have thought your collection of art pieces would also serve as weapons of defense?" Cami said to Pearl.

"I'm still amazed that you were brave enough to fight that giant," Pearl said.

"I'm sorry I broke your vase," Cami said, worried that it was one of her priceless originals.

"Cami," Pearl said, aghast that Cami would even worry about such a thing, "first of all, even if it were priceless, I wouldn't care because you and Josh mean more to me than an old vase. And after that other one was stolen, I stopped by the store when I was in Tillamook and picked up some glass vases on sale for $9.99."

"You didn't!" Cami exclaimed with relief.

Pearl laughed. "I did. That's why it broke so easily. Lead crystal wouldn't shatter like that one did. And I talked to Agent Emerson, who said that he was positive they'd be able to retrieve my other vase."

Cami was happy to hear Pearl's real vase would be returned.

"The important thing is that Wolfgang and Rita are behind bars," Pearl said. "Everybody's safe. We have a lot to be grateful for."

"I still wish I knew where that treasure was, though," Cami said.

"Cami!" Grandpa Willy bellowed.

"I know, I know," she said. "But still, you have to wonder. I mean, we actually found the treasure box. The gold has to be somewhere."

"I want you to leave it alone, Cami. Forget about that treasure. It isn't worth losing your life over," he scolded.

She pulled the key from around her neck. "I just wish I knew what this key went to."

"Whatever it is, it's best locked," Grandpa told her.

Cami sighed but cast a sidelong glance at Josh. She knew she would never give up. She wouldn't actively seek the treasure, but she'd always look for it.

"By the way," Pearl said to Josh and Grandpa Willy, "where did you two run off to this afternoon? Right in the middle of everything, I turned around and both of you were gone."

"We had an important errand to run," Grandpa Willy told her.

"What in the world could have been so important?" she asked.

"Yeah," Cami added, also wanting to know the answer to that question.

Josh and Grandpa Willy looked at each other, mischievous smiles sneaking on to their faces.

"Something's up," Cami said. "What is it? Josh? Grandpa?"

Josh didn't answer, and Grandpa Willy took a long sip of his strawberry lemonade. The sun had nearly disappeared behind the horizon, and the palette of reds and pinks had faded into grays and purples.

"William," Pearl said with piqued interest, "what are you two up to?"

When Grandpa Willy didn't answer, Pearl asked Josh. "I demand that you tell me what's going on right now!"

Josh looked at Grandpa and said, "I don't want to disobey my mother. Should we tell them?"

Grandpa looked disgusted at the thought of having to divulge what he apparently thought was privileged information. "Oh, alright. Good grief!" he exclaimed. "You'd think we'd gone on some top-secret mission or something. Heaven forbid we try and keep a secret from you two!"

Cami giggled. She liked it when her grandfather got all huffy and flustered. The tops of his ears turned red, and he sputtered like a pot boiling over on the stove.

"You want to go first?" Josh asked him.

"Criminy!" he exclaimed. "I suppose so." Grandpa Willy got up from his chair and fished for something in his pocket. He pulled out his hand, but didn't show what he held inside.

Cami and Pearl leaned forward to get a peek.

Grandpa gave a huff and rolled his eyes. "Will you two please relax?"

"It's the treasure!" Cami exclaimed. "He's going to tell us where the treasure is!"

"Horsefeathers!" Grandpa Willy exclaimed. "I'm telling you to forget about that blasted treasure once and for all."

"But the coin and the map," Cami said. "Grandpa, you honestly don't believe there is a treasure?"

Grandpa Willy shut his eyes, as if praying for strength, then, taking a deep breath that he released slowly, he said, "Alright, I'll tell you this, and this is all I know." He gave his granddaughter a level look, which prompted a nod of agreement from Cami.

"My father always claimed that my great-grandfather did find the treasure while he helped rebuild the lighthouse."

"I knew it!" Cami exclaimed. "I knew—"

"But," Grandpa stopped her. Cami clamped her mouth shut. "But there has never been any proof of it."

"Except the coin," Cami reminded him.

"Except the coin," Grandpa admitted with exasperation, "but that could have washed up on shore. We just don't know. I don't think we'll ever know. If he buried it somewhere, even on this property, we have no way of finding it unless we dig up this entire piece of land, and frankly, I have no intention of doing that. So," he gave all of them a warning gaze, "I'd like to consider this matter closed. Alright?"

Cami bit her lip and nodded, even though she knew she'd never stop wondering about the whereabouts of the treasure.

"Besides," Grandpa added, "there's something else I'd like to say that's quite a bit more important than that treasure."

Using the arm of a chair, Grandpa lowered himself onto one knee and faced Pearl.

Everyone remained silent. Cami's heart beat furiously with anticipation and surprise. Pearl's face went white as a sheet.

"Pearl," Grandpa Willy said.

Pearl swallowed but didn't reply.

"I know I'm a pain in the neck sometimes. And I know I can get a little grouchy—"

"A little?" Cami said.

"Shhhh," Grandpa shushed her. "Okay, I can get pretty grouchy at times. And I'm certainly not worthy of you. But . . . well . . ." he began sputtering. "Shoot!" He held out the ring for her. "Pearl, will you—"

"Marry you?" Pearl could barely say the words. She blinked as tears filled her eyes.

Grandpa Willy nodded, then looked down at his shoe.

"Yes!" she cried, causing Grandpa to jump. "Yes, yes, a thousand times yes!"

Grandpa Willy looked up, a smile brightening up his face. "You will?"

"William, I would be honored to be your wife." She held out her arms.

Grandpa Willy reached toward her, and the two embraced, Grandpa Willy chuckling and Pearl crying. Tears ran down Cami's own cheeks.

After they finished hugging, Grandpa turned to Cami. "That's all right with you, isn't it, Cami-girl?"

Cami smiled. "Yes, Grandpa. It is definitely all right with me." Cami sniffed and wiped at her eyes, then jumped to her feet. "Congratulations, you two." She hugged her grandfather first, then she hugged Pearl, whose eyes twinkled with the pure joy she felt inside.

"I guess we should try that ring on and see if it fits," Grandpa Willy said. He took the box from Pearl and pulled out the diamond ring. It was dainty and elegant, classy yet simple. Perfect for Pearl.

He slid the ring onto her finger, and Pearl could barely contain herself.

Mopping at tears on her face, she looked at Josh. "Can you believe this? After all these years, I'm finally getting married."

Josh smiled at his mom. "William's a lucky man," he said.

"It's true, Pearl," Grandpa Willy said. "Are you sure you want me?"

Pearl rested her hand on Grandpa Willy's wrinkled cheek, the diamond on her ring reflecting flashes of brilliant light. "I love you just the way you are."

Grandpa Willy's cheeks flushed bright red as a schoolboy grin grew on his face. "And I love you just the way you are," he replied.

Cami's heart grew warm with joy knowing that neither her grandfather nor Pearl would ever be lonely again.

Josh, who was standing next to her, slipped an arm around her waist and pulled her close. She rested her head on his shoulder, and together they watched the couple in their excitement. Cami realized it didn't matter what age a person was or what station in life they were at, everyone needed to love and be loved. And for some reason, Pearl and Grandpa Willy seemed even more deserving of love than anyone else Cami knew. She also knew that having something as wonderful as two people finding true love would certainly help put the awful memories of the past few days behind them. Now there would be excitement and anticipation instead of nightmares and angst.

Grandpa Willy cleared his throat, then said, "Well, son?"

Josh didn't answer. Cami turned and looked at him, wondering about the strange expression on his face. In the back of her mind, a thousand scenarios played, all of them involving him going back to Pennsylvania and her staying in Oregon.

Josh turned to her and held both of her hands in his.

"Cami, I know how hard it's been for you since Dallin died. You know I understand."

Cami nodded.

"I just can't seem to get you off of my mind, though. You see, I have a problem."

"A problem?" she asked.

Josh nodded. "I've fallen in love with you."

Cami blinked as tears stung her eyes.

"I can't imagine going back to Pennsylvania. I want to be here with you and my mom and Grandpa Willy," he said.

Cami's nose started to run. She sniffed and accepted a tissue from Pearl.

"Anyway, your grandfather asked me to go with him today to pick out a ring for Pearl, and when I was there, I saw one that had your name all over it. And . . . ," he swallowed, "well . . . " He rubbed her knuckles with his thumbs. "Cami, I know it's sudden," he hurried and dropped down on one knee, looking up at her, "but, will you marry me?"

Cami closed her eyes for a moment, relishing the sound of his words.

"Cami?"

Slowly she opened her eyes, looking at the face she had grown to trust and love. Josh had become her best friend and confidant. He seemed to understand her better than anyone else. He listened without judging. He supported without expectations. Just holding his hand made her heart flutter.

"Yes, Josh," she said. "I will marry you."

He raised his eyebrows, as if he wanted to make sure she'd actually said yes.

She nodded.

"You will?" he asked.

"I will," she answered.

Slowly he stood, his own eyes moist with tears.

"You have just made me the happiest man in the whole world," he said.

"The second happiest man in the whole world," Grandpa Willy corrected him.

Josh laughed as he dug into his pocket and pulled out a ring box.

Cami felt lightheaded, as if she would pass out any moment. This seemed like a dream, like a fairy tale. Yet it was real life—her life.

He opened the box and showed her the ring—a beautiful wide platinum band with a large, sparkling stone set in the middle.

"I love it," she whispered. "It's beautiful."

"Let's see if it fits," he offered.

Josh slid the cool metal onto her slim finger. It was a perfect fit.

She admired the ring for a moment before looking up and smiling. "It's perfect."

Josh pulled her into a hug and rocked her gently, then placed a tender kiss on her forehead. "I love you, Cami."

"I love you, Josh," she answered.

They turned and received embraces from Grandpa Willy and Pearl.

"I'm happy for you, Cami-girl. He's a wonderful man. I couldn't have picked a better person for you myself," Grandpa Willy said.

"Thanks, Grandpa," she said.

Pearl was next to hug her. "Goodness sakes!" she exclaimed. "This is almost too good to be true, isn't it?"

Cami chuckled. "It sure is."

They chatted nonstop, talking dates and possibilities. Pearl offered them her cottage to live in so they could have a place of their own. Grandpa announced he was going to build a whole new wing with a master bedroom for him and Pearl. Everything was wonderful and exciting, and Cami couldn't imagine life being any better than this.

"Wait," Josh said. "I have one other thing to give Cami."

The other three looked at him as he brought out another jewelry box from his pocket.

Cami wondered what else he had to give her.

He opened the box, and there was a single diamond-stud earring inside. Cami looked at the diamond, then back at his face, confused.

"I'm sorry we never did find your other diamond earring," he said. "I know that not only were they expensive, they also had great sentimental value to you. I thought that maybe I could give you another earring so you'd have a set again. That way, you'd have one earring from Dallin, and one from me."

Cami felt her bottom lip tremble as she tried to thank him. But words weren't necessary. She threw her arms around Josh's neck and hugged him so hard she couldn't breathe.

"This is the most thoughtful thing anyone has ever done for me," she told him. "Thank you."

She knew without a doubt that marrying Josh was the right thing to do. She knew it in her mind, but more importantly, she felt it in her heart. The Lord had indeed guided Josh to their inn, where he could find his birth mom, rediscover his faith, and put pieces of his life together. But he in turn had helped put the pieces in everyone else's lives together. And Cami marveled at the Lord's hand in the whole thing. If someone would have told her six months ago that she would meet a professor from Pennsylvania and fall in love, she would have told them they were crazy.

And it was crazy. Wonderfully, magically, marvelously crazy.

"I say we celebrate!" Grandpa Willy exclaimed.

"Can we invite Mitch and Ashlyn?" Cami asked.

"The more the merrier," Grandpa replied.

Cami made the phone call and prepared herself for the challenge of telling everyone their news. She prayed that Dallin's parents would understand and support her. But she knew that no matter what they or anyone else said, marrying Joshua Drake was the most important thing in the world to her.

CHAPTER 30

One year later

"So, how do you like it?" Cami asked Ashlyn, who was bouncing her six-month-old baby boy, Elliot, on her hip. He was the spitting image of his father, with a head full of wavy blonde hair and big, blue eyes.

"Cami, the room looks incredible. I love the cranberry-colored walls, and this furniture—is it mahogany?" Ashlyn ran her free hand over the smooth, polished surface of the sleigh bed footboard.

"It is. Josh and I found it at an estate sale when we were back east last month. Isn't it gorgeous?"

"You've done a tremendous job decorating this new wing," Ashlyn said. "How have you done it? I remember how sick I was those first few months when I was pregnant."

"I think it helped to have something to keep me busy and get my mind off the nausea. I'm starting to feel much better now," Cami told her. She was in her third month of pregnancy and couldn't wait until her stomach started to poke out so everyone would know her exciting news. "Let's go join the others. I've been craving Pearl's barbecued shrimp all week."

"I remember having cravings like that," Ashlyn told her.

"How about Oreos and ranch dressing? Ever tried that?" Cami asked.

Ashlyn pulled a face. "You don't actually *dip* the Oreos into the ranch dressing, do you?"

"Of course, that's the best way."

They found the rest of the group in the backyard getting ready to launch into the delicious meal Pearl had prepared. There were two reasons for the celebration. First, to celebrate the grand opening of the new addition to the Sea Rose Bed and Breakfast, and second, to celebrate Pearl's book, *Worth a Thousand Words,* which was on the *New York Times* best-seller list. It was number seven and holding steady.

Like his mother, Josh also showed a flare for writing, and in his spare time from teaching history classes at the high school, he was writing a novel. He figured since he couldn't live out all his dreams of adventure and travel, he could at least write about a character in a book doing it. With his history background, he was writing a fascinating story about an American spy in Berlin during World War II. His friend, Max Simons, had already read the first ten chapters and loved the story, claiming Josh had the makings of the next Tom Clancy.

To say the least, life was good.

Cami felt blessed that the Lord had given her love again in her life. She never thought there would be room in her heart for another man, but she realized her heart had somehow expanded to receive Josh in her life. Even though she was sealed to Dallin, she and Josh had been married and they were very happy. Their faith was strong that everything would work out the way it was supposed to in the eternities, for they both felt that heaven had lent a divine hand in bringing them together.

After dinner, Ashlyn and Mitch left for home to put their baby down for a nap. Grandpa Willy and Pearl, who did practically everything together now, volunteered to clean the kitchen so Cami could relax and Josh could massage her feet. She'd been working double-time trying to get the decorating done for the big grand opening, and she was exhausted.

Josh kneaded the bottoms of her feet with his thumbs, and Cami felt the tension slowly begin to evaporate. Out of habit, she fingered the key she'd found in her mother's diary. The key still hung on a gold chain around her neck.

"You're not thinking about that gold again, are you?" Josh asked.

Cami knew she drove Josh nuts with her occasional quests to find the treasure, but part of her just couldn't accept that it had vanished into thin air.

"I can't help it," she said. "It has to be somewhere."

"Why?" he challenged. "Maybe someone did find it. But it's possible they lost it or buried it without telling anyone where. They could even have been robbed and the gold stolen."

Cami shook her head. "I guess I just can't forget about it until I know for sure."

"We've looked everywhere," Josh said. "We've dug in every cave, looked in every crack and crevice of this house, we've wandered the hills, and even searched the lighthouse. It's just not there. I guess there are some mysteries we'll never know the answers to," he answered.

"I guess," Cami said with a disappointed sigh. Josh was always a good sport to accompany her on her many treasure hunts. He wanted to find it just as much as she did, but he was more of a realist than she was. "Sometimes I get the feeling we're overlooking something. If we'd just look harder, I think we'd figure it out."

"You know how your grandfather feels about that treasure," Josh warned her.

"I know, the T-word isn't even allowed to be spoken, but I can't seem to get that riddle out of my head."

Josh didn't answer, but continued rubbing her feet. All of the sudden, Cami sat up, nearly kicking her husband in the face.

"Did I push too hard? Hit a nerve?" he asked with alarm.

"No, no," she said. "I have an idea. We have to go back into the passageway."

Josh's gaze narrowed. "I don't think that's a good idea."

"Josh," she grabbed his hand, "you're my husband."

"And?"

"And you love me, right?"

"Right."

"Then you have to do this with me. It will just take a minute." She shoved her feet into her shoes and pulled him behind her as she tiptoed through the mansion to the office. The last thing she wanted to do was alert Grandpa Willy to their presence.

"Here," Cami handed Josh a flathead screwdriver, "you're going to have to pry it open."

"Willy's going to regret leaving this last doorway unsealed," Josh told her.

"He's never going to know we did this," Cami said.

Shaking his head, Josh inserted the tool between the wall and the panel and tried to ease it open. After several agonizing minutes, the doorway swung wide.

Josh gave her a concerned look, but Cami just smiled.

"Stop worrying," she told him. "I just want to read the riddle one more time."

"Alright. We'll read the riddle, then we're out of here," he said.

A filtered light allowed them to negotiate the passageway safely until they reached the wall where Cami's mother had written the message in chalk.

It's not just a penny, or even a dime,
To find the treasure, first find the time.

"Okay," Cami said. "What are we missing? What aren't we seeing?"

"I don't know, but if Willy finds out we're here, we're going to be seeing the roof raised."

"Josh," Cami said with frustration, "help me. There's something here. We're just not seeing it." She tapped her toe as she thought. "We know that my great-great-grandfather found the treasure, since we've seen proof of the empty chest."

"How could I forget?" Josh said.

"But where in the world did he put it after that? Did he bury it? Did he hide it?"

"Like your grandfather said, we probably will never know. It was a secret he took to his grave."

"But this note leads us to believe that it isn't that far away if we could just figure out what the riddle means."

She read the note aloud one more time.

Just then, as if on cue, the grandfather clock chimed the hour.

"Josh!" she exclaimed. "The clock! That's got to be it."

"The clock?" he asked with confusion. "What about the clock?"

She went over to the opening in the floor, where the sound of bells rang through. They looked inside the compartment where they'd found the diary, the map, and the key. But there was nothing else inside.

With a huff, Cami leaned against a two-by-four and folded her arms. "It's just not here. Why can't I face that?"

Josh didn't answer her for a moment. He appeared to be in deep thought.

"Josh?" she asked.

He looked at her for several moments, then his eyes lit up. "I have an idea. Let's go." This time he grabbed her hand and pulled her behind him.

She followed him out of the passageway and through the house until they stood side by side in front of the massive, seven-foot-tall grandfather clock.

"Okay," Cami challenged. "Now what?"

"My stepmother had a grandfather clock. Nothing nearly as nice as this one, but it had a panel at the base that opened into the compartment containing the works. Maybe . . ." He knelt down and examined the wood moldings and carved panels at the bottom of the clock. Then he stopped.

"What?" Cami exclaimed. "Did you find something?"

She knelt down next to him and looked at the carved wooden panel. At first she didn't detect anything, but after closer inspection, she saw it—a small keyhole at the top, barely discernable to the naked eye. A person would have had to be at eye level and up close to even see it.

"Oh, wow," Cami said as goose bumps prickled her flesh.

"Now, don't get your hopes up," Josh told her. "This doesn't mean anything is in there."

"I know," Cami said, trying to rein in her excitement. "Still, I might finally know what this key goes to."

"There's only one way to find out," Josh said.

Removing the chain from around her neck, Cami inserted the tiny brass key into the lock.

"It fits," she whispered. Slowly she turned the key and heard a tiny click.

She looked at Josh, whose face was as full of anticipation as a child's on Christmas morning. He wouldn't admit it, but she knew he was every bit as excited as she was.

The tiny door swung open.

Leaning in closer, they peered inside and found . . . nothing.

Disappointment filled Cami. She sat back on her heels with a sigh. *Well,* she thought, *at least I know what the key goes to.*

"I'm sorry," Josh said. "You've got to admit, though, if you wanted to hide gold, this would be the perfect place to do it."

Cami studied the shallow compartment, wishing that there had even been just one gold coin, or even a note. Something!

"Funny," she said, pointing to the back panel, "they've used a different type of wood for this piece in the back."

Josh bent his head and looked inside. "Hmm. I wonder why?"

Cami reached in and ran her hand along the smooth surface of the wood. At the corner, the piece of wood shifted. "Josh!" she exclaimed, giving a firmer push. The entire panel tilted.

"It's a fake back," Josh said. "Can you pull it out?"

The piece was perfectly wedged into place. "No, I can't get ahold of it."

Josh reached in and gave a firm tap on the corner of the panel but couldn't get his fingers under the edge to pull it out.

"Here," Cami said, grabbing a wire coat hanger from the closet. "See if this will help."

Josh hooked the hanger underneath the edge of the panel, gave a little tug, and sure enough, the wooden piece lifted just enough for him to get a grip on.

"I got it!" he announced.

"Got what?" Grandpa Willy's voice came.

Josh and Cami turned to see Grandpa Willy and Pearl standing behind them.

"A . . . well . . . " Cami stuttered.

"We just . . ." Josh looked at Cami for help.

"Oh, alright," she said with exasperation. "We're looking for the treasure!"

Grandpa raised his eyebrows, then a smile creased his face. "The treasure? In there?"

"This key," Cami held up the key, "opened this compartment."

"We just have to remove this back panel," Josh told him.

"Well," Grandpa Willy said, obviously expecting them not to find anything, "let's see what's behind it."

With a shrug, Josh reached back in and grabbed hold of the panel. After a slight tug, the panel came loose.

Silence followed.

"You look, Cami," Josh said.

Cami swallowed. "Okay." She crouched over and reached her hand into the compartment. Then she froze. "Something's in here. It's a bag." The thrill of excitement made her scalp tingle.

Grandpa chuckled. "You just won't give up, will you?"

"She's as stubborn as her grandfather," Pearl teased.

"I'm not kidding," Cami said with a grunt. "It's heavy too." Sliding the bag from its spot deep inside the clock, she pulled it onto the floor with a thump.

Everyone crowded around it to take a look.

"Well, I'll be," Grandpa said, staring wide-eyed at the bag.

"It looks like coins," Pearl said.

"It sure does," Josh added.

"Somebody open it so we can see," Cami said, her breath coming in quick gasps.

Nobody moved.

"Alright, I'll do it," Grandpa Willy announced. Taking a pocketknife out, he slid the sharp blade beneath the frayed rope securing the bag.

And when he spread the bag open . . .

"Gold!" Grandpa cried. "It's full of gold! Gee-whillikers, you found the gold!"

Everyone let out a cheer of delight and surprise.

"We found it!" Cami cried.

Josh hugged her tightly. "*You* found it," he corrected. "You didn't want to give up. And look," he picked up one of the gold pieces, "you actually found it."

"I don't believe it," Pearl said. "There must be hundreds of coins in this bag!"

"It's been here the entire time," Grandpa Willy said. "I never thought it existed, but here it is."

"We found it," Cami said again in disbelief. "We really found it."

* * *

Hand in hand, Cami and Josh stepped out of the kitchen into the moonlit night. Following the stone pathway, they ambled slowly along its winding path as the scent of roses filled the night air.

"Look," Cami said, pointing ahead at the column of light illuminating the path. "Isn't that beautiful?"

"It really is," Josh said, slipping an arm around her waist. They walked to the gazebo and stood inside, the shadows of moonlight creating veiled curtains of silver around them.

"You know we can't keep the gold," he told her.

Cami sighed. "I know. It doesn't seem fair though. It's been on our property for over a hundred years."

Josh chuckled and pulled her close, kissing the top of her head.

"It doesn't really matter," she said. "I'm already the richest woman in the world. I have a wonderful husband who I'm terribly in love with." She kissed his chin. "I have an incredible life that is full and happy." She circled her arms around his neck. "And I'm having a baby." She kissed him on the mouth this time. "Mmm," she sighed with contentment. "Thank you," she said, feeling warm and dreamy inside.

"For what?"

"For helping me have the courage to find happiness again. For fixing a heart that I thought was broken."

"I did that?" he asked.

"Yes." She rested her head on his shoulder. "You did that."

"You know this is only the beginning, don't you?"

She lifted her head and smiled. "Yes, I know."

"I promise you a lifetime of happiness and hidden treasures," he said in his most gallant voice.

"A girl can't ask for any more than that," Cami replied, knowing that without a doubt Josh would hold true to his promise.

ABOUT THE AUTHOR

In the fourth grade, Michele Ashman was considered a "daydreamer" by her teacher and told on her report card that "she has a vivid imagination and would probably do well with creative writing." Her imagination, combined with a passion for reading, has enabled Michele to live up to her teacher's prediction, and she loves writing books, especially books that uplift, inspire, and edify readers as well as entertain them. (You can also catch her daydreaming instead of doing housework.)

Michele grew up in St. George, Utah, where she met her husband at Dixie College before they both served missions, his to Pennsylvania and hers to Frankfurt, Germany. Seven months after they returned they were married and are now the proud parents of four children: Weston, Kendyl, Andrea, and Rachel.

Her favorite pastime is supporting her children in all of their activities, traveling both inside and outside of the United States with her husband and family, and doing research for her books.

Aside from being a busy wife and mother, Michele teaches aerobics at the Life Centre Athletic Club near her home. She is currently the missionary specialist and the teacher of the seventeen- and eighteen-year-olds in Sunday School in the Sandy ward where her husband serves as the bishop.

Michele is the best-selling author of eight books, a Christmas booklet, and has also written children's stories in the *Friend*.